W9-ASR-638

JUL 2 7 2012

By _____

HAYNER PUBLIC LIBRARY DISTRICT
ALTON, ILLINOIS

OVERDUES 10 PER DAY, MAXIMUM FINE
COST OF ITEM
ADDITIONAL $5.00 SERVICE CHARGE
APPLIED TO
LOST OR DAMAGED ITEMS

HAYNER PLD/DOWNTOWN

UNDER OATH

FORGE BOOKS BY MARGARET McLEAN

Under Fire
Under Oath

MARGARET McLEAN

UNDER OATH

A TOM DOHERTY ASSOCIATES BOOK
NEW YORK

This is a work of fiction. All of the characters, organizations, and events portrayed in this novel are either products of the author's imagination or are used fictitiously.

UNDER OATH

Copyright © 2012 by Margaret McLean

All rights reserved.

A Forge Book
Published by Tom Doherty Associates, LLC
175 Fifth Avenue
New York, NY 10010

www.tor-forge.com

Forge® is a registered trademark of Tom Doherty Associates, LLC.

ISBN 978-0-7653-2813-7 (hardcover)
ISBN 978-1-4299-2457-3 (e-book)

First Edition: April 2012

Printed in the United States of America

0 9 8 7 6 5 4 3 2 1

CLEAN

b19926297

This book is dedicated to my loving parents,
Robert and Carol McLean,
for the memories of Golden Beach, magic shows,
and the aroma of hamburgers and hotdogs
on the paper cooker at the base of the North Slope.

It is not the oath that makes us believe the man, but the man the oath.

—Aeschylus, *Fragments*, no. 385

UNDER OATH

1

Presentation of evidence before the Grand Jury of Suffolk County, Massachusetts, against William Joseph Malone. Murder indictment pending. November twenty-first.

DO YOU SWEAR to tell the truth, the whole truth, and nothing but the truth, so help you God?"

Please help me God.

"Miss?" the clerk said.

See nothing, hear nothing . . .

"Miss?" The clerk cleared his throat.

"I do." Jennianne's right hand trembled. *Stop now, save yourself.* She counted thirteen lint specks in the courtroom rug.

"Good morning." Annie Fitzgerald's voice carried across the room and seemed to hover in the air before it landed. Jennianne felt the intensity of the prosecutor's Asian-shaped eyes without even looking at her. She was Fitzgerald's star witness before the grand jury, which meant she had to break the code.

"Please introduce yourself to the ladies and gentlemen of the grand jury." Fitzgerald sounded anxious.

Jennianne peeked through an opening in her yellow bangs, and examined row by row of wooden benches where the public usually sat. They were empty as Fitzgerald had promised. She glanced at the defense table. *Empty, too. Thank God.* She could never do this in front of *him.* Her gaze shifted to the right. Nothing but the dark paneled wall, the American flag, and the elevated judge's bench. And to the left? She spotted the gold-fringed Massachusetts flag, and just beyond that . . . two rows of grand jurors, leaning forward, staring. She resumed counting specks in the rug.

"Please tell us your name." Fitzgerald's voice dropped an octave.

"Jennianne."

"Okay. And your last?"

"Smith." She finally made eye contact with Fitzgerald. Why did she have to be the one to do this? Couldn't Fitzgerald find someone else? Why did they pick this case? Billy Malone would win. He always did.

"How old are you?"

"Twenty-eight." *Too young to die.*

"Where do you live?"

Where do I live? No one was supposed to know about the safe house except Detective Callahan. Billy would find her and kill her. There were three rules of survival: You see nothing, you hear nothing, and you never talk to cops. Jennianne had broken all three.

"Just tell us where you're from."

"Charlestown." Jennianne tried to connect with Fitzgerald by looking through her eyes and into her soul. *You know he's going to kill me. Please don't make me do this. Please, please, please, Annie. Don't.*

"Do you recall November tenth of last year?" Fitzgerald kept her voice steady.

Jennianne knew Fitzgerald would forge ahead at all costs. *Can't you just leave me alone?* She inhaled deeply and nodded.

"Miss, please respond with a verbal answer," the judge said.

"Mmm hmm." Jennianne's mouth went dry; her tongue shriveled. "Yes."

"Do you recall what you were doing at approximately seven P.M.?"

See nothing, hear nothing, never talk to cops. Jennianne shivered. Detective Callahan had tossed her in jail and forced her into this. *Fitzgerald, too.* Her gaze flickered across the rows of grand jurors. According to Callahan, she needed their votes. She closed her eyes and recalled his words as they drove from the safe house that morning: "If twelve or more vote in favor of an indictment, the case will go to superior court."

"What if you don't get twelve votes?" Jennianne had asked.

"We'll end up with a 'no bill,' and if that happens, the complaint against Billy Malone will be dismissed."

"He'd walk free?"

"Yup."

"What'll happen to me?"

Callahan had shrugged. "You'd go back to the projects."

"But, he'll kill me because he knows."

"You'll have to fend for yourself. So, if I were you, I'd do a real knock-up job today."

"Jennianne?" Fitzgerald cleared her throat. "Shall I repeat the question?"

God help me. Jennianne opened her eyes, saw the grand jurors, and closed them again. She felt the sensation of cold air blowing across the nape of her neck, raising the tiny hairs. She pictured an emaciated Trevor Shea sitting behind that splintered easel of his, painting his life away. Ever since they were in first grade together with Sister Peg, Trevor had painted. What were you really doing all these years, Trev?

Without Jennianne's voice, Trevor's case would be tossed into that big box along with the rest of the unsolved murders. Fitzgerald had piled all those dead cases in a heap on the conference table in front of her. *All twenty-six.*

"What happened on November tenth?"

You killed yourself.

"Jennianne?"

2

Four months later

BOSTON HOMICIDE DETECTIVE Mike Callahan leaned up close to the witness and lowered his voice. "Remember what Miss Fitzgerald and I told you to say about how you found the victim?"

Officer Larry O'Neil studied his police report as if preparing for the most important test in his life. Callahan grimaced at the thought of kicking this trial off with a twenty-three-year-old rookie complete with baby face and dimples. And, a virgin to boot. O'Neil would need an escort to the damn stand. At age forty-three, Callahan had twenty-one years of court under his belt and still made mistakes so, O'Neil, he figured would be like a babe in the woods, diapers and all. He recalled his first time testifying before a jury. The defense attorney had his mind spinning in ten different directions, made him say yes to everything, and blew up his report. They lost the case. And now they were going up against Buddy Clancy, the best in the business. He would chew O'Neil up and spit him right out like hard gum.

"Where's that part again?" O'Neil's voice wavered.

"It isn't in your report, Larry." Callahan felt like shaking the guy. They'd gone over this a zillion times.

"Oh yeah, I forgot." O'Neil sucked the tip of his thumb. "So?"

"So you have to talk about the needle and the way Trevor held it in his right hand." Callahan raked his fingers through his thick, sandy-colored hair, long overdue for a cut. "Don't screw up the needle part."

"I won't. I got it. The needle."

"How was Trevor holding the needle?" Callahan laced his hands together and cracked his knuckles.

"You mean in his right hand?"

"Dammit, Larry." Callahan added two more sticks of Big Red to a wad nearly the size of a golf ball. His jaw muscles ached and cracked at the joints. He wished he could coach O'Neil during his testimony, but he'd be stuck in the hallway since all witnesses had to be sequestered until they finished testifying. "Which way . . . how exactly was Trevor holding the needle?"

"Oh, right. I'm sorry, upside down. Upside down."

"Upside down. Good. Now memorize it."

Callahan paced in small circles. Reporters, court officers, lawyers, and spectators jammed the windowless hallway that morning, all snuffling, coughing, or sneezing. It smelled like wet wool and mucky winter boots. Frowning faces lined the benches as if they'd been waiting for a long-lost bus. Fred the custodian leaned against his dry mop in between two CAUTION—WET FLOOR signs. Callahan felt the urge to spill the remainder of his coffee, give ol' Fred something to do for a change. A reporter tugged at the courtroom's locked double doors.

"He'll get off. Malone always does," someone said.

Callahan's throat tightened. He wouldn't let it happen again. Billy Malone was worse than a serial killer. You could catch him, but everyone knew who he was and what he did. They still just turned their backs.

Callahan's cell emitted a high-pitched ring. *The office.* He had no choice but to press the talk button. "I'm busy with O'Neil." He knew it was Captain Murphy, hovering over his ham-and-egg breakfast bagel and coffee.

"Everything on track?"

"Peachy."

"Good. We can't afford another embarrassment. I want an airtight case this time. No missing evidence, no dead witnesses."

"Okey dokey." Callahan hung up. "Bastard."

The case had been a nightmare from the get-go. Callahan had to set up a safe house for Jennianne Smith, his prime witness, and prep her for the grand jury. They narrowly squeezed out an indictment. After that, he endured four months of gathering evidence, cracking uncooperative witnesses, death threats, slashed tires, lack of sleep, lack of help, lack of time. What next? O'Neil forgetting his lines. Callahan regarded the terrified rookie and sat next to him.

"Remember to talk about the path leading up to Trevor's body. Whether you noticed that stuff or not just say it with enough conviction so the jury will believe you. You've got to make them believe you."

O'Neil nodded too fast.

"And beware of Buddy Clancy. He's been around forever. He'll lull you into saying whatever he wants to hear. Listen very carefully to the question before you go blurting out an answer. Okay?"

Again, the rapid nods.

"Don't forget eye contact with the jury. It's very, very important." Callahan frowned. O'Neil sat doubled over at the waist, preoccupied with speed reading again. A ticking bomb. No matter what Callahan advised, he'd explode on the stand.

Callahan withdrew a worn, wallet-sized photograph from his back pocket. It revealed a blond-haired boy with big ears, a gigantic smile, and two missing front teeth. That boy never made it beyond his twenty-eighth birthday. Callahan always kept photos of murder victims in his back pocket while working a case. It was the visual of the living, the boy full of life, full of hope, that gave Callahan his drive, got him through the all-nighters. He stared at the creased picture. Why did he pull this one out more often? Twice as much, perhaps even more?

A flash of red amidst the sea of black and gray coats caught Callahan's eye at the far end of the hallway. That signature red plaid beret could only belong to one person: Annie Fitzgerald. She floated above the fray at nearly six feet tall. Her long, straight hair, which was dark brown, nearly black, shimmered beneath the hat. The crowds broke up, clearing the way for Annie like small animals in the path of a predator.

"Need a hand?" Callahan asked. Annie appeared a bit winded. She struggled with an oversized briefcase in one hand, and a large oil painting wrapped in brown paper beneath her armpit. Callahan knew that painting well. At night, he'd lie awake thinking about it, visualizing the artist's most minute details. In all his years as a homicide detective, he'd never seen evidence like that.

"Here, I'll take the briefcase." Callahan lifted the straps from her shoulder; it weighed a ton.

"Thank you." She gazed at him for a moment, appearing pensive.

Callahan admired Annie's high cheekbones and striking Asian eyes . . . so beautiful beneath those full dark lashes. Annie's mother was Malaysian and her father, Irish. *What a combination.* She was one of the most intelligent women he had ever met. Sometimes he'd sit in the back of the courtroom and watch her argue motions before the judge. She could talk circles around most criminal defense lawyers with her superior grasp of constitutional law. Hell, Annie was smarter than most of the judges, too. She seemed a bit out of place in the criminal courts. Callahan often wondered why she had opted for the DA's Office.

Annie leaned the painting against her hip, removed her hat, and lodged a gold hairclip between her lips. She spoke, but her words came out garbled.

Callahan watched her smooth down that beautiful, silky hair. He ran his hand through his own hair and felt parts of it sticking up. He had to get it cut before testifying.

Annie gathered the mass of hair just below her neck and snapped the clip in place. "Judge Killam is famous for moving cases right along, but they're predicting this rain may change over to snow. If the conditions get hazardous, we may adjourn early. So, I'd say O'Neil, Twomey, and Domenico. However, if O'Neil does a decent job, I may not bother with Twomey. We have to keep it simple, avoid contradictions."

Callahan glanced at O'Neil and rolled his eyes. So that meant Twomey would have to testify. Maybe they wouldn't get to Domenico; he hoped not.

"Where is Twomey?" Annie stood on her tiptoes and surveyed the crowd. "Don't see him."

"He's just getting off a detail."

"Great. Just great. Knowing Twomey, he probably pulled an all-nighter. Better page him now. You'll need to review it with him before he goes on."

Callahan dialed Twomey's number as a tidal wave of people poured into the courtroom. He felt the adrenaline. He would see this conviction through. He promised himself.

"You have that scumbag Domenico on call, right?" Annie lifted the painting.

Callahan released a long sigh. *Don't go there.*

Annie moved toward him until their faces nearly touched. "What's the matter?"

"Nothing."

"What about Domenico?" Annie studied at him as if trying to read his mind. "What's up with Domenico? I need to know everything, Mike."

"Don't worry about it. I've been in contact with him ever since we worked the deal."

"But not today." She released a long sigh. "Without Domenico, we're sunk. He's our link to Malone."

"I told you we should've kept him locked up," Callahan said. "I told you all along."

"Perhaps I should speak with Clancy before we get started." Annie drummed her fingers against the paper covering the painting. "Maybe we can convince Malone to go for manslaughter."

"What?" Callahan almost choked on his gum. "No way. Malone won't plea to anything but a not guilty. Takes his chances with Clancy. You know that."

"I know, I know. What should we do then? We absolutely need Domenico."

She was right. "Get started with O'Neil. I'll head up to Gloucester." Callahan would search every crevice of the North Shore fishing community if he had to. "I'll find Domenico. I'll find him. If he's alive."

3

I **F HE'S ALIVE.** Callahan's words echoed in Annie's mind. Could he be dead? Yes. Could she win this case against Malone without Domenico? No. Forge ahead, don't think about it now.

Annie adjusted the giant oil canvas on the easel and stepped back. The colorful figures haunted her. This one depicted kids on a city playground. They had formed a circle around a freckly little red-haired boy in a blue T-shirt lying on his back in the dirt. He had orange stains around his mouth as if he'd just eaten a bag of cheese curls. A bigger, much older teenager sat on his chest leaning forward, pinning him down. The big one was about to do something. The little boy looked out from the canvas; his gaze met Annie's. Eyes don't scream, but these did. Annie heard them.

A commotion out in the spectators' gallery forced Annie to turn around. A woman sat doubled over in the front row, wailing. Annie recognized her as a member of the group that called themselves Mothers Against Murder, part of the Charlestown After Murder Program. Fifteen had lost sons and one lost a daughter. *All to murder.* Unsolved murders. They were Annie's cases now, her burden. Some had been unsolved for over thirty years, others were around five to ten years old. The fresh ones were under two. The victims' ages ranged from their teens to a couple guys in their fifties.

The group leader, Sandy Finn, walked the woman out. Annie said a silent prayer for her. She wondered which unsolved case it was. Annie had met most of the mothers when she attended meetings in St. Catherine's basement on Tuesday nights with Father Coyne. She had listened to their frustrations with the police investigations, the lack of witnesses, the dead ends. Annie wondered if Trevor's mother would eventually join. Last she heard, the members were planning to visit Mrs. Shea at the psych ward. The doctors had her on suicide watch. *Again.*

"Mornin', Annie."

She jumped at the sound of Clerk Fallon's voice. "Good morning, George."

"They're predicting freezing rain this afternoon, a possible nor'easter. Seems like winter's hanging on forever. Typical March weather in new England. We may have to close court early." He shuffled papers on his table right below the judge's bench. "Ready to go?"

"As ready as I can be." No matter how many hours Annie put in, it was never enough.

"Because he's in one of his moods." Fallon pointed his thumb toward the judge's chambers. "Just rarin' to go." He motioned toward the wall clock, which read five minutes to nine. "I warned Clancy not to be late today. It was the last thing I said to him on Friday, 'Don't be late.'"

Annie sat behind her table. The trial books, legal pads, and her laptop were all arranged. She smoothed her hair again and felt the gold clip in back. Straight. What else could she do? The wait was excruciating. It was when she had nothing to do that the doubts seeped into her mind. Was prosecuting this case a mistake? Callahan had summoned her to the scene shortly after they found Trevor's body beneath the Tobin Bridge in Charlestown. He knew she'd be sucked in. She spun her pen on the table-top until it careened into a legal pad.

Perhaps, Annie thought, she should never have returned. How did she end up in the Boston area again, living in Brookline, when she could practice law anywhere? Her parents were dead; she had no family around. Why had she gotten involved in a case like this? It was all about Charlestown, too, where Annie had spent the first eleven years of her life. This was his fault. *Callahan's.* She should have said no.

Annie gazed at the painting of the kids in the Charlestown playground. Why was she so captivated by it? There was something intimate about Trevor's painting as if she'd been standing right there in that circle of kids. She could smell the grass and mud and a faint odor of cigarette smoke. She'd spent time in that playground as a little girl, but most of it alone, watching the other children play. They rarely asked her to participate; she was too different from them.

Annie recalled her mother and father's tiny bookstore on Main Street in Charlestown called Fitzy's Mysteries. She pictured the shelves stacked to the ceiling with mostly paperbacks. The wall to the right after you walked in contained all the new colorful hard covers. She would open those books in the middle and stick her nose all the way down to the spine, taking in that fresh paper smell. Annie was an only child; when she wasn't in school, she spent most of her spare time with her parents at the store. As they chatted with customers, Annie would make forts out of all the boxes in the storage room in the back. She could still hear the little bell above the door, which tinkled whenever someone came in. People usually entered with a friendly "hello." Most called her parents by their first names. Mrs. White would drop by with a blueberry pie or fresh tomatoes from her garden in August. It was only once a month that the bell would tinkle twice for the two men who always came in and never bought any books. Annie shivered at the memory.

"Dammit all." Fallon banged his coffee mug. "I'll have to stall him."

"Calm down, will yah? Heart attack waitin' to happen." Court Officer Johnny Walsh lumbered down the aisle. "Clancy'll be here any minute. Probably stuck in traffic. Mornin', Annie. It's all jammed up out there."

Annie forced a smile.

"Easy for you to say. I'm the one's gotta go in there." Fallon headed back toward chambers. "Unless you're volunteering?"

"Hell no."

" 'Swhat I thought." In less than a minute, Clerk Fallon trotted back into the courtroom. "Judge wants to see yah, Johnny."

"Oh for cryin' out loud. What does His Highness want from me?" Johnny waddled to the back and stuck his large, speckled head through the chamber door. "Yeah? Alrighty then." He strolled to the telephone on the far wall and fumbled with the receiver.

Annie knew Johnny was nearing the end of his long reign in court-room 812, and could take as long as he pleased.

"Wants the prisoner brought up now." Johnny spoke into the receiver and paused. "Nope, Clancy's not here yet. This oughta be good."

Within five minutes, guards escorted a shackled Billy Malone into the courtroom. His gaze seared through Annie, but she matched it with a menacing look of her own. As she stared at him, another face replaced Malone's, the face that haunted her dreams from the time she was eleven.

Annie looked away from Malone. *Not now. Please don't think about that now.* She focused on the painting of the boy lying in the dirt. *Those terrified, screaming eyes.*

"Good morning, Annie," Malone whispered. His suit jacket brushed the edge of her table as he walked by.

"Take your seat," the guard said.

Malone ignored him and surveyed the audience instead, as if committing the faces to memory. He smiled at his mother in the first row. Annie figured Mrs. Malone had dressed the same as she would for Sunday Mass at St. Catherine's. She wore a pretty gray dress with lace around the collar, hem, and sleeves. Her fingers worked the white rosary beads and silver cross in her lap. Clancy had probably suggested the beads; Annie wouldn't put it past him.

Annie wished Trevor's mother could be seated on the other side of the aisle with another set of rosary beads. In her place, Annie had lined up the Mothers Against Murder with their matching yellow T-shirts. She nodded at them and some nodded back. They should've brought their beads.

"I said take your seat." The guard gripped the back of Malone's wooden chair. "You gotta wait for your lawyer."

Annie looked at Malone's mother again. This time, she was crying. Annie wondered if Mrs. Malone had to pause before deciding which pew to genuflect next to in church. Did she have to see where the Mothers Against Murder were seated first? Would she join them someday?

Malone eased himself down and grinned at Annie. If he could, he'd pull her chair out every time she had to sit down like a polite Irish gentleman. Who would ever know? He looked so dapper in his pressed navy suit and tie. But Annie knew better. Malone was the worst of the worst: a thinker, a plotter, a killer.

Annie scanned the courtroom for Trevor's brother Chris, his only sibling. She needed a representative from the victim's family for the jury to see. Chris had been uncooperative. He never returned phone calls and refused to meet with her. Annie had to find a way to break through his wall.

"All rise!" Johnny spread his arms. "Hear ye! Hear ye! The Superior Court of Suffolk County is now in session, the Honorable Conrad J. Killam presiding." The attorneys and people packed in the gallery stood as the judge emerged from his chambers. He paraded across the rug with long strides, arms pumping, and black robe fluttering. He stomped up three steps to his elevated bench and plunked down in the red-cushioned king-size chair.

"Be seated," Johnny said.

Judge Killam scanned the crowd with eyes set in monstrous sockets. The parallel lines from his comb had been jelled into his steel gray hair.

Clerk Fallon rose. "On the list for Monday, March tenth, is criminal case 12-8996K, which has been marked for trial."

Judge Killam poured himself a glass of water from his plastic brown pitcher. He took a hardy gulp and smacked his lips. "Commonwealth ready for trial?"

"Yes." Annie smiled at the judge. "Good morning, Your Honor. The Commonwealth stands ready for trial, but attorney Clancy—"

"Don't state the obvious, counselor. If attorney Clancy does not appear, I will start this trial without him."

"What?" Malone banged his handcuffs against the table.

"Enough!" Judge Killam raised a hand and scowled at the defendant.

Annie resumed her seat and waited. Every few minutes, the judge jerked forward and ruffled his robe as if threatening to swoop down from his perch and snatch somebody up for sneezing.

The courtroom doors finally banged against the wall. Annie turned to see Buddy Clancy sprinting down the aisle carrying a tattered briefcase, a plaid fedora, and a huge golf umbrella, still half-open.

"I'm getting too ol' for this." Clancy tossed his briefcase on the counsel table, where it skidded and toppled off the other side.

"Good morning, Your Honor, Mr. Clerk, Miss Fitzgerald." He breathed heavily as he folded the umbrella. "I apologize for my tardiness." He took off his coat, revealing a bowtie with American flags all over it.

Judge Killam's jowls and double chin puffed out like a balloon until he looked like he could float up to the ceiling. Annie sat perfectly still. *It was coming.*

"Clancy!" The judge shot to his feet. "You've inconvenienced me and delayed this entire trial. I'm about to declare you in contempt and fine you. What do you have to say for yourself?"

Clancy raised a finger. "It's not my lucky day."

"You're right." The judge slapped his hands on his hips. "It's not your lucky day. In fact, you've started off on the wrong foot."

"Oh dear." Clancy ran his fingers through his thick white hair. "You're not going to believe this, but as my bus was driving past the Boston Garden—the number ninety-two bus—it got hit by a duck boat."

"A what?" Judge Killam's lower jaw dropped several inches.

"A duck boat."

"You mean the big tourist contraptions that drive around the city and end up in the Charles River? Where everybody quacks?"

"It's the God's honest truth, Judge. And it was the duck boat's fault."

Laughter rose from the gallery.

"Now that's a first." He puckered his lips as if suppressing a laugh. "A duck boat, Clancy? You ready for trial?"

"Oh yes, Your Honor."

"Bring in the jury."

The guard unlocked Malone's handcuffs and shackles as Clancy placed his briefcase back on the table.

The courtroom doors banged open again. Annie was surprised to see Trevor's brother, Chris, standing in the open doorway. He looked like a boxer about to enter the ring with his compact muscular frame and gray hooded sweatshirt and sweatpants. He was unshaven and his dark, wavy hair fell to his shoulders. Annie watched him march down the aisle and squeeze into the front row next to the mothers. Chris stared at Malone and Malone winked back.

Judge Killam leaned over his bench and tapped Clerk Fallon. "Call down and tell them to send another court officer for the hallway. Make it clear that no one else is to enter my courtroom." While Fallon made the call, the judge addressed the packed gallery: "This trial will proceed with dignity. If I hear any outbursts, I'll have the responsible party arrested for contempt and fined."

Johnny appeared in a side door. "All rise for the jury."

Annie hoped they'd notice Trevor's painting right away. She and Clancy had battled over it in a pretrial motion. Judge Killam had ruled that she could use it as a visual aid in her opening statement to portray the victim as an artist.

The jurors entered single file. Most of them followed the same pattern. They gazed into the crowded gallery, over at Malone, up to the bench, and, at last, at Trevor's painting. Would it strike a chord with someone? Would they hear those screaming eyes?

4

RACHEL PAINE STARED at the giant painting as she took her seat in chair number one of the jury box. It was so real she could feel the intensity of the moment, the summer heat, the grimy kids. Something was about to happen in that painting, something terrible. The little boy lying on the ground with the red hair and freckles looked right at Rachel as if begging for her help.

"Ladies and gentlemen, we thank you for your service here today," Judge Killam said.

Rachel tore her gaze from the little boy in the painting, and looked up at the judge. She half-listened as he explained their role as jurors and informed them that opening statements are not evidence, but merely a preview of the case. Rachel had been chosen to be the foreperson. She figured the judge had been impressed with her managerial position at one of Boston's top executive search firms. Perhaps he picked her because she was best dressed and looked most attractive in her fitted cranberry suit. Rachel certainly had the ability to lead this mostly working-class jury composed of nine women and five men. Two would ultimately be chosen as alternates and not allowed to deliberate. She was anxious to get started. Jury selection had dragged on the week before. It felt like all they did was sit around and wait.

"Commonwealth?" Judge Killam relaxed into his chair.

"Thank you. Annie Fitzgerald for the Commonwealth."

Rachel watched Miss Fitzgerald approach the jury box with long, graceful strides. She made eye contact with each juror but seemed to gaze longer upon her. She admired the prosecutor's dark, exotic eyes and slim build. *No wedding ring.* Work probably interfered with her relationships as it did for Rachel.

"This is Trevor Shea at age twenty-eight, seven months before he died." Fitzgerald raised a photograph of a young man with the Boston Common as the backdrop. The tulips had been in full bloom. She walked the length of the box making sure each juror gazed into the laughing blue eyes. Rachel noticed Trevor's humorous pose with hands on his hips and a silly grin from ear to ear. He had big Dumbo ears. Trevor's eyes seemed ready to dance right out of the photograph and into the courtroom. *So full of life.* She looked at the painting again. What happened to the little redhead on the ground? Who was he? It didn't look like Trevor. *Tell us about the painting.*

"Trevor Shea grew up over the bridge in Charlestown. His mother, Ellen, is a lifelong resident. Trevor's brother, Chris, is seated right over there in the front row."

Rachel looked and wondered why the brother wore shabby sweat pants. Where was Trevor's mother? Didn't she care about her dead son's trial? Who were all those women in the front row with the matching yellow T-shirts? Rachel felt the intensity of their gazes and stiffened. They were somehow connected to the case, depending on her to make the right decision. Rachel felt the gravity of the job ahead.

"Trevor's father disappeared when he was just five years old, on the little boy's birthday." Fitzgerald gazed into the audience at the victim's brother. "The boys never found out what happened to their dad."

Disappeared? Rachel pictured a young boy blowing out five candles, listening for a key in the front door, footsteps in the hallway. The smoke curling upward from the candles . . . a birthday wish gone bad. What could've happened to him? Rachel looked at the painting again and the frightened little boy on the ground. She could smell the wax and smoke from those birthday candles.

"After that tragic birthday, Trevor's mother struggled. They moved into the Bunker Hill housing project. Trevor and his brother were bused to the other side of the city to attend public school in Roxbury. For the most part, the boys had to fend for themselves."

Fitzgerald centered herself in front of the jury box with her fingers touching as if in prayer. Rachel could hear the raw emotion in her voice when she spoke. She clearly sympathized with Trevor and his family, and all those women in the front row, whoever they were.

Fitzgerald walked up to the painting. "This painting won first prize at the Newbury Arts Festival last year."

Rachel inched to the edge of her seat. *That painting.* Yes, that's where she had seen it, in a color photograph in the *Boston Globe*'s art section. She remembered the full page write-up about the young, aspiring painter from Charlestown.

"The artist, Trevor Shea, possessed a unique talent for capturing a moment. The expressions . . . the eyes . . ." Fitzgerald's voice trailed off. She touched the painting with her fingertip, and gently traced the circle of kids. "So gifted for a street kid."

Rachel felt like she was kneeling in that dirty playground with those dirty children. She could feel the loose gravel embedded in her knees and the prickly blades of burnt-out grass. She noticed a large, fist-sized gray rock off to the side. Even that looked so real, three-dimensional, as if it could be dislodged and fall from the painting right onto the courtroom rug. What was happening here? Who were these kids? Why was the artist killed?

"Art was Trevor's ticket out." Fitzgerald's voice projected across the room as if she wanted to snap people out of the canvas and back to the stark reality of the courtroom. "This painting, right here, was Trevor's lucky break—until he came across another creative genius." Fitzgerald pointed at Malone. "A creative genius in the art of murder."

Clancy popped up. "Your Honor, am I in the right room here? Is this an art gallery?" He spread his arms. "Because it sounds like an art lecture. Perhaps I hit my head on the duck boat and ended up in the wrong place?"

Several jurors laughed.

Judge Killam banged his gavel. "Enough with the theatrics, Clancy. Are you objecting?"

"Of course I am." Clancy addressed the jury. "I rarely object during opening statements, but Miss Fitzgerald's art gallery speech here is both prejudicial and argumentative. It's simply not fair."

"Your objection is to be addressed to me, Mr. Clancy, not the jury."

"Well, then, I object. Officially."

"Yes, I heard you." Judge Killam huffed. "Sustained. Miss Fitzgerald, please refrain from argument."

The judge's ruling confused Rachel. She had liked Fitzgerald's line about Malone. *Creative genius in the art of murder.* What was wrong with saying that? After all, wasn't this a murder trial?

Fitzgerald walked right up to the jury box as if unfazed by the interruption. "The Commonwealth will prove beyond a reasonable doubt that the defendant, Billy Malone, created a masterpiece: the perfect murder. He simply handed Trevor Shea the murder weapon, an overdose of Nine-eleven heroin with the intent to kill him. Malone watched Trevor inject that heroin, watched him die an agonizing death, and then dragged his lifeless body right through the streets of Charlestown."

Rachel studied Malone while Fitzgerald briefed them on the evidence she expected to produce against him. He appeared clean-shaven, rather charming, and didn't really look like a murderer. He seemed comfortable in his surroundings. Perhaps he'd occupied that seat before. Maybe he really was a creative genius.

Fitzgerald positioned Trevor's photograph on the easel near the corner of the painting. "At the conclusion of this case, I will once again address you in my closing argument. At that time I will ask you to analyze all the evidence and return with a guilty verdict against Billy Malone for murder in the first degree.

"Thank you." Fitzgerald made eye contact with each juror before taking her seat.

Clancy rose. "Sidebar, Your Honor?"

Judge Killam motioned both attorneys to the left side of his bench, away from the jury.

Rachel strained to hear what was being said.

The judge faced the jury when the sidebar conference ended. "At this time the defendant has chosen to waive his opening statement as is his right. You must not draw any conclusions regarding the waiver. Commonwealth, please call your first witness."

Rachel was disappointed; she had wanted to hear the other side of the story. Perhaps they were waiting to see what the prosecution had in store for them. In any event, it left her in suspense. She looked at the painting and stared into the eyes of that terrified little redheaded boy.

5

THE COMMONWEALTH CALLS Officer Larry O'Neil." Annie grabbed a legal pad and waited for Johnny to waddle down the aisle and fetch O'Neil. She watched Clancy adjusting a new black bowtie with dice all over it, and pondered why he had picked that one. Was he planning a trip to the casino after court? She wondered what surprises he had in store for her; it wasn't often he deferred his opening statement. Annie hoped O'Neil would remember what to say. She also prayed Callahan would locate their witness, Miles Domenico, up in Gloucester, or all this would be in vain. Malone would simply walk out, looking at her the whole time with that shit-eating grin that said, *"Now get the hell out of Charlestown."*

Annie scanned the front row with all the mothers looking hopeful. She thought about her own mother and sighed. She could almost smell fish—her mother always cooked with that strong fish oil that permeated the house and clung to everyone's clothes. It had been three years since Annie lost her to breast cancer. Was she here in spirit? *Perhaps.* Back then, her mother was one of a few scattered Asians in Charlestown, one of Boston's small neighborhoods, which was almost all Irish. She felt a wave of sadness. Those two men had called her mother a gook every time they came into the bookstore.

"Officer O'Neil!" Johnny yelled into the hallway.

Annie watched the young cop stumble through the doorway. He must've tripped over his own feet. He approached the witness stand with short, quick steps like he needed to find a bathroom—immediately. Perhaps Callahan had been right about not wanting to call O'Neil first. Annie felt it was best to start at the beginning, like telling a story. She looked at the jurors. Annie had successfully hooked them with her opening statement about Trevor and his art. But could she keep them on that hook? She recalled bass fishing with her father . . . the strike on her lure . . . reeling it in with just the right amount of tension . . . keeping the fish on the hook. She missed her father, who died within months of her mother.

"Raise your right hand please." Clerk Fallon raised his own hand and O'Neil copied him. "Do you swear to tell the truth, the whole truth, and nothing but the truth so help you God?"

"I do." O'Neil appeared lost, like he didn't know what to do next. Clerk Fallon pointed to the chair behind the witness stand. O'Neil seemed a bit surprised to be sitting in the lone chair next to the bench.

Annie wondered if they should've practiced in the courtroom. Too late now. She walked to the podium near the far end of the jury box, adjacent to the gallery and away from the witness stand. She had been taught to position herself as far from the stand as possible during direct examination in order to force the witness to project over the jury box. She made eye contact with the attractive foreperson in the cranberry suit with the matching red rectangular glasses. Annie had to win her over.

"Good morning." Annie tried to sound casual to calm O'Neil's nerves. "Please introduce yourself to the jury."

"Um, Larry O'Neil."

"Speak up!" Judge Killam's voice thundered across the courtroom as if he had used a bullhorn. O'Neil gasped and jumped about six inches. His face and ears turned bright red.

Annie felt sorry for O'Neil; the judge had startled her as well. "Where do you work?"

"Patrolman. For the Boston, the Boston Police. Area A."

"How long have you worked there?"

"Um. I'd say . . . a year."

Annie cringed as O'Neil stumbled through the easy answers about his education, training, and experience. She could see his fingers trembling. What would he do when her questions required some thought? Perhaps the jury would sympathize with him; sometimes appearing nervous was a good thing.

"Do you recall Friday, November tenth of last year?" Annie held her breath.

O'Neil stared at the ceiling.

Annie cringed. God help her if he forgot the day of the murder.

"November . . . uh, yeah. The tenth?"

"Yes. Were you working that day?"

"The night shift, starting at ten. I was operating my cruiser on lower Bunker Hill Street in Charlestown and planned to meet up with Officer Twomey, who was patrolling in the vicinity of Collier's Market when the dispatcher said there was a 9-1-1 call—"

"Objection!" Clancy's hand shot up. "That's hearsay. You can't say what somebody else said, Officer."

Judge Killam grunted. "I'll explain the law here, Clancy. Sustained."

"Officer, let's take this step by step." Annie needed to slow him down. O'Neil was spitting out his lines, but forgetting how to deliver them. "As a result of the dispatch, what did you do?"

"Okay. Um, I informed the dispatcher that um . . ." O'Neil rubbed the perspiration from his brow. "I was responding to the call and proceeded to the intersection of Decatur Street and Walford Way and then I took a left-hand turn toward Dupont Street. No, it was a right turn, right-hand turn, and I parked my cruiser over by the Tobin Bridge and stepped out. Well, first I opened my door, then got out. Then, I drew my service revolver with my right hand, carried a flashlight in my left."

Annie took a deep breath. Right, left, left, right. Why was O'Neil concentrating so much on the rights and lefts now? He was still talking way too fast; the words were running together and he'd lose the jury. Annie

had repeatedly told him to speak slowly and concisely. Through the corner of her eye, she caught Malone looking at her.

"What time did all this occur?" she asked.

"Around ten forty."

"What was the weather like?"

"Very cold, gusty. I remember the leaves swirling around."

"What happened next?"

"About twenty feet up from Dupont Street, I discovered the body of a
Caucasian male. I felt for a pulse; there wasn't any. I then radioed in to
the station to report what I found. After that Officer Twomey arrived."

Annie thought he sounded too stiff, too rehearsed. Malone was still
looking at her. "Can you describe the position of the body?"

"It—he was lying on his back. The legs were straight; the arms were
sort of crossed at the chest. No, wait. One arm was up over the head and
the other was lying across the chest. The eyes were bulging out a little,
staring up into space. The mouth was wide open."

"What was he wearing?"

"Jeans and a white T-shirt with paint stains, all different-colored paint
stains."

"Was he wearing anything else, like a jacket?"

"No. No, that was it."

"Did you notice anything near the body?"

"Uhh . . . not that I recall."

Annie stared at him. That was a cue to talk about the leaves and the
path leading from the body and he missed it. She'd have to move on to
the needle. "Was he holding anything?"

"Objection." Clancy rose halfway. "Leading."

"Sustained."

"Did you observe anything else?" Annie had to rephrase her question,
make it open-ended. She hoped O'Neil would know what she wanted.

O'Neil hesitated. "Like . . . you mean, the needle?"

Annie nodded. "What about the needle? Can you describe it?"

"It was a regular one. A hypodermic needle used for drugs, to inject
drugs."

"Do you recall in which hand he held the needle?"

O'Neil studied both his hands. "Uh, I think it was the . . . right."

"Did you make any other observations about the needle?" *Come on.* Annie wished she could slip him a note.

"Not that I recall."

Dammit. She knew he'd forget.

"Are you sure?" she asked.

Clancy raised his hands. "Is he sure? Is he sure?"

"Do I detect an objection?" Judge Killam leaned over his bench.

"You bet! Asked and answered, Your Honor."

"Sustained."

Annie hoped O'Neil would remember later. She decided to try the leaves again. "Did you notice anything else leading up to the body? *Leaving* the body?"

"Objection!" Clancy popped up. "Leading the witness."

"Sustained."

Annie sighed. "What did you do next?"

"I rolled the body over and pulled a wallet out of the left back pocket of the jeans. Me and Officer Twomey looked through the wallet and found a Mass driver's license belonging to Trevor Shea."

"What did the picture on the license show?"

"It showed the same face as the dead, the dead body."

Annie admitted the license into evidence. "What did you do next?"

"Nothing. We just waited and eventually Detective Mike Callahan from Homicide showed up. I told Detective Callahan about the situation, and went back on my patrol."

"Nothing further." Annie watched O'Neil breathe a sigh of relief and sneak a quick glance at the jury like a baby playing peekaboo. Now it was time for the unavoidable Clancy massacre.

Annie grabbed her legal pad from the podium and headed back to her table. Her gaze met Malone's. It wasn't a menacing look that he gave her; no one would notice anything out of the ordinary. It was something else—*a knowing look.* What did he know about her? Annie was thirty-two and Malone, thirty-eight. She had never met him as a child in Charlestown nor had she heard anything about him. She wondered if he'd ever been to the bookstore? If so, had he noticed the little girl helping her parents stock the shelves? Did he spot her reading a mystery in her fort made of boxes? Did he know why they had to shutter the store and leave Charlestown?

6

"OOD MORNING TO all you fine ladies and gentlemen."
Clancy conjured his best grandfatherly smile, and made eye
contact with each juror. He received several smiles in return.
The pretty foreperson in the red glasses mouthed *good morning*. She sat
up straight with her legs slightly angled and close together like a television anchorwoman. Crisp, clean . . . a tad heavy with the makeup
around her eyes. She could be a challenge for she exuded that conserva-
tive aura, and those types were always tough on crime.

Clancy widened his smile for the two old ladies with the tight curly
perms and flowery dresses in the second row. They reminded him of his
great-aunt Adelaide and Sister Theresa, a dark church and incense. He'd
win them over with his Catholic boy charm. The skinny male accountant
with the long face and the crazy-haired techie would most likely overana-
lyze the case, which was a good thing. Too much thinking created more
questions, and questions gave rise to reasonable doubt. *Reasonable doubt*—
his two favorite words in the English language. Hell, they were good in
any language.

Clancy faced Officer O'Neil and adjusted his dice tie. "And a good
morning to you, too, Officer."

O'Neil stiffened. Clancy had cross-examined hundreds of rookie cops;

they were easy to confuse, frustrate, blow up. He'd have to be extra careful with this one. The jurors knew he was nervous, boyishly so. Great-Aunt Adelaide and Sister Theresa might feel the urge to protect him. Clancy had to take it easy, lull O'Neil into answering yes and yes and then pounce.

"Officer, prior to receiving the dispatch you'd been patrolling Charlestown since the beginning of your shift?" Clancy slid out from behind the defense table.

"Yes."

"Your shift began at ten?"

"Yes."

"You covered the Bunker Hill housing project?"

"Yes."

"And the Charles Newtown project?"

"Yes."

"I see. Then your patrol must've included Walford Way and Old Ironsides Way?"

"Yes."

"It's fair to say those two areas are heavily populated?"

"I'd say so."

"And well lighted?"

"With the orange lights." O'Neil rubbed his hands together. "Some dark areas over there."

Clancy noted the confidence seeping into O'Neil's voice. That's just what he wanted to achieve, a false sense of security.

"It's fair to say you didn't notice anything out of the ordinary that night?" Clancy pinched his lower lip.

"I wouldn't exactly say that."

"How many times did you drive down Walford Way?"

"I don't recall."

"It's one of the regular streets on your patrol, isn't it?"

"Yes, but—"

"You didn't see anything out of the ordinary?"

"It depends on how you define out of the ordinary." O'Neil raised his eyebrows as if he was getting the better of Clancy.

It was time for the first curve ball. "Now, Officer, you didn't see anyone dragging a dead body, did you?"

"Somebody dragging a body?" O'Neil snickered. "Not that I recall."

"No one complained about a dead body being dragged through the streets of Charlestown that evening?"

"Someone may've—"

"But it was never brought to your attention?"

"Nope."

"If someone were to drag a corpse from Thirty-six Walford Way to the spot where you discovered it, he or she would've had to drag it through several lighted backyards or right along Walford Way itself, correct?"

O'Neil bit his upper lip. "I would guess so."

"Officer, we don't want you to guess. You're familiar with the area?"

"Uh huh."

"It's fair to say there are no other routes to drag a body from Thirty-six Walford Way to Dupont Street?"

"Probably not."

Clancy glided several steps toward his witness. "You were trained at the police academy?"

"Yes."

"You had special training in crime scene investigation?"

"Yeah?"

"As the responding officer, your responsibility was to protect and preserve the scene?"

"I did that." O'Neil folded his arms.

"Whenever you encounter a dead body, you are to assume that a crime has been committed, correct?"

"Well, yes, until—"

"One of the most crucial things you learn is not to disturb evidence?" Clancy angled toward the jury.

"Right."

"In this case you did not follow procedure."

"I followed procedure."

"You *rolled* the body!" Clancy rotated both arms back in a full circle and then released his fingers like rolling dice.

O'Neil watched Clancy's hands without answering.

Clancy knew jurors hated sloppy cops; so he repeated the rolling motion a bit longer than planned. "You have to answer the question."

"Okay. I moved it a little."

"Just moved it a little? Why, in your police report you said you rolled the body, didn't you?"

"Yeah."

"So you did *roll* the body?" Clancy performed another rolling act. "That's disturbing evidence."

Annie shot to her feet. "Objection."

"Overruled," Judge Killam said.

"I don't know." O'Neil examined his hands.

Clancy stepped closer to the witness stand. "You also groped into the back pocket of Trevor Shea's jeans?"

O'Neil gasped. "I just took the wallet out."

"And then you proceeded to go through that wallet?"

"My partner, Officer Twomey, grabbed the license." O'Neil chewed on his thumbnail. "I think."

Clancy hooked his thumbs behind both suspenders, arched his back, and smacked his lips. "Did you or your partner remove anything else from the wallet?"

"No?"

"You didn't remove any money?" Clancy raised his eyebrows, once at O'Neil and once at the jury.

"There was no money!" O'Neil spoke too quickly, sounding defensive.

"Are you *sure* about that?"

"Objection!" Annie spread her arms. "Asked and answered."

"Yes, I'm sure!" O'Neil's face and neck blushed, even his scalp glowed red through the blond crew cut.

Judge Killam leaned over his bench. "Officer, you are not to answer until I have ruled, is that clear?"

O'Neil flinched when he made eye contact with the judge. "Yes, sir."

"It's Your Honor."

"Yessir. I'm sorry, sir . . . no, I mean, Your Honor."

Clancy smiled to himself. "Did you check the contents of Shea's front pockets?"

"We may have, I don't recall."

"If you checked the back pockets, you most likely checked the front pockets?"

"Probably."

Clancy loomed less than three feet from the witness stand. "Is it fair to say Shea's front pockets were empty?"

"I don't recall."

"You didn't list the contents of the front pockets in your report, did you?"

O'Neil scratched his scalp. "Uh, no."

"After you disturbed . . . uh, I mean, mishandled the evidence, rolled the body, you radioed your dispatcher, correct?"

"Yeah, uh, that's it. I radioed in."

"And you reported what you found?"

"Uh huh."

"I assume you tried to be as accurate as possible?"

"Right."

"You never even mentioned the word *homicide* to the dispatcher, did you?"

"Not to the dispatcher . . . but I, I mentioned it to Officer Twomey and Detective Callahan."

"You did?" Clancy lowered his jaw into an exaggerated look of surprise. O'Neil was making things up on the spot. *Beautiful.* The jury would see right through it. "Are you sure about that?"

"Yes, I remember. I remember it definitely."

"Hmm." Clancy rubbed his chin. "And don't you think that little tidbit would've been important to mention to the dispatcher?"

"Not really."

"I see." Clancy rested his chin on his index finger. "Later on that evening you drafted a report concerning the incident?"

"Yes."

"Did you attempt to be as accurate as possible in that report?"

"Yeah." O'Neil sighed.

"You mentioned nothing about a homicide in your report?"

"No, but—"

"In fact, your exact words to the dispatcher were, 'We have a dead body here—a Caucasian male.'"

"Objection." Annie stood. "There's no question before the witness."

"Sustained." Judge Killam addressed Clancy. "Put a question to the witness."

"But I wasn't finished with my question, Your Honor." Clancy made his response sound like a pout, and glanced at the old ladies in the second row.

"Move along." The judge huffed.

Clancy inched closer to O'Neil. "Were these your exact words to the dispatcher: 'We have a dead body here—a Caucasian male, wearing jeans and a T-shirt with paint stains'?"

"Yeah?"

"Ah, I knew I remembered correctly. And, your next words were, 'It looks like an accidental overdose.'" Clancy paused to let the words sink in. "Accidental overdose. Didn't you say that?"

"I . . . I'm not sure." O'Neil grimaced. "I'd have to check the dispatch tapes to be sure."

"Voila!" Clancy reached into his inner suit jacket pocket and pulled out a cassette tape. "Look what I have here, and I'm happy to refresh your memory by playing it for you." He held the tape up and jiggled it.

"Okay, okay." O'Neil spread his fingers next to his ears as if he didn't want to hear anymore.

"*Accidental overdose.* Weren't those your exact words?" Clancy hovered above him with the tape raised high.

"It wasn't like I saw blood pouring out of the guy. It just looked like a regular overdose with the needle there and everything."

"Right." Clancy smiled.

"People overdose all the time, you know?"

"Yes they do." Clancy could almost taste those delicious words. "People overdose all the time." He walked past the jury and repeated O'Neil's words, "People overdose all the time."

7

CALLAHAN BURST INTO the lobby of the Gloucester Police Station. He had driven up in the freezing rain without a raincoat or umbrella. Nor'easters always rained and snowed sideways, and the trek from the parking lot to the front door left him soaked and chilled from head to foot.

"I need to speak with Chief Turner right now." Callahan spread both hands across the counter. "He here?"

"And . . ." The frumpy, middle-aged desk sergeant glanced up at him, and resumed tapping her computer keyboard. "You are?"

She knew who he was. "Detective Michael Callahan, Boston."

"Do you have an appointment?" She typed faster.

"No, I've been trying him for the past hour. All I get is voicemail."

"Well, I think he might be busy then. You'll have to come back later. Mister . . . ?"

"This is an emergency."

"'Swhat they all say." Her voice was singsongy. *Annoying as hell.* The desk phone rang; she raised a finger.

"But I have to get—"

"Shh." The lady put her finger to her lips. "Gloucester PD."

Callahan paced as the lady babbled into the phone. He wondered how

Annie was doing in court. She had come across a bit edgy that morning. Probably pre-trial anxiety. There was so much riding on this one. The press was all over it, and she would constantly feel the presense of all the mothers in the front row. Callahan tore open another stick of Big Red. He worried about Annie. She'd be all business at the DA's office, often staying late, sifting through yellowed police reports. She kept her private life very private. When he tried to ask her about it, she'd give him short answers, and steer the conversation back to a work-related issue. There was a lot of camaraderie at the DA's office, but Annie didn't seem to partake, and he wondered why.

Callahan tried the chief's line again from his cell phone. Voicemail. *Screw it.* He skirted around the front desk and jogged down the hall. He knew exactly where Turner's office was from prior fights over Domenico. He ignored the shouts from the useless lady at the desk, and barged right into Turner's office.

"I figured you'd show up here." Chief Wallace "the Walrus" Turner leaned all the way back in his leather recliner and sipped coffee from a chipped mug. Both ends of his handlebar mustache were wet and pointy, making him look even more like his nickname.

"Domenico's missing," Callahan said.

The Walrus's lips stretched sideways across his face in a wide, *I told you so* grin.

"You hear anything? Because he was supposed to be in court today."

"Did I hear anything? Like what?" The Walrus rested his mug on one of the police reports littering his desk. Callahan noticed most of the papers revealed overlapping brown coffee rings.

"You know exactly what I'm talking about. Did anything go down around here in the past twenty-four?"

"Always does." The Walrus licked his lips and mustache. "But I'm sure it's all small potatoes far as you Boston guys are concerned."

"I got yah." Callahan knew the entire force suffered from inferiority complexes when it came to the Boston Police. They always brought up how busy they were.

"And your chief's an f'ing blowhard know-it-all. You can tell him I said so."

Callahan agreed, but wouldn't relay the message. "I'm looking for Domenico. Did his body wash ashore? If so, I won't waste any more of your precious time. You look so . . . busy this morning."

"That's right." The Walrus took a long sip of coffee; the right handlebar dripped when he finished. "Seems like everybody wants your man Domenico these days. You'll have to get in line, I guess."

"Thanks for all the help." Callahan headed toward the door.

"You getting in line then? I'm warning you, it's a long one."

"What are you talking about?" Callahan did a one-eighty.

"Like I said, everybody wants that scumbag for something. You, Lawrence PD, Salem, even the feds are all over his ass." He rubbed his hands together. "And guess who got him?" His mustache expanded across his face.

"What the?" Callahan almost lost his balance.

"Heroin, cocaine, Triple Beam scales, glassine baggies, cutting agents, cash, customer lists. Whole nine yards."

"You arrested him?" Callahan felt like flinging that damn coffee mug across the room. "Without telling me?"

The Walrus grinned.

"Where's Domenico now?" He marched up to the desk again. *At least Domenico was alive.*

"Still holding him. In fact, his ride to District should be here any minute." The Walrus glanced at his watch.

"I gotta take him," Callahan said.

"No f'ing way. This guy runs the whole North Shore. He's going up for ten to twenty this time. Drug trafficking."

"Domenico has to be in court." Callahan leaned way over the desk and slapped his palms on the paperwork. "Right now in Boston. You've got to cut him loose."

The Walrus lifted his legs and crossed his muddy boots on top of the desk, right in Callahan's face. "I'm in charge here, and Domenico's not going anywhere with you."

8

ANY REDIRECT, COMMONWEALTH?" Judge Killam glanced at the wall clock and over at Annie.

Annie had to decide whether to ask Officer O'Neil more questions; the jurors looked at her with both anticipation and annoyance. She didn't get all she'd wanted from O'Neil. He left important details out, and might not even remember them on redirect. What would she do? If she asked more questions, Clancy would have another go at it, dice tie and all, and he thrived on cross. Who knows what he'd make O'Neil blurt out this time. What a score for the defense—*people overdose all the time.* Annie couldn't believe O'Neil said that. Malone had also gotten a kick out of it. He had exchanged a glance with her, puckering his lips just enough to let her know.

Annie decided it was best to get O'Neil off the stand at whatever cost. "Nothing further, Your Honor." She smiled for the jury, masking her dilemma. "Thank you."

"We'll take our lunch—"

"*All rise!*"

Annie watched the judge and jurors exit the courtroom. She had to call Callahan and find out about Domenico. She stood and slipped papers into her briefcase. Would her witness show up? She turned and saw Chris Shea parading toward her from the front row.

"Hey, Billy?" Chris leaned over the short paneled rail separating the lawyers' section from the gallery. He made eye contact with Malone and pointed at his brother's painting, which was propped against her table. "Remember little Georgie Hurley?"

Malone glanced at the painting. Annie caught a glimpse of recognition mingled with something else. Shock perhaps? She wasn't sure for he quickly masked his emotion.

"It's a pretty good likeness, huh?" Chris continued pointing at the painting, yet his gaze bore into Malone.

No one moved, including Annie. It felt like a deep freeze had descended upon the courtroom.

"I'll bet your ma remembers Georgie." Chris nodded toward the spectators' gallery without moving his piercing gaze from Malone. "I bet she does."

Malone lunged at Chris. "Leave my mother out of this!"

"Let's go." A guard grabbed Malone's arm.

"Not here, not here." Clancy stepped between Chris and Malone. "Come on, let's go back to the cell. Ignore him. Don't get into it. It's not worth it."

"Keep him away from me." Malone side-kicked a chair. It crashed into the defense table and toppled over. Clancy's papers fluttered to the rug. The guard escorted him out.

Chris stared at the overturned chair. Annie waved a hand in front of his face. When he looked at her, she recalled seeing that same hatred in her father's eyes when those two men came into the bookstore. She suddenly smelled cardboard boxes, felt the cold cement of the musty storage room floor pressing against her bare knobby girl knees. *That look.* She saw it whenever her father handed the crinkled paper bag to those men. The last Monday of the month. *Always.*

"What?" Chris said. His voice snapped her out of the past.

"You and Malone." Annie lowered her voice, people were staring. "What was all that about?"

"I'm not going to testify."

"I'm not asking . . . what about the painting? Who's Georgie Hurley?"

"Don't know nothin'." Chris turned his back on her, and headed down the center aisle.

"No. Wait." Annie opened the short swinging gate, and sidestepped out of the lawyers' section. "I need to know about the painting, Chris."

"We've been through this." He quickened his pace.

Annie followed him. He had refused to cooperate with her and Callahan from the beginning, but, now, she felt a glimmer of hope since he came to court and sat in the front row with the mothers.

"Why won't you talk to me? I'm just asking about your brother's painting." Annie overtook him. "I don't even know who Trevor is."

"You never will."

"Why are you so . . . cold? It's almost as if you want Malone to walk."

He stopped and looked into her eyes. "I do."

"What?" Annie couldn't believe he said that. "But he killed your brother."

"And, this is all a big waste of time."

"Maybe if you would help me—"

"You got no chance in hell. That was a disaster." Chris pointed toward the witness stand. "Clancy made that cop out to be a moron. I'm sure Malone's back there celebrating. Poppin' the champagne. And what's up with them taking money from my brother's wallet?"

"They didn't." Annie hoped she said it with enough conviction.

"Bullshit. Clancy acted like he knew what he was talking about."

"No. It's his way of turning the jury against us. An old trick."

"What a farce." Chris yanked the courtroom door open. "The whole thing." He stepped into the hallway ahead of her. "If you don't know that by now, you don't know nothin'."

Annie despised his tone. *Keep up the pace; challenge him.* "Tell me something I don't know."

Chris lowered his head and walked toward the elevators.

"Come on, are you afraid of me?" Annie sidestepped in front of him and jogged backward. "Do I intimidate you, Chris? Challenge you?"

"Right." Chris snickered. "You think you're so smart, smarter than everyone else. Because why? Because you went to college, some Ivy League school, I bet." He laughed a false, high-pitched laugh. "I'll tell you something." He paused. "I'll toss you a bone, college girl. Okay?"

"A bone." Annie felt like strangling him, but restrained. What did he know about her? "Throw it."

"And then you'll get off my ass?"

Annie didn't respond, but stared him down as she waited.

"Your big witness is a no-show."

"Who?" she asked.

"Your guy from Gloucester. The Italian."

"Domenico." Annie's heart sank.

"That's right. He ain't coming."

"Who told you?"

"Word on the street."

Annie feared the worst. "Is he dead?"

Chris stared at her for a moment. "This case is a dog. Malone is going to beat the system. Always has, always will."

"I'm not giving up, even without Domenico." Annie knew they'd be sunk without him. "If only you would help me," she whispered.

"No way." He pressed the down button for the elevator even though it was already lit. "Malone's gonna walk and then I'm gonna . . ."

"You're going to what? What are you going to do, Chris? Take care of him yourself?" Annie chose a mocking tone.

"Maybe." He pounded the elevator button with the side of his fist as if it would come faster.

"Don't say that. Don't even think it. I can have you arrested."

"Maybe you will someday."

"By then I'll be too late. Do you really think Billy Malone will ever let you take the first shot? Homicide'll be scooping your guts off the sidewalk. The only shot you'll get is right there." Annie pointed to the courtroom down the hall.

"Right over there, huh?" Chris peered in the direction of the courtroom. Annie noticed his eyes had glazed over. "Over there . . . the court-room."

She moved into his line of vision. "Cooperate with me, Chris, or it will always be like this."

His expression hardened. "'An eye for an eye.'"

"'. . . will make the whole world blind.' That's not justice," she said.

"Good one, college." Chris clucked his tongue. "I got one for you, now."

"Really?"

"'Where there's law, there's injustice.'"

His quote surprised her. "Tolstoy."

"That's right, college." The bell above the elevator sounded, and the door opened. Chris stepped in. "Go back to Wellesley or wherever the hell you came from. You don't belong here."

"Excuse me." Annie stuck her arm in the elevator to prevent it from closing. "I'm from Charlestown, the same as you."

She watched him stare at her until the elevator doors closed. *I was there, but you never noticed me, the quiet girl from the bookstore that didn't belong. The store that was forced to close.* Why had her parents bothered with it in the first place? A mystery bookstore in Charlestown? Why not Cambridge? Her parents had loved Charlestown with its rich history and charm, but they were outsiders, neither one had grown up there. They didn't know what lurked beneath the surface.

Annie headed toward the courtroom to prepare officer Twomey. *You don't belong here.* She would always be the girl whose face didn't match her name. So, why had she come back?

9

ELAINE WILSON HAD been assigned to the front row, seat number two of the jury box, right next to the anorexic foreperson, Rachel. Time for lunch—*finally*. What a relief to be heading back into the conference room. It felt good to stretch her legs. Elaine felt wedged in those jury chairs like being crammed into the middle seat of an airplane. She wondered if Judge Killam would notice if she snuck in a bag of peanuts for an afternoon snack.

Elaine was also relieved to get away from that weird painting. Fitzgerald had removed it from the easel after her opening statement, but she'd placed it in full view of the jury box. Malone hadn't liked that. Elaine had seen him whispering to Clancy and gesturing toward the painting. Who could blame him? It almost seemed underhanded for her to make such a big deal over it. So far, it had no connection to the defendant. She recalled Clancy objecting to the art stuff during Fitzgerald's opening. *Bizarre.* The eyes on that redheaded boy with the freckles looked so real. The type that followed you wherever you went. Elaine had turned around right before they left the courtroom. Sure enough, that boy from the painting was watching her. *Eerie.*

Elaine got stuck behind skinny Rachel in the lunch line. That woman's perfume smelled like the lilac spray used to deodorize a bathroom. The smell traveled right up the nose and tingled the inner nostrils. Elaine sneezed twice. Rachel mumbled a God bless you and moved forward a bit too fast, knocking into the guy in front of her. *Germ phobic.*

Elaine grabbed an Italian hoagie, three bags of chips, and a Coke, and waited for Rachel to sit down with her little salad and side cup of fat-free dressing. She shuffled to the opposite end of the long courthouse cafeteria table and grabbed a seat across from Louie Henderson, the seventy-one-year-old retired postman.

"I wonder when it'll start coming our way." Louie set his brown lunch bag down. His full name was written across the top in red Magic Marker.

"What?" Elaine asked.

"The snow. They say we could get over a foot, you know."

Elaine shrugged. He had mentioned the snow three times that morning. "So, what's for lunch, Louie?"

"Baloney sandwich." He unfolded his brown bag and took the sandwich out of the plastic baggie. "See?" He smiled and lifted the top piece of Wonder Bread, displaying three round slices of baloney smothered in mayonnaise and chunks of butter topped with one leaf of wilted iceberg lettuce. "My wife fixed it for me."

Elaine smelled the mayo. She remembered Wonder Bread sticking to the roof of her mouth when she was a girl. She'd have to wedge the tip of her tongue beneath it to pop it out. "These deli sandwiches are free, you know."

"I've had baloney every day for the past forty-eight years." Louie bit into the sandwich. "Why stop now?"

"I guess you got a point." Elaine remembered the taste of warm milk from those school cafeteria cartons. She always washed the ball of Wonder Bread down with it. *Yuck.* She swallowed a mouthful of Coke; it bubbled up her nose. "Why do you think the judge chose that one to be foreperson?" Elaine laced her fingers around the sub, and pointed at Rachel with her elbow.

Louie studied Rachel through the upper half of his black-framed bifocals. "Looks smart."

"Gimme a break. She hasn't even had kids yet. Your typical husband hunter. I'm willing to bet she's not even from here; probably a transplant from New York, maybe Jersey. Lives in one of them penthouses in Back Bay, gets her poofy fake red hair done on Newbury Street, doesn't cook. I bet she keeps a messy house, though. The yuppie types don't have the *time* to clean."

"You would know about that." Louie used his finger to dislodge the Wonder Bread from the roof of his mouth.

"Make for the worst customers." Elaine opened wide and bit into the hoagie; she tasted the tang from the extra oil and vinegar and chopped-up pickles. How would she get all her houses done after court? She'd have to move people around and work the weekend. They'd be alright with it; had to be, no choice. But if she didn't get to them all, she wouldn't get paid.

"They got money though, them yuppies," Louie said.

"Some of 'em. Most just pretend they do. They're all a pain in the ass. Always worried I'm gonna break their stupid knickknacks. Well, some-times I do because they always gotta put stuff on top of a stack of books." Elaine shoved a handful of potato chips into her mouth. "And they're not around for more than a couple years. They get married, have a baby, and move out to Needham or down to Milton. Then I gotta go searching for a replacement. Not worth the hassle. You get many yuppies over in Brigh-ton, Louie?"

"Few. Mostly students from BC or BU 'round where I live."

"You're lucky because the yuppies are taking over, forcing all the good people like us out. They buy up all the affordable places, gut 'em, and the rents go sky high."

Elaine watched the jurors who were seated next to them heading for the restrooms. She leaned close to Louie and whispered, "Do you think that cop stole money from the artist?"

Louie wiped globs of mayonnaise from the corners of his mouth. "Hard to say."

"He must've. Otherwise, why did Buddy Clancy bring it up? The cop looked guilty soon as it was mentioned. Did you see how red his face got?"

Louie chewed and nodded.

"I bet he did it. What's this world coming to when cops start stealing from the dead?" Elaine licked her finger to get the last of the potato chip crumbs out of the plastic bag. "What did you think of the painting?"

"I wouldn't want it up on my wall," Louie said. "He should've painted flowers or mountains. I'm surprised he won a prize. They always pick the weird ones, don't they?"

"Yeah, it's a little creepy for me, but I couldn't stop staring at it." Elaine had zoned out and missed some of the testimony because of that painting. She wondered if it had the same affect on the others.

"The kid had talent." Louie finished his sandwich. "Those children looked real, like a photograph. Can you imagine how good his art would've been if he painted wildlife instead? Like a deer in the woods? Now, I'd buy that."

"I wonder what happened to the artist's mother?"

"She wasn't in court?"

"Nope, only the brother. He was the one in the baggy gray sweatpants who sat there staring at Malone's back the whole time, like he wanted to kill him."

"Oh, right. He didn't look much like the skinny artist. Much bigger with long hippie hair. Tough looking." Louie rolled his mayonnaise napkin into a ball. "Maybe the mother stayed home with the bad weather and all. I wouldn't want my wife out on a day like this."

"No, it doesn't have anything to do with the weather. I've got two grown kids myself, and I can't imagine what I'd do if I lost one of 'em. I don't blame her one bit for staying away."

"Maybe you're right. My wife would feel the same way. We got six kids, eleven grandkids." Louie grinned.

"I wonder what was up with all those women in the matching shirts?" Elaine noticed Louie looking over her shoulder, out the window. "Remember them all? Sitting in the front row near the brother?"

"Do you think they'll let us go early if it starts?"

"If what starts?"

Louie sighed. "The snow, Elaine, the snow."

10

MALONE SCRAPED THE bottom rim of the carton, and licked the rest of his cold tomato soup from the white plastic spoon. The boiled red hot dog had been rubbery and way too salty, but his hunger made him force it down. He was still seething over the confrontation with Chris Shea—a loose cannon. They said he wasn't talking to the other side, so what was that all about? Should keep his mouth shut. He knew his brother was a useless addict.

"Off to a good start, wouldn't you say?" Clancy high-stepped toward the cell and twirled his hat on his fingertips. He looked overly pleased with himself.

"Not at all." Malone flung his orange lunch tray against the cinder block wall. The empty soup carton and plastic fork and spoon scattered across the cell.

"What are you talking about? I'd say we tore that cop up pretty well. The jurors—"

"Why didn't you object again to that stupid painting?" Malone grabbed the tray and threw it a second time. The plastic cracked.

"It's just a bunch of kids. Why so hot under the collar?"

"I don't like it. Object! Get it out of there."

"I already tried. Judge Killam ruled on that, remember? If we make a big ordeal, the jurors will pay more attention to it."

"But it's not fair. She's using it against me. Like I killed Picasso."

"She's building sympathy for the victim. DAs always do that. Unless there's more to it. What was all that hubbub with Chris Shea? I thought he said something about Georgie Hurley. Isn't he dead?"

"Stop." Malone felt the pressure building in his head. "I want that painting out of there." He'd watched the jurors studying it. It wasn't fair. The Chink got away with everything. The judge was afraid to go against her. Nobody else would be allowed to bring art into a courtroom, and this was freaky art. The eyes on that boy seemed to be watching him.

"I'll see what I can do to get the painting removed," Clancy said.

"And you were late. You left me hanging with cuffs and shackles in front of my ma. She shouldn't be forced to see me like that. Callahan already put her through living hell when he arrested me." Malone stomped to the back of the cell. He hated Callahan more than ever. "Why were you so late?"

"I couldn't help it. My bus got hit by that duck boat. Those duck boats think they can hog the road. One time—"

Malone whipped around. "Why didn't you make an opening statement? The DA told her side, which was full of lies and all sorts of crap about that painting. The jurors were expecting to hear from you and so was I. Now they think we got no case; that you had nothing to say. Everyone'll think I hired an idiot for a lawyer. Did you forget to prepare for this thing or what, Clancy?"

"Calm down." Clancy spoke softly, which irritated Malone even more.

"Don't you dare tell me to calm down." Malone gripped the steel bars until his knuckles turned white. "This is my case, my money."

"And you hired me to defend you." Clancy reached into his suit pocket and pulled out a pack of Winstons. "Deferring the opening statement until it's our turn is the right move. We'll have the advantage of arguing our points and focusing on their weaknesses. I practiced law before you were born, so don't second-guess my strategy."

"What strategy?" Malone reached through the bars and grabbed the cigarettes. Thank God he could get away with smoking. At least Clancy was good for something. "Your strategy has been nothing but lines of bullshit since the day I got arrested. At the arraignment you said they had nothing to go on and I'd be out walking the streets. The judge listened to the Chink and I got held without bail."

"The district court judge had no choice with your criminal record. The media would've clobbered him."

"Then you said the case was so weak it would never survive the grand jury. So what happened? I got indicted." Malone tore the plastic wrap off the cigarette pack with his teeth.

"That was just something I said at the bail argument to persuade the judge to release you on personal recognizance. As the saying goes, the Commonwealth could indict a ham sandwich if they wanted to. I told you that."

"You're backpedaling. And all those useless motions?" Malone had suffered through waves of pretrial motions brought by Clancy to dismiss the case or suppress evidence. Judge Killam had half-listened with his massive head lolling up and down. They always came out on the losing end.

Clancy lit Malone's cigarette. "I've had murder cases thrown out as a result of motion hearings."

"Crock a shit. You lawyers use motions to cover your asses and run up the bill." Malone inhaled the nicotine, and trapped it in his lungs for as long as he could. "I really can't believe this. It's not fair." He stomped on the soup container, flattening it. "How come they let all those holy rollers sit out there in the front row? They got nothing to do with me. Can't you do anything?"

"Like what?"

"Get 'em the hell out of there."

"It's a public forum, they have every right."

"I don't care. Do it!"

Malone wished he could reach through the bars and strangle his lawyer. "How did you let them turn this thing into a first-degree murder case? Who testified before the grand jury again?"

"Detective Callahan and Jennianne Smith."

"*Jennianne.*" Malone took another drag. "Get me a copy of the grand jury transcript by tonight or you won't get paid. And get rid of that painting."

11

RACHEL SAT IN her designated foreperson's chair after lunch. She noticed the painting had been taken away. It was probably a good thing; it had been distracting. She smelled the hot peppers and onions on Elaine's breath from her Italian sub. Rachel had offered her a Tic Tac, but Elaine refused as if the offer had been an insult. What was wrong with that woman? Rachel saw her take three large chocolate chip cookies from the dessert tray and stuff another one in her pocketbook. No wonder the country had a problem with obesity.

Rachel suppressed a giggle when she saw Clancy's bowtie. It contained colorful clown faces with giant red noses and cylander hats. She wondered where he found it. What did it mean? Was he wearing it for a reason?

"Commonwealth, call your next witness," Judge Killam said.

Fitzgerald rose. "Good afternoon, Your Honor, ladies and gentlemen. The Commonwealth calls Officer Albert Twomey."

A middle-aged cop clomped down the aisle with mud-encrusted boots. When he turned around to take the oath, Rachel noticed his uniform had wrinkles running up the backside.

"Do you swear to tell the truth, the whole truth, and nothing but the truth so help you God?" Clerk Fallon said.

"I do." The cop's cheeks sagged down below the sides of his nose, forming two purplish pouches. Rachel wondered if he'd been up all night or if he always looked like that. She noted the monosyllabic answers to Fitzgerald's questions about his years on the force. He yawned three times without covering his mouth. Rachel watched him make eye contact with the men on the jury, as if the women weren't important.

"Do you recall November tenth of last year?" Fitzgerald raised her voice as if she wanted to arouse him a bit.

"Yes, ma'am."

"What were you doing at approximately ten thirty P.M.?"

"I joined O'Neil at a murder scene."

"Objection!" Clancy jumped up. "There's no proof anyone was murdered at all. I move to strike the answer."

"Sustained and stricken." Judge Killam turned to the jury. "Please disregard any mention of a murder scene."

"What did you observe when you joined Officer O'Neil?" Fitzgerald asked.

"It immediately looked suspicious to me—like there'd been foul play."

"Objection."

"Sustained."

"Please describe what you saw, Officer." Fitzgerald sounded annoyed.

"Caucasian male lying on back, no pulse, hypodermic needle in hand, and a clear path in the leaves leading from the body."

"How was the deceased holding the hypodermic needle?"

"Upside down. That's what made it look suspicious to me."

"Objection." Clancy raised his hand. "Move to strike the second sentence."

"So stricken."

Rachel couldn't picture old droopy eyes making any pertinent observations. Were the others buying this? She turned around. Some looked as bored as the cop.

"What did you do next?" Fitzgerald said.

"I reached beneath the victim's body and pulled his wallet from the back pocket without disturbing anything. *No one* rolled the body."

"Did you open the wallet?"

"Yeah, just to check ID. We didn't take anything else from that wallet."

"No further questions." Fitzgerald walked back to her table.

"Top of the afternoon to you, Officer." Clancy smiled just like the last time. Rachel perked up. She wondered if he'd make mincemeat out of this one, too.

"On November tenth of last year, you worked a twelve-hour private police detail before your real shift started, correct?" Clancy strolled into the center of the courtroom holding a sheet of paper with writing on it.

"Yup."

"You received double pay for that detail?"

"Yup."

"You have more private details than ninety-nine percent of the police force."

"Seniority."

"Those details are important to you."

"Pays the bills."

"And then some. You made approximately one hundred and eighty-five thousand dollars last year, over fifty percent coming from private details."

"Objection." Fitzgerald raised an arm. "Where's he going with this?"

"Overruled."

"It's fair to say you were exhausted after working your twelve-hour private detail on November tenth of last year?"

"Nope."

"Not even a little?" Clancy cocked his head.

"Nope."

"So then, you were perfectly capable of making detailed observations pertaining to this case?"

"Absolutely."

"What was the weather like that night?"

"Good."

"Do you recall any particulars?"

"Yeah, it was on the warm side for that time of year. Midfifties maybe."

Rachel remembered O'Neil saying it was cold and gusty.

"What was the victim's name?" Clancy sidestepped toward the jury.

Twomey hesitated. "Shea, wasn't it Shea?"

"What was he wearing?"

"I don't recall, but I remember the important things like the needle and the disturbed leaves."

"With which hand did he hold the needle?"

Twomey's eyes shifted from right to left and then back again. "The right."

"Did you know Trevor Shea was left-handed?"

He rubbed his chin. "Yeah, come to think of it, he was holding the needle in his left hand."

"Are you sure about that?"

"Positive."

Clancy glanced sideways at the jury and adjusted his clown tie. "So, you were suspicious from the start?"

"Sure. I knew it wasn't your typical heroin overdose."

"Really?" Clancy wrinkled his brow. "Hmm. You didn't say anything about that when O'Neil reported an accidental overdose?"

"Didn't hear him."

"I thought you were standing right next to O'Neil?"

Twomey shrugged. "It's all right there in my report." He pointed to the crinkled paper in Clancy's hand.

"Oh, you mean this 'ol thing you scribbled up?" Clancy walked the length of the jury box with the report in full view.

Rachel noticed the messy handwriting. It also appeared stained.

"That's my report."

"Were you watching TV when you wrote this?"

"Not that I recall."

"You prepared this report two and a half weeks later? Hmm. Were the Patriots playing?"

Rachel laughed along with several others. Clancy was quick-witted.

"No, sir." Twomey yawned again. "Date's right there on top, November eleven, right when I got off duty."

"Strange." Clancy approached the witness stand. "As I recall, your report was the only one missing for the arraignment on November thirteenth?"

"I wouldn't know about that."

"Why, I had to call your supervisor twice to get it."

"Objection, hearsay," Fitzgerald said.

"Sustained."

Twomey placed his elbow on the stand and rested his chin in his palm. Rachel figured a bomb could go off beneath his droopy eyes and he wouldn't flinch.

"You were standing out in the hallway during O'Neil's testimony?" Clancy motioned down the aisle toward the courtroom doors.

"Sitting on the bench."

Rachel pictured him sprawled across the bench, snoring.

"You were sequestered out in the hallway so you couldn't hear what O'Neil had to say."

"Right."

Clancy gazed at Fitzgerald. "*Someone* must've filled you in over lunch."

"Objection!" Fitzgerald shot up.

"Overruled."

Twomey puckered his lips. "Not me."

"During your direct testimony, you *volunteered* the following statement: 'No one rolled the body.'"

"Right, no one rolled the body."

"That's what came up during O'Neil's testimony. How did you know about it?"

Twomey looked back at Clancy, deadpan. "I didn't."

"Ah. A coincidence then. Nothing further."

"Any re-direct, Commonwealth?"

"No thank you, Your Honor."

"The witness may be excused."

Rachel watched the cap leave the witness stand with the same disinterested expression. The guy was a clown. Maybe that's why Clancy had chosen that tie. Someone had clearly coached him over lunch, told him exactly what to say. It must've been Fitzgerald. She was dealt a poor hand. One cop was inexperienced, the other didn't care. Rachel wondered what she'd do in her shoes. Probably coach the witness. But, was that fair? Was it cheating the system?

12

CALLAHAN CHECKED HIS watch; two thirty already. He hadn't sent word back to Annie, and probably should have by now. The cell phone reception was terrible in Gloucester. The only time his cell had worked was about a mile from the station. He had received a call from their main witness, Jennianne, but could barely hear her through the static. She had been crying and sounded desperate. What next? Callahan could only deal with one witness catastrophe at a time. He wanted to come through for Annie now. It would be a challenge to make it back in time for court, but he would give it his best shot. *He had to.* The Walrus had agreed to let him speak with Domenico, but even that came with a price.

"Get my lunch?" The Walrus stuck his head into the tiny interview room.

Callahan slid a white paper bag and a can of Coke across the table.

"With the bellies, right?" The Walrus opened the Coke, tipped his head way back, and slugged.

"Fried clams with the bellies, a large. Now, where's Domenico?"

The Walrus inspected the bag, opened the carton, and sniffed. It was an exaggerated sniff, too. He nodded to someone out in the hallway.

A cop escorted the ponytailed Domenico into the room. He smelled like dead fish. His bare knees stuck through frayed holes in his jeans, and oil stains dotted his navy sweatshirt. His lips formed a horseshoe-shaped scowl. Callahan hoped Domenico's luck would spill from that upside-down horseshoe. He knew that a guy down on his luck would likely strike a deal.

"Just a few questions." The Walrus dipped three fried clams into the tartar sauce and shoved them into his mouth. He chewed with his mouth open. A glob of the yellow-green sauce stuck to his mustache. "And then we're taking him down to be arraigned."

Now it smelled like greasy fried clams and dead fish. Callahan breathed through his mouth. He slapped a pack of Marlboros on the table and slid them toward Domenico's cuffed hands. Ninety percent of the bad guys smoked. Callahan knew it would take a lot more than a cheap pack of cigarettes, but he had to start somewhere.

Domenico regarded the cigarettes like a dog would eye a sirloin steak. He flicked the pack away. "If you want Malone, I get a free pass."

"You gotta be high." The Walrus grabbed another bunch of clams and swirled them in the sauce.

"I'm sleeping in my own bed tonight." Domenico snorted and spit on the floor right near the Walrus's boots. "And I want two slices of pepperoni pizza right now with a can of Diet Coke."

"You're going away for ten." The Walrus got up and grabbed his food. "Now, lick that off my floor." He stepped out and slammed the door.

"You're an idiot." Callahan pounded his fist on the table. "I'm trying to get you out of here."

"Screw you."

13

"NEXT WITNESS." JUDGE Killam fixed his gaze on Annie.

Annie's heart pounded. It was only five past three. She had banked on an extended lunch break, on Officer Twomey's direct and cross lasting longer. Instead, the testimony flew by and the clock stood still. Should she make her witness announcement? She hadn't heard a word from Callahan, which hopefully meant everything was okay with Domenico. But why hadn't he called or sent a text? Annie recalled when she tried her first drunk driving case in the district court as a third-year law student intern. She had no idea whether the arresting officer would show or not. Annie had learned to brace herself for the judicial tirade.

"Commonwealth?"

Annie curled her toes. Callahan should've tried to reach her either way; now she felt helpless. What if she announced Domenico's name and no one walked through those doors? What would the jurors think? They were all looking at her now, waiting. What about all the mothers in the front row? They were counting on her. Chris has also returned. He had warned her that Domenico wouldn't show up. *Word on the street.* She refused to look over at Malone, but felt his mocking gaze. If Chris knew something, then Malone knew, too. She wondered if anyone kept Clancy in the loop.

"May I have a sidebar, Your Honor?" Annie opted for the easy way out. If she could get the judge to call a brief recess . . .

"No, call your witness."

Judge Killam had forced her hand. *Damn him.* Annie wondered if he got his kicks out of toying with her. Did he forget he was a lowly lawyer once?

Annie took a deep breath, forced a smile, and hoped for the best. "The Commonwealth calls Mr. Miles Domenico."

Johnny slogged down the aisle, and made a show out of pulling the double oak doors as if they belonged in a medieval castle. He stuck his head and shoulders through the opening. "Miles Domenico!" Johnny had perfected his witness announcement over the years. His holler traveled to all corners of the eighth floor, even the bathrooms. Annie figured they could probably hear him out on the streets. Johnny didn't like to search for anyone out there, it would require extra work.

"Domenico? Miles Dommmmmenicoooooo?"

Annie cringed. How long would Johnny stand in the doorway yelling? *Don't look at Malone.* He could probably tell she was avoiding eye contact. Malone would consider that a sign of weakness. *You can't beat me, Annie.*

"Looks like we got a no-show!" Johnny stretched his arms and faced Judge Killam. "Snowing pretty good out there, too, Judge."

Annie's heart sank. She heard a loud sigh from the jury box. It had to be the foreperson in the cranberry suit. Annie stole a glance. *Of course it was.* The woman folded her arms and sighed again. Miss Organization would attribute Annie's witness no-show to being unprepared and sloppy. A strike against her. Jurors held the prosecutor to a high standard. After all, they paid her salary.

"Commonwealth?"

"Sidebar, Your Honor?" Annie smiled at the foreperson. She had to act like there was nothing wrong.

Judge Killam closed his eyes, filled his cheeks with air, and slowly released it. "Approach."

Annie walked up to the bench as casually as she could. Clancy stomped.

"What's going on?" Judge Killam's whisper sounded like a low snarl.

"Your Honor." Annie cleared her throat. How should she respond? Make it sound a little worse than it was? Why not? She really didn't know what happened; they hadn't heard from Domenico. "We suspect foul play, Your Honor." Annie held eye contact with the judge. "Our witness has vanished."

Clancy pursed his lips and placed his fists on his hips. He probably saw right through her slight exaggeration.

"Call another one then." Judge Killam didn't sound the least bit concerned by her dilemma.

"I'm not prepared to do that, Your Honor." Annie knew if the judge began puffing, it would be all over.

"Hey, Judge." Johnny joined the sidebar. "Maybe we oughta all go home now with the snow. Some of the jurors are a bit elderly."

"Enough with the snow already." Judge Killam slapped both hands on the bench. "Commonwealth, where's your witness list?" He fished through papers. "What about Detective Callahan?"

"He traveled up to Gloucester to locate Domenico."

"Ow," Johnny said. "Bet it's bad up that way."

The judge huffed. "I didn't ask your opinion."

Annie knew her chances plummeted every time Johnny opened his mouth. If Johnny wanted to adjourn, Judge Killam would do the opposite.

"Most respectfully, Your Honor." Annie waited for Judge Killam to remove his glowering gaze from Johnny back to her. "I'm requesting a brief continuance until tomorrow morning."

"No way." Clancy fluttered his fingers way up in the air and shook his head, exaggerating for the jury, who could probably hear bits and pieces of the sidebar conference. "We won't go for that."

"Are you objecting, counselor?" Judge Killam rested his forehead in his hand.

"Objecting? I'm requesting an outright dismissal if they can't produce any witnesses."

"We have reason to believe our witness may have been threatened or possibly worse," Annie said.

"Hogwash!" Clancy stomped his foot. "Come on, we all know your guy Domenico has a stack of priors we could paper this courtroom with. Guys like him bolt. The Commonwealth should've kept him under lock and key until he testified. But *no*. You took a chance and now he's gone."

"This is different." Annie stepped toward Clancy. "It's Charlestown. They're experts at scaring witnesses off; it's what they do over there. Even my office received death threats."

"Death threats? Not by my client. He's been locked up awaiting a fair trial for this crock of a case." Clancy gazed up at the ceiling. "Oh such melodrama, Miss Fitzgerald."

"Your Honor, in all fairness." Annie made eye contact with the judge. I need the—"

"Fairness?" Clancy waved his arms. "You wanna talk fairness? Any delay amounts to a violation of my client's Constitutional right to a speedy trial. If the Commonwealth can't produce any witnesses, she must rest her case."

"Speedy?" Annie jumped at the opportunity. "As I recall, you were late this morning!"

"She's right about that, Clancy." Judge Killam's lips formed a tiny smile. "You delayed the whole trial when you were late with your duck boat debacle. So, on that note, I'll grant your continuance, Commonwealth, but you must be prepared to call a witness by nine o'clock tomorrow morning."

"Thank you, Your Honor." Annie breathed a sigh of relief.

"All rise!" Johnny said.

The judge and jury filed out. Annie watched the guard approach Malone with a set of handcuffs. He stood, extended his hands for the guard, yet faced her.

"Rather stuffy in here today?" Malone said, his voice low, yet penetrating.

Who is he talking to? Annie gathered her papers without looking over. Clancy was busy chatting about the ice and snowstorm with Clerk Fallon. Malone was addressing her. *Ignore him.*

"No windows. It's like being stuck in a cardboard box all day."

Annie flinched and turned. Her gaze was sucked into his.

"Wouldn't you say so, Annie?" Malone smiled, maintaining eye contact, while the guard locked his cuffs.

She didn't answer. Could he read her thoughts? At that moment, it felt like it. *Please take him away.*

"Be careful out there." Malone gave her a knowing look. "With the ice and snow, that is. The sidewalks get slippery, Annie." He followed the guard out.

Malone had called her Annie twice.

She shoved a legal pad into her briefcase, and tried Callahan's cell. It went directly to voicemail. What the hell was he doing up there? And what the hell was Malone talking about? He'd mentioned a cardboard box, like the ones from the storage room at the bookstore where she made her forts so many years ago. *Be careful . . . the sidewalks get slippery.* Annie had slipped that day and fallen. *Blood was slippery.*

"Congrats, Miss Fitzgerald." Clancy strolled over to her table. "You won that battle. I knew you would, but I had to put up a fight." He rapped his knuckles on the tabletop. "Hey, I've been itching to ask you something."

Annie regarded him and raised her eyebrows. She wanted to grab her briefcase and run down the aisle, not speak with Clancy.

"What's a nice girl like you doing in a case like this?" he asked. "Why aren't you making the big bucks like your classmates from Yale?"

Interesting question. "Been there, done that." Annie closed her three-ring trial binder. "In New York, Wall Street."

"Jeez, you walked away from that?" Clancy whistled. "And now you want to be a street lawyer like me? I'll be darned."

"No one could be like you, Clancy." Annie squatted and stuffed the binder down into her briefcase. "In fact, I want to be the opposite."

Clancy laughed. "So what brought you back to Boston? No wedding ring, I see."

Annie looked up at him. Clancy was prying. Her instincts told her to act insulted, walk away, make him mind his own business. She could do that or give it right back to him. *Play the game.*

"Divorced?" he asked.

"Wrong, never been married." She lifted the big briefcase to her chair.

"Holy cow. You should be pregnant with your third kid by now." Clancy looked perplexed. "What gives?"

"Are you cross-examining me?" Annie leaned against the table and folded her arms.

"I can't help it, I'm a compulsive cross-examiner."

Annie studied him for a moment. "I have a proposition for you. I ask a question, then you ask a question, fair enough?"

"Shoot."

She looked him square in the eyes. "Is Billy Malone guilty?"

Clancy chuckled. "I wouldn't know, never asked him. My turn. Do you *like* putting people in jail, Miss Fitzgerald?"

"I'd love to put your client away."

"Ah, your ambition is bigger than your compassion."

Annie was taken aback. "If that were so, I'd be back on Wall Street making the big bucks. Besides, I don't need compassion for this case."

"Then you're never going to be a great lawyer."

"Oh *really*."

"Because you don't care about people."

"Me?" Annie blinked. What was he trying to say? Wasn't she on the good side here? He was the one defending murderers. "Have you ever been to the basement of St. Catherine's on a Tuesday night?"

"Mothers Against Murder." Clancy walked back to his table and sat down.

"That's right." Annie nodded. What could he say to that?

"I'm not too popular over there." Clancy stretched a black rubber galosh over his shoe.

"Maybe you should try it sometime and bring your client." Annie slid an arm into the sleeve of her overcoat. "Better yet, why don't you walk back to the front row tomorrow morning and introduce yourself?"

"When was the last time you went on a date?"

"What?" Annie couldn't believe he asked her that. "None of your business."

"It's your game, Miss Annie Fitzgerald. When was the last time?"

Fight back. "How many people has Billy Malone killed?"

"More than six months? A year? Longer?" Clancy cocked his head. "You can't remember?"

"How many has he killed?"

"Holy cow! You need to get out more, meet some nice gentleman, and let him take you to dinner."

"How many?"

"I don't know."

"I bet the mothers do." Annie headed down the aisle. Her cell phone flashed, showing she had a text from Callahan. Before opening the courtroom doors, she spun around and faced Clancy. "Why don't you ask them tomorrow? I bet they know exactly."

14

ANNIE RANG THE bell for the safe house, located about an hour south in Scituate. The early recess bought her just enough time to drive down in the ice storm and check on Jennianne. Callahan was still working on cutting Domenico loose in Gloucester. It didn't look good. Annie wished she could do something to budge that mulish chief up there. They'd already ignored her subpoena; she'd have to think outside the box, and right now her brain was fried.

She rang the bell again and shoved her hands in her coat pockets. It was cold with the wind whipping sideways off the ocean from the east. *Come on.* Annie had called ahead of time, and left a message. After a few frozen minutes, footsteps approached and Jennianne stuck her head through the door. Her face looked pale and drawn, and her long blond hair appeared unwashed and snarled in back. She wore pink sweatpants and a fitted T-shirt, revealing intricate tatoos on both arms.

"Hi," Annie said. "We finished up early today, so I thought I'd take a ride down." She noticed the dark, purplish rings beneath Jennianne's eyes. "You okay?"

"I was sleeping." Jennianne yawned and held the door open. "Didn't realize it was this late. Time is it?"

Annie walked in and checked her watch. "Three thirty." *Had she been sleeping all day?* She noticed an ashtray full of cigarette butts along with several empty cans of Coors Light on the table, and wondered if Jennianne was hungover. "Are you hungry? Shall I pick up a pizza?"

Jennianne waved her off, and slumped onto the couch. "No, I'm not feeling that great today." She rubbed her stomach. "I can't stand it down here."

"I know." Annie sat next to her. "Hang in there. It won't be long now."

"Do you still need me?" Her eyes widened with hope that Annie would say no.

"Absolutely," Annie said. For a twenty-eight-year-old city girl, Jennianne seemed quite naïve, but perhaps she wasn't always like that. Annie imagined Malone had the power to mold people into whatever he wanted them to be. "I can't do it without you."

"I don't know if I . . ." She lifted her bare feet onto the couch and hugged her spindly legs. "I'm sorry. It's just that I'm not going to remember anything right. Maybe it didn't go like I said before. I'm not, like, that sure anymore, you know?"

"You can't back out now." Annie had already been through the same routine with her. Two steps forward, one step back. "Jennianne, just testify like you did before the grand jury."

"That was a long time ago."

"Not really. Only four months. Do I have to show you the pictures again? Remember what Billy did to you?"

Jennianne closed her eyes. "It might not've been from him," she whispered.

"What?" Annie wondered how much power Malone still exercised over her. He was ten years older and, no doubt, controlling. "Do you still"—she touched Jennianne's arm and waited for her to open her eyes—"love him?"

Jennianne rubbed her forehead against her knees. "I don't know. He's got a new girlfriend now anyways. *Stacy.* And she's a wise slut."

Annie sighed. Jennianne was petite, almost waiflike, and she had such pretty green eyes. Most men would likely fall for her. Why had she gotten tangled up with Malone? "Tell me why you went out with him in the first place."

Jennianne twirled a lock of hair around her finger. "You'd never understand."

"Try me."

"It was an honor to be with him."

"Malone is a killer."

"I knew you wouldn't get it. He took care of me." She tilted her head back against the armrest, and stared at the ceiling. "He made me feel . . . like . . . like protected, special." Her lips formed a tiny smile as if remembering the good times. "It was a big deal the night he introduced me to his ma. It was like wicked huge. Not many of his girlfriends got to meet her."

"Did you know he killed one of them? Lydia Thompson. That was pretty special for her. Strangled her with a rope, then rolled her into a carpet pad, and stuffed her into a trunk." Annie watched Jennianne stiffen. They sat in silence for a moment. Annie hadn't prosecuted that one, but Callahan had been the lead detective. The case had been dismissed midtrial, key evidence had gone missing. "How long did you know Trevor?"

"Just about my whole life." Jennianne bit her upper lip. "We went to elementary school at St. Francis and then ended up going to the same public school in Roxbury. We'd ride home on the bus together. Friends for a long time."

"What was he like?" Annie knew Trevor was the key to bringing Jennianne around; that's how she'd found the courage to testify before the grand jury.

"I don't know." Jennianne shrugged. "Trevor was different."

"What do you mean?"

"Like he always said what was on his mind. The nuns didn't get it, so he got in trouble a ton. Plus, he was kind of hyper back then." She cracked her knuckles and sighed. "Trevor was real. Like if you asked him something, he'd always give you the truth."

"What did you think about his art?"

She rubbed both hands through her hair. "Trevor was so talented with a paintbrush. You'd always see him around town with that old wooden easel of his. Always painting something, you know?"

"I can imagine. Wish I could see more." Annie wondered why Chris wouldn't let her see any more of Trevor's paintings. Was it too painful? She visualized the painting with the kids in the playground, and the little redheaded boy. *Georgie.* "Why did Trevor paint Georgie Hurley?"

Jennianne jerked forward. "Who told you that?"

"Chris confronted Billy about it in court. Do you know anything?"

"Georgie died a long time ago." Jennianne chewed on a cuticle. "I didn't even know him."

"Did Trevor?"

"I don't know." Jennianne looked away. "Georgie was at least four years older than we were, so I doubt it. Why don't you ask his mother? I think she's part of that group."

"Mothers Against Murder." Annie remembered one of the mothers breaking down at the very beginning. Sandy had walked arm in arm with her down the aisle. Had she recognized her son in the painting? Annie made a mental note to speak with Mrs. Hurley. She had never seen her at a meeting.

Annie's phone rang. It was Callahan. She pressed the talk button. "I'm down here with Jennianne."

"How is she?"

"Not so good. Nervous." Annie didn't want to go into detail with Jennianne sitting in front of her.

"I've hit a wall. The Walrus won't budge. You'll have to get the judge to intervene if you want Domenico." Callahan's voice sounded hoarse and defeated. "Better line up another witness for tomorrow."

"No." Annie wasn't about to give up even if she had to go up there herself. "Stay with it—for at least another hour or so."

"Seriously?" He huffed into the phone. "I'm wasting my time."

"Just hold out for a little longer. I'm going to try something, and it just might work." Annie clicked off.

She grabbed her jacket and addressed Jennianne. "I have to go now— all the way up to Gloucester from here."

"Be careful," Jennianne said.

"I know." Annie fished her keys from her pocket. "The roads are slippery." She thought about what Malone had said earlier.

"No, be careful of him."

"Who?"

"Billy."

Annie tensed. "He's in jail."

"It doesn't matter."

"That's why we need to win this case." Annie opened the front door; the sleet had turned to snow.

"I think he painted her." Jennianne called out.

"What?" Annie had to step back into the room.

"Lydia Thompson. The one who got strangled. I think she was in one of Trevor's paintings."

15

DOMENICO WON'T GO for that." Callahan sat across from the Walrus, starving. He should've grabbed a box of fried clams for himself at lunch. Why had he agreed with Annie to stay longer? Now it was almost dinnertime. "No jail time," Callahan said, for what felt like the hundredth time. He also had a pounding headache.

"Not a chance." The Walrus folded his hands and rested them on his bulging stomach. He seemed to be enjoying the game.

"Come on! We've got Billy Malone up for murder." Callahan struck the side of his chair.

"I don't give a shit. Domenico's the biggest prick on the North Shore. He'll be out on another score tonight if I hand him over to you."

Callahan hated groveling, but Domenico refused to cooperate unless they offered an outright dismissal of the Gloucester drug charges. If Callahan forced him to testify, Domenico could easily take the stand and claim he'd never met Malone in his life. The Walrus would clock out soon. He was running out of ideas.

Callahan heard shouts in the hallway. Annie burst through the door carrying a big cardboard box, which she dropped on the floor, creating a loud thud, startling the Walrus. Callahan hadn't expected she'd show up in person. He recognized that crazed look in her eyes.

Annie reached into the box, pulled out the top file, and slapped it down on the desk.

"What the hell?" The Walrus jolted to the edge of his chair.

"Paul Kelly. Shot dead in the Ninety-nine Restaurant in Charlestown. Broad daylight. No witnesses."

She grabbed another file and threw it on the desk. "Jack Doulin. Shot in his bed on Harvard Street. Unsolved.

"Let's mix it up." Annie fished through the box. "This one's a woman. Sheila Gorman. Strangled and buried in a Little Princess sleeping bag. She cooperated with the police just once. You don't do that in Charlestown."

The Walrus twirled the corner of his mustache. Callahan could tell he didn't know what to do with Annie as she piled more unsolved murders on his desk. Every name came with a cause of death, location, and that word: unsolved.

"Stop." The Walrus shoved the files. "I get it, okay? But, my hands are tied. We had a major drug bust here. Trafficking."

"Give Domenico a suspended sentence, and let him walk out of here tonight," Annie said.

"No way."

Annie leaned over the desk until their noses nearly touched. "Are you that pigheaded?"

Callahan had to suppress a smile.

The Walrus pointed at the door. "Get the hell out."

Annie didn't budge. She gazed into his eyes, and forced the Walrus to look away.

"And take your garbage with you." The Walrus backhanded a file; papers fluttered to the floor.

"My garbage? You mean all these dead cases?" Annie gathered the files from his desk.

"That's right, get it all out of here."

"Let me ask you just once." Annie enunciated each word as if she spat them. "Are you refusing to help us?"

"You can't have Domenico." The Walrus poked his finger down hard on the desk. "Period."

"Alright. You'll have to face them."

"Who?"

Callahan leaned forward. He had no idea what Annie was up to.

"Jack Doulin's mother. Paul Kelly's mother. Sheila Gorman's mother. They're all here waiting for you: fourteen and counting. I also have channel seven on speed dial." Annie checked her watch. "Mothers Against Murder. Right here in Gloucester. Just in time for the six o'clock news."

16

DRAKE REED GUIDED the motorized dinghy toward the third pier. It shot way up and landed down hard with each swell. The swirling snow and ice and lack of running lights made navigation nearly impossible. Reed could barely make out the pilings near the shore. *Insane.* Why did it have to go down this way? Reed could've come up with a million other ideas, but, as usual, he listened and nodded. That's why he made the biggest cuts when the job got done. He no longer felt the ice pelting against his face; his skin had turned numb, frozen. Just get to the pier. A big wave doused him with seawater; he nearly capsized. *Twenty more yards. Cold and salty.*

The pier looked deserted. Who would be out in a storm like this? Reed lunged for a frozen steel cleat bolted to the edge of the dock. The rocking dinghy nearly tore his shoulder from the socket as he looped the rope in a figure eight. He leaped onto the dock, but slipped on the ice, and cracked his left kneecap against the point of the cleat. Searing pain jolted all the way up his leg. Reed saw stars. He doubled over and threw up. *Don't scream.*

Reed gritted his teeth; he had to clear his mind, work through the pain. He withdrew his gun from the inner pocket of his parka and listened. Water sloshed against the dock and metal tinged against metal. No signs of life. Satisfied, he lugged the canvas bag up from the well and onto the dock. It felt heavier than before, waterlogged.

Reed had staked out the pier the night before. An old bulky fishing trawler clanged against its mooring in the middle of the harbor. The same two fishing boats creaked in adjacent slips on the dock. He had decided to wait on the first boat since its bridge was about ten feet high and offered an unobstructed view of the pier and loading area. His knee throbbed like hell when he boarded the rocking boat. He hobbled up the steps, dragging the canvas bag to the bridge, which housed the driver's seat, gears, and navigational equipment.

Reed allowed time for his eyes to adjust to the musty blackness inside the bridge. He unlocked the starboard side window, and forced it all the way up with his fist. Snow swirled in. Reed was just thin enough to slip out backward and drop down to the lower deck if he had to.

The wait would be about an hour until the meeting. Reed stood with the bulk of his weight on the right leg; any pressure on his left caused shooting pain in the swollen kneecap. He couldn't allow himself the luxury of sitting in the captain's swivel chair or on the floor with his back slouched against the wall. In both cases, it could take him nearly three seconds to rise and point his gun in case of an ambush. What if he stumbled trying to get up with his bad knee and dropped the gun? He remembered when Smitty fell asleep waiting for his victim and never woke up again. He had to remain on high alert, and think all steps through from beginning to end. One tiny screwup could cost him his life or send him to the can for the rest of it.

Reed wiggled his numb fingers and toes. The minutes dragged. He wondered if his nose would turn black from the frostbite; his new nickname would be Blacknose. He'd have to chalk this up as one of the worst jobs of all time, but it would make for a damn good story someday, a story to go along with the nickname. It was so far-fetched, the guys would think he made it up. And, all this for an overdose?

Reed shivered. Malone had made him do some crazy shit lately. Stuff that hadn't even made sense. He'd been working for Malone for years, and had never seen him act like this before. It was like he turned paranoid all of a sudden. Reed had to dig up everything he could on the DA going way back to the story of the guys with the baseball bat at her parents' book-store. He wondered what malone would do with that? Reed never ques-tioned him; he did what he was told. Maybe Malone had reason to be worried. After all, they did find that transmitter hidden in the hanging deodorizer in Malone's truck. He went ape shit over that one. Blamed Taco for being sloppy and letting it happen. He forced the guy to undress in front of everyone and do some nasty things to himself. Reed cringed at the thought of it. They were all told to form a circle around him and watch. Then, Malone gouged his eyeballs out with the claw of a hammer. Reed had to wipe those eyes off the floor with paper towels. He ended up killing the guy after all that, too.

What the hell was up with Malone? It *was* getting harder than ever, nothing like the old days. No one really knew what to do with all those mothers and Father Coyne in the basement church group. Ignore them, he'd advised Malone, they'll go away eventually. That's what everyone thought, but their numbers kept growing. Taco's mother had recently joined, no surprise there. Reed had chopped up the eyeless body and fed it to the fish quite a ways out, beyond the harbor islands. No pieces ever washed up, but word must've gotten back to the mother somehow that her son was dead.

It wasn't just the mothers that bothered Malone, it was something else on top of that. Reed suspected it had something to do with the Shea kid who painted all those whack-ass pictures. Some of 'em even freaked Reed out, and he'd seen it all over the years. The painted shit was weird. *Spooky.* Reed had to avert his eyes when he burned the last one, and he never flinched or looked away no matter how grotesque the scene. It was like he had burned someone alive—*the thing squirmed.* That's why he hadn't burned the others that night. He'd get to it.

Reed finally spotted headlights from a pickup truck pulling into the parking area beyond the boat ramp. A lone figure hopped out of the driver's side and headed toward the water. An orange light near the ramp provided enough illumination for him to see the bowlegged gait, pony-tail, and gun.

Reed hiked the canvas bag over his shoulder; his knee buckled in pain.

He crept back down, waited in the shadows of the dock, and studied the silhouette at the edge of the pier for several minutes to make sure he came alone.

"Hey!" Reed had his weapon drawn.

"Reed?"

"I'm out here, Miles." Reed had to shout over the splashing waves. "We both came alone, we both have a piece. Let's make this easy."

"Where's your car?" Domenico leaped onto the dock.

"Didn't bring one," Reed said.

Domenico scanned the pier. "That the money?" He pointed to the bag with his gun.

"Eighty thousand." A gust of wind with ice pelted Reed from behind. "Gonna count it?"

"It'll blow out here." Domenico squatted over the bag without removing his gaze from Reed or lowering his gun. "In my truck."

"No way. I'm not leaving this pier." Reed wouldn't fall for that.

"So help me, if as much as fifty cents is missing . . ." Domenico loosened the string and reached inside. "I'm on that witness stand tomorrow."

Reed hauled back and booted Domenico in the temple, knocking him off balance. He shoved him sideways with all his strength. Domenico skidded across the icy planks and rolled into the water. His gun came loose when he grasped at the edge of the dock in desperation. It bounced once and sank. *Just as planned.*

When Domenico surfaced, Reed reached down and pointed his gun. "Get in the dinghy."

Domenico struggled into the boat, and doubled over, shivering. Reed got in and stuffed the money bag under his feet. He'd been instructed to bring the full amount in the event of an ambush. Worst-case scenario, he could pay Domenico according to their prior deal.

The sea pounded the dinghy as Reed motored back out into the bay. He kept the gun pointed at Domenico.

"No b-bullet h-holes this way." Domenico's teeth chattered.

"That's right. Not a bad way to go though. Hypothermia is painless from what they say."

Two successive swells nearly capsized the dinghy. Reed gauged the distance to shore. If the thing flipped now, they'd both die. Domenico couldn't swim and make it from here. *No way.* Reed eyed the big trawler, which was moored about a hundred feet away. It wasn't that far, but Domenico couldn't possibly climb up the steel hull and save himself. *Not in this condition.*

"Get out." Reed shoved the gun into Domenico's forehead.

Domenico stood and spread his arms into a Y like an Olympic high diver. His hands flailed as he tried to keep balance. The dinghy rocked.

"What the hell are you do—?" Reed gripped the lip on the side of the boat; they almost tipped again. He had no choice; he'd have to use the gun and kill the guy. Reed fired and missed.

Domenico yelled at the top of his lungs and performed a swan dive into the water. Going out in a blaze of glory. Reed kind of liked that. He didn't bother watching him sink. Instead, he turned the boat around and headed for shore.

A diesel engine roared from behind, and the water lit up all around him. Reed looked back. The trawler lurched forward with a giant spotlight on the bow. Reed already had his small, seven horse motor on full speed.

The trawler closed in. Reed hit the ice water. The steel hull churned him under like a massive snowplow.

17

ANNIE WATCHED THE jury shuffle into the courtroom dressed more casually. The foreperson sported glasses with sleek, rectangular black-and-white frames, which matched her pinstriped pants suit. Annie needed to win her back after yesterday's witness debacles. She watched Clancy adjusting a colorful fish bow tie. Malone poured Clancy a glass of water. *How nice.* And what perfect timing, right as the jurors were entering. He saw Annie watching him and smiled. She thought he looked more confident than ever.

"Be seated," Johnny said. "The Superior Court of Suffolk County is now in session, the Honorable Conrad J. Killam presiding."

"Commonwealth, call your witness." Judge Killam's comb-over appeared perfectly aligned with a fresh application of gel and hair spray. He wiggled in his chair and grinned, like he had just been disconnected from the battery charger.

Annie stood. "Good morning, Your Honor, Mr. Clerk, and ladies and gentlemen of the jury. "The Commonwealth calls Miles Domenico."

"Oh, my turn again." Johnny ambled back down the aisle to the oak double doors, and repeated the same routine as the day before. "Miles Dooooomenico!"

Annie noticed everyone in the courtroom looking back this time. Domenico had been released the night before with a long suspended sentence hanging over his head. If he failed to show up for court, Callahan and she would have no mercy. They'd lock him up and throw away the key. *Please be out there.*

"Ah, look what the cat dragged in!" Johnny pulled the door back.

"Enough with the commentary already," Judge Killam said.

Domenico sauntered down the aisle with his bowlegged gait. Annie breathed a sigh of relief even though he did look like something her cat would leave half-chewed at the front door. His black ponytail shined with grease, and his face looked like he hadn't shaved for a week. Something greenish stained Domenico's Harley-Davidson T-shirt and ripped jeans. Annie would take what she could get at this point.

Instead of walking straight toward the witness stand, Domenico cut in between the two counsel tables. "Canvas floats," he said, as he passed by the defense table. Malone's eyes widened.

Canvas? Did she hear him right? Annie wondered what that was all about. She couldn't tell if Judge Killam and the jurors heard it.

"Raise your right hand, please?" Clerk Fallon waited for Domenico to raise his hand. "Do you swear to tell the truth, the whole truth, and nothing but the truth, so help you God?"

"I do." Domenico winked at Malone.

Annie could tell Malone struggled to maintain his composure. The bitter freeze in his eyes gave it away. He was probably counting on Domenico being a no show. Clancy, on the other hand, seemed overly pleased.

"Good morning." Annie watched the jurors sizing her witness up. They could probably smell him from the jury box. His stench reminded her of a dish of tuna-flavored cat food left out for several days. "Please introduce yourself to the jury."

"Miles Domenico." He sneezed and wiped his nose on the back of his arm.

"Where are you from?"

"Gloucester, Massachusetts."

"Are you currently employed?"

"Yeah, I work part time at the docks." He crossed his arms at his chest, leaning back in his chair.

"What do you do at the docks?"

"Unload the fishing boats."

Annie wouldn't ask exactly what Domenico unloaded from those boats. "Did you make an agreement with Detective Callahan?"

"Uh huh."

"Which was?" Annie had to bring this up now to soften Clancy's blow later.

"I was arrested on these bogus drug charges in Gloucester. He agreed to pull some strings and get me a suspended sentence if I testified today." Domenico shrugged. "So I said I would."

"Okay." Annie flipped a page in her legal pad. Domenico made it sound so easy. "Do you have a criminal record?"

"I, uhh . . ." He snorted. "Yeah."

"Just a minute ago you took an oath?"

"Sure." Domenico yawned.

"What does it mean to you?"

He stared at her and picked wax from his ear. "What?"

"The oath. What does that mean to you?"

"Oh." He wiped the wax on his shirt. *Another stain.* "That I have to tell the truth."

"The truth." Annie nodded toward the jury. She hoped they'd see through Domenico's grime and find his testimony believable. "On November tenth of last year at approximately eleven A.M. where were you?"

"Gloucester Harbor, on a fishing boat."

"What happened?"

"Got a phone call."

"Who called?"

"Objection." Clancy wiggled his finger. "We all know that's hearsay."

Annie addressed the judge. "It's the telephone exception if the witness can identify the caller."

"You're right. Overruled."

"Did the caller identify himself or herself?"

"Yeah."

"Who was the caller?"

"Objection!" Clancy stood this time. "Miss Fitzgerald hasn't laid a proper foundation. It's still hearsay."

"Give her a chance." Judge Killam tapped his gavel. "Overruled."

"Mr. Domenico, who called?"

"Slash."

"Oh, come on, Judge. Objection." Clancy gesticulated without getting up. "This shouldn't come in."

The judge rubbed his chin.

"Since when is a nickname inadmissible?" Annie faced Clancy; she hoped the jurors were getting sick of his annoying objections.

"Sustained."

"It was Billy Malone who called." Domenico blurted his answer out as if he wanted to put an end to the dog-and-pony show. Annie noticed Judge Killam didn't chastise him. Everyone wanted to move on.

"Had you spoken with Malone prior to that telephone conversation?" she asked.

"Talked to him?" Domenico pointed at Malone. "Billy Malone? Jeez, at least fifty times, probably more."

"Liar." Malone mumbled loud enough for the jury to hear.

Domenico's mockery surprised Annie. He acted as if he had one up on Malone. "May the record reflect the witness has identified the defendant?" she asked.

"It may so reflect." Judge Killam studied Malone for a moment.

"What did you and Malone discuss over the telephone?" Annie slowed down her delivery and looked at the jury.

"Objection," Clancy said.

"Once again, your hearsay objection is overruled." Judge Killam regarded Domenico. "Go ahead, answer the question."

"Okay. Slash, I mean, Billy Malone asked if I could get him some heroin, the strongest stuff available."

"What?" Malone extended his arms toward Domenico. "He's a damn liar."

"Order!" Judge Killam banged his gavel. "No outbursts."

"What did you say to Malone when he requested the heroin?" Annie asked.

"I told him I could get some Nine-eleven."

"Nine-eleven? What's Nine-eleven?"

"Very potent heroin from Afghanistan. Twice as strong as the average stuff you get on the street."

"What did Malone say?"

"That he only wanted one bag, which I thought was odd."

"Objection!" Clancy shot up. "Move to strike."

"Sustained." Judge Killam turned to the jury. "The witness's opinion concerning the one bag is stricken from the record. Please ignore his comment."

"What happened next?" Annie glanced at the jury. They seemed interested in what Domenico had to say.

"We agreed to meet at Maria's Sub Shop on Western at three o'clock, then we hung up."

"Did you meet later on?"

"Yeah."

Malone nudged Clancy. "None of this is true." The jurors in the front row turned their heads. Clancy whispered something and Malone nodded.

"Did you see what type of vehicle Malone was driving that day?" Annie asked.

"Black pickup truck. A Ford, I think."

"What was he wearing?"

"Uh." Domenico scratched his scalp. "Definitely jeans, work boots, and I think he had a dark blue sweater or . . . no, it was a sweatshirt with the name of a bar or something on it."

"What happened next?"

"We met up and sat down at a booth. I ordered a large Italian and he had a meatball." Domenico looked up as if visualizing the scene. "Uh, I asked him how business was. He said it couldn't be better."

"What business were you referring to?"

Domenico addressed the jury and pointed a thumb at the defendant. "He controls the drug trade in Charlestown."

"What? I can't believe this bullshit!" Malone slammed his fist on the table.

"Objection!" Clancy raised his arms.

"Control your client, Clancy." Judge Killam pointed at both of them. "And your objection is overruled. I'll allow the testimony."

"What the?" Clancy gaped at the jury in disbelief. "Sidebar, Your Honor?"

"No, your objection will be noted for the record."

Clancy puckered his lips and looked at the jury again. Annie noticed an old lady smiling at him, like a mother offering encouragement.

"What happened next?" Annie had to steal the jurors' focus away from Clancy and back to the witness.

"We ate, made small talk. I told him I got what he wanted, so he asked how much. I said sixty bucks. He said too expensive." Domenico addressed the jury. "You know, he thought I should cut him a break even though my price was wholesale. Out of the goodness of my heart, I sold it to him for forty."

"I see." Annie noticed a few chuckles in the jury box. Domenico was playing it up for them. "What happened after that?"

"He threw forty bucks down, and I gave him a CVS bag with the heroin inside."

"Your Honor?" Annie walked to her table and grabbed a plastic CVS drugstore bag and the empty heroin packet, stamped Nine-eleven in red, and showed them to Clancy. "May I approach the witness?"

"You may."

"I'm presenting the witness with Commonwealth's exhibits C-6 and C-7, previously marked. Do you recognize these?"

"Yup." Domenico pushed the CVS bag aside and examined the heroin packet. "Except the one I sold him was filled with Nine-eleven."

Annie placed the items back on her table. She wouldn't admit them into evidence until Detective Callahan's testimony.

"What happened next?" Annie resumed her position behind the podium.

"I warned him to be careful if he planned on using the Nine-eleven. I told him I knew a couple a guys who OD'd on it and died."

"What was Malone's response?"

"That he don't do heroin."

"No further questions."

Judge Killam gazed at the clock and over at Clancy, who rose for cross-examination. "We'll break a little early for lunch and resume at two o'clock."

"All rise," Johnny said.

Annie noticed Domenico and Malone staring at each other with such open animosity. *If looks could kill.* She wondered what else had gone down between them. The guard hurried over to Malone and escorted him out before Domenico stepped down from the witness stand.

Annie grabbed her legal pad. She wasn't looking forward to spending an extended lunch in a cramped conference room with a guy who reeked of dead fish, but it had to be done. The inevitable Clancy attack was on its way.

18

RACHEL DIDN'T KNOW what to make of this seedy character as she resumed her seat in the jury box following the lunch recess. She wished she wasn't sitting so close in the foreperson's chair; she had to breathe through her mouth the whole time. He smelled like the muck from low tide combined with dead carp. On the other hand, it seemed like he was telling the truth. Rachel could picture the drug transaction going down in the dirty sub shop. The bartering over price sounded just like her negotiations at work. She watched Clancy high-step into center court; his multicolored fish tie was perfect. The jurors had been chatting about his array of ties throughout the lunch break. They were all in for an afternoon treat.

"So, you're a drug dealer!" Clancy sounded impressed.

"I've sold small amounts."

"Let me rephrase that. You're more significant, like a drug wholesaler, supplier?"

"No."

Rachel remembered he'd offered Malone a wholesale price for the heroin, and now he was denying it?

"No?" Clancy scratched his head. "But you're well known as one of the biggest suppliers in the state? The go-to guy for drugs?"

"Nooo."

Clancy strolled before the jury box with his finger to his lips. "You control the entire drug trade on the North Shore."

"Not me."

"Your goal is to take over Charlestown now, isn't it?"

"That's crazy!"

"Your heroin ended up in Charlestown."

"One bag did." Domenico twirled his finger in the air. "Whoop-de-do."

"Five years ago you were convicted of dealing in a school zone. Am I correct?"

"If you say so."

"You sold cocaine? Heroin? Crack? What?"

"Can't recall, got framed for that one anyways."

"I have a certified copy of your conviction here somewhere." Clancy grabbed a stack of papers from his table and fanned through them within inches of Rachel. "Hmm, I have a whole bunch of convictions here." He strolled before the jury box, and moved them up and down and squinted as if his eyesight had dwindled.

Fitzgerald groaned. "Objection."

"Sustained." Judge Killam rubbed his forehead. "Keep your commentary to yourself, counselor."

Clancy licked his fingertips and flipped through more, ignoring the judge. "Oh, here we are." He gesticulated and the stack slipped from his fingers. "Whoops!" Papers scattered everywhere.

Rachel watched one flutter down near the jury box. Did Clancy drop them on purpose to make a show? He *was* old . . . a bit arthritic. Did they slip accidentally?

"Objection!" Fitzgerald pointed at the mess.

"Sustained. Clancy, get those off my floor."

Clancy saluted the judge. "Aye, aye, Your Honor." His knees cracked as he bent down and picked up papers, one by one.

"Oh, there it is. Glad it fell near the top." Clancy winked at Rachel, struggled back up, and walked over to Domenico. "It says right here you were convicted of distributing a class A substance. Heroin is a class A sub-stance right?"

"How would I know?" Domenico rolled his eyes.

"How would you *not* know?" Clancy arced around the witness stand. "You went to jail over Class A, and now you're telling this jury you don't know what Class A is?"

"Objection!" Fitzgerald bolted up. "Argumentative."

"Why, Miss Fitzgerald, that's what we call classic cross-examination." Clancy grinned. "Can't be picked up in the halls of Yale."

"Quite true." Judge Killam smiled. "He may have it."

"So, the bottom line is, Mr. Domenico, you were caught dealing her-oin and landed smack dab in the slammer again?"

"If that's what it says?" Domenico glared. "Yeah."

The slammer? Rachel laughed to herself. Clancy was putting on a show and having the time of his life.

"I'd be happy to show you more." Clancy squatted and gathered more papers. "Wow, you've been busy. Cocaine, cocaine, crack, crack, heroin. Here's a good one. Wait, this one's even better." He reached across the floor. "Ow! My back." Clancy rubbed his lower back and looked up at the old ladies in the second row.

"Poor attorney Clancy." Fitzgerald moved out from behind her table. "The Commonwealth wouldn't want you to hurt your back, so I'll agree to admit all these convictions into evidence."

"Why, thank you kindly, Miss Fitzgerald." Clancy nodded in apparent appreciation as she and Clerk Fallon gathered the papers. Rachel could hear the tension in Fitzgerald's voice. *A Yale educated attorney?* She won-dered why Fitzgerald didn't work for one of the prestigious Boston law firms. Perhaps she couldn't handle the pressure. She came across so fo-cused and serious. Rachel wondered if she liked her job.

Clancy marched toward the witness with his discombobulated papers. "Mr. Drug, I mean, Domenico, your past convictions also include two for larceny, and assault and battery on a police officer, correct?"

"Yup."

"Did I miss any?" Clancy asked.

"That's it."

"Sure about that?"

"Yeah, I'm positive, you named 'em all."

Clancy grinned. "You didn't volunteer to appear here today, did you?"

"I showed up."

"Oh really?" Clancy folded his arms. "Detective Callahan threatened to arrest you on manslaughter charges for the death of Trevor Shea."

"Objection." Fitzgerald raised an arm. "Speculative."

"Overruled."

"That was bogus," Domenico said.

"You didn't mention that part of the deal?" Clancy tapped his foot.

"I wasn't asked."

"Manslaughter. That's rather significant, wouldn't you say?"

"But I didn't kill anybody."

"And neither did my client." Clancy motioned to Malone. "Now, Mr. Domenico, that was a very good deal, but Callahan threw you a bone, too?"

"What are you talking about?" Domenico leaned forward.

"Callahan threw you some money, too, in exchange for your testimony."

"Not that I can recall."

"Ten thousand in advance." Clancy held his palms out and spread his fingers. "And ten thousand after you finish testifying here today—all under the table."

"That's not true!" Domenico's face reddened.

"For that deal you'd say anything, wouldn't you?" Clancy hovered over his witness. Rachel figured he could smell Domenico's sour fish breath.

"I'm telling the truth." Domenico gripped the witness stand and glowered at Clancy.

"The truth!" Clancy slapped his hands on his hips. "The truth is you sold that heroin directly to Trevor Shea. You're the murderer!"

"Objection!" Fitzgerald shouted. "This is outrageous."

"Overruled."

"I didn't even know who Trevor Shea was." Spit flew from Domenico's mouth.

"What?" Clancy spun around and made eye contact with Rachel. "Why, you're telling this jury you've never heard of Trevor Shea, the prize-winning artist?"

"Never."

"Come on, you've been supplying him with heroin for years."

"Objection." Fitzgerald jumped up again. "That's a complete fabrication."

"Overruled."

"Nope." Domenico shook his head. "Never heard that name before in my life."

"*Really?* You do understand your obligation to tell the truth here today?"

"Yeah."

"Have you always told the truth to the jury?"

"Of course. This is ridiculous."

"What about the time you were convicted of perjury!"

"Objection!" Fitzgerald sprang from her chair, almost knocking it over. "Sidebar?"

Rachel watched Fitzgerald and Clancy parade up to the bench. Perjury? She leaned forward and strained to hear what this was all about. She could hear bits and pieces when the attorneys became agitated. Fitzgerald's face turned red, and she kept pointing at Clancy, obviously accusing him of something underhanded.

If the perjury conviction was real, Rachel wondered whether she should discount all of Domenico's testimony. If he lied once, did that mean he never told the truth?

"No way! It's inadmissible. He never showed it to me prior to trial." Annie couldn't believe Clancy managed to find an old perjury conviction.

"I'm using it for impeachment. Her witness just testified under oath that he always tells the truth to the jury. I'm using it to challenge his veracity, and show he's a liar."

"Let me take a look." Judge Killam snatched the conviction from Clancy's hand, and examined it. "It's legitimate, he's got a certified copy here. Miss Fitzgerald, didn't you check his record before putting him on the stand?"

"Of course, but perjury never showed up."

"Clancy, do you know why the conviction never appeared on this man's record?"

"Yes, Your Honor, I'd be happy to explain." Clancy's voice sounded sugary. "Until about a decade ago, the Probation Department up in Newburyport used an outdated filing card system to keep track of criminal records. Those records were eventually entered into a fancy computer database. That perjury conviction fell through the cracks; it was never properly entered into the system. I found it by tediously sifting through old cases, the old-fashioned way."

"You're a classic, Clancy. An A for effort." Judge Killam handed the conviction back to Clancy. "I'll allow it."

Annie gritted her teeth. "Please note my objection for the record."

Annie watched Clancy smile at the jury as he resumed his position, fluttering the paper. "At this time I will introduce Mr. Domenico's perjury conviction into evidence. No further questions."

Annie noticed Malone could barely contain his delight. How could she dig Domenico out of this one? Why hadn't he told Callahan or her that he served time for perjury? Malone must've heard a rumor and sent Clancy up to investigate. She couldn't picture him doing all that extra work on a whim. *No way.*

"Any redirect, Commonwealth?" Judge Killam asked.

"Yes, Your Honor." Annie had to think of at least one or two questions to save face, and get Domenico off the stand as soon as possible. The jurors watched and waited. The foreperson sat with her arms crossed, looking disgusted.

"Mr. Domenico?" she asked.

"Yeah?"

"Did you tell the truth about your dealings with Billy Malone on November tenth of last year?"

"I was tellin' the truth about that."

"Is testifying here today dangerous for you?"

"Very. You risk your life ratting on Billy Malone."

"Objection!" Clancy didn't bother getting up, he just raised a finger.

"Sustained."

"Is it possible you simply forgot about that old conviction?"

"I wouldn't lie about it."

19

ANNIE HAD NO patience for the elevator doors; she turned sideways and catapulted onto the homicide detectives' floor at Boston Police Headquarters. She'd been anxious to speak with Callahan since court ended, but his phone kept going directly to voice mail. Annie breezed past reception, snaked through the cubbies, and barged into Callahan's office.

"What the hell, Mike?" She pushed the door so hard that it slammed against the wall and bounced back, striking her in the hip.

"I had no idea." Callahan sat at his desk about to dip chopsticks into a fresh carton of beef lo mein.

"So how did Clancy know about it then? Huh? I looked like a complete idiot. A complete, stupid, jackass."

"I'm—"

"To make matters worse, Domenico says, 'I wouldn't lie about it.'" Annie gathered her hair and twisted it into a knot on top of her head. "Tells the jury he wouldn't lie about a damned *perjury* conviction. I couldn't even look at them, couldn't even ask another question."

Callahan pushed his food aside and released a long sigh.

"So why am I bothering here?" Annie walked over to the window and pressed her forehead against the cool glass. She felt like crying.

"Annie—" She heard Callahan shove his chair back.

"No, really. Why? Because this case is a loser. We shouldn't have taken it on. I knew it from the get-go. There's not enough evidence to go on. You and I both know it. What are we trying to accomplish here?"

"Maybe I better take the stand after the medical examiner and toxicologist." Callahan walked up from behind and placed a hand on her shoulder. "We'll be a little out of order, but we'll appear more professional that way. Get us back on track."

"Us?" Annie closed her eyes, and kept leaning against the glass. She was so tired, she could fall asleep on her feet, right there.

"Yeah, what?"

"It's not us, it's you, all about you."

"What are you talking about? I've been busting my ass on your case." Callahan removed his hand.

"Oh, so now it's *my* case?" Annie spun around. "Because it went sour?" She felt like choking him. "You're the one who called me out to the Tobin Bridge that night, remember?"

"I did, I know." His balled his hands. "I'm as frustrated as you, okay? Didn't know about the perjury. No idea. If it wasn't on his record?" He moved backward and sat on the edge of his desk. "You know how hard it was to flip that guy? A miracle he showed up today."

Annie opened her mouth and closed it. The question lingered on the tip of her tongue. What about the money? Did he bribe Domenico as Clancy had suggested? Could Callahan really pay that much? Did they have a slush fund? Forfeiture monies? She gave him a long, hard look.

"Why are you looking at me like that?"

Annie knew cops did their thing sometimes, worked backroom deals, bent the rules. She considered who they had to deal with: scumbags like Domenico. Annie was better off not knowing, wasn't she? *Don't ask, don't tell.*

"Are you heading over to the Mothers Against Murder meeting tonight?" Callahan asked. "I'm going to stop by toward the end. We can go together."

Annie considered his invitation for a moment. Callahan rarely missed a meeting. Despite all his flaws, he really cared about all those women. How easy it would be for him to go home and hop into bed right now.

"Why did you become a homicide detective?" she asked. "Maybe you should've been a counselor."

"You're probably right." He walked back to his desk, sat down, and stirred his chopsticks around in the container of lo mein. "My dad was a crime beat reporter for the old *Herald American* back in the late fifties, sixties, and seventies. He'd show up at all the crime scenes across the city and then write about it. Sometimes I'd have to wait in the car while he slipped under the yellow police tape. It was like the Wild West back then. Guys would get knocked off all the time—turf wars."

"It must've seemed so exciting as a kid."

"Oh yeah. My dad knew all the cops and some of the hoodlums from the old Winter Hill gang in Somerville, the Irish gangsters in Charlestown and Southie, the Italian mafia in the North End. We also had all the rackets in the old Combat Zone. I used to read about it and see the old black-and-white pictures of the bodies lying in the streets." Callahan lifted a bunch of noodles with his chopsticks and stuffed them into his mouth. He chewed for a moment. "So, that's all I ever wanted to do was be a cop, a homicide detective."

"Are you happy with your choice?" Annie asked.

He smiled. "Most of the time. Are you coming to the meeting?"

"I may join you later." Annie walked toward the door. "I need some time to myself, to think. It feels like we're missing something, and we're not going to beat Malone unless we figure out what it is."

20

AFTER SUPPER AND before *Wheel of Fortune,* Elaine called her cousin, Liz McCarthy, who lived in Charlestown.

"Hello?"

"Liz, did you know cops pay off their witnesses?" Elaine balanced the phone between her shoulder and ear, and opened the freezer.

"I always wondered about that. I know they pay 'em for information like on that old show *NYPD Blue.* Remember the big fat cop who they'd show naked every once in a while? What was his name again? Began with an S?"

"Yeah, yeah, right, I remember him." Elaine could picture the guy naked in the shower, but couldn't think of his name offhand. She grabbed the Ben & Jerry's Chocolate Peanut Butter Swirl. "We're talking serious money here, Liz. I'm not supposed to discuss it, but between you and me, it looks like a cop on my murder case paid off a witness to testify. Can you believe it?"

"Is that so?"

"S'what the defense lawyer said."

"Who, Buddy Clancy?"

"Yeah, know him?"

"Uh huh. His office is right on Main, lives up on School Street. I met his wife, Margaret, couple times. Nice lady. See him walking his dog all the time around town. They wear matching bow ties."

"I can picture it—he's a character alright." Elaine loved his fish tie.

"I'll say. Gets all the thugs as clients."

"'Cause he's good." Elaine fished through her drawers for the stainless ice cream scoop. "You been watching the news about the case?"

"Pretty much."

"What's up with those ladies with the matching yellow T-shirts? One of 'em was interviewed on TV yesterday, but I only caught the end of it. They're always sitting in the front row."

"They're all in Mothers Against Murder down at the church." Liz sighed. "I guess they call it the Charlestown After Murder Program now. Anyways, they all lost sons to murder. Might be a couple a daughters was killed, too."

"Okay, yeah, makes sense now." Elaine wondered why Fitzgerald hadn't explained who they were in the beginning. She'd have to remember to tell Louie. Her mind drifted back to the bribe again. "Clancy seemed pretty convincing about that payoff. It didn't sound like he made it up, had the numbers down and everything."

"I'm sure he was right. How much was it?" Liz asked.

"Twenty grand."

She whistled. "How come so much?"

Elaine grimaced as she pictured Domenico in his ratty dock clothes. She remembered the fishy stench, too. "The guy was a drug dealer from Gloucester. Knew he could get money out of the cops. They got some kind of slush fund, I guess. I'm surprised the press didn't go crazy over it. That's tax money, you know. Our money."

"How did the guy that got paid off do?"

Elaine laughed. "It backfired on them. The idiots. The drug dealer got up there and lied, committed perjury. Clancy figured it all out and had a field day."

"Well, you'd have to pay me an awful lot to testify against that one."

"Billy Malone?"

"Yeah, a real bad apple, Elaine. Big time. I know that for a fact. Remember when he got arrested last fall?"

"I recall hearing something about it."

"It was all over the news, made all the papers. Somebody got shot during his arrest. It was a pretty bad scene."

"Hmm, funny nobody mentioned that." Elaine found the scoop and tore the cardboard lid off the container. "You sure?"

"I think so. Might've been a cop was shot."

"Really? You'd think I'd remember that. Huh." Elaine grunted. She had to use her muscles; the ice cream was hard. "Well, he's probably guilty then."

"Oh, I would say so."

21

ANNIE TORE THROUGH Roxbury, and hopped on the Expressway, only to get off a few exits north in Charlestown. Her Ford Mustang hydroplaned twice on black ice. She crossed Main Street and drove up Monument Avenue, a narrow street lined with expensive brownstones, trees, and gas lamps. At the peak of the hill, she gazed up at the tall, lighted Bunker Hill Monument, which memorialized the first major battle of the American Revolution. This is what the tourists saw every day, and, for most, it *was* Charlestown. The pristine landscaping, the happy young mothers walking with their baby strollers, diaper bags tucked underneath. *Charlestown.* But what did Trevor, the artist, see? *Not this. Not this at all.*

Annie continued down the other side of the hill until she faced row after row of the drab brick units of the Bunker Hill housing project, the largest in the city. She squeezed into a parking spot near the bus stop on lower Bunker Hill Street, and walked down a block to the church. It was eight thirty; the meeting would be wrapping up soon in the basement. Maybe they were finished and cleaning up. She hesitated at the front steps. Why had the case spiraled out of control so fast? How could she face all the mothers again and answer their questions? *What do you think the jury will do? Is Malone going to take the stand?* She didn't have answers.

Annie spotted one of the tiny lower basement windows close to the ground; she could take a quick peek. She squeezed in between a row of prickly bushes at the side of the church, stumbling in her heels. Annie knelt in the frozen dirt, and peered through the mud-streaked window. There they were, sitting in a semicircle on gray metal folding chairs, eating Mary's brownies with the mint frosting and Joann's strawberry cheesecake. Father Coyne tilted on the edge of his chair, and listened to Sandy rattling on about something, probably the trial. He was a good, devoted priest; the kind you don't hear about. Callahan sat opposite the priest, and took off his jacket. I appeared like he had just arrived.

Annie couldn't go down there. Let them pray for their dead with Father Coyne. She flipped around, stretched her legs out in front, and leaned her back and aching head against the cold cinder blocks. She knew she should make an appearance. Annie owed them explanations. She also had to speak with Mrs. Hurley about her son, Georgie, who Chris claimed was in the playground painting. Her nylons snagged on the prickers to her left. Clancy's words popped into her mind: *What's a nice girl like you doing in a case like this? Why aren't you making the big bucks? No wedding ring?*

Why *did* she choose this path? She visualized her father's eyes every time he had to slide that brown paper bag across the tiny counter. Her father was so kind, everyone loved him, respected him. He and her mother worked day in and day out at that damn bookstore. Annie tensed. *They minded their own business.* And, once a month when her father had to hand over that bag, Annie remembered feeling scared. She could smell the cardboard boxes of her fort again. She dug her fingers into the dirt. Tears trickled down her cheeks. She dug harder until she hit something hard. It felt like wood.

Annie used her fingernails and pried up a piece of plywood frozen into the ground. Something scurried away, a mouse, perhaps a rat? What was under there? She bent over for a closer look. More compacted dirt, broken glass, an old potato chip bag. *Ugliness.* That's what Trevor saw, all that ugliness. He looked and painted what was beneath the plywood, what people didn't want to see, what they were afraid to talk about.

Annie closed her eyes and saw the circle of kids in the playground. The little boy Georgie lying on his back; the eyes that screamed. And, those kids in the circle? What were they doing? Watching something about to happen. What were they thinking? Were they afraid? They were taking part, participating like they belonged. Annie had always been an outsider in Charlestown. The girl whose Asian eyes never matched her Irish name. Would she have joined those kids, if asked? She belonged at Yale and in New York, so why had she come back here?

Annie jumped to her feet and brushed dead leaves from her coat. Chris lived a few blocks away. *Find him, get through to him.* She needed Chris to understand Trevor. She couldn't win without Trevor, and Annie had to win.

She walked up the sidewalk. The orange lights helped, but certain areas were dark; she felt vulnerable, exposed. A drunk sitting on a stoop yelled something and started following her. She picked up the pace, turned a corner, and ran into a gang of teenagers playing street hockey and drinking beer.

Someone whistled.

"Look at that. Nice ass!" A hockey puck shot between her legs.

"I want some."

"How much for all ten of us?"

Annie ran; only a few more buildings to go. They were jeering at her, more whistles. Someone hurled a beer can; it bounced in the street ahead of her. *Find Chris and get the hell out of here.*

Annie skipped up his front steps; the door flew open. She jumped.

"You." Chris loomed in the doorway.

Annie struggled to catch her breath. "This a bad time?"

"It's always a bad time." Chris gripped both sides of the door frame, blocking her entrance.

"Can I? Come in?"

"No."

Annie stalled. She couldn't turn around and face the street kids again. God knows what they could do to her. She felt so out of place in her rumpled skirt, ripped nylons, and dirty hands. She scratched her head and yanked a brown leaf from her hair; Maybe she did look like a hooker. *How much for all ten of us?*

"Why are you here?" Chris's words came out measured.

"Where are the rest of Trevor's paintings?" she asked.

Chris stared at her with lips pressed in a thin line.

"I need to learn more about your brother. Why was he killed, Chris? Why?" Annie moved toward the door in an effort to get in. He didn't budge. What was wrong with this guy? Why wouldn't he cooperate? "Show me Trevor's paintings."

"Not available."

"What about Lydia Thompson? Trevor painted her, too. She was Malone's girlfriend. He strangled her and got off. I know there's a connection, Chris."

"Got no clue," he said.

"I can get the paintings, subpoena them as evidence."

"You think you can do anything, don't you, Miss Yale?"

"I can." Annie stared him down.

"You think you're above us? If we won't give you something, you'll simply take it?" Chris laughed. "Just like the cops, huh? Like Callahan. You're not one of us."

"I spent the first eleven years of my life in Charlestown. Don't tell me that. I'm trying to prosecute your brother's case. Put an end to this insanity, this ridiculous code of silence you have out here." Annie motioned in the direction of the street kids.

"Put an end to all this? *You?*" Chris folded his arms. "How will you go about it? Race out here in the middle of the night and stomp your little high heels until you get what you want?"

"Listen to yourself, Chris. You're talking crazy. I know you lost your brother and I'm sorry. But I'm busting my ass here."

"Tell me, where's Jennianne Smith right now?"

"In a safe house." Annie pictured the frail girl twirling her hair on the couch. "At least Jennianne's brave enough to stand up to Billy Malone, and Trevor's not even related to her."

"Poor Jennianne." Chris grasped the door frame. "I feel sorry for her, you know that? All alone out there. A lost cause."

Annie should've gone down there and visited Jennianne again. Callahan had been too busy to check up on her. She suddenly had a bad feeling.

"What did you do to her?" Chris said. "Tell me."

"Nothing. What are you talking about?"

"You know exactly what I mean. What did you do to Jennianne to make her snitch?"

Annie felt uneasy. "We just talked to her."

"We." Chris looked into her eyes and shook his head. "Pathetic. I bet you don't even know the extent of it, what Callahan's capable of. But it doesn't matter, you're just as bad."

"I'm not—"

"Go on, get out of here. Leave."

Annie turned around and stumbled back onto the sidewalk; she couldn't deal with any more of his bullshit. She'd rather take her chances with the street kids, who were still looming close by somewhere in the shadows. She felt their presence and broke into a fast jog.

"Annie." She heard sneakers running on the pavement behind her. "Wait up."

Chris caught up with her. "You're not safe here. I'm coming with you."

"Thank you." She was both surprised and relieved.

"It's not the street kids I'm worried about." He looked into her eyes. "It's Malone."

22

ELAINE NOTICED THE men leaning forward as the next witness strutted down the aisle with high heels clicking and hips swinging that morning. Even Judge Killam craned his neck from the bench. The woman appeared to be in her midthirties, with dark hair, shaped into a shoulder-length bob. She wore a large gold pendant that settled into her deep cleavage. Her red suit looked expensive and showy, and it matched her shiny shoes and fingernails. Clerk Fallon greeted her with an extra wide smile as he read the oath.

"Please introduce yourself to the jury." Fitzgerald walked to her spot behind the podium.

"Dr. Katherine Joyce."

"What is your occupation?"

"I'm an assistant medical examiner for the Commonwealth of Massachusetts."

Elaine almost laughed out loud. No wonder this woman got all snazzed up for court. She worked in the morgue chopping up dead bodies all day. *Morticia.* Elaine craned her neck to see if Morticia wore a wedding ring. *Nope.* Who'd want to come home to a wife smelling like formaldehyde every day? Elaine thought back to dissecting the slimy, gray, fetal pig in high school biology class. Thank God she grew up to be a housecleaner.

Elaine missed most of Morticia's background, but did hear Harvard thrown around a couple times. It figured. She carried herself off all high and mighty, definitely Harvardish.

"What happened when you arrived at the scene in Charlestown?" Fitzgerald asked.

Morticia cocked her head. "Trevor Shea, the deceased, was lying on his back when I arrived. His left hand rested across his chest, palm down, while his right hand rested above his head, holding a syringe. I observed a fresh track mark on his right arm and vertical scrapes and scratches on his back."

Fitzgerald had Morticia identify several pictures of Trevor as he lay there, dead, with his eyes wide open. Elaine wished someone had closed his eyes.

"Did you look for any other track marks besides the one you mentioned?"

"Yes and I only observed one on the victim's right arm."

"Did you make any observations about Trevor's right hand while you were at the crime scene?"

Morticia raised an enlarged crime scene photograph showing Trevor holding the syringe. "Here, the deceased is holding the syringe loosely in his fingers. I was able to remove it with ease. You see, when someone dies, the hands undergo what we call cadaveric spasm, which means a stiffening of the hands. So, if someone is gripping an object at the time of death, that grip will remain tight after death due to cadaveric spasm. Likewise, if an object is placed in a person's hands after death occurs, you will not observe a tight grip."

"Objection, move to strike." Clancy popped out of his seat. Elaine noticed his bow tie had what appeared to be a tangle of yellowish gray worms on it.

"Overruled," Judge Killam said.

Fitzgerald nodded at the judge. "Did you form an opinion regarding Trevor's grip on the syringe?"

Morticia faced the jury. "If the deceased had been holding the syringe in his right hand before death occurred, his grip should've been much stronger. I would've had more difficulty extracting the syringe from his fingers. Thus, I concluded that someone must have placed the syringe in Trevor's right hand postmortem, or after death had occurred."

"Objection," Clancy said.

"Overruled."

Elaine studied Malone, who showed no emotion. What Morticia was saying made sense. Perhaps someone did try to rig the body to make it look like he overdosed out there under the Tobin Bridge.

Trevor's brother sat next to those yellow-shirted mothers in the front row with his arms crossed and lips puckered. He looked like he was about to leap from his seat and choke Malone. Elaine wondered if he had come out to the crime scene. She wondered how much the brother knew. What were they saying about the case on the streets? She'd have to get more info from Liz. All this court stuff didn't really tell her anything.

Next, Morticia took them step-by-step through the autopsy procedure at the city morgue. There was so much cutting and sawing. Elaine shivered as she imagined herself lying naked on that cold stainless steel table. The autopsy photographs were gruesome, so dehumanizing.

"Did you make further observations regarding the scrapes and scratches on Trevor's back?" Fitzgerald placed a hand on her own back.

"During the autopsy, I discovered sand, bits of blacktop, and gravel embedded into the flesh."

"Did you form a medical opinion as to the origin of the marks on Trevor's back?"

"Objection."

"Overruled. This is expert testimony." Judge Killam frowned at Clancy and smiled at Morticia. "You may answer, Doctor."

Morticia batted her eyelashes at the judge. "I formed the opinion that someone dragged Trevor's body along his back over a paved surface like a street or sidewalk. The wounds were inflicted postmortem, meaning, after death had occurred."

Elaine watched Clancy writing in his legal pad. She wondered what he would come up with on cross. She examined the tie again and wished she could get a closer look.

"What is your opinion regarding the needle mark you observed on Trevor's right arm?"

"The track mark on the deceased's right arm was inflicted antemortem, before death occurred. It appeared fresh due to the coagulation of blood in and about the wound, which had just begun to scab over."

Fitzgerald cleared her throat. "Do you have an opinion regarding the approximate time that the track mark was inflicted in relation to Trevor's death?"

"Yes, that track mark was inflicted between five and ten minutes before death occurred."

"Did you observe any other marks or bruises on Trevor's body?"

"Yes, I observed a lump about the size of a quarter on Trevor's forehead, approximately two centimeters above his right eye. Further examination revealed that the skin in the center had been perforated. I also observed a small blood smear in that area."

"Did you form an opinion concerning the origin of that lump?"

"It appeared as if the lump originated via contact with a hard object. The wound was inflicted antemortem or just before death occurred."

"Doctor, based upon the autopsy and any additional observations you made of the deceased at the scene, do you have an opinion regarding the time of death?"

Morticia faced the jury. "In my opinion, death occurred at approximately nine fifteen P.M. on Friday the tenth of November."

"Doctor, do you have a medical opinion regarding the cause of death?"

"Pulmonary congestion, or in lay terms, heart failure, caused Trevor Shea's death."

"As part of your autopsy and medical investigation into Trevor's death, did you examine the toxicology report?"

"Yes."

"Based upon your examination of the toxicology report and your autopsy, do you have a medical opinion regarding the cause of Trevor's heart failure?"

"Objection," Clancy said.

Judge Killam wrinkled his brow. "No, she may have it. Objection overruled."

"In my medical opinion, a lethal dose of heroin caused Trevor's heart failure, which resulted in death."

"What does it look like when someone is experiencing heart failure due to a drug overdose?"

"Usually the victim will undergo rapid convulsions, have difficulty breathing, clutch at his heart, and collapse."

Elaine peered out at all the mothers again while Fitzgerald introduced the death certificate into evidence. She wondered how many of them had had to struggle through a trial before. Perhaps they never got that far. She wondered how many had had to identify their dead children at the morgue. Elaine was lucky she'd never had to go through that. She thought about her robust sons and couldn't even fathom it.

"No further questions. Thank you, Doctor." Fitzgerald tucked her legal pad under her arm and walked back to her table.

"Cross?" Judge Killam drained the rest of his water and smacked his lips.

"If I may, Your Honor?" Clancy said.

"Go ahead."

"Thank you." Clancy smiled as he approached Morticia. "Good afternoon, Doctor. You look lovely today."

"Thank you." She pushed her hair back from her face.

"I've always admired your work. I need only clarify a few things."

Morticia smiled. Elaine didn't like her lipstick color, a dark rusty brown.

"Did you know that the responding officers rolled Trevor's body before you arrived on the scene?"

"No."

"Detective Callahan didn't tell you how they rolled the body?"

"No."

Clancy cocked his head. "Really? He left that part out?"

"He did." She wrinkled her brow.

"Well, that changes things, now, doesn't it?" Clancy circled toward the witness.

"What do you mean?"

"After rolling the body, the officers had to put it back the way it was, right?"

"Objection." Fitzgerald jumped up.

"Overruled."

"I'm not sure." Morticia frowned. "I can only testify about what I observed when I arrived upon the scene, not what happened before."

"Absolutely, Doctor. It's possible the syringe became dislodged from Trevor's hand when the officers rolled the body?" Clancy made a rolling motion with his arms.

"I wouldn't know."

"But, it's possible?"

She shrugged. "I suppose so. Yes."

"Then it's also possible that one of the responding officers placed that syringe back in Trevor's hand?"

"Sure, but I wouldn't know."

"Makes sense and that would account for the absence of a tight grip for your . . . cadaver spasm?"

Elaine laughed. *Cadaver spasm.*

"*Cadaveric.*" Morticia corrected him. "It's possible."

"This theory jells with your conclusion that someone must've placed the syringe in Trevor's right hand postmortem, or after death had occurred?"

"Well, it does, I suppose."

Elaine shifted in her seat. Clancy was right. She looked at Malone. No telling who could've placed that syringe in Trevor's hand. It could've been anyone. The cops did roll that body. She remembered Clancy's dice tie. *Clever.*

"You observed a wound on the deceased's forehead?" Clancy tapped his own forehead.

"Yes."

"It drew blood?"

"Yes."

"Did you tell us what caused the head wound?"

"No, I can't tell you the exact cause of the wound, but I can speculate that the deceased hit his head on something."

"Is it fair to say that his head injury could've occurred when he had his heart attack?"

"Possibly."

Clancy paced in front of the jury with his hands behind his back. "So the head injury could've occurred within a minute or so before death?"

"Yes."

"Lots of sharp objects in the area where Trevor's body was discovered?"

"Not right next to the body, that I could see."

"The area consisted of overgrown grass, weeds, pricker bushes?"

"I believe so."

"Some big rocks?" Clancy raised an imaginary rock with both hands.

"I can't recall."

"It was near a street?"

"Not too far."

"Trevor could've fallen during his heart attack and hit his head on the curb?"

"Possibly."

"Or on a rock?"

"Maybe."

"A piece of wood?"

"I suppose anything's possible."

"In fact, he could've fallen due to the heart attack, and writhed on the nearby blacktop, clutching his chest?"

She sighed. "Perhaps."

"That would account for the scrapes and scratches and bits of gravel in his back?"

She shrugged again. "It's possible."

Elaine pictured Trevor injecting himself with heroin, clutching his chest, and falling against the curb. What Clancy was saying made perfect sense.

"Did you know Trevor had a history of heroin abuse?" Clancy asked.

"I knew he had used in the past, but I'm not aware of the history."

"Trevor also abused cocaine?"

Morticia pursed her lips. "I believe so, but I'm not certain."

"Cocaine abuse can lead to heart failure, correct?" Clancy patted his chest.

"Yes."

"What about heroin abuse? Can that cause one to have a heart attack?"

"Yes."

"Is it possible Trevor could've simply died of a heart attack due to his past history of drug abuse?"

"It's possible." Morticia tilted her head.

"Have you conducted autopsies on people who have died of accidental heroin overdoses?"

"Yes."

"How many?"

She gazed at the ceiling. "I'd say over fifty, maybe more."

"In your opinion, Trevor Shea's death occurred at approximately nine fifteen P.M. on the tenth of November?"

"Yes, according to my calculations."

"Ah. I have the highest degree of faith in your calculations, Doctor." Clancy gave her a big smile. "Thank you. Have a pleasant afternoon."

"You too, Mr. Clancy."

Elaine wondered what Clancy had up his sleeve about the time of death. Everything else made sense. As he passed by the jury box, Elaine got a closer look at his tie. A bunch of yellowish gray entangled worms. It looked like brain matter. *Brain matter.* Is that what it was supposed to be? Did he get it at a Halloween store?

"Any redirect, Commonwealth?" Judge Killam glanced at the clock. It was lunchtime. Elaine's stomach growled.

"No, Your Honor."

"Then the witness may be excused, and we'll take our luncheon recess." Judge Killam smiled at Morticia. "Thank you for your time here today, Doctor."

"You're welcome." She held his gaze. Elaine watched Morticia making eye contact with the male jurors as she left the stand. She didn't waste time with the women.

. . .

"Did you see the way that morgue doctor dressed for court? You could see all the way down her blouse when she leaned forward. I think she looked like Morticia from the *Munsters*."

"You mean the *Addams Family*?" Louie sat and placed his lunch bag down on the cafeteria table.

"Whatever, same thing." Elaine took a bite of her turkey gobbler and chewed. "Bet she dressed like a hussy on purpose."

"I thought she was quite bright, especially with all that schooling." Louie took out his baloney sandwich. "Too good lookin' for the morgue, if you ask me."

"Ah, she was plastic looking and not that smart. Clancy got the best of her, and she didn't even realize it. I don't think she cares much about the case. It was an excuse to get all dolled up and out of the morgue."

"Think so? I thought he took it easy because he thought highly of her."

Elaine snorted. "No way. And his bow tie? Looked like brain matter to me."

"A brain tie—perfect for a doctor." Louie bit into his sandwich as if it was a filet mignon.

"Only Clancy would think of that." Elaine rolled her eyes. "Those ladies in the yellow shirts? In the front row?"

He nodded and looked at Elaine as he chewed. She watched him sticking his index finger into his mouth to dislodge the ball of Wonder Bread.

"They're all in a support group, you know. From Charlestown. Lost their children to murder."

"How'd you know that?" Louie had his mouth open, ready to take another bite.

"Got a cousin lives in Charlestown."

"Wow. Give 'em credit for coming to court in the snow and all. I saw on the news it's going to be unseasonably cold tonight, below freezing."

"Louie you missed your calling, I swear."

"What?"

"You should've been a meteorologist."

23

AFTER LUNCH, **RACHEL** watched a stout man with thick bifocals plod up to the witness stand. As Clerk Fallon swore him in, she noticed that one shoulder appeared much higher than the other.

"Please introduce yourself to the jury and tell us what you do." Fitzgerald walked across the courtroom with her legal pad.

"Dr. Benjamin Stubbs. I'm a forensic toxicologist. I work at the Forensic Toxicology Laboratory at the University of Massachusetts, which handles over five thousand cases per year submitted by the Office of the Chief Medical Examiner for the Commonwealth of Massachusetts."

"What does toxicology entail?"

"It's the study and analysis of body fluids for the presence of alcohol, poisons, and/or drugs in the body."

"What types of tests do you perform?" Fitzgerald asked.

"We detect drugs and their metabolites in blood, urine, and postmortem tissue. Metabolites are the breakdown products formed in the body."

"Doctor, please describe your educational background."

Rachel removed her glasses and rubbed her eyes. She would have to force herself to concentrate for the rest of the afternoon. This witness had a flat voice, the type that could easily lull her to sleep. It would probably take him an hour or so to testify that Trevor had heroin in his blood-stream. Dr. Joyce had already told them, but Fitzgerald had to drill it into their heads as if they were stupid. No wonder trials took so long. She glanced around at her fellow jurors, whose eyes were glazing over. Only Elaine appeared somewhat interested. She probably didn't get it the first time around.

Rachel had overheard some of her colleagues quietly discussing parts of the case with each other. They seemed reluctant to include her because she had been chosen to be the foreperson. Were they afraid she'd report them for discussing the case prematurely? She'd just as soon start talking about it now to hasten the process. She looked around again. What were they thinking?

So far, she thought Fitzgerald's case against Malone was weak. It seemed like she tried so hard, but nothing went her way. There had to be more to the prosecution's case. Clancy's cross-examinations made her shed doubt on all the witness testimony so far. He reminded Rachel of her grand-father who had died when she was only twelve years old. They shared the same taste in bow ties, except Clancy's were a bit more creative. She also noticed gumdrops on Clancy's table.

Rachel's gaze shifted from Clancy to Malone. She wished she knew more about him. Did he have a criminal record? Had he stood trial for murder in the past? She needed more answers, and it was up to Fitzgerald to provide them.

"The court will be in recess for the rest of the afternoon."

Rachel jumped at the sound of Judge Killam's voice. She had missed the boring doctor's entire testimony. Clancy must have decided not to cross-examine him.

"Please be back here at nine tomorrow morning. Do not discuss this case with anyone or read any newspaper articles or watch any television programs about it. Go outside and enjoy the day before it snows again," the judge said.

"Not so fast, Rehnquist. I'm slowing down these days." Clancy gently tugged on his dog's leash and patted his back. Everyday he enjoyed tying a matching bow tie around Rehnquist's collar and taking him for a walk throughout Charlestown. He'd adopted the golden retriever from a rescue shelter as a puppy; someone had abandoned him following one of the southern hurricanes. On a whim, Clancy named him after the deceased Supreme Court Chief Justice, William Rehnquist. They walked from his law office on Main Street toward the Charlestown Community Gardens, where he hoped to share a late afternoon coffee with his childhood friend, Jimmy Nunn, a retired barber. Clancy was relieved to be out of court a tad early. Everyone had been falling asleep during the toxicologist's testimony; he'd counted multiple yawns in the jury box.

Clancy paused at the spot where Annie's parents had operated their bookstore so many years ago, Fitzy's Mysteries. A florist's shop occupied the space now. He remembered browsing in the narrow aisles where the bookshelves reached all the way to the ceiling. It was where he bought his first-edition, signed Robert B. Parker mysteries. He still had them. It was a shame when they were forced to close the store and leave. He shuddered at what had happened to Annie's father. Rehnquist lunged.

"I'm coming. You just want your cookies. I know you too well." He scratched the dog's ears and forged ahead, stopping every half a block for somebody to say hello and pat Rehnquist.

"Hey, you're out early." Jimmy held the greenhouse door open. "I have coffee and peanut butter cookies. Here, grab a seat." Clancy sat in an old lawn chair looking out over the barren garden plots. "I've just finished watering my tomatoes." He pointed to a row of seed trays on a potting shelf in the greenhouse. "It's going to be a great growing season this year. I can tell already. How'd it go today?"

"Long." Clancy fed Rehnquist a cookie and took one for himself.

"I don't know how you do it. It seems like you've been defending bad guys forever. Why don't you retire and take on easy stuff like writing wills?" He poured Clancy a cup of black coffee from a chipped pot.

Clancy sipped the stale coffee and fed his dog another cookie. "Somebody's got to do it, right, Rehnquist?" No matter how much he despised his clients at times, he couldn't imagine doing anything else. It's what he'd been doing since passing the bar exam so many years ago. He liked being a street lawyer, the underdog, a defender of the constitution. He had started out with simple drunk driving and car theft cases, graduated to bank robberies, and then handled most of the big murders. Won some, lost many.

"It must be hard seeing all those Charlestown mothers in the front row."

Clancy rubbed Rehnquist's belly. "I pray for every single one of them."

"I hear they might be getting a new member."

"Who?"

"Gloria Reed. Her son, Drake, went missing a couple nights ago. I've heard rumors that it's related to your case, something to do with that drug dealer from Gloucester."

Clancy wondered what had gone down. Malone had been in a sour mood ever since Domenico testified; he hadn't expected him to show up. Had Drake Reed tried to take out the witness? Had his plan backfired? Clancy fed Rehnquist another cookie. He hoped Malone wouldn't try anything else.

24

DO YOU SWEAR to tell the truth, the whole truth, and nothing but the truth, so help you God?"

"I do." Callahan raised his right hand and sat in the witness chair. He peered into the audience, and zeroed in on all the mothers in the front row. Callahan knew them all. He'd seen them vomit, heard their screams, and had lit countless cigarettes in shaking fingers. *God help the mothers.* He noticed Malone sitting next to Clancy with his pressed suit. *What a fraud.*

"Please introduce yourself to the jury." Annie sounded confident, ready to go. She looked sophisticated in her slim black suit with her hair pulled up. Callahan admired the silky strands dancing next to her cheekbones.

He smiled at her. "Michael J. Callahan."

"Where are you from?" Annie smiled back.

"South Boston." Callahan repositioned himself, angling his shoulders a bit toward the jury. He caught Malone's cold stare, and felt the years of mutual hatred between them. Callahan reminded himself to stay neutral; jurors could sense bad blood and may consider him a biased witness.

"What's your occupation?"

"Homicide detective. Twenty-one years with the Boston Police." Callahan noticed a few raised eyebrows in the jury box. They were impressed.

All those years. To him it felt like one long, gray blur that smelled like coffee.

Annie guided him through his lengthy training and experience. "Have you been qualified as an expert in the field of homicide investigation?"

"Yes, I've testified as an expert in homicide investigation over forty times in the courts of the Commonwealth, and about a dozen in the U.S. District Court." Callahan knew these were standard questions, which established his expertise and allowed him to use opinion testimony later on. Only experts could render opinions, and those carried a lot of weight with the jury. He scanned the box. More than half were women. *Good.* He usually connected with the women. He'd managed a quick trip to the barbershop; no hair sticking up today. The old ladies liked the clean-cut look. The men could go either way, though, and the minorities were the hardest to win over. So many didn't trust cops.

"Do you recall November tenth of last year?" Annie said.

"Yes, I do." He gazed at Malone.

Judge Killam slurped his water.

Annie waited for the judge to wipe his mouth as the jurors seemed distracted. "Where were you at approximately ten forty-five P.M.?"

"At my desk facing a pile of paperwork with a brand new cup of coffee. That's when the phone rang." Callahan admired the pretty red-haired foreperson in her snazzy rectangular glasses. Her lips formed a tiny, flirtatious smile. Callahan maintained eye contact with her for a few extra seconds. He'd made a connection.

"As a result of the telephone call what did you do?" Annie raised her voice; she probably noticed the eye contact and would razz him later.

"I responded to the intersection of Decatur Street and Walford Way in Charlestown, underneath the Tobin Bridge. Upon my arrival I observed two police cruisers, an ambulance, the yellow police tape." Callahan remembered a small crowd had gathered in a semicircle, gawking.

"What happened next?"

"I observed the body of the victim, Trevor Shea. He was lying on his back in a T-shirt and jeans." Callahan saw Chris in the front row and decided to eliminate the part about Trevor's mouth gaping open, something had crawled inside, some small varmint. "And, there were paint stains on his clothes, lots of paint stains, all different colors."

"Did you take any photographs?"

"Yes." Callahan reached down, grabbed his stack of enlarged photos, and handed several to Annie. He waited for her to show Clancy, who objected and called a sidebar. Callahan rubbed his eyes. *Here we go again.* Clancy had already filed a motion to exclude all pictures of Trevor's dead body because they were inflammatory and could turn the jury against his poor, innocent client. Judge Killam had denied his motion, but Clancy lived by the old motto: if at once you don't succeed, try, try again.

Callahan waited for Clancy to lose again, and when he did, Annie admitted the crime scene photos into evidence.

"What else did you observe?" she asked.

"I noticed a hypodermic needle in Trevor's right hand. The needle part was positioned up toward his thumb." Callahan grabbed a clear plastic bag containing the needle from a cardboard evidence box next to the witness stand. "This one." He held the bag up for the jury to see.

Annie introduced the needle into evidence. "In which hand did Trevor hold this needle?"

"The wrong hand."

"The wrong what?" Clancy blurted his question without getting up.

"Clancy, you heard him." Judge Killam grimaced. "Are you objecting?"

"Of course. Objection! Move to strike. Speculative."

Annie sighed. "But this is all part of Detective Callahan's expert opinion."

"No foundation." Clancy waggled a finger.

"Sustained."

"Please describe what you observed about the hypodermic needle." Annie sounded impatient.

"Okay." Callahan realized he had jumped ahead of himself; the law always required baby steps. Another reason why trials took forever. He faced the jury. "Trevor had a fresh track mark on his right arm." He raised an enlarged photograph of Trevor's arm. "If Trevor had just injected himself with the needle in his right hand, the track mark would naturally be on the left arm. I also learned that Trevor was left-handed. Therefore, I formed the opinion that Trevor was holding the needle in the *wrong* hand."

"I see." Annie paused. "Did you notice anything else about the needle?"

"Yes, it was held loosely and upside down." Callahan raised another close-up shot. "Meaning, if Trevor had just injected himself, the needle would've been positioned the other way around."

"I see." Annie scanned the jury box to see if they understood. "What happened next?"

"I noticed a slight bulge in the right front pocket of Trevor's jeans. I reached in and withdrew what appeared to be an empty glassine bag stamped 'Nine-eleven'."

"Nine-eleven?" Annie acted as if she'd never heard the word before. "What's Nine-eleven?"

"Very powerful heroin from Afghanistan."

"Detective, have you made any drug arrests involving the possession and distribution of heroin?"

Callahan knew she wanted to reveal his expertise in narcotics. "Hundreds."

"What's the difference between regular heroin and Nine-eleven?"

"Twice as powerful. Nine-eleven is twice as powerful."

"If someone took a large dose of Nine-eleven heroin what would happen?"

"It would most likely kill them."

Callahan shot a quick glance at Clancy. He expected an objection, but didn't get one. Instead, the crusty old lawyer listened with his chin pointed upward; his lips revealed the trace of a grin. The gears were cranking in that crazy brain of his. No objection from Clancy meant a storm was brewing for cross-examination.

"What did you do with that empty bag stamped Nine-eleven?" Annie asked.

"I placed it in a sealed envelope to be fingerprinted and sent to the drug lab for analysis." Callahan knew he couldn't testify about the trace amounts of Nine-eleven heroin found in the needle and the bag. They'd get the hearsay objection. Annie would call a witness from the lab for that.

"What happened next?"

"I rotated Trevor onto his stomach. His T-shirt was soiled, damp, and ripped in several places. I observed fresh scrapes on his skin in the form of vertical lines running from his low back to his shoulders. I also saw dirt and small pebbles embedded in his back." Callahan produced all the photographs of Trevor's back, and Annie admitted them into evidence.

"What did you do next?"

"I examined the area surrounding the body, and noticed the leaves were disturbed, forming what looked like a path." He raised and spread his hands about shoulder-length apart to demonstrate the width. "A path going from Trevor's head off toward the street. I intensified the light and, yeah, I saw a definite path running at an angle from Trevor's body all the way to Decatur Street." He moved his hands down at an angle.

"Approximately how wide was this path?"

"One and a half feet. The width of a human body." Callahan blurted the last sentence and waited for the reaction.

"Objection." Clancy rose. "Move to strike."

Judge Killam wrinkled his brow. "Overruled."

Annie nodded at the judge. "Based upon your observations regarding the condition of Trevor's back and the path in the leaves, did you form any opinions, Detective?"

"Objection!"

"Overruled."

Callahan cleared his throat and looked at the pretty foreperson. "I formed the opinion that Trevor was dragged on his back by the feet or ankles to the location where we found him."

Annie flipped a page in her yellow legal pad. "What did you do next?"

"Let's see." Callahan scratched his forehead. "I radioed the station requesting our fingerprint expert, and had a conversation with the assistant medical examiner. I also assigned two detectives the task of canvassing the area."

"What does canvassing mean?"

"Going around the neighborhood, asking questions, checking out whether anyone saw anything unusual."

"What happened next?"

"At that point, Trevor's brother, Chris, came running up. He wanted to touch the body. I, along with two officers, had to restrain him." Callahan watched the jurors zone in on Chris sitting in the front row. He stared at Malone's back and scowled.

"Did Chris say anything?"

"Yeah." Callahan focused on Malone. "Chris yelled and it was at the top of his lungs. We were still holding him back, too. He said—"

"Objection!" Clancy jumped to his feet. "That's hearsay. You can't say what somebody else said. You should know that by now, Detective."

Callahan stiffened. Clancy was good at getting under his skin. Don't get riled, he reminded himself.

Annie stepped forward. "And, attorney Clancy should know that's an excited utterance made in response to a shocking event." Her lips formed a tiny smile. "An exception to the hearsay rule."

"Miss Fitzgerald is right," Judge Killam said. "Overruled. She may have it."

"What did Chris say in response to seeing his brother's dead body?"

Callahan faced the jury. "Chris yelled, 'Malone! Come out here! Come out, Malone. I'm going to f'ing kill you, you son of a bitch.'" He watched the jurors look from Chris to Malone and back. He wished he could re-play Chris's screams that night. They were blood curdling. *Truthful.* The evidence hadn't been gathered at that point, but Callahan didn't need any more. He knew who did it. He gritted his teeth.

"Detective?"

Callahan missed Annie's next question, but guessed what it was. "Yes. Sorry. So, we were trying to calm Chris down when their mother, Ellen, showed up." Callahan gazed at the mothers in the front row. Two were crying. "She was screaming, too. Just screaming." He remembered the poor mother running down the dark street, in her light blue night-gown and bare feet. Ellen was overweight, nearly obese. One of her breasts had slipped out and flapped against her white skin; she didn't even know it.

"What did Trevor's mother do?"

"Ellen did a swimming dive over the police tape and almost landed on Tre . . . on her son's body. We had to hold her back." Callahan bowed his head. "Had to preserve evidence."

"What happened after that?" Annie's voice sounded soft.

"Father Coyne showed up." Callahan acknowledged the priest sitting with the mothers in the front row. "He's the parish priest from St. Catherine's." Callahan remembered how Father held her for a long time that night. Ellen's wails still echoed in his ears. She blamed herself, they all did, really.

Poor Ellen. Her husband had simply vanished one day. Callahan had learned he was a bookie. He probably had gotten behind on payments or crossed the wrong guy. Callahan guessed somebody killed him and got rid of the body. Ellen was one of the weak ones. Callahan wondered if she'd ever recover.

"What happened next?" Annie said.

"Trevor was ziplocked into a body bag and taken to the morgue. I looked around for his jacket because I thought it was odd that he'd be dressed in only a T-shirt and jeans in November."

"Objection, move to strike."

"Sustained." Judge Killam turned to the jury. "Please disregard Detective Callahan's opinion about the jacket."

"Do you recall what the approximate temperature was that night?"

"It was a clear, cold night. We could see our breath. I'd say, approximately thirty-five degrees, maybe less."

"What were the next steps in your investigation?"

"I obtained a search warrant, and at approximately one fifteen A.M., I, along with several detectives, performed a search of Thirty-six Walford Way, which was an apartment being rented by Jennianne Smith."

"What happened when you executed the warrant?"

"Miss Smith let us in. She appeared all disheveled with bruises on her face." Callahan recalled the terrified look in her eyes. He could tell she knew something or had witnessed something horrible. She was paralyzed by fear that night, and Callahan knew if he acted quickly, he could capitalize on it. *He had her.*

"We also found a smashed lamp in the living room, and a broken telephone cord in the kitchen. The plastic end of the cord remained in the wall outlet. I gathered evidence consisting of beer cans, cigarette butts, a plastic CVS bag, and an artist's sketch pad."

Callahan paused while Annie admitted the items into evidence. "I also recovered this blue New England Patriot's jacket from the Bunker Hill Laundromat, but that was the following morning." He reached into a plastic bag and retrieved the jacket, and Annie admitted it. He hoped Chris would later testify that it belonged to Trevor, and he had seen him wearing it earlier that evening.

"Did you search Trevor and Chris Shea's house that night?"

"We did." Callahan looked at Chris; their eyes met. He recognized that aura of mistrust in the way Chris rolled his shoulders back, crossed his arms, and cocked his head slightly to the left. He was raised in Charlestown, listened to the street talk, and had learned to hate the Boston cops early on. But, there was something else about Chris that Callahan believed he caught glimpses of, an element picked up from the streets of Charlestown that Callahan had witnessed in some of the most hardened criminals. It was fear, pure and simple, and Chris masked it well.

"Can you describe your search?"

"Had a warrant, so we knocked and announced our presence, but no one answered. We let ourselves in through the front door, it was unlocked." Callahan eyed Chris again. "We heard noises coming from below, in the basement. I drew my service revolver and headed down the stairs."

"What happened?"

"I got down there and I—" Callahan remembered the strong odor of oil paints and turpentine when he reached the bottom step. "I saw Chris. He looked like he was about to destroy one of his brother's paintings."

Annie grabbed the painting, which showed the Charlestown playground scene. She walked right up to the witness stand with it. Callahan leaned forward and identified the painting. For the first time, he zoned in on the name "Snich" sketched by the artist into the powdery dirt below the circle of kids.

Annie turned toward the judge. "At this time I move to introduce this painting into evidence."

"Objection."

"Overruled."

"Sidebar, Your Honor?" Clancy said.

"Approach."

Annie circled the judge's bench to join Clancy on the other side. Callahan thought about the name "Snich" again. It was a tiny detail, which could only be seen by viewing the painting up close. It looked like it was written by a kid with sloppy penmanship. Was it somebody's nickname? *Maybe, maybe not.*

As the lawyers continued arguing at sidebar, Callahan made eye contact with Chris. Annie was right. They had to break him if they ever wanted to come up with a motive for Trevor's murder. That night in the basement, Chris had been facing the painting with his back to Callahan. He was talking to it at first, rambling, and, then, he began yelling at it. *You stupid, stupid asshole, idiot, moron. Selfish bastard. You couldn't stop, couldn't quit. You wouldn't listen to me. You had to keep going.* Chris had snapped a long, pointy paintbrush in half across his knee.

When the sidebar ended, Judge Killam addressed the jury. "Attorney Clancy's objection is sustained. The painting will not come into evidence at this time."

Annie leaned the painting against her table. She looked agitated. "What was Chris doing when you first arrived in the basement?"

"Looking at Trevor's painting." Callahan paused. He'd left out the part about Chris talking to himself in his report. He'd never mentioned it to Annie, either. After all, it was just jibberish, but it could be interpreted the wrong way. People might get the impression that Trevor was just a drug addict, that his death was accidental, another ordinary overdose, but Callahan knew better. The DA's office would never have indicted Malone for murder.

"What else did Chris do?" Annie asked.

"He broke some paintbrushes, grabbed a matte knife, and slashed at the painting. I grabbed him before he destroyed it." He picked at a hangnail, and caught Chris's piercing gaze. *He knows what I'm omitting. Isn't it better this way?* He recalled Chris's death threat against Malone at the crime scene. *Don't we both want the same result here?* Callahan refused to make eye contact with Chris again as Annie asked him more details about his investigation, including his trips to Gloucester to speak with Domenico.

"Based on all the evidence, I obtained an arrest warrant for the defendant. At approximately six thirty P.M. on that Sunday, we proceeded to Twenty Pearl Street in Charlestown where Malone lives with his mother." Callahan decided not to get too detailed about Malone's chaotic arrest. Besides, the judge wouldn't let him testify about Sergeant Amidon getting shot. Thank God he had survived. Amidon would never regain full use of his right arm. It didn't seem fair to keep that testimony from the jury, but the judge had ruled it could prejudice the defendant's case. *Always protecting Malone.*

"Shortly after our arrival, I placed the defendant, William Joseph Malone, under arrest for murder."

"Nothing further, Your Honor."

"We'll take our lunch break now," Judge Killam said.

25

"ICE JOB UP there, Mike," Annie said. "Now, we need to talk about Clancy's grenades. They're coming. Lunch?" She grabbed a fresh legal pad from her briefcase and looked up to see Callahan studying Trevor's painting, which was still leaning against the table.

"I can't believe the judge wouldn't allow it into evidence," she said.

"Why not?" He squatted and was now at eye level with the circle of kids.

"He bought Clancy's argument that it was too prejudicial." Annie had a feeling the judge would rule against her, but every time the jurors saw the painting, it would get them thinking.

"Figures. They always have to bend over backward to protect the bad guys; God forbid Malone gets portrayed in a negative light." Callahan sighed. "Come here a minute." He motioned her over. "What do you make of this?"

Annie moved closer, and Callahan pointed at "Snich" sketched into the dirt of the playground below the circle of kids. She had wondered about it before. Why had Trevor included that barely legible detail in his painting?

"What do you think it means?"

"Somebody's nickname? Possibly one of the kids?" Annie traced a finger over the letters. "It also sounds like *snitch*. A snitch is a bad thing in

Charlestown. Anybody labeled a snitch wouldn't last too long; they'd disappear, end up dead. Maybe the kid in the middle who's about to get beat up was a snitch."

"Didn't Chris say that's Georgie Hurley?" Callahan appeared to be studying the kids in the painting.

"Yeah and Georgie Hurley is dead."

"One of our unsolved cases." He snapped his gum.

"That's right and I just took another look at the file after Chris brought it up. Thin folder. A scribbled police report in faded pencil and a one-pager from the medical examiner. Georgie got beat up in the playground up on Bunker Hill Street and apparently died from a crushed skull. No witnesses. All dead ends from the get-go."

"No mention of motive?"

"Nope."

"Perhaps Georgie was a snitch?" Callahan tapped the red-headed boy in the painting.

Annie stared at the terrified eyes and felt the familiar chill. Trevor had captured the moment. That little boy knew he was about to die. Annie felt a lump forming in her throat. *That poor little boy.* Maybe he had done the unthinkable, maybe he'd been a snitch, talked to a teacher or a cop. The kid sitting on him was about to kill him, and the others were standing by in a circle. *Participating.* Not offering help. *Silent witnesses.*

"Look, there's a rock over there." Annie pointed to a gray rock near the circle of kids. It looked 3-D, as if she could take it from the painting and hold it in the palm of her hand. "I'm wondering if that's also symbolic. Georgie's skull was crushed."

Callahan nodded, and traced the rounded edges of the rock with his finger.

"Could be the murder weapon." Annie wondered if they were reading too much into the painting, searching for clues that weren't there.

"Have you met Georgie's mother? Maybe she could shed some light?" Callahan asked.

"I haven't."

"Neither have I. Artists do things for a reason. Sometimes the answers can be found in the subtleties, like that." Callahan pointed at the word "Snich" again. "Make any headway with Chris about whether Trevor painted Lydia Thompson?"

"No."

"I've been asking around, but no one claims to have seen a painting like that," he said.

"Snitch." Annie whispered it and made eye contact with Callahan. "Why would Malone bother with Trevor? He wasn't a rival drug dealer or anything like that. He was a street artist. Harmless." She knew they were thinking the same thing. "Do you think Trevor was a snitch? Could that be it? What if he was an informant against Malone?"

Callahan closed his eyes and pinched the bridge of his nose. "The narcs would've told me. D'Ambrosi would've said for sure. They know I've been banging my head gunning for Malone. For years."

"But that's Boston PD. What about the feds?"

"Shit. I don't know. Maybe." Callahan checked his watch. "I'll run over to Center Plaza and ask."

"Ask?" Annie couldn't help herself; she laughed. "Ask who? The receptionist?"

"Seriously. I've worked on a bunch of stuff with the FBI. They want Malone almost as bad as I do."

"And, you're doing this when?"

"Right now."

"Oh no you're not. We have to prepare for cross." Annie didn't like the idea. *What if something happened and he didn't make it back? Move to dismiss, Clancy would say.* "Can't you do it after court?"

"I'd like to know now." Callahan curled his lips over his teeth.

Annie knew what that meant: there was no changing his mind. "Go now and hurry up. Watch your time because you absolutely, positively have to be on that witness stand when Judge Killam comes back from lunch."

"I will." He sounded annoyed. "Try and find Chris in the meantime. I've seen him a few times at Dippell's Deli. I think Chris knows exactly what Trevor was up to before he died. It's all making more sense now."

26

"EXCUSE ME." ELAINE maneuvered around Rachel and her tiny salad like a middle linebacker. She beelined toward the lunch table and sat next to Louie. She was famished; the damn line took forever. "What? *Another* baloney sandwich, Louie?"

"Same." He breathed on his oversized bifocals and wiped the spots with a cafeteria napkin.

"Your sandwich looks good." She lied. The mayonnaise had soaked through the bread again. How could he give up a fresh hoagie for a soggy baloney sandwich? Elaine noticed Louie had saved the paper bag from the previous day. His wife probably washed and reused the sandwich baggie, too.

"If it's free, I'll take it." Elaine raised her meatball sub in the air. A glob of spaghetti sauce landed on the table with a splat. She opened her mouth wide and took as big a bite as she could manage.

"They're predicting another storm this week, you know. Could get six to eight inches."

Oh boy, here we go again with the snow. "So much for an early spring." Elaine talked as she chewed. "Typical March weather."

"I should be getting ready to plant my peas and lettuce, but with the snow and the trial?" He shrugged. "Don't know when I'll get to it."

"Speaking of the trial, what did you think of that Detective Callahan?"

Louie examined his sandwich as if he couldn't decide which corner to sink his teeth into. "He was okay, I guess."

"No way. That one's a charmer. He knew exactly when to throw out the smiles and where to plaster on the sympathy. Way too smooth for me, but the others may've been sucked in. That Rachel drooled over him—made me sick. Girls like that have no business being on a murder case, and she's supposed to be in charge here? Gimme a break! I wonder if Judge Killam saw her behaving like that? Although, I caught him leaning over the bench a few times, peeking down that cleavage."

"I didn't see it. You sure?"

Elaine didn't answer. Louie was probably too busy worrying about the next batch of snow to notice anything. She took another big bite and chewed. "I'm willing to bet Callahan's in cahoots with the cop who stole money from the artist. Wouldn't put it past him for a second."

"Really? I don't know, Elaine. He seemed on the up-and-up. He had a point about the needle being in the wrong hand, like somebody placed it there to make it look like an overdose. Thought he did a good job with that."

"Do you really believe everything you hear? Who's to say Callahan didn't switch it himself and then take a picture?" Elaine noticed his blank expression. She gazed out the window at the blue sky and smiled. "Let's put it this way, Louie. How many times has the weatherman gotten it wrong?"

27

HEAR ANYTHING ABOUT an undercover FBI gig on Malone?" Callahan talked to D'Ambrosi on his cell as he ran toward the Government Center.

"Not lately." D'Ambrosi paused. "But heard something about Malone finding a bug in his truck. Wasn't us or the Staties, I know for a fact. We all figured it was them."

"When?"

"Sometime within the last year or so?"

"Before Trevor's murder, you think? Before last November?"

"Mmmm . . . maybe."

"Anything else that could possibly link the feds in?"

"I'll ask around." D'Ambrosi exhaled into the phone. "Your trial's getting a little hairy, huh?"

"What do you mean by that?"

D'Ambrosi didn't answer.

"Seriously. What?"

"Mike, I mean, is it possible this kid just overdosed? Because I know he had a problem. We bagged him a couple times."

Callahan gritted his teeth; even the guys from his own department had doubts. "Malone did it, and I'm beginning to think Trevor was a snitch for the feds. It makes sense, gives us motive."

"Huh." D'Ambrosi paused. "Could be big if it's true."

"It would tip the scales." Callahan approached the lobby door. "I'm in front of their building. Going to speak with Bertrand."

"That guy?" D'Ambrosi grunted. "He won't give you squat."

"Gotta try." Callahan wrapped up the call and flashed his badge to security. He had to accomplish his task and be back up on the witness stand in forty-five minutes. The more he thought about it, the more he became convinced the feds were running their own show on Malone. The Walrus up in Gloucester had mentioned something about the feds wanting Domenico, too. If he could prove Trevor was an informant, they'd win the case. The jury needed motive.

Callahan walked with an air of authority right up to Agent Bertrand's semi-open office door. He knocked and stuck his head in. "Got a minute?"

Bertrand rose from his leather chair with hands on his hips. He was tall, about six-five, with a long rectangular face, and wispy silver hair.

"What are you doing here? I'm in the middle of something."

"This is important."

"And so is this, Officer Callahan." Bertrand motioned to a neat stack of papers. The only other items on the desk were an engraved brass nameplate, a matching pencil holder, and a sparkling Waterford crystal clock.

"It's about Billy Malone." Callahan knew he had called him *officer* instead of *detective* on purpose. *Cocky son-of-a-bitch.*

Bertrand yawned. "Excuse me." He yawned again, this time louder and longer. "That's right, you arrested him again. How many times is this?" Sarcasm dripped from every word.

Callahan's mood soured. "In case you missed it, he's on trial right now for first-degree murder. We have information that the victim, Trevor Shea, was one of your informants." He didn't have any specific information, only a hunch.

"Come again? Who?"

"I said, *Trevor Shea.*"

"Not one of ours." Bertrand answered too quickly.

"You sure?"

"Very. But, since this is for *you,* Officer, I'll have my assistant check our Christmas list sometime later on this week or next."

"Christmas list?"

"To see if we sent him a holiday card this year." Bertrand grinned. "Don't you send your informants cards? Acknowledge all the hard work they've put in over the year?" He tapped his forehead. "Oh, wait, I'm sorry, maybe it's not in your budget. Shame."

"Trevor was dead last Christmas."

"Dead? Yes, yes, your *murder* victim." Bertrand shrugged one shoulder.

"Trevor was an artist, a good kid. If he snitched for you, and Malone found out, he'd kill him for sure. If you cooperate with us, we'll sink Malone this time, destroy his entire operation."

Bertrand stared him down. "Do you have a short memory or are you just plain stupid?"

The bastard had called him *stupid.* Callahan fought hard to control his rage. "Can't we let bygones be bygones and work together on this?"

"I vowed never to share with an idiot like you again." Bertrand pointed at Callahan. "Not even a damn pencil. Your last case against Malone went south because of sloppy police work and you dragged us right down with you. Years of busting our asses over here—all flushed down the shit can."

"That had nothing to do with sloppy work and you know it." Callahan pointed back. "Malone got to the guy in charge of evidence. It was a bribe. Don't we all have the same goal here?"

"Not really. My goal is to stay the hell away from you." Bertrand sneered. "I've never heard of Trevor Shea and we don't have any files on Malone. End of story. Now, get the hell out of my office."

"Bullshit no file on Malone. You want him as bad as we do. You're lying."

"Believe me, I'm not. Your dead artist was not one of ours. I wish he was though. We'd be thrilled to have one less scumbag on payroll."

Callahan saw red. He swung his fist across Bertrand's desk, knocking the papers and Waterford clock across the room. The clock smashed. "I'll have you arrested! Obstructing justice."

"Arrested?" Bertrand picked a piece of the clock off the floor. "Good idea."

28

"**M**OVE TO DISMISS!**" Clancy announced.

Annie cringed as Judge Killam puffed. *May lightning strike and put me out of my misery.*

"Where? Is? Detective? Callahan?" Purple veins popped out in Judge Killam's forehead.

Annie had never seen him this angry. She felt about an inch tall, and didn't even know if her voice box would work. It might be better if it failed her altogether. She refused to even glance in Malone's direction. He was probably grinning. *Rejoicing.* What could she say?

"Miss Fitzgerald? If I don't get an answer in two seconds, I'll dismiss this case."

"Sidebar?" Her voice worked, but it squeaked.

"No." Judge Killam leaned forward. "No, no, no." His whole face and neck resembled a swollen red, black, and blue mark. She'd seen corpses look better.

"But this is non-public information, Your Honor."

"Whoa." He raised his hand. "You represent the Commonwealth. The public has every right to know what happened to your star detective, so why don't you fill us all in right now?" The judge spread his arms as if encompassing the entire courtroom and the world beyond.

Annie knew the gallery was almost full behind her. Thank God the jury couldn't hear this. How could she couch it in the best possible light? Given the circumstances?

"We're waiting?"

"Detective Callahan was . . ." Annie's voice trailed off.

"Was *what*?"

"Detained."

"That's it?" Judge Killam banged his gavel. "Then I'll grant attorney Clancy's motion to dismiss."

"No. Wait." Annie had no choice. The press would be all over this one. "He was arrested."

"Arrested." Judge Killam's jaw dropped open. "You're telling me he was arrested? Detective Callahan is a member of the force. He *is* the police. What'd he do, arrest himself?"

"The FBI arrested him, Your Honor." Annie couldn't mention the informant theory in front of Malone and Clancy. "Because he went over there during lunch and accused them of, of . . ."

"Holy Toledo!" Clancy laughed. "This is good stuff. Accused them of?"

"Yeah, accused the FBI of what?" Judge Killam leaned forward, way over the bench.

Annie took a deep breath. "Not cooperating in a homicide investigation. I can't say any more than that."

"Wow!" Clancy raised both hands in the air and slowly turned around in a circle. "This case is akin to a small car stuffed full of clowns. With each passing day, we think it's gotta be empty, but one more clown always pops out. I strongly urge you to dismiss, Your Honor."

Judge Killam shot him an evil look. "Clancy, stop playing it up for the press."

"I'm not, Your Honor. I'm simply flabbergasted because we spent all morning on Detective Callahan's direct examination. I'm prepared to cross-examine him right now. It's not fair to my client or me." Clancy placed his hands on Malone's shoulders, and Malone nodded, vigorously. "First of all, we had to suffer through a long lunch break. Any more delay

will lessen the impact of my cross. Cross-examination is supposed to follow direct. How can I possibly do my job?"

Judge Killam exhaled. "You didn't suffer through lunch, Clancy. I saw
you eating steak tips at the Federalist. Your motion to dismiss is denied."

"What the hell happened?" Annie burst into Boston Police Chief Warren
Steele's office. The large-framed chief had been standing over the desk,
yelling at Callahan, who sat facing him. Captain Murphy leaned against
the wall with his arms crossed.

Annie had interrupted the chief, midsentence. The chief's eyes widened and then retracted to slits.

"Who do you think you are?" His voice rumbled. Chief Steele was a
yeller, grew up in the Bronx, and had risen through the ranks in the
NYPD. Now, he reigned in Boston with an iron fist and ended up with the
nickname Old Ironsides. Annie barely knew the guy, and had never imagined barging into a meeting like this.

"I'm Annie Fitzgerald." She spoke with authority and looked him right
in the eye.

Callahan rose halfway from his seat. "Annie—"

Upon hearing Callahan's voice, Annie felt the urge to strangle him. She
lunged toward him, and didn't give a shit about the chief. They'd have to
hold her back.

"Hey! What're you doing?" the chief yelled.

Annie refrained from grabbing Callahan around the neck, and shook
the back of his chair instead. She shoved her face up close to his. "You
just publicly humiliated yourself, my office, and this department."

"Lay off. This is police business!" Chief Steele skirted around his desk,
tipping over a Styrofoam cup. Coffee spilled through the lid's drinking
triangle onto a report.

"It's every bit my business." Annie slammed her fist on the desk. "It's *my*
case, and you're not going to tell me what to do." Her words were drowned
out when Captain Murphy stepped into the fray, and everyone started
yelling at once. She raised her voice higher and joined in.

Callahan finally jumped out of his chair and shot his arms straight up like a football umpire. "Stop!" All he needed was a whistle. "My bad."

Annie and the men stopped shouting.

"I've been working around the clock on the Malone case, and I lost it with Bertrand." He turned to the chief. "You gotta know the guy—total asshole. Got under my skin."

"Why didn't you come to me before confronting Bertrand?" Captain Murphy yelled. "I know more people over there than you do. Now you've burned our bridges over your lunatic obsession with Malone. I knew this case was a loser from the very beginning. I told you so. The kid just over-dosed. We should a dropped it. I told you so. I told you."

Annie placed a hand on her forehead. No one believed in their case; even she had her doubts now.

"Enough!" Chief Steele barked at Murphy. "We're going backward again, and there's nothing we can do about it now. Game over."

"What do you mean over?" Callahan said.

"Siddown." Chief Steele pointed to the chair. "I spoke with Bertrand's boss. They deny having any files on Malone, and claim that Trevor Shea was never one of theirs."

"He's lying!" Callahan gesticulated and hit the downed Styrofoam cup, sending it spinning and spewing more coffee.

"I said siddown and listen!" Chief Steele got right in his face.

Callahan slumped down.

"They've agreed to drop the charges against you if you pay for the clock and we agree not to pursue this matter further. I gave him my word. *My word*,"—spit flew from the chief's mouth—"that they wouldn't be hear-ing from you again. And, you're banned from *all* federal buildings. Don't even go to the damn post office. Got it? We're trying to improve rela-tions."

Callahan stared hard at the chief. Annie cringed. She could tell he was about to blow up, and that might be it for him.

Instead, Callahan gritted his teeth. "That's called obstruction of jus-tice." His words came out slow and measured.

Chief Steele sat down in his big office chair, and stared at Callahan with an icy gleam in his eyes. "No, it's called politics. Now everybody, get out!" He pointed at the door.

Callahan was the first to storm out and slam the door behind him. Annie followed and slammed it again. She caught up to him in the hallway.

"The hell with this case! Why should I bust my ass and ruin my career over it?" Callahan tore the wrappings from five sticks of Big Red and stuffed them into his mouth. "Go ahead and dismiss it. Bottom line: we got no motive, we got no case."

"What?" Annie knew he was right, but had to rise to the occasion. "You wanna give up now? So, Malone wins. And Bertrand wins? I can picture them both smirking. Mike, we have to see this through at all costs. There's no going back now. I've won plenty of criminal cases without proving motive. The evidence against Malone will speak for itself."

"But, if it's a close call, the jurors'll want their hardy dose of motive. This is one of those cases where they'll want to know *why*."

Annie didn't want to admit it, but she had witnessed the skepticism in their eyes. This one would be tough to prove beyond a reasonable doubt. She racked her brains as they made their way through the building and out to the street. They had to start thinking outside the box.

"I'll send the FBI a blanket subpoena requesting all files, documents, tape recordings, and other information pertaining to Malone and Trevor Shea," she said. "I don't care what the chief says, I'm going to pursue this." Annie would stand up to Bertrand, too, and suffer the consequences later.

Callahan rolled his eyes. "Bertrand will ball that subpoena up and eat it for lunch."

"Good, let him choke then. He'll probably have the U.S. attorney file a motion to quash my subpoena on the grounds that it interferes with a federal investigation."

"According to Bertrand, they're not investigating anything." Callahan beelined toward his car in the parking lot. "We're prosecuting a murder case here. You'd think they'd have to comply."

"A federal investigation usually preempts whatever the state has on its plate. But, I'll request a private in-camera review of their files in the judge's chambers."

"You mean a federal *non-investigation*."

"Right." Annie sighed. She had to refocus. "I should take advantage of the extra time and prep Jennianne for her testimony. Maybe she can shed some light on the informant theory."

Callahan grimaced. "She's a basket case. Maybe we should get her up on that stand sooner rather than later."

Annie had already considered the option. "Her testimony will have a much greater impact if she goes last."

"But Malone's on the offensive. I can feel it. If he discovers her location, she won't be around to testify at all. He's done it before, he'll do it again."

"Jennianne's not here." Annie spoke to Callahan on her cell; it was seven o'clock. She stood on tiptoes and peeked in several darkened windows of the safe house. "Car's gone."

"You check up the street? I told her not to park out front."

"Yeah." Annie felt a twinge in her stomach, like she knew something bad had happened.

"I can't believe this. Check the pubs."

"But, where do I start?" Annie trotted toward her car.

"Do a GPS search and start with the closest." Callahan exhaled into the phone. "I'll head down now and help you."

"Give me a half-hour. Maybe she ran out for cigarettes."

"Maybe." He sounded skeptical. "I'll tie some things up here in the meantime."

Annie used her GPS and began the search at Jamie's Pub in North Scituate. *No luck.* Finding Jennianne this way seemed futile. Barker Tavern, Satuit Tavern, Mill Wharf. No sign of her. Annie finally struck gold at T.K.O. Malley's near the harbor when she spotted Jennianne bellied up in the back bar, holding court with two scraggly barflies. They were in the process of tossing back brown shots.

"What are you doing here?" Annie wedged herself in between one of the barflies and Jennianne. She smelled whisky.

"I got bored." Jennianne slurred her words. She was dressed in low-rise skinny jeans, which exposed her pierced belly button in the front and an intricate tattoo running down her backside.

"What can I get you, honey?" The forty-something bartender grinned at Annie, revealing a wide gap between his front teeth.

"Nothing, thank you." Annie turned away and placed a hand on Jennianne's shoulder. "Come on, I'm taking you home."

"One more for the road." Jennianne snapped her fingers and gestured to the empty shot glasses for refills. The barflies cheered. "I'll meet you back there."

"No way. You're not driving."

"But I drive better drunk."

"Don't tell me that." Annie ignored the buzzing from the barflies. "It's not safe for you to be out like this."

Jennianne looked around. "I don't see nobody I know. You can't make me anyways."

"Come on, let's go. I'll take you out for something to eat."

"And smokes?"

"We'll stop and get some."

"How 'bout Chinese?"

"Fine." Annie paid the balance of the tab and guided Jennianne off her stool and out of the bar. She was so drunk, she could barely walk. "We'll get takeout. Let me get you home first."

"No way. I can't go back yet. It's the same as jail." Jennianne stumbled off the curb. "Let's get a scorpion bowl."

"You've had enough." Annie opened the car door and helped her in. "Hang in there. In just a few more days, it'll be over and we'll fly you down to Florida to stay with your mother."

"I'm already dead, so just let me have some fun."

"From what I can see, you're very much alive." Annie got in and started the car.

"Because Billy already tried killing a witness."

"What?" Annie faced her.

Jennianne fumbled several times with her seat belt before making it clasp. "Yeah and it got all screwed up, and now he's really pissed off. Gonna take it out on me."

"What are you talking about?" Annie figured it was all in her head, a natural part of her anxiety over testifying.

"He's after me." Jennianne hiccupped.

"No, too much risk." Annie started the car and drove onto Front Street. "The trial's going well. Billy hasn't threatened or touched any of our witnesses. He's not that stupid."

"Yeah he did. You're so wrong." Jennianne sat upright and then teetered into Annie. The odor of alcohol on her breath was practically intoxicating. "The fishing dude from Gloucester."

"That's Miles Domenico and he already testified." Annie masked her concern. She hadn't told Jennianne anything about Domenico or his testimony. "So, what are you talking about?"

"Billy sent Drake Reed up the night before to kill your guy, but something happened, and word is, he's dead now. Then he stole Billy's money out a some canvas bag. You don't steal Billy's money."

"Who's Drake Reed?" Annie knew he was Billy's right-hand man, but wanted to see what Jennianne knew.

"Billy's friend. He'd do anything for Billy. That's why . . . I can't do this."

"If Reed's dead, he can't come after you." Annie would make a call to Callahan to start an investigation on Reed. "Look, no one's coming after you. But, you can't be careless about it, either. You can't be out in public, getting drunk in bars."

"Don't you get it? Billy's got others besides Reed. People'll do anything for him." Jennianne knocked her head against the side window. "All he has to do is ask."

"That's not true."

"Sure it is and you know it. They're afraid to say no."

"And that's why we're doing all this." Annie tightened her grip on the steering wheel. "Billy preys off people's fear. Year after year it will get worse, and he will get more brazen because no one will have the guts to stand up to him."

"His old girlfriend is dead, so is Trevor, I'm next."

"How many paintings did Trevor do?" Annie glanced at Jennianne, who was staring out the window. "How many?"

"Maybe he'll kill me the same way as her, with a rope."

Annie bit her lip until she tasted blood.

"There it is." Jennianne pointed to the Peking Palace. "Can we get the egg rolls? Can we go now? I'm wicked hungry."

Annie swerved into the parking lot. She'd feed Jennianne and get her into bed. Trevor, his artwork, and the informant theory would have to wait. Besides, she was exhausted and couldn't think straight. She thought about Clancy and his remark about the circus clown car. Annie could visualize it: tiny pink car, clowns with giant red balls for noses, faces painted white. She wondered how many more clowns were going to jump out.

29

CALLAHAN RESUMED THE witness stand at nine A.M. He hadn't slept at all the night before. It seemed like the world had turned against him, except Annie. Now he had to face Clancy. He tried his best to appear confident. No matter how much he studied his reports and felt prepared, Clancy had the ability to rattle him and rattle him good. The old codger knew every trick in the book. He gazed out at all the mothers sitting in the front row. *Keep going,* he reminded himself. *Do it for them.*

"Attorney Clancy?" Judge Killam said.

Clancy rose from his table and sauntered up to the jury box. "Good morning, ladies and gentlemen." He grinned, looking very grandfatherly. "I hope you all had a pleasant afternoon off yesterday. But, it's about time we get on with this, eh? With all the delays, I'll be a hundred before we finish." Most of the jurors smiled back; Callahan could tell they liked him.

"You may start your examination now." Judge Killam moaned.

Clancy nodded at the judge and adjusted his bow tie imprinted with dollar bills. Callahan wondered why he had chosen the money tie. He'd find out soon enough. Clancy always had some theme.

"Top o' the morning to you, Detective." Clancy bowed.

"Morning." Callahan ignored the showmanship and forced a smile.

Clancy took a moment and studied Callahan. "Trevor Shea's death was an accidental overdose?"

"Not at all."

Clancy pinched his lower lip, appearing perplexed. "But the responding officer said so, didn't he?"

"He's not a homicide detective." Callahan kept his voice even.

"Oh!" Clancy tapped his forehead. "That's right, Officer O'Neil *rolled* the body before you arrived?" He made the rolling motion with his arms.

"He didn't hurt anything, just checking for ID. Standard procedure."

"But, aren't all officers trained not to disturb a dead body upon discovery?" Clancy rubbed his chin.

"Well, it depends. Sometimes it's necessary to touch the body to see if he or she has a pulse or to attempt revival. In this case, no harm was done."

"Detective, it's fair to say that the scrapes you described on Trevor's back could've come from a variety of sources, like a tackle football game?"

"Based on my observations, the scrapes and dirt resulted from someone *dragging* the body." Callahan stretched out the word dragging, mimicking Clancy.

"But you have no evidence *prooving* the body was dragged to that location." Clancy sounded like a physics professor.

"Nobody caught it on videotape, sir," Callahan said. Several jurors giggled.

Clancy zigzagged toward the witness stand. "The officers who canvassed the neighborhood reported back to you, Detective, correct?"

"They did."

"That would be Detectives Mannix and O'Connor?"

"Yes."

"They questioned people who lived nearby?"

"Yes."

"Near where Trevor overdosed? Where you found the body?"

Callahan's antenna shot up. *Trick question.*

"Objection!" Annie said. "That's two different questions, Your Honor."

"Sustained."

"They questioned people near the location where Trevor's body was discovered?"

"Yes."

"Approximately forty-five people were questioned?"

"Sounds about right."

"And no one saw anything out of the ordinary?"

"Of course they didn't. They've had the highest unsolved murder rate in the country. It's Charlestown's code of silence." Callahan's jaw tightened.

"Detect—"

"They don't hear anything. They don't see anything."

"Detective—"

"And nobody talks to cops."

"I'm not looking for your opinion here, just the facts. No one saw or heard anything out of the ordinary?"

Callahan paused and stole a glance at the jury. They had to know what he was referring to. "That's correct."

"The first arrest you made was Jennianne Smith?"

"Correct."

"She's the girlfriend of Billy Malone?" Clancy pointed to his client.

"Yes." Callahan looked at the emotionless Malone. "Well, she *was*." Malone would kill Jennianne before he'd ever take her back.

"You held Jennianne for two days in a filthy jail cell?" Clancy waved two fingers in the air.

"It wasn't that filthy."

"You relentlessly interrogated the poor girl?"

"I asked a few questions."

Clancy crept closer. "A few questions took you two whole days?"

"Yes."

"You threatened Jennianne with a murder charge?"

Callahan stiffened. "Never."

"It's a fact Jennianne changed her story several times until you were satisfied."

"No."

"You and Miss Fitzgerald made a *deal,* didn't you?" Clancy stressed the word *deal* and pointed at Annie.

"Objection!" Annie popped out of her seat.

"Overruled." Judge Killam banged his gavel. "It's cross-examination. Answer the question, please."

"We had booked Jennianne on minor drug charges." Callahan shrugged again. "We would've dismissed those anyway."

"Ha!" Clancy charged forward. "So you're admitting those charges were trumped up. Jennianne should never have been arrested and held in that filthy cell for two whole days."

"I'm not saying that."

Clancy snickered. "Once you *blackmailed* Jennianne, you arrested my client?"

"Objection!"

"Overruled."

"We also received additional information."

"Oh right, pardon me. You made that pact with the perjuring drug dealer."

"Objection as to form." Annie gesticulated.

"Sustained."

"You also threatened Domenico?"

"I never *threatened* anyone." Callahan gritted his teeth.

"Oh, come on, these people weren't born yesterday." Clancy thumbed toward the jury.

Callahan didn't reply; that's what Clancy wanted him to do.

"You gave the drug dealer a suspended sentence in exchange for his testimony at this trial?"

"Sure." *Keep it short and sweet.*

"You also paid him off." Clancy fingered his money bow tie.

"What?" Callahan felt the heat rising in his face.

"Ten grand up front and ten thousand after he came here and said what you wanted him to say."

"That's a lie!" Callahan jumped up. "You're making that up!"

"You're under oath, Detective." Clancy's voice thundered across the courtroom. "You're telling this jury you did *not* pay Domenico a total of twenty thousand dollars?"

"I never offered him money, never paid him a dime!" Callahan shouted; spit flew from his mouth.

"Order!" Judge Killam banged his gavel twice. "Sit down, Detective, and move along, Clancy."

"When you made that sweetheart deal with Domenico, were you aware he had a prior conviction for *perjury*?" The word *perjury* rolled off Clancy's tongue like butter.

Callahan glanced at Annie. "No, I was not."

"Really?" Clancy cocked his head. "Didn't you check his criminal record, Detective?"

"It didn't show up." Callahan knew the strategy was to make him appear crooked and sloppy. Jurors despised crooked cops and sloppy work.

"Now Detective, if you had known about that perjury conviction, would you have considered Domenico less reliable as a witness?"

He paused before answering. Clancy was doing his best to paint him into a corner. "I questioned Domenico at length. Based on my years of experience as a detective, I formed the opinion he was telling the truth about Malone's purchase of the Nine-eleven heroin up in Gloucester on the very day of Trevor's death."

Clancy flipped his head at the jury in disbelief. "You arrested my client at his mother's house, correct?"

"Yes."

"And, that would be his mother right over there with the rosary beads between her fingers?" Clancy pointed back into the gallery. The jurors looked at Mrs. Malone, perched in the front row in her blue flowered dress and coifed white hair. And, yes, there they were, the white rosary beads with the silver cross dangling off the end. It caught the light and flashed back at Callahan. He felt like a vampire being fended off by the cross.

Callahan nodded at Mrs. Malone; he knew where Clancy was going.

"A harmless, churchgoing lady, wouldn't you say, Detective?" Clancy walked toward Mrs. Malone.

"She's got a few outstanding parking tickets, Clancy." He couldn't resist blurting that one out.

"So, when are you going to arrest her?"

"When is she going to join Mothers Against Murder?" He stretched his arms in the direction of the mothers sitting in the front row on the opposite side.

"All right, all right," Judge Killam said. "That's enough."

"You and your fellow detectives busted down poor Mrs. Malone's door without even knocking?" Clancy made a shoving motion with his hands.

"While we were arresting her sons who we believed were armed and dangerous."

"You had your weapons drawn?"

"Yes."

"And you and your detectives used foul language in her presence?"

"As I recall, it was her sons who used foul language."

"I don't curse," Malone blurted.

Clancy nodded at his client. "Did you personally search that sweet little old lady's underwear drawer?"

"We were looking for weapons." Callahan kept his tone as businesslike as he could.

"And you found a bazooka?"

Several jurors laughed.

"No."

"Hand grenades?"

"Panties." Callahan answered frankly to end Clancy's charade.

"I see." Clancy winked at him in full view of the jury. "And your search included spilling all Mrs. Malone's flour and sugar on the kitchen floor, dumping the contents of each drawer in her house, tipping her trash cans upside down?"

"That's standard procedure. Like I said, we were searching for weapons."

"Did you find any weapons at all?" Clancy stretched his arms out wide over his head.

"No."

"Did you clean up the mess for Mrs. Malone?"

"No, that's standard procedure, too."

"When my client had his hands cuffed behind his back, you smashed his head against the floor, didn't you?" Clancy loomed over Callahan, invading his space.

"No, I did not."

"In fact, you shattered Mr. Malone's nose right in front of his mother. Blood gushed onto her white rug and you smeared it all over his face."

"That's not true." Callahan raised his voice.

"Are you telling this jury that my client did not receive a broken nose during his arrest?" Clancy slowed his delivery, placing emphasis on each word.

"When we were cuffing *your client,* he lunged forward to break free and fell, face-first into the coffee table. It was his own fault."

Clancy walked toward the jury box and then spun around. "Oh! Speaking of arrests, weren't *you* arrested over at FBI headquarters during lunch yesterday? Isn't that why we were delayed?"

"Objection!" Annie jumped up, knocking a book to the floor. "That's prejudicial and irrelevant."

"Sustained." Judge Killam scowled at Clancy before turning toward the jury. "Please disregard the question."

Callahan noticed all eyes widen on the jury panel. Clancy just had to slip that one in. He knew they'd all go home and look for it on TV.

"Detective?" Clancy walked along the edge of the jury box. "You've been out to get my client for a long time."

"No. He's simply been a suspect before."

"Yes, even when he's *innocent.*" Clancy stared at Callahan. "How many times have you arrested Mr. Malone?"

"I don't know."

"I'll bet you do. I bet you know precisely. And how many times has he been convicted from your spurious arrests?"

Callahan didn't answer; his mouth felt bone dry.

"Zero." Clancy made an O with his fingers and thumb, and held it up before the jury. "Now Detective, you said you found an empty packet of Nine-eleven heroin in Trevor's pocket?"

"Yes."

"That's awfully strange." Clancy scrunched up his face. "Why, Officers O'Neil and Twomey must've missed it?"

"I don't know."

"You planned to have it fingerprinted and analyzed, am I correct?"

"Yes."

"But you did not hand it over to the fingerprint expert when he was at the crime scene?"

"I dropped it off at the lab the next day."

"After you met with Miles Domenico?"

"Once I got done up in Gloucester? Yes."

"Let's face it, Detective," Clancy said, wagging his index finger. "You never found that empty packet of Nine-eleven heroin in Trevor's pocket."

"I did too." Callahan gripped the edge of the witness stand.

"Miles Domenico gave it to you to set my client up, didn't he?"

"That's not true!" Callahan clenched his teeth.

"Captain Murphy is planning on retiring next year from his position as the head of the Homicide Unit?"

"I believe so."

"And you're gunning for that position, Detective Callahan?"

"There's no position available at this point; he's still on the force."

"A conviction in this high-profile case would certainly help your crusade."

"Objection!" Annie hit the table.

"Overruled."

"No." Callahan leaned over the stand. "This is ridiculous."

"You'd do anything to frame Mr. Malone, like planting evidence and lying under oath."

"Objection!" Annie flew out of her seat. "Objection!"

"Overruled."

"No!" Callahan bolted up and pointed at Clancy. "You and your client will do anything to keep the code of silence! Anything!"

"Order!" Judge Killam struck the gavel. "Sit down right now, Detective, or I'll hold you in contempt."

Callahan sat down hard. It felt as if the judge had publicly given him a spanking. The jurors were looking at him with frigid eyes.

Clancy stared at him. "I have nothing further, Your Honor."

Callahan picked at a hangnail, drawing blood along the side of his thumb. Clancy had humiliated him, attacked him personally. Years of placing his life on the line, dealing with scumbags, pulling all-nighters, sacrificing relationships. All for what? This was even worse than getting arrested by Bertrand.

"Any redirect, Commonwealth?" Judge Killam addressed Annie.

"Yes." She walked into the center of the courtroom, and smiled at the jury as if she had everything under control. Callahan wished that was the case.

"Detective Callahan, how big is Charlestown?"

"Only one square mile."

"How many murders remain unsolved in Charlestown?"

"Objection!" Clancy shouted. "This has nothing to do with my client or this case."

"Sustained."

"What is a code of silence murder?"

"Objection." Clancy stood again. "Prejudicial."

"Sustained."

Annie gazed at the jury. "No further questions."

"Recross?"

"I'm satisfied, Your Honor," Clancy said.

"Then the witness may be excused, and we'll take the rest of the day off. Have a pleasant weekend."

"Thank you, Your Honor," Callahan mumbled. When he got up, he made eye contact with the pretty foreperson. Was she still with him? The big lady sitting next to her gave him a nose sneer. They probably all hated him now.

"The court will be in—"

"Recess!" Johnny announced. "All rise."

Callahan ran up to the defense table as soon as the judge and jury left the room. "I'm warning you." He stuck a finger into Clancy's chest. "Watch your back."

"Is that a threat?"

"Take it any way you want."

Annie stepped between them.

"He just threatened me." Clancy turned toward the gallery. "I have witnesses."

"And you slandered him." Annie stepped in between them. "You have no evidence to back your accusations."

"We'll see about that."

"Come on." Annie placed a hand on Callahan's back. "Let's go. It's not worth it."

"Tell your client to go to hell!" Callahan shouted at Clancy before marching down the aisle.

Annie chased after him. "Calm down, okay? We still have reporters sitting out there."

"But he accused me of lying under oath, planting evidence, and bribery of all things. Why didn't you ask more questions to give me the chance to redeem myself?"

"I thought it would be best to let it go at that point. I wasn't about to risk another Clancy attack."

Callahan would've preferred taking the risk. "It'll be all over the papers. With my arrest and everything? I could lose my job."

"Clancy can't prove any of it." Annie lowered her voice. "Did you look into the Drake Reed thing?"

"Reed's missing." Callahan unsnapped his cell from the case on his belt and turned it back on. "I spoke with his mother, and she hasn't heard from him in several days. Hasn't been home." He wondered how Jenni-anne received the information that Reed had been ordered up to Glouces-ter to attack Domenico, yet, somehow, the plan had backfired. What had gone down? Would Domenico now be the focus of a murder investiga-tion? The press would have a field day . . . and so would Clancy.

Callahan opened two pieces of Big Red and started chewing. "I'm worried about Jennianne getting through this weekend alive. Malone is capable of anything.

"How about sending her to Florida to stay with her mother?"

"Too risky. Malone may have people down there watching the place. I'll have a cop stationed outside the safe house around the clock." He turned toward Annie. "We need to get her on that witness stand. I got a bad feeling."

30

ON SATURDAY AFTERNOON, Annie parked on Green Street in Charlestown and walked up the hill to the Hurleys' house, a dark brown triple-decker. She spotted a lighted electric candle in the window on the third floor and wondered if that was Georgie's old bedroom. She had phoned several times, leaving messages for Mrs. Hurley, but never received a return call. She walked up the front steps, rang the bell, and took a deep breath. It was always hard speaking with a murder victim's mother.

A woman with short white hair came to the door. She was pale and wore no makeup. Annie recognized her as the one who left the courtroom crying on the first day of the trial. "Mrs. Hurley?" she said.

"Yes?" Her voice sounded scratchy and a bit uncertain.

"Hi, I'm Annie Fitzgerald. I saw you in court on Monday and wondered if we could sit down and talk for a moment."

Mrs. Hurley hesitated. "My husband stepped out . . . ahh . . . I'm not sure."

"I can come back if that's better for you?" Annie wondered why she felt more comfortable with her husband present.

She peered over Annie's shoulder and scanned the street. "That's okay, you can come in. It's all right. Here." She held the door open and they walked through a small parlor to the kitchen. "Would you like a cup of tea? I was just about to put the kettle on."

"Sure." Annie sat at the round wooden table. A collection of porcelain bird plates and a large crucifix adorned the wall.

Mrs. Hurley turned on the gas stove, and pushed a red tea kettle over the blue flame. The dishwasher hummed. Annie thought about her own mother, who always had to have her afternoon tea. She would put the kettle on the stove in the tiny back kitchen at the bookstore. Annie used to hear that kettle whistle when she played in her cardboard forts in the adjacent storage room. *Tea and cookies. And, a baseball bat.*

"I'm Marie, by the way." She smiled slightly and sat at the table. Neither spoke for a moment.

Annie would have to start. "Marie, I'm sorry if I upset you in court. I didn't know."

Marie nodded and pressed her clenched fists to her lips. Tears rolled down her cheeks. Her body shook.

"I'm so sorry." It was all Annie managed to say, she couldn't imagine losing a child. She waited for Marie to wipe her eyes and face with a napkin. She blew her nose; the tears kept coming.

"I can't." She gasped. "Go." She gasped again. "Back."

"I understand."

Annie waited, but Marie kept crying. The kettle steamed.

"I'll get the tea." Annie got up and poured water into the cups that Marie had set on the Formica counter with the tea bags ready to go. She carried them over to the table and set them down. Marie rested her forehead on her arm and sobbed. Her body convulsed.

Annie heard the front door open and close, followed by the sound of heavy footsteps.

"What's going on?" A burly man walked into the room. He wore a long-sleeved plaid shirt and jeans. She figured he was her husband.

Annie rose. "I'm—"

"Why the hell are you here?" He addressed Annie and placed an arm around Marie's back. He had a thick Boston accent.

"I'm sorry, I tried to call."

"And we didn't call you back, did we?" he shouted.

"No I . . . I'll leave." Annie got up and headed toward the door. "I didn't mean to intrude."

"Wait outside. I'll be there in a minute. Gotta calm her down."

Annie stepped outside and paced along the sidewalk. She felt like an outsider. Mrs. Hurley was steeped in sorrow, it was clear. She couldn't imagine walking around in her shoes.

Mr. Hurley came out a few minutes later. "I didn't mean to get hot in there, but Marie, she's been to hell and back. Maybe she never came back, actually. I think she's still there." He had a loud, gruff voice.

"I can't imagine," Annie said.

"No you can't until it happens to you. I should've never let her go to court with them ladies. Big mistake. She's not coming back and can't answer none of your questions." He grabbed a pack of cigarettes from his shirt pocket and lit up.

"Did she know about the painting?" Annie was reluctant to bring it up. "It was featured in the *Globe*."

"I didn't tell her and I wouldn't let her look at it neither. Whether those ladies told her, I don't know. The Shea kid shouldn't have painted that. It's killing us. If he wasn't dead, I'd be suing him. You bet I would."

"Did you see it?"

Mr. Hurley shoved his hands on his hips. "I took one look and ripped up the newspaper, ripped it to shreds." He puffed his cigarette and looked up toward the candle in the window. "She was home that day when Georgie died, home with the kids. It was sometime after school, close to summertime. We got four kids, had four. Well, in my book, we got four, it's just that one of 'em ain't with us no more. The rest are grown, married, all that."

Annie watched him smoke for a moment and pace along the sidewalk.

"So the cops come to the house and Marie answers the door. I wish it had been me." Mr. Hurley shook his head. "So they make her go down to the morgue and ID Georgie." His face contorted and eyes filled with tears. "Ten years old with his head bashed in. *My son.* Only ten years old. She had to see that? What mother should ever have to see that? She ain't never been the same."

Annie felt like crying as she witnessed the anguish in Mr. Hurley's eyes. She imagined the red-haired boy with the freckles from the painting. What had that sweet-looking boy appeared like at the morgue? She forced the tears back.

Mr. Hurley wiped his eyes on the back of his hand. "I know you gotta do your job, but it ain't changing nothing. Them ladies you got all lined up there? You're giving them false hope. That guy's gonna get away with it just like the last time and the time before that. You wait and see." He snuffed his cigarette out on the sidewalk and started up the front steps. He opened his door and faced Annie again. "I got no problem with you here. No disrespect, okay?" He held a palm up. "You're just, you're just . . . putting people through hell and I don't even think you know it." The door slammed behind him.

Annie felt heavy-hearted as she climbed back into her car and started the engine. If she could turn the clock back and start all over again, would she take this case on? She drove down Main Street and passed the location of her parents' old bookstore without slowing down. There were so many things she wished she could change and couldn't.

31

RACHEL FILED INTO the courtroom at nine A.M. Monday morning and sat in her assigned seat. Elaine accidentally elbowed her again. She didn't even mumble an apology. *That woman has some sort of complex.* She strutted around the jury room like an authority on everything. What did a housecleaner know about anything besides which bottle of bleach to use for a bathtub ring?

"Do you swear to tell the truth, the whole truth, and nothing but the truth, so help you God?" Clerk Fallon said.

"I do."

Rachel noticed the next witness was completely bald; his head reflected the courtroom lights.

"Good morning, sir." Fitzgerald skirted around her table. She looked sharp in her fitted black suit. "Please introduce yourself to the jury."

Rachel glanced at attorney Clancy with his new bow tie, a black-and-white swirly design, and wondered why he had chosen it.

"Good morning." The witness nodded at the jury. "Sergeant Frank Sutton."

"How are you employed?" Fitzgerald asked.

"I work for the Boston Police, specializing in fingerprinting." Sutton spoke with authority as he described his qualifications. He had published a book on fingerprinting and taught classes on the subject at Northeastern University. Rachel wished they could shorten the background information and focus on the substance. The guy from the drug lab had droned on and on the week before. Rachel had caught Elaine sleeping twice. *And she snored.*

"Sergeant, please explain what fingerprinting is?" Fitzgerald smiled.

"Certainly." Sutton lifted an enlarged black-and-white fingerprint onto an easel near the witness stand. "Fingerprinting is the science of using the friction ridge patterns on the fingertips for purposes of identification. You see, a person's fingerprint is unique and will remain unchanged for the duration of his or her lifetime. Prints are left on various surfaces by perspiration, natural oils in the skin, or by other substances on the fingers. Latent fingerprinting is the technique of preserving and identifying these prints."

Rachel wondered if Sutton would provide the forensic evidence Fitzgerald desperately needed to nail Malone. So far, the prosecution's case seemed a bit shaky. Rachel still couldn't get over the witness who committed perjury. He was nothing but a drug dealer with his own agenda. Why should she believe a word he said?

"How do you gather fingerprints?" Fitzgerald glanced at the jury, making eye contact with Rachel.

"Powder is sprinkled on the print or applied with a soft brush. The print is then lifted with adhesive tape and sent to the lab for development and enlargement."

"What happens after the print comes back?"

"A comparison is made between the unknown fingerprint and previously identified prints on file." Sutton used a wooden pointer on the two enlarged fingerprints to describe the ridge arrangements found on each finger.

Rachel stared at the giant prints, and took another look at Clancy's tie. Sutton's black-and-white patterns of arches, loops, and whorls from the fingerprints looked exactly like the tie. *Clancy and his ties.* Every morning Rachel looked forward to the tie of the day.

She had liked his money tie, and wondered if Detective Callahan had really bribed the drug dealer. Callahan had vehemently denied it. *Twenty thousand dollars.* It boiled down to Callahan's word against Clancy's. Someone had to be exaggerating or lying. Could she trust the detective? Rachel had liked Callahan at first and felt flattered by the way he looked at her more than anyone else. There was something magnetic about his green eyes. In the right light, they glowed. Rachel had imagined herself having a wild, passionate fling with him. She even considered looking him up after the trial, but her fantasy had waned during Clancy's cross-examination.

"Sergeant, did you dust for fingerprints on any of these items that Callahan provided at the lab?" Fitzgerald raised her voice, which forced Rachel to refocus. She had missed several questions and answers.

"Yes, I lifted two latent fingerprints from the plastic CVS bag, and an additional fingerprint from the empty packet of Nine-eleven heroin."

Fitzgerald walked to the evidence table and had Sutton identify both pieces of evidence. "What did you do next?"

"Performed a computer search using FBI fingerprint files and found several matches. I then obtained the original fingerprint cards for Billy Malone and Miles Domenico, and made comparisons with the prints I had lifted."

"What were the results of your comparisons?" Fitzgerald gazed into the jury box.

"Objection!" Clancy said.

"Overruled."

"A latent fingerprint lifted from the empty packet of Nine-eleven heroin matches Malone's right index finger." Sutton raised a fingerprint card for Malone and an enlarged latent fingerprint, and pointed out the identical pattern of arches, loops, and whorls.

Rachel studied Malone, who was whispering something to Clancy. Clancy shrugged as if he didn't care about the testimony.

"Did you find any other matches?" Fitzgerald asked.

"Yes, I found a fingerprint which matched Malone's middle finger on the plastic CVS bag. I also matched another fingerprint lifted from the same bag with Miles Domenico's right index finger."

That lying drug dealer again. Rachel sighed. Maybe he was telling the truth about handing Malone the heroin in the CVS bag? Did they really meet up in Gloucester? She couldn't decide.

"Nothing further," Fitzgerald said, after she introduced the latent prints and fingerprint cards into evidence.

"Cross?" Judge Killam zeroed in on Clancy.

"You're hiding evidence from this jury!" Clancy charged toward Sutton.

Sutton stumbled backward, almost taking out his easels. "What? I'm not hiding anything."

Clancy's eyes bulged. "You left out the body!"

"The body?"

"Detective Callahan dragged you out of bed late at night to dust for prints on the body."

"Well, yeah." He paused. "Part of the job."

"Oh, come on, Sergeant. That was a bit unusual, wouldn't you say?"

"Not really."

"You must be aware of Detective Callahan's obsession with Mr. Malone?"

"Objection!" Fitzgerald jumped up.

Judge Killam pinched his lower lip. "Overruled. Answer the question, sir."

"No." Sutton crossed his arms. Rachel thought he looked and sounded defensive. He wasn't answering truthfully.

Clancy grinned. "Callahan ordered you to dust for prints possibly left behind on Trevor Shea's skin."

"He didn't *order* me." Sutton sounded flippant this time. Rachel wondered if the fingerprint guys were called to all murder scenes. She didn't realize they could find prints on a body in the first place.

"You must've used fluorescent lighting to search for evidence of fingerprints left behind on Shea's skin?" Clancy zigzagged toward the witness.

"Yes."

"Once you locate a fingerprint on the skin's surface, you employ the Kroma-something method to lift it?"

"Kromekote." Sutton grimaced and addressed the jury as if he now had one up on Clancy. "We press a Kromekote card against the surface of the skin for about three seconds. We then apply fingerprint powder and the card is later processed along with the powder to develop the latent impression. This print will look like a mirror image of the actual fingerprint, and is then photographed and reversed to avoid confusion. This technique allows us to lift prints up to an hour and a half after they were left behind on the skin's surface."

"Thank you for your thorough explanation, Sergeant. So, did you lift any fingerprints from Trevor Shea's skin?"

"One. From his right wrist."

Rachel watched Sutton wipe his hands along the side of his pants, leaving a wet mark. She also detected perspiration forming on his bald head, probably a good surface to lift a print or two.

Clancy smacked his lips. "I bet you deliberately declined to tell us about your search results for that fingerprint."

"Not at all." Sutton's face flushed. "The results were irrelevant."

"Irrelevant?" Clancy fluttered his hands above his head. "Perhaps irrelevant to you, sir, but not to my client."

"Objection." Fitzgerald rose.

"Sustained." Judge Killam frowned. "Please put a question before the witness, counselor."

"In fairness to Mr. Malone and this jury, please tell us who that additional fingerprint belongs to?"

Sutton cleared his throat. "It came back negative, meaning we were unable to find a match using the FBI filing system."

"Holy cow! So, that fingerprint lifted from the body of Trevor Shea did not belong to Mr. Malone?"

Sutton's gaze flickered downward. "No, it did not."

"Meaning no match?"

"Right, no match."

"Hmm. That print did not belong to one of the responding police officers?"

"Correct."

"Why, that's huge!" Clancy spread his arms wide.

"Objection!" Fitzgerald slapped her table.

"Sustained."

"I'm sorry, I got carried away. Well, actually, blown away."

Judge Killam leaned forward. "Clancy!"

"You're telling us that *someone else* touched Trevor Shea's body within an hour and a half before you lifted the print?" Clancy blinked several times at Sutton.

"Yes."

Rachel leaned forward. *Someone else touched the body?* This was new. She looked at Fitzgerald. Why hadn't they been informed? It seemed odd. Rachel had a bad taste in her mouth. She studied Malone in his gray suit jacket and pressed white shirt underneath. Rachel regarded Fitzgerald again, and hoped she had an explanation.

Clancy filled his cheeks with air and slowly released it. He made eye contact with Rachel, strolled to the evidence table, and picked up the syringe.

"Here's another gigantic detail you left out." Clancy walked toward the jury box with the syringe raised high. "You found yet another fingerprint that you didn't bother telling us about!"

"A partial."

"A partial fingerprint where?"

"On the syringe."

"The syringe." Clancy waved the syringe in the air. "You mean the syringe recovered from the scene that Trevor was holding?"

"Correct."

Rachel noticed that Sutton failed to hold Clancy's gaze. *Where's all your confidence now?*

"The only fingerprint lifted from this syringe matched up to Trevor Shea, didn't it?" Clancy dangled the syringe in front of the jury.

"Yes." Sutton folded his hands.

"You did not find any fingerprints belonging to Mr. Malone on that syringe?"

"No, I did not."

"Thank you, Sergeant. No further questions." Clancy placed the syringe back on the evidence table.

"Any redirect, Commonwealth?"

"Yes, Your Honor." Fitzgerald stood without leaving her table. "Sergeant, please describe the exact location of the fingerprint you lifted from Trevor's wrist."

Sutton turned toward the jury and held up his arm. "It was right here in the area where one would take a pulse." He rubbed the underside of his own wrist.

"Nothing further."

Rachel admired how Clancy could step into the ring, throw a few punches, and sit back down. He had successfully tarnished the Commonwealth's theory that Malone or one of his henchmen placed the syringe in Trevor's hand to make his death appear like an accidental overdose. Maybe that's all this was, *accidental*. In addition, someone had touched Trevor's wrist, perhaps to take a pulse. Rachel studied Malone again. Was Detective Callahan obsessed? And, if so, was he obsessed for good reason? How many times had Malone gotten away with murder?

32

THAT'S NOT WHAT you said in front of the grand jury, Jennianne." Annie checked her watch, it was nearly ten p.m.

"It's not?" Jennianne cocked her head.

"Here, reread page twelve." Annie handed her the grand jury transcript
once again. They had been prepping for Jennianne's testimony for nearly
three hours. Annie had to hone in on the details, make sure Jennianne's
order of events and descriptions were consistent with what she said before. Annie wished Jennianne hadn't testified before the grand jury, then
there would be no transcript for Clancy to trip her up with. But she and
Callahan had been worried that without Jennianne, Malone may not
have been indicted. The case against Malone screamed classic overdose at
the time. The grand jurors could've gone either way. *No looking back now.*

"Finished?" Annie had to leave Scituate soon and head back up to Boston, but she had to make sure Jennianne had her facts straight. The whole
case hinged on her testimony. If Jennianne could get it right, the jurors
would be able to piece the whole thing together. "Let's go over that part
again."

"I can't do this no more!" Jennianne flung the transcript across the table.
"Why can't they just let the jury read the stupid transcript? Why do I have
to say it all over again? It's not fair to me."

"That's against the rules. We always need a live witness at trial. Attorney Clancy has to have the opportunity to cross-examine you." Annie had explained all this before.

"I can't face Billy tomorrow."

Here we go again. "Don't look at him. Just take the oath, sit behind the witness stand, and keep your eyes on me and the jurors if you can. When it's attorney Clancy's turn to ask questions, focus on him. You have to concentrate and pretend Billy's not there."

Jennianne pulled several white threads from a frayed hole in her jeans. "That's impossible."

"You can do this." Annie tried to say it with as much zeal as she could muster. What if Jennianne fell apart? They'd have no case and Malone would walk within . . . hours. She visualized the look of defeat on all the mothers' faces. *Malone wins again.* They were sinking to new lows in the courtroom. Annie had witnessed the negativity in the jurors' eyes and in their body language during Clancy's cross-examination of Sutton. He'd made it look like she and Callahan were hiding damaging information. *So not true.* If they had gone through all the negative fingerprint results, Sutton's testimony would've taken hours upon hours. In hindsight, Annie wished she'd at least brought up the unknown fingerprint they lifted from Trevor's body on direct examination to lessen the impact of Clancy's cross. She'd been beating herself up over it for the rest of the day.

"Billy's gonna win." Jennianne snuffed her cigarette stub in the ashtray.

"No." Annie squeezed her hands into fists and dug her fingernails into her skin until it hurt. What else could she do? She closed her eyes and racked her brain. All she could see were fingerprints, black-and-white fingerprints . . . *Clancy's tie. Trevor's limp wrist.*

"Who called nine-one-one?" Annie blurted the question out and watched Jennianne closely for a reaction.

"I don't know." She extracted another cigarette without making eye contact.

Push her. Annie leaned forward. "Someone who was not at your apartment on the night Trevor died left a fingerprint behind on Trevor's wrist. I'm willing to bet money he or she dialed nine-one-one from the pay phone up the street. If it wasn't for that anonymous call, the cops wouldn't have discovered Trevor's body that fast."

"So?"

"And you know who it was."

"What?" Jennianne jerked her head up; she looked pale, *more so than usual.*

Annie repeated herself.

"I don't know nothing about that."

Jennianne knew. Her defensive tone gave it away. Annie had to tread delicately and draw a name out of her.

"Why are you looking at me like that?" Jennianne tapped her pack of Virginia Slims and dislodged another cigarette. "I'm tired. I want to go to bed."

"You're protecting someone."

"No, I'm not." Jennianne's gaze shifted. She stuck the cigarette between her lips and lit up.

Annie had to get a name, and she knew Jennianne could be easily manipulated. There was too much at stake to let this go. She watched her smoke for a minute. If Jennianne was protecting someone, they had likely been in communication by phone or text at some point around the time of Trevor's death. It was worth a try.

"Jennianne, Detective Callahan can get your phone records tomorrow morning. We can easily go through them and figure it out on our own." Annie gathered her papers from the table.

"No." Jennianne tapped her cigarette on the edge of the ashtray. "He can't do that."

"Sure he can. Easily."

Jennianne leaned her head against the back of the couch and inhaled the cigarette. "He can't be involved at all."

"Who?"

"Trevor would never want him to . . . you don't get it still."

"Try me."

"He was one of Trevor's best friends since we were kids." She squeezed her eyes shut. "This guy stayed wicked straight, you know? He's married with a wife and they got two little kids. Shit, he even has a job."

"This is a murder trial." Annie had to get tough, rattle her a little. "If you don't tell us, that's obstructing justice, a criminal penalty that comes with jail time."

"I don't give two shits about that. I'm already screwed. Let Callahan come down and arrest me." She exhaled a long stream of smoke. "He done it before."

"But Jennianne, perhaps this guy witnessed something that could tip the scales in our favor, send Billy away for good."

"He didn't."

Annie was running out of options. *Think.* "Okay, if you say he didn't see anything, so be it." She paused. "I'd like an opportunity to at least speak with him. I want to know more about Trevor's paintings. How about a compromise? Give me his name and number and I promise not to call him as a witness. Billy will never find out."

"You can't keep nothin' from Billy."

"You said Trevor painted Lydia Thompson. Maybe he saw the painting, too."

Jennianne concentrated on her cigarette. "I don't know."

"Come on, just give up his name, Jennianne. There's no harm in that. If you force us to go through your phone records, then all bets are off. I'll subpoena him as a witness by tomorrow afternoon, and we'll let the chips fall where they may."

"You'll just end up killing him then because they'll find out."

"So help me now. Who is it?" Annie whispered.

"If I give you his name, will you promise you won't make him a witness? Because they'll kill him."

"Yes, I'm just going to ask him a few questions." Annie gazed into Jennianne's eyes as she made her promise, *a promise she probably couldn't keep.*

"Paul Garrity."

33

"COMMONWEALTH CALLS JENNIANNE Smith." Annie twisted her fingers, and tried as hard as she could to mask her emotions in front of the jury. She hadn't felt this anxious in ages. Would Jennianne fold under pressure? The gallery was packed that morning in anticipation of her star witness. This time Annie had taken Trevor's painting of the kids in the playground and leaned it against her table facing the witness stand. She hoped it would help get Jennianne through her testimony.

"Jennianne Smith!" Johnny hollered into the hallway. "Come on. We're all waiting."

Everyone looked back as Johnny escorted Jennianne into the courtroom. She angled her face toward the floor, hiding behind her long hair. She wore a simple blue dress with a satin ribbon tied in a bow around her waist. A size zero, no doubt. Annie noticed again how frail she'd become over the past several months. Jennianne stumbled halfway down and Johnny grabbed her arm to prevent her from falling. *Just don't look at Malone.* Annie knew Jennianne would crumble if she did.

"Raise your right hand?" Clerk Fallon said.

Jennianne raised her left.

"Your other right." The clerk smiled at her.

Jennianne looked confused for a moment, but switched hands for the oath.

"Do you swear to tell the truth, the whole truth, and nothing but the truth, so help you God?"

Jennianne opened and closed her mouth without saying a word.

"Miss?"

"I do," she mumbled without looking up. Clerk Fallon guided her to the witness stand, pulled the chair out, and motioned for her to sit.

"Good morning." Annie positioned herself near the painting, hoping Jennianne would look at it. She heard Malone rustling in his seat and ignored him. She couldn't even glance in his direction fearing that Jennianne would follow her gaze and freeze up. Annie pictured Malone grinning a devilish grin. "Please introduce yourself to the jury."

"Jennianne Smith." Her voice came out raspy and barely audible.

Judge Killam leaned over the bench. "Miss, you'll have to speak up so they can hear you way over there." He pointed to the far end of the jury box.

Jennianne nodded once without looking at the judge.

"Now tell us your name again." Judge Killam sounded like he was addressing a child.

"Jennianne Smith."

"Where are you from?" Annie would provide the jury with the basics and get through this as efficiently as possible. She felt her heart pounding in her chest.

"Charlestown." Jennianne hunched and hugged her arms.

"Where do you live in Charlestown?"

"Thirty-six Walford Way."

"Who do you live with?"

"My mother. But, you know, she's . . . she's down in Florida." She didn't make eye contact with anyone.

"Are you familiar with Trevor Shea?" Annie knew she couldn't start right in with the night of the murder. She had to ease Jennianne into it and talking about Trevor was the best way.

"Umm. Yeah."

"How well did you know him?" Annie watched Jennianne sucking her knuckle.

"All my life."

"Tell us a little about Trevor when he was younger?" Annie smiled and gestured toward the jury box. She hoped Jennianne would follow her lead and look at them, too. They had always practiced with a pretend jury in the room in Scituate.

"Um . . . Trevor was a funny kid, like sort of a goofball with his big ears that stuck out. Used to fool around in class, make everybody laugh when he did stuff."

Annie softened her voice. She noticed Jennianne concentrating on the painting. "What did he do?"

"Things like holding his pencil between his lip and nose as long as he could. Um, make funny faces. He'd just blurt stuff out. Like whatever came into his mind. Like when everybody's thinking the same thing, but nobody says it?" Jennianne peeked at the jury for the first time. "The nuns, they didn't like that. Always yelling at him, you know?"

"What was he like later on?" Annie asked.

"Was always wandering around, looking at things that nobody else cared about, doing this or that. Making paintings. Like, a free spirit type."

Annie took a deep breath and exhaled. This was perfect, way better than she'd anticipated. Her gut told her to move on, but it was also important to educate the jury about the victim since Chris refused to do it. Annie decided to dwell on Trevor for just another minute or so; she needed the crucial sympathy vote.

"Are you familiar with Trevor's art?"

"Yup."

"Tell us a little about it." Annie watched the jurors; they seemed mesmerized by Jennianne now. It was going so well.

"Well . . . he . . . Trev was wicked talented. I could watch him paint for hours on whichever street corner he picked. You'd look over his shoulder and it was like perfect, like better than a picture."

Annie walked to her table and grabbed the giant painting depicting the circle of kids in the playground. "Do you recognize this?"

Jennianne nodded. "He won a prize for that and was even in the newspaper."

"Did you see him paint any of it?"

"I remember him doing that one near the playground over by the church. He would set up his easel every day in the same spot like for a couple weeks."

"Your Honor, at this time I move to introduce this painting into evidence." Annie angled the painting toward the jury.

"No way," Malone said.

"Objection." Clancy walked around his table. "Sidebar." The judge motioned them both up to the bench.

"Your Honor," Clancy whispered. "Once again, I'm objecting on grounds of relevancy. The prejudicial impact of this painting clearly outweighs any probative value."

"I disagree." Annie looked up at Judge Killam. "It serves to educate the jury about the victim. He was a talented painter." Annie really wanted the jurors to examine the painting up close during deliberations and connect with Trevor on another level.

"It's already been well established that Trevor Shea was a talented artist." Clancy tapped his index finger on the side of the bench. "This painting is disturbing. It shows a kid being bullied. The jurors may think my client's the bully here, and we have not established any connection between the kids in this painting and Mr. Malone whatsoever."

Judge Killam rubbed his chin. "Once again, I agree with attorney Clancy. The painting cannot be admitted into evidence."

"But Your Honor?"

"Commonwealth, your objection will be noted for the record."

Annie leaned the painting back against her table, facing Jennianne. The jurors must be wondering why Judge Killam wouldn't allow it into evidence. She resumed her position near the podium, and watched Jennianne gnawing at her cuticles.

"Jennianne, did Trevor ever have a drug problem?"

"Used to."

"What do you mean?"

"He was into heroin for a bit, but had got cleaned up. Did the metha-done thing, went to rehab, really started getting his act together." Jenni-anne studied the painting again. "Trevor was making something of himself and we were all rooting for him. That's why . . ." Her voice trailed off.

"Did Trevor ever draw or paint a portrait of you?" Annie knew the an-swer would make a good transition to the night of Trevor's murder.

"He started one."

"When?"

Jennianne crossed her arms and huddled over the witness stand. "That night."

"Which night?" Annie held her breath.

"Um, last fall." She fiddled with a section of her hair. "You know."

"Are you referring to November tenth of last year?"

"Mmm hmm."

"Do you remember what you were doing around seven P.M. on that day?" Annie tried to soften her voice; she sensed Jennianne's fear. They had to get through this.

"Uh." Jennianne kept her face pointed down. "Was home."

"Did you have a boyfriend at the time?" Annie noticed several jurors with creased brows, scrutinizing Jennianne.

"Yeah. I was seein' Billy Malone," she mumbled. "Not no more though."

"What happened that evening?" Annie's mouth turned dry.

"Well . . . Billy called to tell me he invited some people over to my apartment. He said to buy a case of Bud and get cigarettes."

"Did you?"

"Yeah, I went to the packy."

"What happened when you got back?"

"He was already there. At my place. With his brother Frank. Billy had got a key so he could let himself in." Jennianne gazed at the painting.

"What were Billy and Frank talking about when you first arrived?"

"Objection!" Clancy jumped to his feet. "Hearsay."

"Sustained."

Annie didn't mean to draw the objection from Clancy; she felt herself rushing. *Slow down.* "Focusing on Billy, what did he say?"

"He was talkin' about Trevor right before I came in the door and then stopped quick."

"What did he say exactly?"

"Um. I'm not sure, but like he couldn't deal with him no more, I guess, something like that."

"Objection!" Clancy rose again. "Speculative. Move to strike."

"Sustained."

Jennianne looked away from the painting and chewed on her thumbnail.

Annie ran her tongue back and forth across her lower teeth. She had practiced this over and over with Jennianne. She warned her against using words like *guess* or phrases like *I'm not sure.* Jennianne had to be specific with her answers or else Clancy would pounce and crucial testimony would get barred. She looked at the jury. They would have to read between the lines.

"What happened after that?" Annie asked.

Jennianne looked at the painting again. "Billy threw a fit because I got Genesee instead of Bud. It was on sale. Umm, and they helped theirselves to beers without even thankin' me or nothin'. Frank was pissed off, too, because he said I got the cheap shit."

Judge Killam cleared his throat. "Watch your language."

"How well did you know Frank?" Annie glanced at the jury.

"Pretty good." She grimaced. "I never liked him though. Sometimes he would pat me on the ass when his brother wasn't lookin'. Thought it was funny, but it made me feel sleazy."

Annie nodded. She was surprised Jennianne had volunteered that part about Frank. *Just don't look at Malone. Keep staring at the painting.*

"Did anyone else come to your apartment?" Annie placed a hand on her hip.

"About seven thirty, Trevor did."

"Who invited him?"

"Not me." Jennianne shrugged. "Must've been Billy or Frank."

"Objection." Clancy waved. "Speculation again, Your Honor."

"Sustained."

"What did Trevor do?"

"He just like whipped out this big sketching pad and started drawing me."

"Is this the pad?" Annie walked toward the witness stand, and raised an artist's pad with a dark pencil drawing of Jennianne.

"Yeah, there it is. That's me." Jennianne appeared caught up in the moment. "He was going to turn it into a painting."

"Your Honor, at this time, I move to introduce this pad into evidence." Annie showed it to Clancy. It was a simple sketch, nothing prejudicial like the other painting.

"No way." Malone nudged Clancy. "That can't go in, right?"

"Objection." Clancy leaned over his table. "Relevance again."

"Overruled. The evidence is admitted."

As Annie carried the pad over to Clerk Fallon to be labeled, she noticed Malone looked even more perturbed than Clancy. *Good.* Perhaps the tides were turning.

"Why was Trevor drawing you that night?" Annie asked.

"Billy just like out of the blue asked him to do a painting of me. It was weird."

"Did they pay Trevor?"

"Billy was gonna pay him after." Jennianne tucked her hair behind her ear. "They were like acting wicked nice and stuff. They even gave him a beer."

"Did you know ahead of time that Trevor would be sketching you?"

"Nope because I would've done my hair better. I kinda knew something was up because it wasn't my birthday or nothing, and Billy and Frank never gave a crap about Trevor or art. Never."

"Objection." Clancy bolted up. "Move to strike again. This isn't fair."

"Sustained." Judge Killam peered down at Jennianne. "Miss, please refrain from speculation. Just answer the question before you."

Annie was thrilled Jennianne had blurted the part out about her suspicions. The jurors would certainly dwell on it. "What happened after that?"

"Um, everybody smoked and drank for about twenty minutes. Made small talk, tellin' him how good he was, yah know, while he was sketching me. Then, Billy and Frank went to the kitchen."

"What did you do?"

"I got up to go to the fridge to get another beer, but they told me to stay with Trevor 'til he was finished. But I hung back and listened in. I knew something was fishy."

"Objection, move to strike."

"Sustained."

"Did you hear anything?" Annie had gone over this part many times.

"Yeah, I heard Billy say, 'Let's get this over with quick, I can only put up with this faggot for so long.' Then I went back to the couch just in time because they came in."

"Were they carrying anything?"

"Yeah, Billy was carrying a CVS drugstore bag."

"What happened next?"

"Billy told me to go back in the kitchen and get more beers. I told him, since they were just in the kitchen, why didn't they get their own beers. He yelled at me to shut the F up and do it. When I was getting the beers, I heard Billy say, 'You done good, Trevor. It looks just like her. I got something for yah.'"

"Did you get the beers?"

Jennianne nodded. "I did what I was told."

"What did you see when you went back into the living room?" Annie clasped her hands; they were almost done.

"Trevor was holding a bag of heroin. Billy was telling him to go ahead and cook it up. There was a syringe and a cooker spoon on the table."

"Do you know where the syringe came from?" Annie stepped toward the jury.

"No, I was surprised by that."

"Did Trevor have a syringe or cooker spoon when he came in?"

Jennianne looked down. "Not that I noticed."

"Was he carrying a CVS bag?"

"Objection," Clancy said. "Leading."

"Sustained."

Annie had to reword her question. "Was Trevor carrying anything when he showed up at your apartment that evening?"

Jennianne shrugged. "Not that I recall."

"What happened next?" Annie felt like reaching across the courtroom and hugging Jennianne. She was getting through this and keeping her facts straight.

"Trevor tied up his arm real tight, cooked up the heroin, and shot it up." Jennianne's voice cracked.

"Did anyone else have heroin?" Annie asked.

"Nope, just Trevor. Billy and Frank don't do heroin."

"Did they offer you any?"

"There wasn't none left."

"What did Trevor do after injecting the heroin?" Annie glanced at the jurors, who were listening intently.

"Leaned his head against the back of the couch. Closed his eyes like he was enjoying it for a minute."

"Did anything happen after that?" Annie held her breath.

"Did it ever. When Trevor got up he looked like . . . just really out of it."

"Can you explain?"

"I don't know. Like walking funny, sorta wobbly. Yah know, like his eyes glazed over and stuff. He took a few steps, then he stopped and just stood there in the middle of the living room like a total zombie."

"What happened next?"

Jennianne looked above the painting, toward the back wall. "I remember he grabbed his chest with both hands. It was wicked scary. His face went all out of whack. His mouth was wide open, like he couldn't breathe. He was shaking, too. After that, Trevor, he . . ."

"What? What did Trevor do?"

"Just dropped to the floor."

"Tell the jury what you did after you saw Trevor drop to the floor."

"I yelled, 'Oh my God, I'm going to call nine-one-one.' And then Billy . . . and then Billy." Jennianne looked at Malone for the first time and blanched.

"What did Billy do?" Annie jiggled the painting, hoping to distract her from Malone.

"When?" Jennianne regarded Annie as if she had no clue what she was asking.

"After you yelled, 'Oh my God, I'm going to call nine-one-one.' What did Billy do?"

Jennianne's gaze shot back to Billy. Her eyes widened. Annie panicked. *Please get yourself together.*

"Jennianne?"

"It's all happening so fast."

"Is that what he said?" Annie moved closer to the witness stand.

"No." Jennianne squeezed her temples like she had a migraine.

"Do you need a moment to collect your thoughts?" Annie felt desperate.

Jennianne scanned the spectators' gallery. With shaking fingers, she reached into her handbag and took out a pack of Virginia Slims and a hot pink lighter. Annie was speechless.

"What are you doing?" Judge Killam craned his neck. "Miss, there's no smoking in my courtroom."

"Oh." Jennianne looked up at the judge with a vacant expression. "I wasn't going to smoke."

"Are you feeling okay?" Annie pointed to the water pitcher on the clerk's table. "Would you like some water? Do you need a break?"

Jennianne gave Annie a hard look. "What if you don't get twelve votes?"

"Pardon?"

"If you don't get twelve votes does Billy go free?"

"Objection." Clancy stood with his hands on his hips. "We've had enough of this charade."

"Because he's from Charlestown." Jennianne pointed into the gallery off to the right. "And I know him." She pointed to someone on the opposite side. "He's from Charlestown, too."

"Miss, Miss!" Judge Killam stood. "That's enough. There's no question before you."

"And she's from Charlestown." Jennianne ignored the judge. "I seen her on the street."

"Commonwealth!" Judge Killam addressed Annie and spread his arms. "Control your witness!"

Jennianne closed her eyes and covered her ears. "Don't hear nothing. Don't see nothing. Never talk to cops."

"Enough!" Judge Killam hammered his gavel three times and faced the jury. "You are to completely disregard this witness's unresponsive statements. This court is in recess."

34

JENNIANNE!" ANNIE SHOVED the door to the ladies' room with both hands and barged in.

A woman finished washing her hands and pointed to the first stall. Annie peered underneath and recognized the blue shoes and dress.

"Is she alright?" Callahan caught the door after the other woman scurried out.

"Just go. I'll handle it."

He looked taken aback.

"Leave us alone," Annie said.

Annie watched Callahan shake his head and step out. She had snapped at him, but couldn't help herself. She heard the sound of vomiting and the splash as it struck the toilet water.

Why now? Annie grasped the ceramic sink. She wanted to yank it from the wall, throw it down, and shatter it into a million pieces with a baseball bat. She pictured those puckered lips, that look of pure joy, flash across Malone's face. *She had come so close to beating him.*

Annie heard Jennianne cough and spit several times. She marched to the first stall, and gripped the top of the worn brown metal door. She turned and whacked it hard with her hip. The door flung open, striking Jennianne in the foot as she knelt on the cement floor over the bowl. *Pathetic.* She twisted around, and Annie noticed the vomit near the corner of her mouth and all over the toilet. *Next time, lift the seat.*

"What just happened in there?" Annie stared hard at Jennianne, forcing her to avert her gaze.

"I don't know." She wiped her mouth on her sleeve. "I just don't know about this."

"Did someone threaten you?"

"I . . . I can't go on." Her head bobbed forward, nearly striking the toilet.

"But you've got to. Without you, we have no case."

"Do I have to say what happened next?" Jennianne addressed the rust-colored water in the bowl.

"That's the most important part," Annie said.

"I can't go through with it in front of him."

Annie clenched her fists and refrained from shaking her. "Remember what he did to you?"

"I got a bad feeling about this. He's gonna win. I can see it in his eyes."

Those satanic eyes of steel. Why do they always win? So close.

Jennianne heaved over the bowl. Nothing came out.

"Pull yourself together." Annie stepped over Jennianne's legs and flushed the toilet. She couldn't stand looking at the floating chunks of vomit anymore, and the stench was nauseating. "You almost got to the important part, just another minute more." Annie leaned over her. "I don't get it. You already told the whole thing to the grand jury."

"But he wasn't there watching me." Jennianne gazed into Annie's eyes. "If I stop now, he'll spare me. I know that look—if I go on, I'm dead."

"We have you in a safe house."

"But all his people are watching me from the audience."

"You're paranoid."

"They're everywhere."

"No way!" Annie shouted.

"They're gonna get me."

"How can they find you if you don't go out?"

Jennianne spread her hands on both sides of the toilet seat and leaned over the bowl. "I'm a rat," she whispered.

"No." Annie struck the metal stall. "You're not a rat. You took Trevor Shea off the pile of dead cases."

"Dead cases . . ."

Annie tilted her head back and ran her fingers through her hair. She had to convince Jennianne to get back up there at all costs. "You want to turn your life around?"

Jennianne nodded at the toilet.

"You're so young, Jennianne. You have your whole life ahead of you. We'll get you in night school, back on your feet again. I know you want better for yourself. I can help you. You want kids someday, don't you?"

Jennianne sniffled. She was crying now.

"Think about Trevor. You've known him since first grade. You owe him this much, Jennianne. You don't want Malone to get away. We have that bastard by the throat. We're so close. So close, we can strangle him." Annie pictured her hands closing around Malone's neck, cutting off his air, his face turning a grotesque shade of blue, and then gray.

Someone clapped right outside the bathroom stall. Annie turned around. It was Chris. How did he get into the ladies' room? Where was Callahan? He must've left in a huff after she yelled at him.

"Bravo!" Chris raised his arms and clapped louder. "Where do I sign up? You could talk Trevor right out of the grave." He addressed Jennianne and pointed at Annie. "Don't trust her."

Annie gasped. "What's wrong with you? You won't lift a finger to testify for your brother. Now you barge in here and try to destroy his case?"

Chris ignored her and made eye contact with Jennianne, her face was streaked with red tear tracks. "She's not one of us." He pointed at Annie again. "When she's done with you, Jennianne, she'll throw you out with the trash. We take care of our own."

"Bullshit, not one of you." Annie stepped toward Chris until their faces nearly touched. "I grew up in Charlestown."

"You and your family bolted, ran away when things got a little hairy. You're a sellout." Chris jerked away. "Look what you're doing to her. She's a wreck."

Jennianne was wedged next to the toilet and wall, on all fours, hyperventilating.

Annie inhaled and forced herself to ignore Chris and soften her words. "I know it's hard, Jennianne, but I have to keep you under oath. I've got to. You need to understand that you always pay a price when you testify because someone is not going to like what you say."

"Don't do it," Chris said.

"Will you shut up!" Annie shouted. "Or I'll—"

"Or you'll what?" Chris grinned, mocking her. "Come on, what are you going to do to *me* now?" He clutched his chest.

"Please, Miss Fitzgerald." Jennianne gasped for air. "I can't do this."

Annie stared her down. "You can and you will."

"I'm begging you, please let me off the hook. I'll do anything else for you, anything."

"Jennianne, you don't have a choice. Tomorrow morning, you're either on the stand or under arrest."

Jennianne's eyes widened. "For what?"

"Conspiracy to commit murder."

"Wow." Chris raised his arms. "I can't believe this."

Jennianne gripped the toilet paper holder with both hands. "But I didn't . . ."

"Blackmail!" Chris stuck his face close to Annie's. "You'll do whatever it takes."

"I didn't kill Trevor." Jennianne sobbed. "Annie, you know that's not true."

Annie stared her down. "I'll decide what's true."

35

JENNIANNE HOISTED THE bedroom window all the way up and straddled the sill. She relished the cold night air, the freedom. She had been curled up in bed, smoking a cigarette when she felt the urge for a drink. Nicotine didn't cut it. *Just say what happened next. Annie will decide what's true.* She couldn't trust Annie no more. Why had she ever? Chris was right; she's not one of *us*. Not now, not ever. What had she been thinking when she gave up Paul Garrity's name? What would Annie and Callahan do? Arrest him right in front of his family?

Jennianne needed something to relieve the pressure, and help her think . . . *or not think at all.* They had a cop car stationed out front. Was it to protect her or to keep her locked up? *Annie will decide what's true. Escape,* her instincts screamed. Jennianne zipped her black leather jacket all the way up, and threw her pocketbook down to the ground. The keys jingled when it landed. She twisted onto her stomach, dangled both legs out the window, and slowly inched herself down until she hung from the sill by her fingers. Jennianne released her grip and dropped about six feet to the hard ground. Pain flared in her right knee. *Alcohol will take care of it.* She glanced up and wondered how she'd get back in. *Screw it and screw Annie, too.*

A chilling sea gust whipped Jennianne's hair as she circled the backyard toward her car. It was parked far enough away from the cop that he wouldn't notice nothing. She pulled away from the curb with the lights off, and drove to the Cumberland Farms near Scituate Harbor for two packs of Virginia Slims and a scratch ticket. After that, she swerved into the parking lot of T.K.O. Malley's without signaling. A car following close behind nearly rear-ended her.

Jennianne grabbed a seat at the bar and dangled her purse over the back of the stool. The bartender winked at her.

"I'll have a shot of tequila with a lime and salt and a Madras."

"My kinda girl. Tab?"

"Sure." Jennianne noticed the stares directed at her from several men at the bar. It wouldn't take long before the free drinks rolled her way. She shook salt on her hand, licked it, and downed the shot. The burning sensation felt good. She sucked the lime and sipped the cold Madras.

Jennianne scanned the bottles of booze with their colorful labels along the top shelf behind the bar. What next? *Annie will decide what's true.* What is true, Trevor? If that's what you painted, tell me? I'm already dead, just like you. Jennianne pictured Trevor perched behind his easel in that flimsy lawn chair with the frayed blue straps. She had promised to get him a new chair before he fell through the old one. *Empty promises.* She drained the Madras; the ice touched her lips and then clinked against the glass.

"That guy over there wants to buy you a drink." The bartender pointed with his elbow and Jennianne nodded without looking.

"Rum and Coke."

Jennianne watched him make the drink without acknowledging the donor. She went back to imagining Trevor. His flat metal paint box would be opened on the ground next to him. On his left, he kept his wax paper pallet where he'd mix all those beautiful colors. His paintings were vibrant, full of life. Better than life, so detailed and telling. Trevor always saved the eyes for last. They'd be sketched lightly in pencil, just empty sockets for so long. When he started filling in the eyes, Jennianne knew he was almost finished. Trevor used a dab of every single color—except black—when he created them. Thoughts, fears, the soul itself poured out through those textured eyes. Jennianne remembered the painting of the girl wrapped in the rubber rug pad. That was her, Billy's old girlfriend, Lydia Thompson. *We take care of our own.* The orange streetlights reflected off her golden brown irises like a low-burning flame, one that was about to be snuffed out. There was another face in that reflection, too, the shadow of a face, and a terrified scream.

"Another shot?" A disheveled man with greasy hair invaded her space.

"Whisky." Jennianne pictured Lydia's eyes again. *God, Trevor.* She tipped her head back and drained the shot. Blue, hazel, green—she'd seen multiple eyes come to life on Trevor's canvases. He never had anyone model for him, except for her, that one time. She remembered when he set his easel up on Harvard Street in front of a brownstone. Jennianne would go out of her way to watch him create that painting. It showed a heavyset man sitting on his stoop, smoking a cigarette. Those eyes were a deep, haunting gray. A knowing gray, bursting with color. *The colors of fear.* Jennianne had peered over Trevor's shoulders as he painted that man's terror. Trevor hadn't known she was there. *No.* Of course he knew. Trevor knew everything. *How did you see?* You were one of us, Trev, and we take care of our own like Chris said. *What made you see these things?* What made you so different?

Jennianne went back to her rum and Coke. It was strong, mostly rum. She recalled the portrait that Trevor had sketched of her on the night he died. It looked just like her, the long hair, high cheekbones. She wondered how Trevor would've filled in her eyes at the end. Why had he agreed to do it for Billy? She never found out how much he was going to get paid. Did he need the money? Was Trevor back on heroin? She had been baffled by the whole arrangement; she knew Trevor didn't like Billy. *Don't go out with him, Jennianne,* he'd warned on numerous occasions.

The greasy man babbled in her ear; his breath smelled like tacos. Jennianne mumbled disinterested answers to his questions. He touched the skin beneath her sweater on her lower back. She tensed and pulled away. Most men thought of her as an easy, dumb blonde. She used to be smart in school way back when. Billy thought she was smart, and he used to love her. A lump formed in her throat.

Jennianne's cell phone rang. When she looked down to check the number, she saw double, and had to concentrate. It was Detective Callahan. She hesitated. If she answered, he'd hear the noises from the bar in the background. *Don't answer. We take care of our own.*

Jennianne pictured Trevor sitting behind his easel again, paintbrush between his fingers. Could she testify for him? Could she be Trevor's voice? *Where are all your beautiful paintings, Trevor?* She wondered if Paul knew; he'd been Trevor's best friend forever. They used to watch him paint together; Jennianne had always liked Paul. *God, I'm so sorry, Paul.* Annie would destroy him; she was so desperate to win. Annie needed to get her hands on more paintings, but she'd never find them. Perhaps Chris had destroyed them all. *You just couldn't stop your brother from painting—no matter how hard you tried.*

The cell phone rang again. *Callahan.* Jennianne also noticed two text messages from him, which she didn't bother to read. She shut the phone off. *Let him come find me.* Her legs felt wobbly and she crashed into a chair on her way to the bathroom. She should probably call Callahan back. He'd make sure she got home safely. That guy with the taco breath made her nervous; he looked kind of familiar. She felt nauseous for a moment. Could he be from Charlestown? Jennianne used the bathroom, and fluffed her hair in front of the bathroom mirror. No, he just wanted a one-night stand. She could use that tonight. *Just a few more drinks and maybe he'd look better.* She'd have to find him some Tic Tacs.

"I'll have another Madras." Jennianne tried to speak as clearly as she could when she resumed her seat at the bar.

"You sure? How about a glass of water instead." The bartender scooped ice into a glass and poured water from one of his taps. "Here."

"Thanks." Jennianne drank the cold water. "But, I'm good enough for one more."

"Don't worry, I'm driving her home." Taco breath placed an arm around her back, his fingertips stroked her skin again.

Jennianne wanted the drink. "Yeah, I'm going with him."

36

NO ONE ANSWERED when Annie banged on Chris's front door. The house appeared dark, empty. *Go home, get some rest.* She visualized Trevor's painting of the circle of kids in the playground. She had to get her hands on more. She yearned for Trevor's paintings. If she could find them, she would beat Malone.

Annie walked back to her car and grabbed a flashlight from the glove box. She approached a front window, stood on tiptoes, and shined the light inside. Nothing but scattered clothes and furniture. She peered through every first-floor window. No paintings. As Annie circled around the back, she spotted a bulkhead attached to the building. She remembered Trevor's art studio had been located in the cellar.

Her cell phone rang. Annie unzipped her jacket pocket and looked at the screen. It was Callahan. She ignored him and walked toward the old bulkhead. Could she get in somehow? Take a quick peek? The phone rang again. *What does he want?*

Annie rolled her eyes and answered. "Did you locate Trevor's friend, Paul Garrity?"

"I did, but let's discuss it first. He's got a wife and kids, so—"

"We need to haul him in."

"I'm more concerned about Jennianne right now. She's not answering calls or texts."

"She's probably sleeping."

"I sent the officer to her door, and she's not responding." Callahan paused. "I'm worried."

Annie bit her lip. She hoped Jennianne hadn't done anything drastic. "Tell the cop to break in and check."

"Okay." Callahan sighed. "You were pretty tough on her today."

Annie tensed. "I was doing my job."

"Right." He clicked off.

Annie zipped the phone back into her pocket. Who was Callahan to pass judgment? She squatted next to the bulkhead and examined it. He's the one who likely bribed Domenico. And, what about all his interrogation tactics? Annie gritted her teeth and walked to the other side of the bulkhead. There were several rusted spots near the top. She struck the largest spot with her metal flashlight as hard as she could. On the second try, the rust disintegrated, creating a hole large enough to insert her arm all the way to her shoulder. Annie felt around with her fingers, found a dead bolt, and forced it open. She withdrew her arm and yanked the bulkhead door up from the outside.

"Don't do it," Annie whispered to herself as she shined her light down the cement steps into a yawning cellar. She took a step down anyway. *Why are you doing this?* Annie took another step and continued until she reached the bottom. It smelled like mold mixed with turpentine. She stopped and listened, and heard only faded street noises in the background. She shined her light in a wide arc. The small unfinished cellar contained a gray cement floor with exposed beams all around. Someone had tacked old newspaper clippings up and down the wood. She took a closer look at the yellowed paper. They were mostly stories about crimes and some contained photographs of old crime scenes. Annie removed several and stuck them in her jacket pocket.

Her cell rang; the loud ring tone startled her. Annie reached in her pocket and flipped the switch on the side, silencing it. She should've shut it off before.

A light shined in her face. Annie flinched. *Chris?* No, it was her flashlight beam reflecting back from a full-length mirror leaning against the wall. She breathed a sigh of relief. *Thank God.*

Annie continued moving forward, searching with the light. Off to the right, she spotted a workbench littered with paintbrushes, razor blades, and wax paper pallet pads, some used, some new. Canvas board, a hammer, rulers, and other artist tools had been laid out. This was Trevor's space. She felt his presence.

Annie sneezed twice and stood still, holding her nose. She had to stay quiet. The mold and dust were making her stuffy. She sneezed again. What if Chris was upstairs? What if he heard her? What would she say if he came down and found her? *What the hell are you thinking? Why are you down here?* Something above her creaked. She turned off the light and held her breath. Annie felt chilled as she stood alone in the dark. All old houses make noises, she convinced herself. *Another creak.* Was she losing her mind? Lawyers weren't supposed to be sneaking around in old cellars. *Get out now.*

Annie switched the flashlight on again as she turned around to head back out. She froze when the beam danced across a giant unfinished oil painting propped on top of an old cane chair. Annie tiptoed closer and examined the canvas. It was a portrait, half-finished. The short hair . . . big ears . . .

"Trevor," she whispered. "You were making a self-portrait." Annie touched the canvas. The clothes, hair, and most of the face had been filled in with paint. He had used such an array of colors, making the facial features so vivid. The eyes and lips remained sketched in pencil. *Eerie, yet so beautiful.* Annie's fingers trembled as she traced the cheek and the textured hair. She closed her eyes and imagined Trevor dabbing the canvas with his paintbrush. This was his last work, she knew it. She pictured Trevor examining his face in the mirror as he painted. What did you see in yourself? What were you trying to say?

"Where are the rest of your paintings, Trevor?" she asked.

Someone grabbed her arms from behind, just below the shoulders. Annie screamed and twisted her body, but the hands held her tighter. She dropped her flashlight, it rolled across the floor, and came to a rest next to the mirror. The beam bounced back, creating a subdued, eerie illumination.

"What are you doing here?"

Annie recognized Chris's voice. "Get your hands off me," she said.

"You're trespassing." His words sounded like a low growl.

"You're hiding evidence. I demand to see your brother's paintings."

"Where's your warrant?"

"I knocked, you didn't answer."

"So that gives you the right to break in through the cellar, and sneak around with a flashlight? You think you're above the law, don't you?" he whispered.

"No," Annie said.

"You decide what's true. Remember? What makes you any better than Malone? Actually, you're worse because you have the law on your side."

"I'm not like him. You don't understand me."

"Oh I do. You're obsessed." He pointed to Trevor's self-portrait. "Like my brother. It's what killed him."

"Why do you hate us?" She twisted around; their faces nearly touched. His eyes glittered in the low light.

Chris stared at her. "I didn't hate Trevor. Only you."

"You hated everything Trevor stood for, his art, his message."

"What do you know about my brother?"

"That he wanted things to change around here." Annie felt her phone vibrating in her pocket. "And so do I."

"You don't belong." Chris continued holding her arms. "You never did."

"Let go." Annie kept her voice even and maintained eye contact.

Chris loosened his grip. Annie moved her hands up along his bare arms, over his neck, and through his hair.

"Annie—"

She grabbed his hair in her fists, forced his head forward, and kissed him hard on the lips. Chris tensed and then she could feel him letting go, giving in to her. Annie felt a burst of passion as she kissed him for several minutes.

She finally looked over Chris's shoulder, and her gaze locked onto the penciled-in eye sockets of Trevor's self-portrait. *No eyes,* yet it felt like he was watching her, studying her.

She jerked her head back, pushed Chris away, and tore across the cellar. Her hip struck a table and knocked something over; glass shattered. She barreled up the stairs, into the crisp night air, and kept running. *What the hell was she doing?* Her phone vibrated again.

37

JENNIANNE USED THE bathroom and stumbled out of T.K.O. Malley's. The taco breath guy creeped her out. She'd find another bar and have one more for the road. She leaned against a parked truck and scanned the street. Where was her car? She had to find it and get out of there before Taco realized she'd bolted. Her head felt dizzy as she made her way across the street to the parking lot. She spotted her car at the far end.

The door had been left unlocked—easier that way. Jennianne plunked down into the driver's seat and rested her head on the steering wheel. She could fall asleep right there. Should she find another bar or go home? The image of Trevor painting behind his easel popped into her mind.

"Trev, what should I do?" Jennianne's throat tightened and she started to cry. "Why? Why? Why do you keep painting? I can't do this no more, Trev." She sobbed. "I'm sorry. He's gonna kill me if I do. Don't you get it? You do, you get it, but you always keep going."

Jennianne wiped her face on her sleeve, and fished the keys from the pocket of her leather jacket. She stuck the key in the ignition, but it wouldn't fit. She jabbed it in the hole several times, no luck. Jennianne threw the keys against the windshield and cried again.

"Go to hell, Trevor. I hate you. I hate Annie. I can't do this." Jennianne hyperventilated as she sobbed. "Maybe I'll just kill myself like you did."

After several minutes, Jennianne grabbed the keys again and studied them. Maybe she had tried the brass door key by accident. She selected one of the silver keys and jammed it in. It worked; the car started. Jennianne breathed a sigh of relief. "I'm sorry, Trev." She wiped her eyes again. "I'll go home now, okay? I'll do this for you."

When her seat belt wouldn't clip, Jennianne threw it aside, and lit a cigarette. She backed out of the parking spot with one hand on the wheel, and decided she was good enough to drive.

Headlights shot through her driver's side window. Was it Taco? No way, he was still drinking at the bar. It didn't look like a cop car. If it was, Callahan could take care of another drunk driving arrest. He owed her.

Jennianne drove away from Scituate Harbor and turned off Front Street; the car behind her made the same quick turn. Was it following her? No, she decided, it was her imagination, just the lights reflecting off the dirty windshield, making it hard to see the road. She increased her speed and it did the same. Could it be that creep, Taco? No, she suddenly remembered her pocketbook. She'd left it dangling from her bar stool. Perhaps someone was trying to return it. She pulled over and stumbled out; her legs felt wobbly.

"What d'yah want?" Jennianne placed both hands on her hips and waited; the high beams blinded her. The driver's door opened and a thin figure stepped out. Jennianne shaded her eyes, struggling to see through the lights. It definitely wasn't Taco, he was on the fat side. The figure started walking toward her . . . carrying something, small, shiny. *Not her pocketbook.* Jennianne froze as panic crept up from her stomach to the back of her throat. She had a bad feeling. *Run. Get back in the car. Call Callahan.* Her cell was in her pocketbook back at the bar's. Find a pay phone. She didn't know Callahan's number. *Dial 911.*

Jennianne raced back to her car and dropped her cigarette. She twisted the ignition key, causing a resounding grinding of gears. She shifted into drive and jammed her foot on the accelerator. The tires squealed as she jolted forward. Her speed rose to sixty, then seventy. She spun out around the first sharp curve, but regained control. When she glanced back, the other headlights were gone. Jennianne continued speeding ahead and looking back. Nothing but darkness. Her chest pounded. *Cigarette. Need lighter.* She stuck her hands in both jacket pockets. *Had it fallen out? Find another one.* Jennianne opened the glove box and felt around. She remembered seeing one stuck between all the folded papers. She found it, but her fingers trembled so much that she couldn't get the lighter to flick on. She looked down at her thumb. *Come on. Come on.*

Jennianne felt a hard thud; her body lurched forward. She looked up and screamed as her car careened off the road.

An image hovered in her mind. A hand, a paintbrush, dabs of color filling in a void. *Eyes coming to life.*

38

I **THINK WE** *found your girl.* Callahan cringed as he replayed the words of the Scituate cop over and over in his mind. He rounded a curve in the road and the scene unfolded. The ominous flashing red and blue lights: cop cars, fire trucks, an ambulance. He drove onto the sandy shoulder and parked. It smelled like low tide as he stepped from his car. A gust blew off his baseball cap, but he didn't feel like retrieving it. Callahan walked with a robotic gait toward the scene. People called to him, but he blocked the voices out.

Spotlights illuminated Jennianne's mangled car; it had sailed off the road, over an embankment, and struck a tree. The driver's side corner was smashed in; a circle of white crushed glass adorned the windshield in the shape of a basketball.

Callahan spotted the telltale black blanket placed over a long, bumpy shape. He squatted next to it and pulled the corner back. *Jennianne. Those big green eyes.* They were wide open, staring up at him. *Terrified and beautiful at the same time.*

He felt numb as he stared into her eyes. He barely noticed the dried blood on her forehead. He should be used to this by now. He'd seen so many dead bodies. *Why you, Jennianne? We failed you. You were right all along.* He pictured her doubled over and crying when he had her cornered in that tiny interrogation room. They had used her. This was bound to happen. *You were so innocent.*

A car door slammed, the sound of someone running came from behind. Callahan turned to see Annie heading toward him in a pair of jeans and a T-shirt. He had called and left her a message about the accident. The Scituate Police must've filled in the rest of the details.

Callahan's instincts told him to hide Jennianne's face. *Protect Annie.* He stood and grabbed the end of the blanket, lifting it up to fold over her head. It fell sideways. Jennianne's face was still exposed. *Cover it. Don't let her see the green eyes.* Callahan lifted the corner again, but Annie ripped it from his hand.

"Don't you dare." Her gaze burned into Callahan. She squatted and pounded the pavement with her fist until her hand bled. "No! No! No!" She looked up at Callahan. "I hate you."

"Annie—"

"She's dead. Dead!" Annie gripped each side of Jennianne's leather jacket, and gazed at her face for a long time until finally resting her head on Jennianne's chest. "I'm so, so sorry, Jennianne." Callahan heard Annie sobbing, hyperventilating. He waited for a moment and then placed a hand on her shoulder.

"Don't you touch me. You repulse me." Annie shoved his hand away. She crossed herself and covered Jennianne back up with the blanket.

"I don't know what happened," Callahan said.

Annie jumped up and faced him. "This is your fault. It's your fault she's dead."

"Annie—"

"Where was the cop? Huh? Where was the cop? Tell me now."

"Right outside."

"She wasn't supposed to leave the house. Don't you get it?"

"I know. I told him that."

"So what's she doing out here then?" Annie pointed at the blanket. "On the side of the road. Dead."

"She must've snuck out."

"Not acceptable."

"I know."

"*You know.*" Annie shook her head. "You know nothing." She emphasized each word.

"Me?"

"Yeah, you. This is all your fault." She hauled back and shoved him in the chest with both hands; he almost fell over backward.

"Whoa." Callahan spread his arms to regain balance. "When Jennianne went missing, I tried to call you. You wouldn't pick up. I was down here looking for her. Where the hell were you?"

Annie came after him again, throwing punches on his shoulder with her bloody fist. "You didn't protect her."

"I did my best." The accusation stung.

"Look at her, you dumb shit, she's dead." Annie pointed at the corpse again. "How's that protecting her? How? Tell me how?" She screamed.

Callahan seethed. "Maybe she couldn't take you anymore! I heard you yelling at her in the bathroom today. Jennianne cracked because of you, Annie. You've been applying pressure since day one."

"No! You're the one obsessed with Billy Malone. *You.*" She lunged at him again, this time a full-on hit to the chest with her head. "Clancy's right. You'll do anything."

"Me?" Callahan turned and marched toward his car. He couldn't take it anymore.

"Yeah, anything to win." Annie followed him; he heard her footsteps closing in. "It's all you. You dragged me into this, remember? Called me out to the scene? Maybe this was just an accidental overdose. And now we got somebody else dead."

"Leave me alone." Callahan quickened his pace.

"Did you bribe Domenico?"

He spun around. "You're accusing me of bribery now?"

"Yeah I am and I want to know. Did you pay him off just to nail Malone? Did you?"

Callahan opened his car door and climbed in.

Annie grabbed the top of the door. "Bertrand was right to arrest you. You're nothing but a crooked cop."

Callahan removed her hand and slammed his car door.

"A crooked cop, do you hear me? A moron. A bastard. That's what you are. Because you killed her."

Callahan started the car.

She picked up a stone and whipped it at his windshield.

Callahan watched her turn and jog crookedly down the side of the road. She wiped her face with her fists. Annie was hysterically crying again, he could tell. He struck his forehead against the steering wheel. His ears rang. What the hell was happening? To Annie? To him? They were both unraveling, and Jennianne's green eyes were still wide open under that blanket.

39

CLANCY RESTED HIS briefcase on the defense table, and sat down to remove his wet galoshes. His bus had been on time, which meant he was early for once. The courtroom doors opened and slammed against the wall, the sound of hurried steps followed. Clancy knew it had to be Annie without looking back. Those steps were too determined to be anyone else.

"Good morning, Annie." Clancy stood as he always did for women. He turned around and smiled at Annie, but she didn't return the smile. She stomped toward him with head and shoulders slanted forward, arms swinging. He worried about her. Annie had trouble in her eyes, something deep down in the soul. Clancy had noticed it from the day they met. Annie reminded Clancy of his niece, Sarah, another talented lawyer with a turbulent past. They were both too young to carry the weight of the world on their shoulders.

Annie barged right up to Clancy and crossed her arms.

"What's the matter?" he asked.

"Jennianne Smith was killed last night."

Clancy felt paralyzed like he'd been sucker punched in the face. He couldn't find the words to respond.

"She's dead."

Dead. God no. "I'm so sorry." Clancy braced himself for the worst. "How did it happen?"

"Car wreck."

"A two-car accident? Anyone else killed?"

"No, just *her.*" Annie glared. "The car went off the road and over a bank. Head through windshield. How did your client discover her location?" She exhaled. "I guess we'll have to do better next time."

"What do you mean by that? Was she forced off the road?"

"It's under investigation as we speak."

"Any evidence?" Clancy prayed it was just an accident. The timing was suspect.

"We both know Billy Malone will do absolutely anything to get off."

Clancy recognized the truth in her statement. "Does Judge Killam know?"

"Not yet."

Clancy nodded. "I'd like to have a brief word with my client first."

"Jennianne Smith is dead." Clancy wrapped his fingers around the cold steel bars of the holding cell.

"What happens next?" Malone leaned against the cinder block wall.

The questions Malone didn't ask unnerved Clancy. *Doesn't he want to know what happened? How and when?* He searched Malone's eyes for a trace of knowledge, and came back with nothing.

"You knew what she was going to say. You read the grand jury transcript."

Malone shrugged. "So?"

Clancy wondered what Jennianne Smith meant to Billy Malone. Did he ever love her? She loved him until the moment she died. Clancy witnessed that look in her eyes, right before she broke down on the witness stand. It was a mix of love and fear. *What a shame.* Malone exuded power over women like no other. Clancy had seen many come and go over the years. *No one ever dumped Malone.*

Clancy looked at his client with disdain. "Jennianne was your girl-friend, you were intimate. Don't you even care that she's dead?"

"I asked you a question." Malone moved forward and shoved his face as close as he could to Clancy's. "What happens next?"

"I'm asking the questions today. Did you have anything to do with Jennianne Smith's death?" Clancy knew he sounded accusatory. He rarely took that tone with his clients.

"Not a thing." Malone's face resembled a porcelain mask, devoid of emotion.

"Doesn't look good." Clancy gave him a hard look. "I'm sorry for her, and I'm sorry for her family." He turned his back on Malone and walked away.

What really happened the night before? Clancy wished he knew. Did Jennianne get drunk or high and simply drive off the road? Did she miss a curve? Was the trial pressure too much for her? The forces had been working against that poor girl from the beginning. Clancy could feel the intensity streaming out of Annie the day before. Malone had also driven Detective Callahan to the brink of madness. Poor Jennianne had been trapped somewhere beneath the rubble. He visualized the pretty girl, brushing the long blond hair from her pretty green eyes. She never had a chance.

As Clancy entered the courtroom, he couldn't stop thinking about the possibility that his client had taken the law into his own hands. Malone knew what Jennianne was going to say if she found the courage to take the stand, and he didn't like taking chances. This is where it became tricky being a criminal defense lawyer. Over the years so many people had asked Clancy how he could defend murderers and get guilty guys off. I'm defending the Constitution, he would reply, making the state prove its case. After all, he'd seen his share of overzealous cops and prosecutors. It was his job to jump up and down on the scales of justice to maintain the balance. God forbid that one innocent guy lost his freedom. Clancy sighed. He could make his job sound so idealistic, but it was never that simple. *Far from it.* There were too many complicated ethical choices when it came to defending some of his clients. Clancy felt for all the mothers in the front row. Many times he'd gone to bed with a heavy heart.

Clancy reentered the empty courtroom, and sat behind his table. He stared into the vacant jury box. He would take Rehnquist, his golden retriever, for a long walk that night to think things over. In a few minutes he'd have to face an angry judge. He would need that porcelain mask.

Annie felt nauseous and delirious. She hadn't slept at all. She'd been wandering the hallway, looking for the court officer. Several times she forgot who she was looking for. The ghastly image of Jennianne's pale green eyes frozen in death loomed in her mind. *Jennianne. Why did you leave the house?* Annie kept asking herself the same questions. Why hadn't she answered Callahan's calls? What had she been doing with Chris?

Annie finally found Johnny in a vacant conference room sneaking a smoke. "We need to conference an urgent matter in chambers." She chose not to tell him what it concerned. Annie wanted to inform the judge herself.

Johnny took a long drag. "Can it wait a few minutes?"

"No, it's really important."

"Every damn thing you lawyers do is really important." He carefully snuffed the cigarette out to save the rest for later. "Alright, come on. Clancy here yet?"

"Yeah." Annie followed him into the courtroom where Clancy was sitting alone at his table. What would Judge Killam do? The future of the case looked grim. He'd probably declare a mistrial and Malone would be released. She pictured Malone floating above her like a giant Thanksgiving Day Parade balloon with those ominous black eyes twinkling in victory. She loathed him now more than ever.

"Does he know yet?" Clancy gestured in the direction of the judge's chambers.

"No, I waited for you to inform your client of the heartbreaking news," Annie said. "I hope he handled it okay."

Clancy frowned. Neither spoke as Johnny walked to the back to inform the judge.

After several minutes, Johnny poked his head from the door. "Go on in, he's waiting for you."

Clerk Fallon greeted them at the entrance to Judge Killam's chambers and held the door open wide.

"Have a seat." Judge Killam, dressed in a suit and tie, motioned to the chairs across from his mahogany desk. He sat in a large leather chair behind the desk and sipped a cup of coffee. Bookshelves, diplomas, and various other certificates adorned the walls. An adjacent table held framed photographs of the judge back when he was in the marines and several pictures of his family on the ski slopes.

Annie slumped down in a chair. Her head throbbed.

"Would anyone care for coffee?" Judge Killam lifted his mug.

"No, thank you," Annie said.

"How about you, Buddy?"

"No, thanks, Judge."

"Well, you're all doing a terrific job out there. I enjoy having good lawyers in my courtroom." He smiled.

Annie wished they were present for something else, *anything else*. Without the black robe, Judge Killam seemed to be on the same level as the attorneys.

"I'm curious, have you reached a plea bargain?" Judge Killam rubbed his hands together.

"It's Jennianne Smith." Annie's voice sounded hoarse; she cleared her throat.

"Ah, yes. Not an easy witness. Do you have her under control today?"

Annie's jaw tightened. "She is. Very much so, in fact."

"Good. I can't have outbursts in my courtroom."

Annie leaned forward. "It's not your courtroom because this is Charlestown. They can find anybody. They can control anybody. They can kill—"

"Whoa, whoa." Judge Killam raised his hands.

"Anybody."

"Annie?" The judge wrinkled his brow.

"Jennianne Smith is dead," she said.

"What?"

"She was killed in a car accident last night."

He wiped his brow. "Does it look like foul play?"

"Under criminal investigation." Annie looked at Clancy.

The judge sprang to his feet, lifted a heavy law book, and slammed it onto his desk, spilling his coffee.

Johnny rushed in. "Everything okay?"

Judge Killam's face flushed. "Your client had something to do with this." He pointed at Clancy. "I know he did. That son-of-a-bitch won't get away with it this time."

"You have no proof." Clancy raised his voice. "I just spoke with him and he denied it."

The judge swatted the air. "I don't believe you or your client."

Clancy jumped up. "You're calling me a lawyer? I mean, liar? I resent that and request you resign from this case at once."

"Siddown!"

"I will not."

"Come on." Annie addressed Clancy. "We all know Billy Malone's M.O. He needed to control my witness, so he found a way to kill her."

"No." Clancy spun toward her. "He denied any wrongdoing. Must've been an accident."

"Right, an accident." Annie snickered. "Did they find a syringe in her hand?"

Clancy waggled a finger. "Good point, Miss Fitzgerald. Let's figure that out before we go pointing fingers."

"Enough!" Judge Killam banged the book again, and addressed Annie. "What do you want me to do?"

Annie was caught off guard and had to think of something fast. She didn't want the judge to declare a mistrial. But without Jennianne, they had no case. Malone knew that. She racked her brain. If only they had more evidence, more witnesses.

"It looks like you'll have to declare a mistrial," Clancy said.

"I didn't ask you, counselor."

"But under the circumstances, Judge?" Clancy spread his arms.

"I can use the grand jury transcript." The idea popped into Annie's mind and she simply blurted the words out without giving it much thought.

Clancy's face contorted. "You can't use that."

"One more word out of you, counselor, and I'll have you escorted out of here." Judge Killam marched across the room from the window to his desk about ten times. Annie held her breath; she had him thinking.

"Here's what I'll do. The jury will be excused for the rest of the week. We'll see what happens with the accident investigation. I'll hear arguments Monday morning regarding the admissibility of the grand jury transcript. You may fax your written briefs to my chamber over the weekend, preferably by two o'clock Saturday."

"Thank you, Your Honor," Annie said.

"One more thing," Judge Killam called out as they were heading toward the door. "I'm issuing a gag order. You're not to discuss any of this with the press. Is that clear?"

"Yes, Your Honor," they both said.

"And so help me." Judge Killam looked at Clancy. "If this poor girl's death is linked at all to the defendant, he will pay dearly."

40

A T 8:30 A.M. on Monday, Annie hurried up the Center Plaza steps two at a time in her high heels, lugging her heavy brief-case. She wished she had gotten an earlier start to avoid the in-evitable reporters stationed outside the courthouse. All weekend, the *Globe* and *Herald* had run front-page spreads. Both papers mentioned Charles-town's code of silence, and suggested Jennianne had been murdered for being a snitch. Annie quickened her pace when she saw the television vans. She kept her face pointed down and wore her hair pulled back, tucked neatly under her beret. Maybe they wouldn't notice her.

"Miss Fitzgerald?" A female reporter scrambled toward her with a camera-man in tow. "Was your lead witness killed for what she was going to say?" She stuck a microphone under Annie's chin.

"No comment." Annie circled around the reporter and increased her speed.

Two more closed in. "Was this another code of silence killing?"

"Anyone charged?"

"Did Malone order it?"

"I can't comment on the case." Annie pushed through the pack and into the building.

"Is Malone going to walk?"

A court officer waved her around security, and escorted her through the crowded hallway. Annie slipped into an elevator, and squeezed against the wall, gripping the handle of her briefcase with both hands. She cringed at the thought of the upcoming motion hearing. She hated arguing motions before judges, especially Judge Killam. She'd take a jury any day over a judge. In front of the jury she could employ her acting skills and art of persuasion, but arguing before a judge forced her to stand still and discuss meticulous case law.

Annie halted at the courtroom doors. It was so hard to go in there. Her stomach ached. How could she face all the mothers in the front row? She hoped they weren't in yet. *And Chris?* Annie had kept herself isolated all weekend researching and writing her motion. She hadn't even called Callahan after their fight on the night Jennianne died. Annie took a deep breath and forced herself to walk in. The gallery was already filling up, and the mothers had taken their regular seats. Annie nodded at them and kept going. What could she say? *One more dead, another mother for the group.*

Annie unpacked her briefcase and sat down. She hadn't seen Chris and she wasn't about to turn around and look for him. What would she say to him? Should she apologize for what happened in the basement? And, would she have to apologize to him for Jennianne's death? Annie had never felt so conflicted in her life. *And guilty.* If only she could do it all over. But would she do anything differently? She didn't know.

Annie stared at her legal pad where she had underlined her best arguments in red marker. She'd labored through the weekend reading over a hundred pages of case law from the United States Supreme Court and the Supreme Judicial Court of Massachusetts down to the lower levels of the federal and state courts. What if she lost the motion? Would she have to dismiss the case? She watched the guards escort Malone to the defense table. He mouthed "good morning" to her. *She hated him.* Clancy came in and said hello, but Annie barely acknowledged him.

The gallery rose shortly after nine when Judge Killam assumed the bench. Annie had never seen it so jam-packed for a motion hearing. The case had certainly evolved into the most highly publicized murder trial Annie had ever prosecuted. According to rumor, the case was about to receive national attention from *60 Minutes*. They were probably present, taking notes with the rest of the reporters out there. Judge Killam had banned television cameras from the courtroom from the very beginning.

Annie looked at Malone, appearing gallant in his tan suit and red tie. The bastard winked at her. He knew everyone would blame her if the case went sour. Annie wished she could somehow connect him to Jennianne's car accident. No doubt he was involved, but could they ever prove it?

"Good morning." Judge Killam's voice thundered throughout the courtroom, sounding louder and more powerful than ever. The very survival of the case teetered on his decision and he knew it. "I received written briefs from both sides over the weekend addressing the issue of whether the prior recorded testimony of a witness appearing before the grand jury is admissible at trial. Commonwealth, since this is your motion, I'll hear from you first."

"Thank you, Your Honor." Annie walked around her table with her legal pad and stood before the judge. The jury box was empty. She had to concentrate. "May it please the court, at issue is whether the prior recorded testimony of the Commonwealth's primary witness, Jennianne Smith, now deceased, is admissible at trial. According to *Commonwealth v. Bohannon*, prior recorded testimony is admissible when it is established that the witness is unavailable to testify and when the prior testimony is deemed reliable. In this case, Jennianne Smith—"

Judge Killam raised a finger. "You've established that the witness is unavailable. I have her death certificate here. Now explain how her prior testimony is reliable."

Annie bit her lip. She had to exercise patience; she was about to do just that before the interruption. "First of all, I'm only planning on reading a small portion of the transcript. Jennianne was almost finished testifying—"

"I don't care how short the prior testimony is. You didn't answer my question, how is it *reliable*?"

"Jennianne's prior testimony is reliable. She testified before a Suffolk County grand jury which consisted of twenty-three people on November twenty-first of last year. She was duly sworn, and court stenographer Aimee Wallace recorded her testimony. The grand jury proceeding is very formal. I presented this case to the grand jury and called Jennianne to testify about the—"

"Come on, counselor." Judge Killam placed both hands on top of his head. "Don't tell me how a grand jury works. Get to the point. How is her testimony reliable?"

"Throughout this case, Jennianne's version of the events remained consistent."

"How can you prove that?"

"I attached the sworn affidavit of Detective Callahan to my memorandum of law. He swears under the penalties of perjury that Jennianne's story never changed from the very first time he spoke with her about the case. In addition, she passed a lie detector test administered by Carol O'Brien, one of the finest polygraph examiners in the state. I've attached—"

"Polygraph results are inadmissible, you know that." Judge Killam grimaced.

"Your Honor, I'm aware that Jennianne's test results can't be used at trial, but the fact that she passed adds to her reliability as a witness. She's told the truth from the very beginning."

Judge Killam squeezed his lower lip and shook his head from side to side. "You may say that her testimony is reliable, but defendants have a constitutional right to confront witnesses against them."

"Yes, Your Honor—"

"That's why we have vigorous cross-examinations in the courtrooms. What do you say to that?"

Annie had expected the question. "According to *Delaware v. Fensterer*, the United States Supreme Court held that a defendant is not entitled under the confrontation clause of the Constitution to a cross-examination that is effective in whatever way and to whatever extent the defense may wish. At the grand jury proceeding last November, the jurors were very active participants. Four jurors vigorously questioned Jennianne to test the reliability of her testimony. If you allow the prior testimony, this jury will be able to listen to those questions and hear how she responded. They will then draw their own conclusions about the credibility of Jennianne's prior testimony."

"Wrap it up, counselor."

"Yes, Your Honor." Annie referred to several other leading cases that she had cited in her brief until the judge cut her off.

"Is the witness's death connected to this defendant in any way?" Judge Killam pointed at Malone.

Annie wished she could say yes. "Not at this time."

"I'll hear from Attorney Clancy."

Annie sighed. That's all he wanted to hear. "Thank you, Your Honor." She resumed her seat, and wondered if the judge had already made up his mind.

Clancy marched into the middle of the courtroom, wearing his yellow bow tie with a curled rattlesnake on each side. Annie had seen him wear it before. It was his constitutional, *Don't Tread on Me* tie.

He spread his arms wide. " 'The right of cross-examination is one of the safeguards essential to a fair trial.' " Clancy turned around and addressed the packed gallery. "That is a direct quote from famed Supreme Court Justice Harlan Fiske Stone in *Alford v. United States.*"

"Clancy, there's no need for theatrics. This is a motion hearing, not a closing argument," Judge Killam said.

"Oh, Your Honor, when important constitutional rights are at stake, I will grab a bullhorn and shout from the mountaintops if I have to."

"I can picture it," the judge mumbled. "Get on with it."

"If Jennianne Smith's prior recorded testimony is allowed into evidence, it will be a violation of Mr. Malone's absolute right to confront witnesses against him as spelled out in the Sixth and Fourteenth Amendments of the United States Constitution. Article Twelve of the Massachusetts Declaration of Rights also provides that every person held to answer for a crime has a right to meet the witnesses against him face-to-face."

"Okay Clancy, I see you know your basic constitutional law, but can you be more specific here?"

"In this case, my client was not present at the grand jury proceeding, and he was not represented by counsel. As you are aware, even if Mr. Malone had a lawyer present, he would not have been allowed to question the witness."

"I know that. Tell me more about the case law. According to Miss Fitzgerald, the Fensterer case holds that the defendant is not entitled to a cross-examination in whatever way and to whatever extent he may wish. How do you respond to that?"

"Why, clearly, Fensterer is easily distinguished from the present case."

Judge Killam leaned over his bench and squinted. "How?"

Annie knew the judge was testing Clancy on his knowledge of the law. He didn't have a legal pad or his typed brief with him.

Clancy smirked like a student who knew all the answers. "In Fensterer, the prior recorded testimony of the unavailable witness came from a probable cause hearing at which the defendant was present and represented by counsel. In that case, the defendant had every opportunity to conduct a thorough cross-examination of the witness at the probable cause hearing."

"Why is that different?"

"Because in Malone's case there was no probable cause hearing. In the very beginning, the Commonwealth had a choice. They could've conducted a probable cause hearing or obtained an indictment via the grand jury in order to get this case into superior court. They chose the latter. It is common knowledge and a general rule of practice that when the Commonwealth chooses to have a probable cause hearing, they're attempting to preserve the testimony of a witness just in case the witness becomes unavailable later on. But they failed to take that precaution. Now, they want to have their cake and eat it, too."

"Are you saying there was no cross-examination of the witness Jenni-anne Smith?" the judge asked.

"That's right."

"But several grand jurors cross-examined this witness. I assume you've read the transcript?"

"Yes, many times over, Your Honor, and that's not what I'd call cross-examination."

Judge Killam scratched his head. "So, you're saying the cross-examination conducted by the grand jurors was ineffective?"

"Yes."

"In what way?"

"I've been in practice for forty-four years. Almost forty-five. No disrespect intended, but the grand jurors who questioned Jennianne Smith were laypersons with no trial experience. They may have been good accountants or housewives or firemen, but none were lawyers. Even for lawyers, the art of cross-examination takes years to master." Clancy rested his hands on the back of Malone's chair. "My client hired me to represent him due to my many years of experience as a trial attorney and for my reputation as a vigorous cross-examiner. If he wanted laypersons asking questions of the Commonwealth's witnesses, then he would be representing himself. But he chose not to. He is on trial for first-degree murder here."

Judge Killam gazed at the ceiling for a moment. "Are you finished?"

"If you admit this prior testimony into evidence, it will be an error of constitutional magnitude and a miscarriage of justice." Clancy maintained eye contact with the judge.

"Thank you." Judge Killam rose and addressed the audience. "You will have my decision by eleven A.M."

Annie sat back down in her seat. She felt drained of all her energy, unable to move, unable to think.

41

AS A SEQUESTERED witness, Callahan couldn't hear any trial testimony, but Judge Killam had allowed him to sit in the courtroom for the motion hearing. Instead of following the crowd out, he headed down the aisle toward the counsel tables.

"Coffee?" Callahan placed his hand on the back of Annie's chair and waited for an answer. He hoped she'd acquiesce; they needed to talk their issues through. They had about an hour until Judge Killam would announce his ruling.

Annie sighed. "Sure."

"Come on then. My treat."

Callahan noticed Annie's slumped shoulders and listless gait as they walked from the courthouse to Dippell's Deli. She had argued her motion with zeal, but now she appeared pale and deflated.

"Great job this morning. You made some excellent points." Callahan placed a coffee and blueberry muffin in front of Annie on a small corner table next to the window. "If it was up to me, you'd win." He set his black coffee and frosted cinnamon roll down, and sat across from her.

"Thanks." Annie gazed into his eyes for a long moment. "I'm sorry about the other night. I really lost it." Her voice cracked. "I didn't mean some of the things I said."

"I know. I'm sorry, too." He blew on his coffee. "It's Malone, he's getting to us. He just keeps on killing. I can't stop him."

She leaned over the table. "Why do you keep trying? Why not take the easy way out like Officer Twomey? Transfer out of Homicide, and load up on private details?"

"I'd make more money that way, buy a big house somewhere." Callahan had friends who were raking it in, even taking vacations.

"Why not?"

Callahan visualized his mother passing the time away watching television in her recliner with that dull look on her face. He closed his eyes for a moment and could practically smell the baked ziti being reheated in the basement of St. Catherine's for the Mothers Against Murder meetings. The metal folding chairs would be arranged in a semicircle.

"Well?" Annie cocked her head.

"My mother lost a child, my brother. His name was Brendan."

Annie frowned. "I didn't know. When was that?"

"Long time ago. I was only five years old, and he was just a baby. Car accident."

"What happened?"

"They never found out. The other driver left the scene. Mom was taking us all to Carson Beach in the old Chevy station wagon." Callahan remembered the heat, the dog sitting on his lap, and then it was all a blur. "She was never the same after that; she shut us all off, really."

"I'm sorry, Mike."

"That's why I keep going—for the mothers. They never get over losing a child, whether it's a baby or a grown man. So, I do what I can."

"I admire you," she whispered.

"At some point I lost my way. Clancy was right. I have no life outside of chasing Malone down. No wife, no children. Now, I've become obsessed at the expense of others like Jennianne."

"We both pushed her." Tears formed in the corners of her eyes. "If it wasn't for us, she'd be alive."

Callahan reached across the table and touched her fingertips.

"I thought about it all weekend, played the events over and over in my mind. I actually threatened her. What was I thinking?" Annie dabbed at her eyes with a napkin. "She just . . ." Her voice trailed off.

"Don't blame yourself, and let's not rehash what happened." Callahan rubbed her hand.

Annie poured cream and sugar into her coffee cup, and stirred the spoon in a figure-eight pattern. "I'm not sure what to do now. I feel completely out of it and lost."

"About the case?"

"That and just about everything else." Annie blew on her coffee and sipped it.

Callahan ate most of his roll and watched Annie pick little pieces of blueberry from the muffin. He wished he could read her mind. She had demons.

"What is it, Annie?" he asked.

She raised her eyes in question.

"Why are you so . . . hard on yourself?" Callahan leaned over the table. "What happened to you?"

"What do you mean?" She set her coffee down and drew her arms into her body. *A defensive move.*

"When you were young. I know some bad things happened . . . at your parents' bookstore. What did you see?"

"Mike, this isn't the time to be bringing that up; whatever happened, I got over it." She drew her lips together and examined her reflection in the coffee spoon.

"I don't think you did."

"I moved on. I'm a lawyer now." Annie peered out the window and then met his gaze again.

"And you're back in Charlestown. You could be with a big firm making all kinds of money. I picture you in New York."

"I suppose." She massaged her forehead.

Callahan wanted to help her more than ever. Whatever went down obviously still impacted her. Annie had turned into a workaholic, rarely had boyfriends. Would she ever meet someone and get married? Would she end up like him? He hoped not.

"What happened?" he asked. "I'm sure I could find out, but I want to hear it from you. I care about you, Annie."

She gazed into his eyes for a moment. "We had a storage room in the back of the bookstore. I made forts out of cardboard with all the boxes; it was a special place where I'd go and read. On the first Monday of the month, two men would always come by late in the afternoon. They were making collections for security, and you had to pay up. If you owned a business, you had to pay."

"True." Callahan waited for her to continue. It had happened in his neighborhood in South Boston, too. People had to make payments to whichever crime boss controlled the area.

"So, one day—it was summer, the storage room was hot. I heard the bell above the door ring twice. I looked out and could see all the way down the last aisle. My dad was doing something behind the register. The store was empty. My mother was out." Annie inhaled, her cheeks filled with air. She exhaled slowly. "The bell rang two times because, you see, one had followed the other through the door. The second one carried a shiny wooden bat with pretty red lettering all in cursive."

Callahan cringed; he feared what was coming next.

"I felt something was wrong, so I ran down the aisle. The man looked at me first, then he raised the bat way above his head, and gripped it with both hands together." She raised her hands above her head. "He brought it down with all his might. I remember those red cursive letters swirled off the tip of that bat." Annie brought her fists down on the table as if swinging a bat herself. "The man swung that bat down until it struck my daddy on the head. I can still hear the crack. I can still see the horror in his eyes before he fell. I remember feeling frozen. Both men looked right at me and walked out." She closed her eyes. "I ran over there to help him, but slipped on his blood and fell. I slipped and fell." Her lips trembled.

"I'm sorry, Annie." Callahan held her hand as they sat in silence.

Annie reopened her eyes. "My dad lived, thank God. The police interviewed him at the hospital when he regained consciousness after a few days.

He said it was a random attack and told me to say the same thing. *Don't see anything, don't hear anything, and never talk to cops.*" She shook her head.

"Code of silence." Callahan rubbed her arm. "I'm glad you told me," he whispered.

"My dad didn't pay them that month because he needed the money for my Catholic school tuition." She sipped her coffee. "We never spoke of it after that. My parents closed the bookstore and moved out of Charlestown."

"I think I'm beginning to understand you, why you're here," Callahan said.

"After all these years, I couldn't let it go." Annie checked her watch. "We have fifteen minutes left. What if I don't win the motion?"

Callahan swallowed his coffee. "That means we won't get the end of Jennianne's testimony into evidence. The jurors simply won't hear the rest. The judge will be broadcasting the message that under the law it's beneficial to kill off witnesses."

Annie raised her finger. "With one caveat."

"Which is?"

"You don't get caught."

"Right." Callahan finished the rest of his roll. "The justice system's all screwed up. It's what makes my job so hard. Criminals get the white glove treatment as soon as they set foot in a courtroom. Lawyers like Clancy make us cops out to be idiots. The judges and politicians don't know what goes on in the streets." Callahan licked white frosting from his fingertips. He'd risked his life so many times out there, wound up in the emergency room with all sorts of injuries, and had to deal with constant verbal abuse. If he dared use his gun, Internal Affairs, *the tin collectors*, would squeeze the last breath right out of him. "It's a thankless job."

"I know." Annie drummed her fingernails on the table. "We have two options."

"Dismiss the case or keep going."

"Exactly." She gripped her cup with both hands. "If we dismiss, Malone wins today."

"And if he did kill Jennianne to stop her from testifying, then his plan worked."

"And long lives the code of silence." Annie pursed her lips. "Let's forge ahead, and do our best, despite Judge Killam's decision. He may not rule against us. It'll be a close call."

Callahan didn't have high hopes. "What's your plan?"

"I'll rest my case, but reserve the right to call rebuttal witnesses." Annie attacked her muffin.

"Okay. I'll be out there twenty-four/seven digging up whatever I can find, chasing all the loose ends." He flipped his phone open. "We have to figure out how to approach Trevor's friend, Paul Garrity."

"I'll do it," Annie said.

"How?" Callahan hoped she wouldn't barge into Garrity's home, and go gangbuster on him.

"Quietly. I promised Jennianne I wouldn't make him testify, and I'm going to keep that promise."

Callahan nodded. "I have to return a call from the Walrus up in Gloucester."

"Really?"

"Yeah and he never calls me out of the blue. Something probably happened with Domenico."

"Hmm." Annie drained her coffee. "Oh, I forgot to tell you that I checked out Trevor's old art studio in the basement. I found an unfinished painting."

"You did?" Callahan couldn't believe she hadn't told him. It must've been sometime shortly before Jennianne died. "What was it of?"

"Trevor. He was working on a self-portrait before he died." Annie finished the rest of her muffin. "I'm convinced, if we peel away all the layers of this case, we end up with Trevor's paintings. There's got to be more out there. I'm hoping Garrity can help us."

"Did you ask Chris where they might be?"

Annie looked away and rapped her knuckles on the table. "I didn't have a chance. He's blaming us for Jennianne's death now, I could tell by just one look from him at the motion hearing. Chris will never help us now.

He refuses to testify, and I can't force him. God knows what he'd say." She got up from the table, and brushed the crumbs from her skirt. "Let's go."

Callahan balled up his napkin and tossed it on his plate. He wondered how Annie convinced Chris to let her into the basement in the first place.

"Mike?"

"Yeah?"

"Can you buy me another muffin? I'm still hungry and I don't have any cash on me."

He smiled. *Typical woman.*

42

"ALL RISE."

Annie and Clancy stood with the rest of the gallery as Judge Killam ascended the bench. Even though Callahan and she had discussed how they would move forward despite a loss, Annie held out hope for a win. The judge knew as well as anyone that Malone was a master at beating the system. Wouldn't it make sense to side with her and let the last bit of Jennianne's testimony in?

"Be seated," Johnny said.

Clerk Fallon called the case and everyone looked at the judge. He surveyed the room like a despot from the olden days. This was his kingdom and he made the rules.

Judge Killam cleared his throat. "The Commonwealth's motion is denied. Allowing Jennianne Smith's prior testimony into evidence will violate the defendant's constitutional right to confront witnesses against him. I have a copy of my decision for both of you here." He handed two stapled packets to Clerk Fallon.

She lost. Annie felt like someone had plowed her over.

"Nice job," Malone whispered to Clancy.

"Commonwealth?"

Annie stared at the judge with her mouth open. Why had he ruled

against her? He could've saved the case; it was within his power. Callahan was right; they bent over backward and did flips for the criminals.

"Are you prepared to call another witness, Miss Fitzgerald?"

"Since my primary witness is dead . . ." Annie turned around and
looked at Chris sitting in the front row. She raised her eyebrows, giving
him one last chance to change his mind and take the stand.

Chris sat back and folded his arms across his chest. His gaze told her to
get lost. He had control over her now. What if he told someone about how
she bullied Jennianne in the ladies' room? Drove her over the edge? What
if he reported what had happened in his basement? How she broke in?
That she kissed him?

"I have no choice but to rest my case," Annie said. "I reserve the right
to call rebuttal witnesses."

Judge Killam nodded. "Attorney Clancy?"

"Your Honor, at this time I'm making a motion for a directed verdict."

"I'll hear you."

Annie resumed her seat. This was a standard motion, argued before
the judge every time after the Commonwealth rested. The defense usually lost. She only saw them prevail in one case due to an overwhelming
lack of proof against the defendant. Annie prayed this wouldn't be the
second time. Judge Killam wouldn't end the case now. Would he?

"There's no reason for the jury to sit through any more of this nonsense." Clancy gestured toward the empty jury box.

Annie knew he was showboating for Malone and the audience. *Always
shilling for business.* She hoped the judge saw right through it.

"My client is standing trial for something that's not even close to murder at all. The evidence presented by the Commonwealth points to a classic drug overdose. Absolutely nothing supports a first-degree murder
indictment here. For justice's sake, you must direct a verdict of not guilty
and end this charade right now."

"Commonwealth?" Judge Killam turned to Annie for a response.

"This is not a charade." Annie marched past Clancy, right up to the
clerk's table where the evidence was laid out. "In the light most favorable
to the Commonwealth, the evidence has demonstrated each element of

first-degree murder." She picked up the syringe and the empty bag of heroin. "Here we have the murder weapon and the ammunition." Annie fanned through photographs of Jennianne's apartment and raised several. "And, the crime scene." She highlighted testimony from Domenico, the medical examiner, and other key witnesses. "Do you really want to take this case away from the jury, Your Honor?"

"No." He tapped his gavel. "The defendant's motion for a directed verdict is denied."

"What?" Malone pounded his fist on the table.

"Please note my objection for the record," Clancy said.

"So noted." Judge Killam glared at Malone. "Attorney Clancy, are you ready to present your case?"

"May I have a moment with my client before you bring the jury back in?"

Judge Killam regarded the clock. "We'll break for lunch now and resume at two o'clock sharp."

Clancy finished his ham sandwich as he walked down the hall toward the holding cells. When he arrived, Malone was pacing, his lunch sat on the orange tray, untouched. *Tomato soup again.* Clancy anticipated another mess judging by his client's scowl. He decided to begin on a positive note.

"It's great we won that motion, huh? The judge wouldn't allow the grand jury transcript in." Clancy forced a smile. "I spent all weekend researching that one. Now it's our turn, so we have to decide—"

"It's *our* turn." Malone grinned, showing all his teeth. "I'm just tickled pink." He picked up the tomato soup and whipped it across the cell. It splattered and dribbled down the cinder block wall. "It shouldn't be my turn at all! I shouldn't be here!"

"What's going on down there?" The guard got up from his lunch table and walked toward them. His gaze fixed on the tomato soup–covered wall and then on Malone. "I can have you arrested for that."

"We'll clean it up, no trouble," Clancy said. He would love to see Malone arrested on that one. "Everything's under control now."

"It better be gone soon as I'm done with my lunch." The guard snorted and headed back. Malone gave him the middle finger.

"What's under control?" Malone jammed his hands on his hips and circled around. "Nothing's under control; this freak show of a case is spinning way out of control. It's way over your head, Clancy, that's for sure."

"I disagree, they don't have enough evidence for a guilty verdict." Clancy ignored the insult. "It's going well for us. Remember, Domenico perjured himself and we can offer reasonable explanations pointing to an overdose for everything they have so far."

"I'm getting bad vibes from that jury. The old bitches in the second row hate me; they'd send me to the electric chair if they had the chance." Malone spat on the floor. "Now they're gonna think I killed off a witness. Why did you let the newspapers print up all those lies? Why didn't you get my story in the papers? It's all bullshit. Not my fault she got drunk at a bar and drove off the road. You know the jury's gonna read that shit and believe it."

"The judge has instructed them not to."

"Like they're gonna listen to him? It's not fair to me." He slapped his hand against the wall.

Clancy hoped it hurt. "We can ask the judge to declare a mistrial. I've already discussed the option with you, but maybe we should re—"

"No mistrial. *I said, no mistrial.*" Malone glared. "You know they'll try this thing all over again. Who knows what Callahan'll concoct the second time around."

"Okay. We got twenty minutes to strategize. Remember, the jurors have heard only one side of the story."

"My girlfriend's testifying."

"What?" Clancy felt his heart flutter; he hated surprises.

"Stacy was at Jennianne's place that night. She'll tell you all about that stupid addict artist. She'll get up there and prove Callahan's a lying sack of shit."

Clancy wished he had retired a year ago. "Why didn't you tell me that in the first place?"

"I thought we'd be in better shape than we are at this point. I wanted to spare her from having to go through with it. If you'd done your job right, I'd be walking the streets right now, smelling the flowers."

"Is that what you think? That I haven't been doing my job?"

"You obviously don't know what you're doing! I shouldn't be here! You know I've been framed and you're letting them get away with it." Malone kicked the lunch tray.

"Maybe we better part ways right now." Clancy turned to leave.

"We both know that fat bastard Killam won't let you walk away at this point. Besides, if I lose, I'll blame it on my useless, senile lawyer and I'll get a new trial."

May he rot in jail someday. Clancy clenched his teeth and breathed in and out a few times before turning around. He had to exercise patience. "What did your girlfriend witness that night?"

"Everything."

"What do you mean by everything?"

"That I didn't give Trevor no heroin. He brought it that night like I told you."

"What's this one's name?"

"Stacy Black."

"Well, she's not on the witness list." Clancy sighed. "Fitzgerald will throw a willy. Killam might not allow it."

"Do what you have to do." Malone smacked his lips. "I want her to testify."

"I'll do my best. Any more surprise witnesses you want to tell me about?"

"No, the jurors'll hear the truth from Stacy, my mother, and me. That's it."

Clancy's mouth dropped open. "You're not taking the stand. We discussed this already, remember?"

"You sure as hell can't stop me."

Clancy closed his eyes and took a deep breath. "As your attorney, I'm strongly advising you not to take the witness stand. You have the right to remain silent. You'll get destroyed on cross."

"I'm getting up there no matter what, and I want you to tell them so in your opening statement."

Clancy couldn't stand it when clients told him how to do his job. "I'd rather not announce your plan in my opening just in case you change your mind. That would look bad for us, don't you think?"

"I'm not changing my mind on this." Malone picked up his plastic soup spoon and snapped it in half.

Clancy had to cover himself. "You'll have to sign a statement that you're taking the stand against my advice, and you want me to announce it up front."

"Whatever."

Stupid bastard. "If you and Stacy are off kilter on one tiny detail, the jurors will sink their teeth into it," Clancy said.

Malone shrugged. "I'm not worried about that. Me and Stacy both know what really happened."

"What about your brother, Frank?"

"No way. The idiot'll sink us both by trying too hard and then saying the wrong thing. Frank's got his own case to worry about."

Clancy had to agree with his client on that one. Frank had been arrested on conspiracy charges in connection with Trevor's murder. He would be tried separately later on. With Malone insisting on taking the stand, it was best not to have Frank as well. Clancy knew they would end up contradicting each other.

He half-listened as Malone described what his girlfriend looked like. He turned and headed down the hall at a brisk pace.

"She'll be looking for you," Malone called out.

"Hey!" The guard waved at Clancy. "Did you clean up the mess in his cell?"

"Make him do it." Maybe he'd make Malone lick it off the wall. He had to find the girlfriend and get her story straight, and then supplement his witness list. He was running out of time.

"Um, excuse me." An attractive brunette waved him over to a bench near the courtroom. She wore a short black leather skirt with a tight pink sweater, black stockings, and bright red high heels. The girlfriend. Clancy wondered to what extent she had discussed her testimony with Malone during visiting hours at the jail the night before.

"Miss Black?"

She nodded and smacked her gum, chewing with her mouth open.

"I'm Charles Clancy but everyone around here calls me Buddy." When they shook hands, she pulled away a bit too fast.

"I know who you are." She sounded curt, her words carried an edge.

Clancy assumed a businesslike tone. "Mr. Malone just informed me you're planning to testify on his behalf. Is that so?"

"Yeah." She fished in her pocketbook, pulled out a little round mirror, and applied orangy lipstick. "I was wondering when you was gonna talk to me."

"Well, I just found out about you." Clancy sat next to her on the bench. He didn't even have time to grab his legal pad. He'd have to wing it. "Tell me what you witnessed on November tenth?"

43

"S TACY WHO?" ANNIE squinted at the paper and wondered if she was awake or dreaming. Had she fallen asleep at her table?

"Black," Clancy said.

Annie bit her cheek. It hurt, so she was awake, unfortunately. "This is ridiculous. What's she going to testify about?"

"That she was present at Jennianne Smith's apartment on the night—"

"What?" Annie bolted from her seat nearly knocking over her chair. "No way! That's bullshit!" She flung Clancy's handwritten witness list across her table; it fluttered to the rug. She couldn't believe he was pulling this now. "No way in hell. Judge'll never allow it. I don't even have a record on her."

"That's easy enough. There's her date of birth." Clancy gathered the paper and pointed to a date. "You can run a record in five minutes' time if you want to use it for impeachment. I won't make you run from court to court and gather all her certified convictions, if she has any. Hey, she may be clean, never know. I haven't run across a Stacy Black before." Clancy rubbed his chin. "I don't recall, anyway."

"Fat chance considering the crowd she runs with." Annie gestured toward Malone, who was being escorted into the courtroom.

"Let's make a quick call to probation," Clancy half smiled. "They'll run a record for us. I'm willing to stipulate—"

"That's the least of my worries. I have no idea who this is or what she'll say." Annie jiggled the back of her chair with force, knocking it against the table. She wanted to throw it across the room, and accidentally hit Malone, who seemed overly pleased with himself that afternoon.

"Like I said, our witness's name is—"

"No, just forget it. I have a better solution. Judge Killam will be starting up in exactly four minutes." Annie pointed at the clock. "I'll make it easier on both of us."

Clancy raised his eyebrows. "How's that?"

"I'll object and object and object until my face turns purple."

"Ah, come on." Clancy shuffled over to his table. "It's just one extra witness, not like I'm adding a dozen."

Annie plunked down hard, angling her chair away from Clancy and Malone. She rustled papers, ignoring both, until Judge Killam entered the courtroom. She wouldn't let him get away with this one.

"Are there any other matters that need to be addressed before we bring the jury back in?"

Annie rose and slapped her hands on the table. "Oh yes, Your Honor."

"What is it now?" He sighed.

"Attorney Clancy added a surprise witness to his list only five minutes ago and I'm objecting."

"What next?" Judge Killam rolled his eyes at the ceiling. "Clancy?"

Clancy raised a finger. "I reserved the right to supplement my—"

"It's too late now!" Annie faced Clancy. "And, I'm willing to bet your witness sat in the back row taking notes throughout the whole trial."

"That's not fair, I just—"

"I bet you knew all along."

"I did not."

"Enough!" Judge Killam whacked his gavel. "I won't have attorneys fighting and interrupting each other in my courtroom. Is that clear? Now, attorney Clancy, why didn't you add this witness to your list earlier?"

"May God strike me, I just found out about Stacy Black during the lunch break. She approached me in the hallway and told me in a shaky voice what she'd witnessed. I was alarmed and asked her why she hadn't come forward earlier. Fact is, she was scared to death but felt she had to do the right thing."

"What's the basis of her testimony?" Judge Killam asked.

"She was present at Jennianne Smith's apartment on the evening of November tenth, the night Trevor Shea died."

Judge Killam rubbed his brow. "Why was she present?"

Clancy gestured toward his client. "She's Mr. Malone's girlfriend and—"

"No way!" Annie raised her arms straight up in the air. "I've heard it all now. Two girlfriends?"

Judge Killam raised a palm. "Hold on."

Annie stepped toward the judge. "But she's clearly lying, no way was she there. I'm getting railroaded here."

"Miss Fitzgerald, can you prove this witness wasn't there?"

"If she's Billy Malone's girlfriend, she's a biased witness. She'll say anything he tells her to."

"She may be biased, but who can say she wasn't there?" the judge asked.

"Jennianne Smith never mentioned her." Annie knew she couldn't have been there. *No way.*

"As I recall, Jennianne was never specifically asked about this woman," Clancy said.

"And now we can't ask, can we, because Jennianne's dead. *Dead.*" Annie glared at Malone. "My hands are tied."

"I'm sorry about Miss Smith's tragic accident." Clancy softened his voice. "However, my client has a constitutional right to present witnesses in his own defense. Your Honor, if you deny him the opportunity—"

"I know what the law says, Clancy. I will allow this witness to testify, but she will not take the stand first due to your late supplementation." He turned to Annie. "If you don't think she was present, you will have the opportunity to cross-examine her."

"May I be heard?" Annie placed a hand on her hip.

"My ruling stands."

"But, in all fairness!"

"Are you objecting?"

"Yes, I'm objecting and I wish to be heard."

"Your objection has been noted for the record and that will be all on the subject."

Annie felt as if she was being punished for raising an objection when Clancy should've received the brunt of Judge Killam's wrath. She sat back down and forced herself to take deep breaths.

"Attorney Clancy, are you planning to give an opening statement?"

"Yes."

"Are the jurors ready?"

"All set, Judge." Johnny leaned against the wall, sucking on a plastic straw.

"Well, don't just stand there. Go get 'em. I need a fresh pitcher of water, too."

Johnny stretched his arms and cracked his knuckles. "Whatcha want first, Judge, the jurors or the water?"

"Your Honor, I'll get the water." Clerk Fallon grabbed the pitcher and headed toward the judge's lobby.

Annie snuck her phone from her pocketbook and sent a quick text to Callahan, asking him to dig up whatever he could on Stacy Black. She put it away without waiting for a response. Judge Killam hated seeing phones in court.

She doodled in her legal pad as they waited for the jury. What would they think now? Had any of them read the papers or listened to the news about Jennianne's car accident? How could they avoid it? Would they connect the dots and suspect Malone?

"Chief Turner, please?" Callahan jogged down the courthouse steps toward Government Center as he waited for the receptionist to connect him to the chief up in Gloucester. He knew the Walrus would make him wait on the line for a few minutes.

The phone line finally clicked over. "Turner," the Walrus said.

"Callahan here, returning your call."

"Why, ain't this special. Getting off your high horse to return *my* call." He snickered. "Got your problems down in the big city, now, don't you?"

Callahan sighed. "What's up?"

"Malone giving you a hard time? Killing off all your witnesses again?"

Callahan felt like hanging up. Is that why he called? To taunt him?

"I see Clancy gave you a black eye in court, too." The Walrus bellowed his signature hiccupping laugh.

"Laughing at your own jokes again. That how you entertain yourself all day up there with nothing to do?"

The laughing stopped and Callahan heard static on the other end. "Hello?" He wondered if the Walrus had hung up.

"Some little kid found Drake Reed's corpse all mangled up on Good Harbor Beach. It was the torso and legs, head and arms missing. The gulls were enjoying the picnic."

Callahan stopped walking. They found the body, and in Gloucester of all places. Reed had been reported missing by his mother since around the time Domenico testified.

"Poor kid was out walking his dog on the beach. He'll have nightmares the rest of his life, thanks to you."

"Thanks to me?"

"Yeah, you put the whole thing in motion with this drug-overdose-turned-murder case of yours. I should never have given up Domenico. *Never again.* Now we got a warrant out for his arrest on this one. *Murder.*"

"How do you know this was Drake Reed's torso?"

The Walrus laughed. "Can't tell yah, but it's him alright. We got positive ID."

"What do you have on Domenico?" Callahan asked.

"Can't tell yah that, either, but we know Reed was one of Malone's men. Looks like he's been dead since around the time you came and snagged Domenico. I figure they were running some side deal, and it went down bad against Reed."

Callahan's mind raced. So, they were looking for Domenico. Is that why the Walrus had called? Did he think Callahan could find Domenico? "I'll keep my eye out for him; if I hear anything—"

"Feds are all over it. We came down your way to check out Reed's apartment, and I had a run-in with an Agent Bertrand. I actually found somebody who pisses me off more than you. Know him?"

Callahan stifled a laugh, imagining the two of them going at it. "Yeah."

"Well, he ran this bullshit that he's got jurisdiction over us. Federal investigation. Thought I'd let you know."

"Why me?"

"Because I have to get in the apartment, got a murder to solve. Maybe you have some connection over there?"

"With the feds?"

"Right. I did you a favor, remember? Quid pro quo."

"Sure. I'll head over there myself. See what I can do."

The Walrus grunted and hung up.

Callahan couldn't believe it. What was Bertrand up to now? How did he know about Reed's death so fast? The feds definitely had an ongoing investigation on Malone. What was going on? He picked up his pace and ran toward his car, which was parked outside the Area A police station. A text from Annie came through on his phone.

Callahan read it twice. She wanted information on a Stacy Black? He couldn't believe Clancy was adding her as a witness and the judge allowed it. If they had tried to pull something like that, it would have been denied in a heartbeat. He had wanted to go to Reed's apartment in Charlestown, and now he had to do this, which would take the rest of the day and all night.

Callahan hopped in his car and headed toward the Charlestown bridge. Perhaps he could kill two birds with one stone.

44

THE AIR FELT stifling when Rachel entered the packed courtroom. She couldn't believe the judge hadn't declared a mistrial with all the publicity. Instead, he had given them a long speech on Wednesday, warning them not to read the papers or watch the news. Rachel had spotted a *Herald* headline over the weekend and couldn't resist. She recalled those bold, black letters: FOUL PLAY SUSPECTED IN WITNESS'S DEATH.

Rachel had quickly scanned the article and learned that Jennianne Smith had been killed in a car accident the night after she testified. The article went on to provide a history on Charlestown's code of silence. It described Malone as an Irish mob boss, who the police suspected had committed multiple murders and obstructed justice in previous cases. She wondered how many of her fellow jurors had read the article or caught the story on the news. No one admitted it when Judge Killam asked them that morning. Rachel wished she hadn't read it.

"Good afternoon, I hope you enjoyed your lunch." Clancy stood before them for his opening statement. He appeared casual with one hand in his pocket. He walked the length of the jury box as if out on a Sunday stroll, and stopped in the center, making eye contact with each juror.

"I'm going to make a promise to all of you . . . yes, a promise." His voice tapered off. "I promise that I will expose the truth." He adjusted his rattlesnake bow tie. Rachel had seen that curled snake on a flag. *Don't tread on me.* It was a symbol for liberty, coiled and ready to attack.

"I will lead you to the truth, and thus prove my client's innocence." Clancy's voice boomed across the courtroom.

Rachel heard the resolve in Clancy's voice; those were strong words. He seemed sincere and now he'd made a promise. Despite all the courtroom theatrics, she couldn't imagine Clancy going back on his word. She had to ignore that *Herald* article.

"As His Honor emphasized early on, my client, Mr. Malone, doesn't have to testify. He has a constitutional right to remain silent and force the Commonwealth to prove its case. In fact, I don't have to prove anything; the burden of proof rests solely with the Commonwealth." Clancy looked at Fitzgerald and then walked the length of the jury box.

"Most defense lawyers advise their clients against taking the witness stand and I'm one of them. I tell 'em lawyers have a way of twisting whatever you say, putting words in your mouth, making you lose your cool." Several jurors nodded, including Rachel. "See, you know what I mean." Clancy smiled.

"You know, I really can't believe Mr. Malone was forced to stand trial at all. The prosecution has laid its cards on the table and there is still no evidence that Trevor Shea was murdered at all. I'm sorry for the family, I truly am, but the fact is that Trevor was a heroin addict, in and out of drug treatment programs."

Clancy walked behind his client's chair. "Mr. Malone insisted from the very beginning that he would take the witness stand at all costs, and he's been patiently awaiting the opportunity. Why? Because he wants to broadcast the truth. That's right, the bare-boned truth. And in testifying before you, under oath, he will proclaim his innocence." Clancy made eye contact with each juror.

"Mr. Malone will take the stand and tell you exactly what happened on November tenth. He will swear he had nothing to do with the death of Trevor Shea. He had absolutely no reason to harm Trevor in any way, shape, or form. In fact, he liked the artist and his paintings. Mr. Malone will share his own theory about what may've happened to Trevor—a theory the police refused to investigate."

"Objection." Annie leaned forward.

"Overruled."

Rachel wished Annie hadn't interrupted; it was Clancy's turn now. *Just let him get on with it.*

"Speaking of the police, you've only been provided with half the picture, maybe less." Clancy raised his voice as he marched across the courtroom, positioning himself in front of the jury again. "Detective Callahan has it out for Mr. Malone, and you're about to find out why. As you're listening to the testimony, ask yourselves, was this normal police procedure or the work of a vindictive, overzealous cop?"

Rachel had her doubts about Callahan. She studied Malone in his dapper tan suit. Had this man committed multiple murders as the article suggested? Was it up to her as leader of this jury to convince the others and put an end to the violence? Was this the one time Malone *didn't* do it? Rachel's mind kept drifting back to the article as Clancy outlined more of his case.

Clancy positioned himself close to the jurors and near the center of the box. "The Commonwealth failed to tell you something else." He had lowered his voice to a whisper. "Something crucial . . ."

Rachel moved to the edge of her seat; she could barely hear him.

"There was another witness in Jennianne's apartment on the evening of November tenth."

"Objection, sidebar!" Annie pounded her table as she scurried around it. Several papers fluttered to the floor.

Annie had yelled so loudly, she startled Rachel.

"Approach." Judge Killam waved them to the other side of the bench.

Rachel watched Clancy and a red-faced Annie arguing at sidebar. Judge Killam didn't appear amused with Clancy's last comment, either. Rachel strained her ears and caught bits and pieces. Annie had a loud whisper, sometimes the words came through. It sounded like they were accusing each other of hiding a witness. After a few minutes, Rachel watched Judge

Killam pointing to their respective tables and motioning them away from the bench.

When the sidebar ended, the judge twisted around toward the jury box. "You are to completely disregard attorney Clancy's last statement about the Commonwealth's failure to tell you about a witness. Remember, this is an opening statement. What you're hearing is not evidence. Attorney Clancy is merely telling you what he expects the evidence will show."

"Thank you, Your Honor." Clancy resumed his spot before the jury. He smiled as if he'd just enjoyed a relaxing cup of afternoon tea with Annie. "I'm planning to introduce you to another witness who was present at Jennianne's apartment on November tenth. Her name is Stacy Black."

Who? Rachel couldn't believe it. Why hadn't Fitzgerald called this witness? No one mentioned a Stacy Black before.

"Miss Black volunteered to come forward as a witness. She wasn't subpoenaed, and hasn't made any deals in exchange for her testimony. She's simply here to tell you the truth." Clancy pressed his palms and fingers together as if in prayer. "The truth. Yes, that's all I can hope for, pray for, in this case. That you'll listen carefully, recognize the truth, and refrain from sending an innocent man to jail." Clancy moved his pressed hands rhythmically to and fro.

"Thank you."

Rachel watched Clancy resume his seat. She gazed at the women in the yellow shirts. According to the *Herald* article, they were from Mothers Against Murder, and probably hated Clancy. They looked united, waiting for justice. Did Malone kill all their children?

45

"THE DEFENSE CALLS Mrs. Mary Malone," Clancy said.

Elaine watched the defendant's mother approach the witness stand. She wore a floral-print lavender dress, probably her Sunday best. Her white hair looked freshly permed in tight, short curls. She held her right hand high in the air when Clerk Fallon read the oath. Elaine had noticed her sitting behind her son in the front row throughout the trial, fingering her white rosary beads with the silver cross.

She couldn't believe Fitzgerald had been hiding a witness. How could she be that underhanded? Elaine thought Clancy made some great points in his opening statement, and looked forward to the defendant's case.

"Good afternoon, Mrs. Malone." Clancy sounded like a gentleman. "Please introduce yourself to His Honor and the ladies and gentlemen of the jury."

"Mary Grace Malone."

"Where do you reside?"

"On Pearl Street in Charlestown."

"Are you married?"

"Widowed."

"Mrs. Malone, if you don't mind telling us, what happened to your husband?" Clancy tilted his head to the side.

"He was murdered, shot in the chest. God rest his soul."

Murdered? Elaine watched Malone cross himself.

"I'm very sorry for your loss, Mrs. Malone." Clancy paced for a moment. "Do you have any children?"

"Yes, my two sons, Billy and Frank. We also had a baby girl, Elizabeth, who died at birth."

The poor woman. Elaine felt sorry for her. She leaned back in her chair and stretched, accidentally bumping Rachel with her elbow again. It was going to be a long afternoon, and Rachel had doused herself with more perfume over lunch. Elaine kept getting the sensation of having to sneeze. Her mind drifted to the events that had unfolded over the weekend. Jennianne Smith's car accident had been the lead news story. If Jennianne had kept her mouth shut and not testified against Malone, would she still be alive? Elaine's cousin Liz was convinced that Malone had hired somebody to go down to Scituate and run the girl off the road. Elaine hadn't realized she was in a safe house to begin with. Why weren't they told? She learned more about the case watching TV and talking with Liz. Didn't they deserve to know all the facts? After all, they were the ones making the big decision here. Elaine sighed and forced herself to tune in again, she'd missed several questions and answers.

". . . and a member of St. Catherine's Catholic Church where I'm a Eucharistic minister and sing in the choir."

St. Catherine's. Elaine gazed at the row of women with the yellow shirts. Liz had mentioned they were from the Mothers Against Murder group run out of the same church. Did they know Mrs. Malone? Did they bear a grudge against her? Had Malone been accused of murdering any of their sons or daughters? Is that why they were there?

"Directing your attention to Sunday, November twelfth of last year, what were you doing at approximately six P.M.?" Clancy asked.

Mrs. Malone glanced at her son. "I was busy preparing a nice corned beef dinner for Billy and Frank. At that time I was probably making the mashed potatoes, which they preferred instead of boiled."

"Were you celebrating any special occasion?"

"My birthday."

"What time did your sons arrive?" Clancy asked.

"Let's see, Billy and his friend, Drake Reed, came over first at about five past six, and Frank arrived just before six thirty. Frank brought a lovely bouquet of pink carnations for my table."

"How nice." Clancy smiled. "At some point, did Drake Reed leave?"

"Uh, yes, just before we sat down for dinner." Mrs. Malone rubbed her arthritic knuckles.

"Did you enjoy your birthday meal?"

"We never had the chance to eat; my dinner ended up completely spoiled."

"What happened?"

"Just after we said grace, the Boston Police bashed through my front door. It was horrifying, like army troops storming into my home. I thought we'd all be killed. At some point I heard them yell out, 'Police!' Then they kept saying they'd blow our heads off if we moved."

"Objection, hearsay." Annie stood.

"It's certainly not hearsay." Clancy stepped toward the judge. "I'm not offering it for the truth of the matter asserted."

"I agree. Overruled."

Elaine didn't get half the legal jargon. Why couldn't they just talk normally and not hide stuff all the time? It was getting annoying.

"Where were the police when they kept saying they'd blow your heads off?" Clancy turned his hand sideways and extended his index finger, mimicking a gun being pointed at his own head.

"They were in the living room. We couldn't see them from where we were sitting in the dining room," Mrs. Malone said.

"What happened next?"

"They forced my sons to walk out one by one into the living room with their hands up. I closed my eyes and prayed they wouldn't get shot. I've never trusted the Boston Police."

"Objection, move to strike the last sentence."

"Sustained." Judge Killam turned to the jury. "Please disregard Mrs. Malone's opinion testimony."

There they go again. Elaine sighed. So what if she didn't trust them?

Maybe Mrs. Malone had good reason. Elaine wondered what had happened to her husband, Billy's father. Why had he been shot?

"Did you witness any part of the arrests?" Clancy wrinkled his brow.

"Yes. After Billy walked into the living room, I heard a loud crash followed by the tinkling of breaking glass. I ran over to see if my son was still alive and saw Detective Callahan kneeling on him with his knees digging into Billy's back, cuffing his hands. After that, he lifted Billy way up high by the hair and smashed his face into the floor. No reason for it, far as I could tell. Just slammed my son hard as he could into the floor. Right in front of me."

"What happened to Billy after Callahan slammed him down?"

"It makes me cringe to this day. I could hear the bones crackling, splitting. Awful. Then Billy's blood started gushing out all over the floor and white rug. I didn't care about the rug, just him. Sounded like he couldn't breathe. He was wheezing and the blood was all over his mouth, dripping off his chin. As it turned out, that detective broke his nose real good."

"Did anyone attend to Billy's broken nose at the house?"

"They took a dirty dishrag from my kitchen sink and mopped the blood from his face and neck. Detective Callahan told someone to do it just in case anyone had a camera outside."

"Objection," Annie said. "Hearsay."

"Sustained as to any statements made by Callahan."

Elaine could picture the detective saying that. What was the point of smashing his face in front of his mother? And with handcuffs on? Police brutality.

"What happened after the arrests?" Clancy asked.

"Three officers searched my home up and down."

"What did you observe?"

"They barged into every room and tipped all my drawers upside down, including my very personal things, toiletries, and junk drawers." Mrs. Malone waggled a finger as if the police were sitting out in the audience. "They spilled my sewing box, needles and all, across the bedroom rug, pulled all the books out of the bookcases, tore the covers from my bed. They even slid the mattress onto the floor. Let's see . . . they also took dishes out of the cupboards, smashed a few, emptied my sugar and flour jugs onto the floor. What else? What else?" She tapped her chin.

"Take your time," Clancy said.

"Oh, they broke several glass picture frames, shattered an antique Hummel my mother had given me as a child, and, and . . . a hole was shot right through my living room window."

Annie rose halfway up, but sank down without objecting. Elaine wondered why she had changed her mind. Did the police really fire a shot through Mrs. Malone's window? Someone could've been killed. She studied Annie for a moment. Clancy was right, she and Detective Callahan were trying to hide all the bad stuff.

"Did the police find anything during their extensive search?" Clancy raised his hands.

"Not a thing. They left empty-handed." Mrs. Malone pursed her lips. "And, I forgot to mention, they used filthy language in my presence. Please don't ask me to repeat it."

"Don't worry, Mrs. Malone. I wouldn't want to embarrass you." Clancy clasped his hands together. "Did the police clean up after themselves or reimburse you for the items they destroyed?"

"No, and it took me the best part of a week to get my house back to normal again. Some things like the Hummel couldn't be replaced."

Clancy nodded. "No further questions."

Elaine imagined the mess—a whopping cleaning bill. She watched Annie making notations in her legal pad as Clancy resumed his seat. The women in the yellow shirts whispered amongst themselves. The case was a roller coaster. Sometimes Elaine felt so angry at the police that she wanted to let Malone off to prove a point. On the other hand, Liz said Malone deserved to go to jail if not for this case, then for all his other murders.

She also wondered whether Jennianne just got drunk and fell asleep at the wheel. The girl was losing it that day in court, that's for sure. Besides, Liz said she heard Jennianne was mixed up with the wrong crowd in Charlestown, a big party girl covered in tatoos. She turned around and caught Louie's eye. What was he thinking?

. . .

Annie took one last glance at her notes before leaving her legal pad on the table and marching into center court. She had been taught never to carry a pad during cross-examination. Notes were both inhibiting and distracting. Annie had listened with intensity to Clancy's direct examination. She had to be on constant alert for objections and any statements she could use against the witness. She saw right through Clancy's strategy: attack the cops, inflame the jury. Who would they believe, a little old lady with rosary beads or Callahan?

"Good afternoon, Mrs. Malone." Annie smiled at her.

Mrs. Malone nodded once, and knotted her fingers together.

"You mentioned Billy and Frank came over for dinner?"

"That's right."

"Drake Reed came with them?" Annie cocked her head.

"Yes."

"Had you invited Mr. Reed over for your birthday meal?"

"Well, actually, no." Her gaze bounced over to Malone and then back to Annie. "But it was no bother because we had plenty of food. I didn't mind one bit."

"Drake Reed brought a gun with him, didn't he?"

"Objection." Clancy grimaced.

Judge Killam rubbed his chin. "Overruled."

"I didn't see any gun." Mrs. Malone bit her upper lip. "Because I would've asked him to leave if he had one. I don't allow guns in my house."

Annie had no evidence that Reed had been carrying a gun, but she wanted to dangle the possibility in front of the jury because Mrs. Malone had mentioned that somebody shot a hole through her living room window. Judge Killam had ruled that the shooting of Sergeant Amidon couldn't come into evidence for it would prejudice Malone's case. Annie had to figure out how to delve into the mystery behind the window getting shot.

Annie glided toward the jurors. "Mr. Reed changed his mind about dinner, didn't he?"

"He ended up leaving before we sat down."

"Did he tell you why he decided to leave?"

"Objection." Clancy remained seated. "Hearsay."

"Sustained."

"But I was happy to be alone with my sons, anyway," Mrs. Malone said.

"Don't answer when you hear me say 'sustained.'" Judge Killam smiled at Mrs. Malone. "Okay?"

"Oh dear, I'm sorry." She nodded.

"Did Mr. Reed have any private conversations with either Billy or Frank?"

"I can't say it was private, but they went into the living room while I was in the kitchen cooking." Mrs. Malone shifted. "It seemed perfectly normal to me."

"Prior to that evening you hadn't seen your sons for at least four days, correct?"

"Yes, but that wasn't unusual; they're both real busy."

"With jobs?" Annie glanced at the jury, making eye contact with the attractive foreperson.

"No, busy with other things. Looking for jobs, I guess."

"I see." Annie paced for a moment. "By the time your sons came to dinner on November twelfth, had you heard about Trevor Shea's death?"

"I heard something about it in the church vestibule that morning."

Annie guessed Mrs. Malone may have had suspicions after the police questioned her about Billy's whereabouts that Saturday. "Did you ask your son, Billy, if he was involved?"

Mrs. Malone hesitated and glanced at the defense table. "I asked Billy if he knew about it, I believe. He said it was a drug overdose."

"Were you aware Billy had been dating Jennianne Smith at the time?"

"They'd been dating, I knew that, but it was rocky. I didn't like her much. I thought she was a bad influence on my son. She was covered in those tatoos."

"Did Jennianne's name come up that Sunday evening at dinner?"

"Well, yes, because I heard she'd been arrested. I figured it was for the drugs again and I was right. You know, that's why I really didn't like her for Billy. So, I asked about it."

"What did Billy tell you?"

"He said she'd been arrested, and that they had broken up because of it. Billy didn't like her doing all the drugs. That's why he broke up with her. My sons aren't involved with that nonsense." Mrs. Malone raised her chin. "They don't do drugs."

Annie regarded her for a moment. "Your sons may not do drugs, but they sell drugs, don't they?"

"Objection." Clancy jumped up. "Calls for speculation."

"Overruled."

Mrs. Malone's eyelids fluttered. "Not that I'm aware."

"I see." Annie had to tread lightly. She decided to dangle the drug dealer part out there. If she pressed further, Mrs. Malone would dig her heels in and feign that she had no knowledge. Perhaps that's why she was so involved in her church activities, keeping herself busy, ignoring what her sons were up to.

Annie walked toward her table and spun around when positioned near the center of the jury box. "One last thing. The Boston Police never shot a hole in your window, did they?"

Mrs. Malone opened her mouth to answer, but Clancy stood and thrust his hand up.

"Don't answer that. Objection." Clancy skirted around his table. "Sidebar, Your Honor?"

Annie cast a bewildered look at the jury as she approached the bench to make it appear like Clancy was attempting to cover up information.

"Your Honor?" Clancy whispered to the judge. "You know this isn't fair. Miss Fitzgerald is dredging up the Sergeant Amidon shooting. You've already ruled against it coming in. Remember?"

Judge Killam smirked. "You blew it, counselor. Your witness implied that the police shot a hole through the window, and Miss Fitzgerald has the right to set the record straight."

"But, Mrs. Malone didn't specifically state that the police shot her window. She merely alluded to her window being shot."

Annie raised a finger. "She might as well have said it. Mrs. Malone included the window along with a laundry list of items the police tipped upside down or destroyed. It's only fair the shooting come in now."

"No way. If you let that in, Judge, I'm demanding a mistrial." Clancy's nostrils flared. "It's extremely prejudicial."

Judge Killam rubbed his forehead. "I'll allow limited questions about the window under the circumstances. I'll instruct the jury there is no evidence linking Malone to that event. Your request for a mistrial is denied, Clancy."

"Note my objection for the record." Clancy huffed, but Annie watched him smile for the jury on his way back to the defense table.

Annie resumed her former position and waited for Judge Killam to finish instructing the jury. Mrs. Malone's testimony had worked to her advantage. She could never predict what a witness would say and neither could Clancy. People often blurted things out under pressure. Clancy must have instructed Mrs. Malone not to mention anything about the window, but it just slipped out.

"Commonwealth?" Judge Killam nodded at Annie.

"Once again, Mrs. Malone, the Boston Police didn't shoot a hole through your living room window, did they?"

"I'm not sure who did it."

"Do you recall how that bullet hole ended up in your window?"

"Objection," Clancy said.

"Overruled."

"After my sons were arrested and cuffed, a shot came from outside. Everyone ducked down."

Annie noticed several jurors exchanging curious glances. "Is that when the bullet entered your living room?"

"Yes, it came right through the window." Mrs. Malone demonstrated by moving her hand across her body.

"When did Drake Reed leave your house again?" Annie asked.

"Objection."

"Overruled."

"About forty-five minutes earlier."

Annie walked toward the witness stand and stopped. "Are you sure you didn't see him carrying a gun?"

"Objection." Clancy rose. "Asked and answered."

"Sustained."

"Where did Mr. Reed go after he left your house?"

"I don't know, but I'm certain it wasn't him. The only ones I saw with guns were the police."

Mrs. Malone had volunteered too much information again. Annie considered herself lucky. She must've had it in her head that a police officer stationed outside had fired a shot through the window, and had aimed at Billy, but missed. Annie didn't buy it. They wouldn't miss and hit one of their own. Annie paced for a moment; she needed time to think. She decided to go for it.

"Did anyone get shot when the bullet entered your living room?" Annie asked.

"One of the—"

"Objection!" Clancy shot up. "Don't answer that."

"Sustained."

"Sidebar?" Annie asked.

"No."

"I see. Thank you, Mrs. Malone. I have no further questions." Annie studied the jurors. They would have to read between the lines. Someone must have read something about Sergeant Amidon getting shot during the arrests.

"At this time we'll break for the day." Judge Killam smiled at Mrs. Malone. "Thank you for your time."

Annie breathed a sigh of relief when the judge and jury left the courtroom. She had managed to get through the day. That morning she had had her doubts. Annie felt the tension in her neck and lower back as she gathered her papers. She fished a bottle of ibuprofen from her briefcase, and swallowed three pills without any water. Now she had to get in touch with Callahan and figure out what to do next. She needed to find Trevor's friend Paul Garrity and persuade him to talk.

Annie entered the hallway with her head lowered to avoid the reporters.

"Hey." Chris stepped in front of her, blocking her path to the elevators.

"How come Malone's girlfriend's allowed to testify when she's been sitting back there taking notes? And why didn't you just tell the judge she wasn't there that night?"

Annie couldn't believe he was speaking to her again. "Chris, I objected to her testimony on several legal grounds. Judge Killam simply doesn't want his head handed to him by the appeals court for failing to allow a potential witness to testify in a criminal case."

"That judge always rules against my brother. Stacy Black's a liar—she wasn't there." Chris spread his arms.

"If she really wasn't there, the jury'll know she's lying by the time I'm finished with her on cross."

"But I know for a fact." Chris had raised his voice, causing a camera crew to look over and head their way. "What's she going to say?"

"Don't know. She refuses to speak with me. I'm sure Malone instructed her not to. She can be as uncooperative as she wants."

"I told you the legal system sucks." Chris kicked an empty Styrofoam coffee cup that someone had left on the floor. "Why don't you just give up?" He headed toward the elevators.

"I need you on that witness stand." Annie caught up with him. She knew if the judge let Clancy add a witness now, it would make it easier for her to add a rebuttal witness even though she had rested her case.

"Out of the question," he said.

"Why?"

"I told you from the beginning."

"But things have changed. Look what he did to Jennianne. It's wrong, Chris. Please help me."

His face contorted. "Don't go there."

"I have to. Do you want Malone to win?"

He turned and stared at her for a moment: "*You* killed Jennianne."

"No." Annie maintained eye contact. "I did what I had to do."

"Like you did in my basement." Chris slipped into the elevator as the doors were closing.

46

ELAINE WATCHED RACHEL shove her way through a crowd of people, and dash down the courthouse steps. "That girl has a pair of sticks for legs, way too skinny." She pointed an elbow at Rachel.

"Well . . ." Louie hesitated. "I don't pay much attention."

"Not healthy. Are you taking the T today?" Elaine adjusted her pocketbook strap across her shoulder.

"I always take the Green Line out to Brighton. Can't drive, no parking around here."

"I'll walk over to Government Center with you. Could use a little sunshine after being cooped up in that courthouse." They headed toward the T Station.

"Might as well enjoy it now." He turned his face toward the sun, and shielded his eyes. "They're predicting a cold front, you know, coming down from Canada. Going to get worse before it gets better. We can expect a deep freeze over the next two nights. With this heavy cloud cover we're sure to have some accumulation. It's going to—oh look, there's a crocus." Louie pointed to the tiny lavender flower in one of the dormant flower beds next to the sidewalk. "Now that's a sign of spring."

"So much for the crocuses with all the bad weather you're predicting."

Elaine's lower back ached from sitting all day. During Mrs. Malone's testimony she had also been struck by a charley horse in her right thigh. All she could think about was getting up and walking it out; it had been tough to concentrate. The afternoon seemed to drag on forever. She breathed in the scent of fried Italian sausages, onions, and red peppers from the stand up ahead. Her stomach growled. The cheers of a crowd echoed from Faneuil Hall Marketplace. Elaine peered over her shoulder; a large circle had formed around a clown on stilts juggling bowling pins. She thought about Clancy and his clown tie.

"It's a living shame what them cops did to Mrs. Malone's home," Elaine said. "They'll trash a place, you know."

"How do you know?" Louie said.

"They ripped my neighbor's house to shreds looking for stuff against her grandson. Did the same thing with the flour and sugar. I felt so sorry for her that I volunteered to clean the place up for free."

"That was nice of you. I wonder why they do that to people?"

"To make their lives miserable, Louie." Elaine slowed her pace. "What do you think about the prosecution hiding a witness from us? Imagine that? They got caught red-handed though. Malone's got himself a good lawyer."

"Clancy's a character, alright; I love his bow ties. Wonder where he gets them? Oh look." He pointed at a wispy cloud. "That's a mare's tail. It's a sign that bad weather's coming."

Elaine ignored the weather comment. "I wonder what this new witness will say. Could put a whole different twist on the case, you know? I wish they told us more about how the window got shot up, too."

"That came out of nowhere," Louie said. "Like those clouds."

"Exactly. Fitzgerald tries to hide the bad stuff." Elaine raised her eyebrows. "I heard a police sergeant got killed, too, when they arrested Malone."

"Really? I don't recall hearing anything about that. I wonder why they didn't tell us right off the bat? That would make a big difference to me." Louie gazed at the sky again. "I thought one of the cops did it, aiming at Malone. Seems like they're out to get him all the time."

"Amen." Elaine recalled the intensity in Detective Callahan's eyes when he was testifying. They circled around a young homeless man collecting cans near the T entrance. "You see a lot of that these days, Louie. So young. I blame it on all the drugs coming from Mexico."

"Mmm hmm."

"That's what bothers me about this case. They want us to believe Trevor was a heroin addict and then miraculously came clean? I don't buy that for a second."

"I thought he went to a treatment center?" Louie removed his wallet from his back pocket, and pulled out a train pass.

"Don't matter. You can go to a dozen centers. Can't break a heroin habit. I oughta know—got a niece who's addicted to it. She's been in and out of rehab, but lives on the streets most of the time. On methadone and skinny as a rail, too. She won't make it past forty."

"Shame."

"It is. The ex-husband's got custody of their three young children. They hardly ever see their mother."

Louie shook his head as he pushed through the turnstile. Elaine retrieved her pass and followed him down the stairs to the subway.

"Heroin addicts mix with some real shady characters, drug dealers, you name it. Anybody could've whacked Trevor or given him a bad batch of drugs," Elaine said.

"I never thought about that. Maybe it was Domenico? He gets his heroin from Afganistan."

"You're right. And then you have Jennianne Smith, another admitted heroin user." Elaine lowered her voice. "Did you read the papers this morning, Louie?"

"What?" He cupped his hand next to his ear as a train came into the station. The brakes squealed.

Elaine raised her voice. "Did you read the newspaper?"

"Oh. They said it would turn again by suppertime."

"Turn?"

"Cold. The temperature's going to drop by thirty degrees."

"No, I'm talking about the headlines. What do you make of Jennianne Smith getting killed in that car accident?"

"Oh. I flipped past that. We're not supposed to read the newspapers or watch television, remember?"

"Yeah, yeah, I know. But I'm sure everybody else did, except for you."

"Well, I wouldn't want to get caught."

Elaine pictured him hiding in his closet, reading the weather section with a flashlight. "I'm surprised they didn't stop the case."

"Why? Do you think Malone had something to do with it?" Louie lowered his voice.

"It's under investigation, but if he had her killed no one will be able to prove it."

"I suppose." Louie pointed at a train. "B line's here. Don't forget to dress warm for tomorrow."

Callahan parked next to Drake Reed's red triple decker on School Street. A man stood on the sidewalk right outside wearing jeans, a Patriots sweatshirt, and a baseball cap. Callahan could tell by his clean-cut look that he was a federal agent. Bertrand was most likely inside, tearing the place apart. Callahan hadn't decided what to say . . . yet. He walked past the agent and up the three front steps.

"Excuse me? You looking for somebody?" the man said.

"Police business." Callahan flashed his badge.

"Wait, I have to run it by—"

Callahan ignored him and walked through the front door, closing it behind him. A gray-haired woman stood at the other end of the mud-room. Callahan almost didn't recognize Reed's mother. She looked like she'd aged ten years in a week's time.

"Hello, Mrs. Reed," he said.

She nodded and blinked several times as if fighting back tears.

"I'm sorry for your loss, I really am." He extended his hand. "Detective Mike Callahan, Boston PD. We met briefly."

"Yes, I know."

Callahan felt her cold fingers when she shook his hand. The banging sounds of drawers being opened and shut came from upstairs.

"Are you with them?" she asked, pointing toward the stairs leading up.

"No, I'm here in connection with the Malone case going on now." Callahan watched her fiddling with a key ring, which contained a single brass key. She'd probably let Bertrand in.

"The artist." Her words were barely audible.

"Yeah." Callahan wanted to jump right in and ask questions. Maybe she knew something about Trevor and why Malone had been out to get him. But his instincts told him to hold off for the time being. "It's not easy."

"No, it's not," she whispered.

Heavy footsteps pounded down the stairs.

"Oh, no!" Bertrand crossed his arms back and forth when he saw Callahan. "This is a federal investigation. You have no business here."

Callahan simply stared at him as did Mrs. Reed.

"Are you deaf?" he said. "Scram."

Callahan breathed in. He had to control himself this time, especially in front of Mrs. Reed. "I believe this may be related to the Malone case. I have certain information from Chief Turner in Gloucester."

Bertrand cackled. "That bozo doesn't know what he's talking about."

"I have the right to look around."

"No, you don't." Bertrand grinned. "It's all classified. Now get out before I arrest you again."

Callahan handed Mrs. Reed a card. "Again, I'm sorry for your loss." He turned his back on Bertrand and walked out.

47

THE DEFENSE CALLS Stacy Black." Clancy stood in the center of the courtroom that morning, and tried to appear as controled as possible. He adjusted his shamrock bow tie, which matched his suspenders.

Stacy strutted down the aisle. She wore a tiny dark purple skirt without stockings and a tight silver top with black sparkles on it. It looked like her nightclub attire. Clancy figured it was all she had to dress up in.

"Do you swear to tell the truth, the whole truth, and nothing but the truth, so help you God?" Clerk Fallon said.

She raised her right hand. "Yeah. I do."

Clancy almost wished her testimony had been barred. This could potentially blow up. It was up to him to make her story credible.

"Please introduce yourself to His Honor and the ladies and gentlemen of the jury," Clancy said. He had instructed Stacy to smile, appear humble, and make eye contact with the jury, especially in the beginning. His advice probably went in one ear and out the other.

"Stacy Black." She chomped on gum.

Clancy cringed. He couldn't believe she was chewing gum. Did she have it under her tongue when he spoke with her a few minutes ago? Had she just put it in her mouth? Clancy should've instructed her not to have any. She should've known better.

"Where are you from?" he asked.

"Charlestown."

"How long have you lived in Charlestown?"

"I grew up there."

"Do you have a relationship with the defendant?"

"Billy's my boyfriend." She gazed at Malone and smiled.

Clancy noticed the pride in Stacy's voice. She was clearly in love with him as Jennianne had been. Was she afraid of him? Intimidated? Would she do anything for him? Had he coerced her into testifying?

He decided to move along. "Do you recall November tenth of last year?"

"Mmm hmm." Stacy chewed the gum with her mouth wide open.

Clancy hoped she wouldn't blow a big bubble and pop it. "What were you doing in the afternoon?"

"Me and Billy was watchin' a movie from eleven 'til four at my place, and then he was talking about how he was gonna break up with Jenni-anne."

Clancy thought she sounded rehearsed. "Was Billy with you the entire afternoon?"

"Absolutely." She crossed her arms.

Clancy glanced over at Annie scribbling notes on her legal pad. She hadn't objected to his leading question.

"What happened after the movie?"

"We took a walk up Bunker Hill to Collier's for subs and brought 'em back to my place."

"What happened next?"

"Billy left." Stacy still hadn't made any eye contact with the jury. Instead, she kept giving Malone seductive looks.

"What time was that?" Clancy asked.

She shrugged with one shoulder. "Around six."

"What did you do for the rest of the evening?"

"Well, I knew Billy was going to break up with Jennianne that night.

He was going over there, you know, to do it? So, I just decided to show up." Stacy smirked and looked at Malone again.

"You decided to go over to Jennianne Smith's house at Thirty-six Walford Way?"

"Yeah, I wanted to make sure it happened." She snapped her gum.

"What time did you arrive?" Clancy asked.

"Around seven thirty."

"Who was present?"

"Um, Billy, Frank, Trevor, and Jennianne." Stacy examined her chipped fingernails; she still hadn't made any eye contact with the jury.

"What happened when you first arrived?"

"The bitch started into me and picked up a beer can—"

"Miss!" Judge Killam leaned over the bench. "You will refrain from using that language in my courtroom."

"What language? Oh, you mean, *bitch*?"

Clancy cut in. "Miss Black, what happened?"

"So, Jennianne started going after me, accusing me of stealing her boyfriend and shit—" She glanced up at the judge. "Sorry . . . *stuff*. So, she was screaming at me like crazy, like I couldn't even get half of what she was saying. Threw a beer can at me. She was probably on something."

"What did you do at that point?" Clancy had expected an objection from Annie, but figured she was holding off on purpose. The more his witness blabbed, the more ammunition she'd have for cross.

"Jennianne started going after me, so Billy had to jump in the middle to try and stop her. She just couldn't take the fact that he was breaking up with her for me." She placed her hand on her chest. Clancy wondered how much of this was true. It sounded plausible.

"Did anyone else react or do anything?"

"Yeah, Trevor was sitting on the couch and then he got up. I remember him saying, 'This is way too much for me, man.'"

"Were you familiar with Trevor Shea?"

"Yeah, I knew who he was. He was a friend of Jennianne's. They used to party together." She rubbed her nose.

"What did you observe Trevor do after he got up?"

"He grabbed his drug stuff off the table and got out of there."

"What kind of drug stuff?" Clancy hooked his thumbs beneath his suspenders.

"Bags of heroin, a syringe." She shrugged. "He was, you know, a druggie, an addict. He always had that kinda stuff with him."

"Objection!" Annie shot to her feet. "Speculative. Move to strike."

"Overruled."

"Was Trevor wearing a jacket when he left?" Clancy asked.

"Nope, no jacket."

"Did you see anyone injecting heroin that evening?"

"Nope."

"Did you see Trevor inject any heroin?"

"I don't recall, but he was always getting high, so maybe he did, I don't—"

"Objection!" Annie jumped up again. "Highly speculative, Your Honor."

"Sustained."

Clancy loved how Stacy just slipped that in. Perhaps she was smarter than she looked. "Did you observe Trevor walk out the door?"

"Yeah, like I said, he just up and left."

Clancy faced the jury and raised his voice. "Was Trevor Shea alive when he left the apartment?"

Stacy raised an eyebrow. "I would say so if he walked outta there."

Clancy wished she had merely answered yes instead of being sarcastic. "What time did Trevor leave the apartment?"

"At eight o'clock."

"Did you see Billy or Frank Malone with any heroin that evening?"

"Nope." Stacy smiled at Billy. "Trevor was the only one with heroin. My boyfriend had nothin' to do with Trevor Shea dying. Nothin'."

"Objection."

"Sustained."

"No further questions." Clancy smiled at the jurors before heading back to his table.

. . .

Rachel noticed Fitzgerald's taught facial muscles as she passed by Clancy and strutted into center court for what was bound to be a face-off. She wore an attractive pin-striped gray suit.

"Stacy Black?" Fitzgerald continued walking toward the witness stand.

"That's my name." Stacy wrinkled her nose.

"You came forward as a witness just yesterday, am I correct?"

"If you say so."

"I'm not the one testifying." Fitzgerald motioned to herself. "Please answer the question with a yes or no."

Stacy rolled her eyes. "Yeah."

"You refused to speak with me?"

"Attorney Clancy said I didn't have to talk to nobody if I didn't want to."

"I see." Fitzgerald glanced at Clancy. "Were you aware that Judge Killam ordered all witnesses to be sequestered?"

"Nope."

"So no witness can listen to another's testimony and change her story to fit the facts, isn't that so?"

"How would I know?" She huffed. "I'm not a lawyer."

"In fact, you've been in the back of this courtroom taking notes." Fitzgerald pointed to the rear of the gallery.

"I didn't take no notes, and I didn't think it was against the law to sit in the back of a courtroom. For your information, I didn't come forward 'til yesterday because I was afraid to, okay?"

"Afraid? Afraid of whom, your boyfriend Billy Malone?"

"No, him over there, Chris Shea." She pointed at Trevor's brother seated in the front row.

"Bitch," Chris said.

"Order!" Judge Killam banged his gavel.

"He didn't threaten you." Fitzgerald dragged out her words, sounding contemptuous.

Stacy leaned over the witness stand and sneered. "He didn't have to. *We're* from Charlestown."

Rachel zeroed in on Trevor's brother. He sat there, staring at the witness, with a scowl on his face and arms crossed. Is that really why this woman hadn't come forward earlier? Had he intimidated her somehow? If Malone was so powerful, wouldn't he protect her? Rachel wondered if Trevor's brother and Malone had a past. She sensed a strong undertow in the case and it had everything to do with Charlestown. Detective Callahan had referred to it earlier. *Charlestown, only one square mile . . . they don't hear anything, don't see anything, and nobody talks to cops.*

"Where did you watch that movie again?" Fitzgerald asked.

"My place."

"What time?"

She sighed into the microphone, which made a loud scratching noice. "I already told you all this."

"Pardon me, Miss Black, I'd like to hear the information again."

"It was the afternoon, eleven to four." She picked off flakes of red polish from her fingernails.

"Billy was with you the entire time?"

"Never took my eyes off a him." She smiled at Malone.

"Even while Billy had lunch with Miles Domenico up in Gloucester?"

Clancy raised a finger. "You mean, the perjurer?"

Judge Killam banged his gavel. Rachel laughed at Clancy's little jab; she liked his green shamrock tie.

"What did you do between the time the movie ended until you went over to Jennianne's apartment?"

"Nothin', got subs and just hung out." She raised her eyes at Malone.

"What time did you go to Jennianne's?" Fitzgerald placed a hand on her hip.

"I walked over around sevenish or so."

"Had you ever been to Jennianne's place before?"

"Nah uh." Stacy wrinkled her nose. "I never hung out with her."

Rachel had noticed the difference between the two women. Both city girls, but Jennianne had seemed more vulnerable, like a victim. She was also much prettier. Stacy Black was a tough cookie. Both had a relationship with the defendant. Rachel gazed at Malone, and he made eye contact with her. Malone's eyes commanded power, the kind of power that could hypnotize a woman. Rachel could tell both girlfriends were in love with him. Would this one say anything to please him? Had he instructed her what to say?

"What rooms were you in?" Fitzgerald moved toward the witness.

"Only the living room."

"Can you describe it?"

She rolled her eyes. "I don't remember no exact details. I was paying most of my attention to Jennianne who was clobbering me."

Rachel couldn't imagine Jennianne leading the attack. One shove from Stacy would likely send the waiflike Jennianne flying across the room.

Fitzgerald took several more steps, angling toward the witness stand. "Where was Trevor sitting?"

"On the couch."

"What color was the couch?"

"Maroon." Stacy stuck her chin out. "The rug was maroon, too. I remember not liking it much."

Rachel knew Fitzgerald was challenging her on the details, trying to trip her up. So far, it wasn't working.

"Where was the TV located?"

She shrugged. "I don't know, behind me someplace. I was too busy being hit."

"What type of beer can did Jennianne throw at you?"

"Genesee."

"Did you see heroin on the table?"

"I saw drug stuff, yeah."

"A Walgreens bag?"

"No." Stacy grinned as if she knew Fitzgerald was trying to trick her. "CVS, it was from CVS."

"Did Billy touch the heroin?"

"Billy don't do heroin."

"But he sells heroin, doesn't he?" Fitzgerald motioned toward Malone.

"Objection." Clancy stood.

"Overruled, answer the question, Miss," Judge Killam said.

"Billy don't sell it neither."

"After you ran out, did you go home?"

"Billy ran out after me and we both drove back to my place."

"How long was Billy there?"

"All night." She smiled at Malone.

Fitzgerald paced for a moment with her index finger against her lips. "Did you walk or drive home?"

"Drove."

"In your car?"

"Yeah."

"Hmm." Fitzgerald made eye contact with Rachel. "A minute ago you said you walked over to Jennianne's house, but now, you drove home?"

"Um. Wait. No, that's right, me and Billy walked home."

"So, where did you leave your car?"

"My car?" Stacy looked at Malone and pursed her lips.

"Yes." Fitzgerald cocked her head.

"It would've been parked on the street that night in front of my place."

"What kind of car do you drive?"

"Buick."

"What color?"

Stacy made eye contact with Malone again. Rachel noticed a change, a worried look in her eyes.

"What color is your car?"

"Uh. Olive. Sort of."

"Olive? You mean green?"

"Yeah, I guess." Stacy shrugged and looked down.

"What year is it?"

"I don't know, I don't remember." She shifted in her seat.

"You don't remember the year? Did you drive here today?"

"Yeah. Well, no."

"Is that a yes or a no?"

"No."

Rachel listened and watched carefully. Fitzgerald had latched onto something and pressed her. With each question, she moved forward, until she was almost hovering over the witness stand.

"Why didn't you drive your car?"

Stacy looked at Malone as if he could provide her with an answer. "My car, it's . . ."

Fitzgerald stared at her. "What?"

"In the shop."

"Why?"

"Objection." Clancy waved his arm. "Relevance?"

"Overruled," Judge Killam said. "Answer the question."

"Somebody rear-ended me."

"When?"

"Last week sometime."

"What shop is it in?"

"In Somerville. Bob's Auto."

Fitzgerald placed both hands on her hips and continued staring at Stacy Black. "No further questions."

Rachel watched Fitzgerald resume her seat, and write something down in her legal pad. She wondered why Fitzgerald had zeroed in on the car like that.

"Sidebar, Your Honor?" Clancy said.

"Approach."

Instead of watching the lawyers argue again during the sidebar conference, Rachel focused on Malone. There were two completely different versions of what happened the night Trevor died. Who should they believe? She wished Jennianne Smith could have finished her testimony. What was Jennianne about to say before she made eye contact with Malone and fell apart? Malone must've ordered Stacy Black to testify for him. Rachel was convinced that she would say whatever that man wanted her to say. She was clearly under his spell. Should all of her testimony be ignored? Rachel thought back to the drug dealer who had perjured himself. These witnesses had their own agendas, yet they had sworn to tell the truth, the whole truth, and nothing but the truth.

"We'll break for the day," Judge Killam said, after the sidebar conference. Once again, he warned them not to discuss the case or follow the news.

"All rise."

Rachel was surprised they weren't continuing through the afternoon. She felt an elbow in the chest. *Elaine again.* "Hey, watch out."

"Fake, just what I thought," Elaine mumbled.

"Excuse me?" Rachel said.

Elaine grinned and faced the other way.

Rachel sighed. For some reason that woman hated her; she could sense it. Rachel had attempted small talk on several occasions, but Elaine had rudely ignored her. *Jealousy, no doubt.*

Rachel wondered if any of her fellow jurors were secretly discussing the case. People seemed to be avoiding her. They were probably worried she'd tell the judge because she was the foreperson.

She turned and exchanged eye contact with Malone before leaving the courtroom. She hoped to hear from him in the morning. After all, Clancy said he was so anxious to prove his innocence. She wondered what Fitzgerald would do to him on cross.

48

WHAT THE HELL is going on now?" Malone said to Clancy as soon they were back at the holding cell. He hated being kept in the dark when the lawyers were whispering during those sidebar conferences. This was *his* trial. Didn't he have the right to know?

"We're taking the rest of the afternoon off."

Malone balled his fists; he hated delays. "Why?"

"I want you to take advantage of this time to decide once and for all whether you're going to take the stand in your own defense."

"Clancy don't tell me this delay was all your idea?" Malone wished he could shake his senile lawyer. He rested his forehead against the bars. "I told you. I signed your damn papers. You even told the jury, remember?"

"I know, but if I were you, I'd reconsider. Even after I announced you'd be testifying, you can still change your mind. I'll rectify it in my closing argument."

"What are you so afraid of?" Malone gripped the bars with all his strength.

"It's never good when the defendant takes the stand. Stacy's testimony went better than I thought; your mother made a positive impression. Let's quit while we're ahead. I'll rest and make my closing in the morning."

"Quit? You wanna quit?" Malone yelled. "You outta your mind?"

"No, come on, you know what I mean." Clancy placed his hands in his pockets and paced in front of the cell. "I'm afraid you'll incriminate yourself."

"What? You think I *did it* now? No way. I'm saying what really happened."

"But Stacy said it all."

"I was watching that jury. They didn't like her. Why did you let her chew gum and wear that ridiculous hooker outfit?"

"I didn't know she—"

"You're not doing your job." Malone circled his cell; his temples throbbed. "Why did you let her cop that pissy attitude? Now I gotta get up there or this jury'll hang me."

"I disagree. If I rest our case first thing tomorrow, it'll give the other side less time to work with. We don't want them digging up anything else they can use against you at this point."

"Like what?" Malone had placed his feelers out there. He knew Callahan had been asking questions about Stacy, but no one gave him squat. Fitzgerald had been followed as well.

Clancy cracked his knuckles. "You never know. Why take the chance?"

"I'm not going to jail for the rest of my life. That jury needs to hear from me." Malone shoved his face up against the cold bars. "Do you hear me?"

"I've been practicing law for—"

"Don't give me that crap. You got your head so far stuck up your ass."

"I've got to go." Clancy turned and started walking away.

"No, you're not going anywhere. I'm not done here. What was up with all those questions about Stacy's car?"

Clancy faced him again. "Why don't you tell me?"

"No, I hired you. You're supposed to be the lawyer here. I'm asking you a question."

"I have no idea about her car. All I know is your girlfriend looked awfully nervous when asked, and Fitzgerald picked up on that. Maybe they have an ace up their sleeve? That's why I have a bad feeling about you taking the stand." Clancy tipped his hat and walked away. "Think about it."

49

AT FIVE PAST seven that evening, Annie whisked through the main entrance of the Boston Public Library in Copley Square, and turned left toward the old section. This is where Paul Garrity, Trevor's old friend, had reluctantly agreed to meet at seven. She didn't even know what he looked like. He said he'd find her.

Annie wanted to stop and browse as she passed by the giant wall of new releases. She wished she could grab a mystery, find an isolated seat, and read until closing time. She crossed the outdoor center courtyard and entered the ornate McKim Building, her favorite. As Annie climbed the grand staircase, she admired the Chavannes murals, representing the disciplines of poetry, philosophy, and science. She would have to come back again after the trial.

Annie entered the long reading room with its fifty-foot carved ceiling and sat at the last table at the far end as instructed. She glanced around at the other people sitting at various tables, reading and researching. Was Garrity one of them? Annie grabbed a small notepad and pen from her pocketbook and waited. Now it was nearly ten past the hour; she hoped he hadn't left.

"Miss Fitzgerald?" A voice whispered from behind.

Annie turned to see a tall, thin man in his late twenties wearing a faded blue Red Sox cap, sweatshirt, and jeans. He must've come from the stacks, for she hadn't spotted him at one of the tables. He sat opposite her.

"Thanks for coming." Annie smiled in an attempt to place him at ease.

"I can't be a witness." He looked over his shoulder for a moment and scratched the back of his neck. "And I only have a minute to talk."

"I won't make you testify." She recalled her promise to Jennianne. "I just need some answers." Annie wondered how useful this meeting would be. She decided to get right to the point. "Was Trevor an informant for the FBI?"

"I don't know." Garrity chewed on the edge of his thumbnail. "I got something for you though."

Annie held her breath, knowing she couldn't push him.

"But it's not here." Garrity looked away. "You're going to have to get it yourself somehow. Got a family; can't take any risks."

"What is it?" she whispered.

"A really big painting that Trevor gave me on the day he died." Garrity pinched his lower lip. "It was weird. You know, as if Trev knew." He ran his tongue across his front teeth. "I could tell he just wasn't himself. I thought maybe he was on something." He shrugged. "Maybe he was. So I . . ."

"You found him, and placed the 9-1-1 call, didn't you?" Annie needed to know.

Garrity closed his eyes and nodded. "I was too late. Jennianne sent me a text. She told me where she thought they took him, by the bridge. It was by the bridge."

"What's the painting of?" Annie asked.

"Billy Malone," Garrity whispered and gazed into her eyes. "I think you need it. I should've got hold of you way before this, but I guess I was, you know, afraid to. It's crazy."

"Where is it now?" Annie felt her heart beating faster.

"My aunt's house in Somerville. I almost brought it back home, but thank God I didn't because I got broken into. Got this feeling somebody was looking for it. It was still in the bed of my truck mixed in with my work stuff. I hadn't brought it in yet. Didn't know what to do with it."

"I have to get it tonight, especially with Malone taking the stand in the morning. It may be helpful."

"Well, the house is empty. My aunt and uncle are down south for the winter, but I have a copy of the key for you and the address." Garrity reached into his front pocket and pulled out a single silver key and a slip of paper. "Here." He looked relieved when he handed her the warm key.

"Thank you." Annie felt her heart pounding.

"Least I can do for Trev, you know? So, it's ah, upstairs. The second bedroom on the right under the bed. It's framed, like on the canvas board."

"Okay."

"Good luck." Garrity got up and paused. "Be careful because Malone's probably got somebody watching you around the clock. He's got his people everywhere."

Annie remembered that's exactly what Jennianne had said. "Do you know where the rest of Trevor's paintings are?"

Garrity shook his head. "You need Chris for that."

Annie tied her hair back with two heavy-duty elastics, and secured the remaining strands with bobby pins. She had changed into a pair of black running pants and slipped on her hooded black ski jacket. She peered out her third-floor apartment window in Brookline and scanned the street below. A young couple walked along the sidewalk, holding hands. They were followed by a fast-paced businessman carrying a briefcase. Did Malone really have people watching her? He kept an eye on her in court. Wasn't that enough?

Annie zipped her jacket and headed out the door and down the stairs of her building. Was she crazy doing this alone? Should she request a police escort? Callahan was down on the South Shore with the Scituate police investigating all the auto body shops in the area on the hunch that Jennianne's car had been hit and forced off the road. Annie considered asking Chris for help, but what would he do? Take the painting and run? She didn't trust him. He often looked at her in that knowing sort of way.

Why had she kissed him in the basement? She had clearly crossed the line and compromised the case.

Just do it and get it over with, she told herself. *Stop being paranoid.* Stop thinking about Chris. She kept her head down as she walked up the block.

Annie decided to take her car and drive around a bit first. She checked her rearview mirror several times to see if anyone was trailing her; it didn't feel like it. *No way.* She drove on Storrow Drive along the Charles River and got on the expressway, heading north, past Somerville, and exited in Malden. She took several turns on side streets until she was convinced no one had followed her. Annie plugged the address into her GPS, drove back on the expressway, and headed south again, getting off at the Somerville exit. She turned on the radio to calm her nerves.

Make it quick, she told herself as she pulled up to the address Garrity had provided. She pulled her hood up, felt for the house key in her pants pocket, and grabbed her flashlight. It was nine forty-five. She decided not to lock the car just in case she had to make a quick getaway. She shoved the car keys into her jacket pocket. Go in and come right back out. Annie's sneakers squished into the mud along the side of the house making a slight sucking sound. Otherwise, it was relatively quiet. She could hear the rush of traffic on the expressway in the distance. A faint smell of skunk wafted in the air.

Annie spotted the back wooden steps leading up to the small deck and rear door. She looked around, and noticed lights on in various houses. This was even scarier than breaking into Chris's basement. Bad thoughts crossed her mind as she climbed up to the deck. What if Garrity worked for Malone and this was a setup? She pictured Malone and the way he stared at her with those dark, brooding eyes. At times, he leaned forward and squinted with such concentration as if formulating a plan. Annie's fingers trembled when she inserted the key in the lock. Was Malone brazen enough to go after a prosecutor? Jennianne had been terrified of him, and rightly so. Annie shuddered. What was Malone thinking about when he stared at her? He knew she wouldn't give up no matter what obstacles he created for her. It all came down to willpower and survival.

Annie glanced up at the dark house. A dim light shone through one of the windows toward the front. Was someone inside or did they leave a light on because they were away? Garrity would not have sent her to an occupied house. Annie turned the key in the lock and slowly opened the door. The hinges creaked when she walked in, even her breathing sounded extra loud. What if she got caught? This was not a break-in, she reminded herself. Garrity had provided a key and asked her to retrieve something for him, that's all.

Annie rotated the knob and quietly closed the door behind her. She stood in the dark for a minute, just listening, before turning the flashlight on. The beam revealed a tall, wrought-iron coatrack with jackets and umbrellas dangling from it. This was a small mudroom. It smelled dank and musty like any unoccupied house would. She moved her light around and spotted the entranceway to the kitchen. *Find the back stairs.* Garrity had said they were located somewhere off the kitchen. Annie tiptoed onto the linoleum floor, and circled around an oval island with two stools around it, toward a pair of brown French doors. She slid the doors open, and found a pantry.

Annie hated being here. It didn't feel right. Something was going to go wrong; she had a bad feeling. The refrigerator started humming, which startled her. Where was that staircase? She took a deep breath and shone her beam up and down in a circle. She walked diagonally to the other side of the kitchen and pushed a swinging door, which led to a small dining room. There were newspapers and boxes stacked up high on the table. *No stairs.*

Annie reentered the kitchen, and spotted a gap next to the refrigerator, which she hadn't seen before. She walked over and spotted the narrow staircase leading up. *Almost there.* Visions of Malone filled her mind again. Annie willed herself to keep going, and climbed the steep old staircase. Garrity had instructed her to go to the first bedroom on the left. Annie stepped into the hallway, pushed the first door open, and walked toward a four-poster bed. She squatted and shone the flashlight underneath, which illuminated a large, flat object toward the head of the bed. Annie's heart raced. She lay on her stomach, and stretched her arm under. It felt like a painting stretched on canvas board, which had been wrapped up in trash bags and secured with duct tape.

Annie dragged the painting out from beneath the bed, and sneezed twice from the cloud of dust. It was quite cumbersome. She wondered if all of Trevor's paintings were life-sized and eerie. The self-portrait from the basement had been larger than life. The penciled-in eye sockets could practically swallow someone. Annie wanted to rip the plastic off and take a look at this one. *No, get it out of here first.* She tucked the painting under her right arm, held the flashlight in her left hand, and headed out of the bedroom toward the stairs.

Annie banged the canvas board against the wall several times on the way down. She tripped over her feet on the last step and nearly fell onto the kitchen floor. She couldn't wait to get the giant painting back to her apartment and unwrap it. Light shone from beneath the swinging door that led to the dining room. Annie froze. There were no lights on in that room before. She hadn't turned any on. That meant someone else . . . footsteps pounded in the other end of the house. She panicked.

Annie eyed the pantry. *Hide in there.* She turned off her flashlight and squeezed through the French doors with the painting. She shuffled to the opposite end and crouched down in the corner in between the shelving. Annie maneuvered the painting at an angle in front of her. She crouched, removed her jacket, and covered herself with it.

Annie listened. The house sounded quiet again except for the steady ringing in her ears. Someone must've come in through the front door while she was upstairs. Who was it? Something rattled in another part of the house, followed by the thuds of doors opening and closing. Annie wished she had something to defend herself with. Next time she vowed to carry a small spray can of Mace. *Always next time.* The footsteps clomped louder, sounding like heavy boots. Annie guessed they belonged to a man. The kitchen lights went on. Annie cringed as she heard boots crossing the linoleum and stopping.

The French doors to the pantry rattled open. *Stay right there, don't come in.* She heard a click and the light came on. The ringing in her ears escalated. Someone panted, like he'd been running, searching for something or someone. Annie tensed. He was going to find her. She smelled card-board boxes and visualized the storage room in her family's bookstore. This time Annie wasn't safe. Had she ever been safe? Would she ever be safe again? *Please don't look behind the painting. Turn around, go away.* The guy snorted and coughed. The seconds dragged on. Annie heard shuffling, the French doors rattled again. The footsteps retracted.

Where was he going? The footsteps pounded up the stairs. Annie heard him right above her. He would be heading through the hallway and per-haps taking the front staircase back down. What if he searched the house again, and, next time, looked behind the painting? Annie couldn't risk it. She grabbed her jacket, lifted the painting, and headed into the bright kitchen toward the mudroom. The flashlight would have to stay behind.

Annie banged the painting against the center island in the kitchen. He probably heard her. *Keep going. Run.* She headed into the mudroom, lost her balance, and grabbed the coatrack. It fell over, crashing against the wall and onto the floor. She turned the doorknob to get out, but it wouldn't move. Annie had relocked the door after she got in. She twisted the silver lock with her trembling fingers and thumb. *Stuck.* She forced it until it fi-nally moved. As she opened the outside door, she heard footsteps pounding down the back stairs.

"Hey, who's down there!" a man yelled.

Annie bolted outside and leaped off the deck. She dodged around the corner of the house as fast as she could. The big painting slowed her down. *Just get to the car.* Her jacket slipped from over her arm and fell. Annie stopped to pick it up, losing time. She ran along the sidewalk to her car. She opened the door. *No keys. No keys.* They'd been in her jacket pocket.

She looked over her shoulder; he'd be coming any second. *Keep running.* Annie gripped the painting with both hands and ran off the sidewalk. She cut between houses, and ran along a chain-link fence. She darted under a deck and hid behind two plastic garbage barrels. Her lungs hurt from breathing so hard. A siren wailed nearby.

Annie caught her breath first and then called Callahan. It rang three times before he picked up.

"Hey there," he said.

"Where are you?" she asked.

"Heading back from Scituate, almost home. Why?"

"Can you come pick me up? I lost my car keys."

"Sure." He paused. "Are you at the office?"

"No, I'm hiding in a dark alley behind a garbage can in Somerville."

He laughed. "Good one."

"No, really. I'm crouched behind a garbage can with one of Trevor's paintings. It smells like throw-up here, so hurry."

50

THE DEFENSE CALLS Billy Malone." Clancy stood and motioned to his client.

Elaine watched Malone get up and walk around the defense table toward the witness stand. He nodded at Fitzgerald as if they were old friends. She didn't acknowledge him. Elaine thought she looked more tired than usual that morning. She had gray rings beneath her eyes.

Clerk Fallon stood before Malone. "Raise your right hand, please. Do you swear to tell the truth, the whole truth, and nothing but the truth, so help you God?"

"I do." Malone smiled briefly at the clerk and took his seat behind the witness stand.

"Please introduce yourself to the jury." Clancy said.

"Good morning." Malone shifted and looked at Elaine. "I'm William Joseph Malone."

"Please tell us a little about your childhood." Clancy's voice sounded sugary.

"Sure. I grew up on Corey Street in Charlestown with my mother, father, and brother. We were pretty tight, you know, ate all our meals together, went to church every Sunday at St. Catherine's. My father worked down the Navy Yard until it closed and then he struggled to find a job after that."

Elaine caught several grimaces on the faces of the women sitting in the front row. She imagined them all in church together, avoiding eye contact with the Malone family on the way back from communion.

"What do you do in your spare time?" Clancy asked.

"I volunteer with the underprivileged kids at the Boys and Girls Club, organizing pickup basketball games for them. I'm currently looking for a job, but I can't seem to find one without a high school diploma."

Elaine studied Malone. His voice sounded soft. He made eye contact with everyone on the jury, including her. He didn't sound like a vicious killer or a major drug dealer. In fact, he came across quite articulate for a high school dropout.

"Why did you drop out of high school?" Clancy furrowed his brow.

Malone faced the jury. "It's a long story. Basically, I did well in school until my father was murdered, shot in the chest my junior year. Me and my dad were real, real close, so it shook me up pretty bad. I actually witnessed him bleeding to death on the sidewalk outside the Celtic Tavern where they just left him to die. I quit school after that and never went back."

Elaine wondered why his father was murdered. What had he been involved in? Perhaps Liz would know. Regardless, it must have impacted Malone's life. She felt a trace of compassion for him.

"Did the police ever arrest the people responsible for your father's murder?" Clancy sidestepped toward the jury box.

"No." Malone crossed his arms.

"Who was in charge of the investigation?"

"Detective Michael Callahan." Malone raised his voice.

"I see." Clancy pursed his lips. "How did you get along with Detective Callahan?"

"I did my best to cooperate, but Detective Callahan had some other high-profile investigation at the time, so he let my father's case fall right through the cracks." Malone looked right at Elaine.

"What did you do when Callahan dropped the ball?"

"I reported Callahan to his superiors and called the press. I know he got some flack for it, too. From that day on, he's been out to get me."

"Objection." Fitzgerald stood.

"Overruled."

"Have you had any contact with Detective Callahan since the time he dropped your dad's case?"

"Yeah, he's done his best to arrest me for any trumped-up charge he can think of. One time, after I was found not guilty for one of his phony arrests, he pointed a finger at me and said, 'I'll get you. The next murder to go down in Charlestown is on your back, no matter who did it.'"

"Objection! Move to strike." Fitzgerald stretched her arms wide.

"Overruled."

Elaine believed Malone; it made sense. Callahan had come across as overly aggressive on the witness stand. Clancy had done a nice job bringing that out on cross. She found herself rooting for Clancy.

"Directing your attention to November tenth of last year, what were you doing during the day?"

"I was with Stacy Black all afternoon. We watched a movie, and then had subs."

Elaine listened to him repeat most of what they had already heard from the second girlfriend. He was quite the charmer. She imagined the two women exploding with jealousy.

"Did you see Miles Domenico on November tenth of last year?" Clancy placed his hands on his hips.

Malone shook his head. "Absolutely not."

"Do you know Miles Domenico?"

"I'm familiar with him."

"In what context?"

Malone sighed. "A few years back he tried to channel his drug trade into Charlestown through me. I refused to do it. He has a nasty reputation, and I wanted nothing to do with him. I told him there would be trouble if he attempted to bring his drugs into my hometown. I know for a fact he's been trying his hardest to work his way through Charlestown into Boston. I know he worked a deal with Callahan to get rid of me."

"Objection, move to strike." Fitzgerald jumped up. "Speculative."

"The last sentence will be stricken from the record," Judge Killam said.

"Did you ever purchase Nine-eleven heroin from this Domenico character?" Clancy raised his voice.

Malone leaned forward. "Never."

"Did you plan on killing Trevor Shea at Jennianne Smith's that evening?" Clancy asked.

"No, I didn't even expect to see him." Malone looked at Fitzgerald.

"What happened when you arrived at Jennianne's?" Clancy rubbed his chin.

"When I got there I told her we had to talk." Malone turned and faced the jurors again. "I was about to tell Jennianne that her drinking and the drugs were getting way too much for me, and that I wanted out. But, before I could tell her, Trevor showed up. She must've asked him over."

"Objection." Fitzgerald said. "Move to strike the last sentence."

Judge Killam faced the jury. "The last remark shall be stricken from the record."

Clancy nodded. "What happened next?"

"We had a beer and a smoke. My brother Frank had come over, too. We were going to stop by my mother's after, so that's why he was there." Malone gestured toward his mother in the audience. "Then Trevor pulled out a sketch pad and started making a picture of Jennianne." Malone shrugged. "I didn't think nothing of it. He was always drawing and painting stuff."

Elaine wondered why Trevor was over there in the first place. No one 'fessed up to inviting him. Jennianne could've asked him—they'd been friends for years. Elaine scratched her cheek. It was also believable that Malone would've invited Trevor if he had planned to kill him. But why was Malone's brother really there? If this had been a preplanned murder, as Jennianne had suggested, perhaps he was there to help Malone get rid of Trevor's body later on. That would make sense. It seemed like Malone forced the explanation as to why his brother was there; it wasn't natural. He should've left it alone.

"Did you observe Trevor doing anything else?" Clancy asked.

Malone nodded. "He pulled out a CVS bag from beneath his jacket."

"Did you see what was in it?"

"Yeah, a bag of Nine-eleven heroin, a syringe, cooker spoon, lighter. The whole nine yards."

Clancy made eye contact with Elaine. "What happened next?"

"Trevor cooked up the heroin. That's when Jennianne began yelling. She didn't want him shooting it up. He wasn't going to listen to her though. It was like he had to have it, you know? Trevor was a serious drug addict." Malone looked into the gallery at Chris. Elaine watched Chris grip the edge of the bench until his knuckles turned white. He appeared to be fighting the urge to jump up and strangle Malone right in open court.

"Did you see Trevor inject the heroin?"

"Right into his arm. Then he closed his eyes for a while and just sat there enjoying it."

"What happened next?"

"Then Stacy came and all hell broke loose between the girls. I told her not to. Jennianne was real jealous."

Elaine recalled the fight scene from Stacy's testimony.

"What did Trevor do?" Clancy asked.

"He grabbed his drug stuff and walked right out the door," Malone paused. "Actually, he took off without picking up his garbage."

"What do you mean by that?"

"Trevor left his empty heroin bag on the floor, which I picked up and threw away. He had no respect for Jennianne's place."

"Did you handle the CVS bag?" Clancy painted to the CVS bag on the clerk's table.

"Yeah, and I picked up his beer can and cigarette butts. He took the syringe with him."

"What time did Trevor walk out the door?"

"Around eight, maybe a little before. Me and Stacy ended up taking off around eight thirty or so."

Clancy paced for a moment. "Can you describe your relationship with Trevor?"

"I liked him. He had a great sense of humor." Malone faced the jury and made eye contact with Elaine. "I would never have done anything to hurt Trevor. I had no reason to."

"Did you murder Trevor Shea that evening with a deadly batch of Nine-eleven heroin?" Clancy raised his voice and articulated his words.

"No way, absolutely not."

Clancy nodded. "On Sunday, November twelfth at approximately six P.M., where were you?"

"At my ma's house on Pearl Street in Charlestown."

"What were you doing there?"

"We were celebrating her sixty-fifth birthday." Malone smiled at his mother. "She looked beautiful, too, with a pretty new dress on, and her hair all done up. The dining room table had a white linen tablecloth with this big bouquet of flowers, candles going. You could tell she worked all day trying to make everything perfect."

"And how did it go?" Clancy glanced at Mrs. Malone and her rosary beads.

"We thanked the Lord for the food on our table, and I was just about to carve the corned beef when we heard this thunderous crash, followed by the sound of falling plaster and broken glass coming from the living room. My ma clutched her chest like she was having a heart attack. We all thought we were going to be the victims of an armed home invasion."

"What happened next?"

"We all froze until somebody yelled from the living room: 'Police! Drop your weapons!' My ma told them we were unarmed and begged them not to kill anyone. It took a minute or so before they responded, but then the same voice said, 'Billy Malone, you'll come into the living room slowly with both hands in the air. No one else is to move until instructed by us to do so or we'll blow your f'ing heads off, including the old lady.'" Malone bowed his head. "That was my ma they were talking about."

"Take your time," Clancy said.

Elaine noticed Mrs. Malone crying in the gallery.

Malone took a deep breath. "When I entered the living room with my hands up, there were six loaded guns pointed at my head. Then, Callahan and another cop bounded at me like a pair of rottweilers. Callahan struck me in the back of the head with a nightstick that sent me flying headfirst into the corner of a coffee table. He leaped on my back with his knees, and knocked the wind right out of me. He cuffed my wrists as tight as he could. Then he grabbed hold of my hair, lifted me up about four feet, and smashed my face into the floor. He did it four to five times, all in front of ma. I begged him to stop."

"Did anyone attempt to stop Callahan?"

"My ma screamed when all the blood spurted out. It took three officers to finally pull him off me. He got this crazed look in his eyes. If they hadn't stopped him, he would've killed me right there in front of my mother."

"Objection, move to strike," Fitzgerald said.

"Sustained. The last sentence shall be stricken from the record."

Elaine wouldn't be surprised if they were trying to kill him.

"Your Honor, may I approach the witness?" Clancy grabbed several photos from his table.

"You may."

Clancy showed the pictures to Fitzgerald and handed them to Malone. "Do you recognize these?"

"Yeah, that's what I looked like after Detective Callahan got through with me."

Clancy admitted the photographs into evidence. "Did you seek medical attention for your injuries?"

"About five hours later the cops took me to Mass General, where they treated me for a broken nose and concussion."

"At this time, Your Honor, I'd like to introduce Billy Malone's medical records into evidence."

"Any objection, Commonwealth?"

"I've already stipulated to their admission." Fitzgerald sounded impatient.

"So admitted."

Clancy resumed his position in front of the jury. "Once again, Mr. Malone, did you supply Trevor Shea with a batch of Nine-eleven heroin with the intent to kill him?"

Malone gripped the podium. "I did not."

"No further questions." Clancy headed back to his table.

"Cross?" Judge Killam regarded Fitzgerald.

"Oh yes, Your Honor." She stood and stared at Malone like a lioness about to rip her prey into shreds. Elaine savored the showdown.

"Hold on." Judge Killam raised a finger. "It's a little early, but we'll take our luncheon recess now, and you can cross-examine the defendant in the afternoon."

"All rise!"

Elaine was relieved. She was starving and so was everyone else—stomachs were growling in all directions.

Clancy watched Malone attack his turkey and cheese sandwich in the holding cell. He hadn't seen him eat this much in ages. No tomato soup today—always a good thing.

"See?" Malone spoke with his mouth full. "I was right all along about taking the stand. That went pretty good. I think they actually felt sorry for me at one point."

"Perhaps." Clancy noticed the smug grin, which Malone hid so well from the jury. His client was a great actor; he would've made a terrific lawyer. "Let's get started. We only have an hour."

"For what?" Malone tore open a bag of salt-and-vinegar potato chips with his teeth.

"We have to prepare for cross."

Malone waved him off. "I'm gonna eat and then enjoy a smoke or two."

"Fitzgerald is out for blood."

"So what?" Malone slugged back half his Coke. "I can handle anything that bitch throws at me. Bring it on. I'm not worried about a thing." He belched.

Clancy cringed. That attitude had buried many a client in the past. He paced outside the cell for a moment without replying. "What are you going to say if they find the car?"

Malone looked like he'd been struck over the head with a two-by-four. He spread his arms and gripped the bars. "Hell are you talking about?"

"I hear that Callahan's been out searching body shops for a car on the South Shore. An olive green one. Does that ring a bell?"

"What are you implying, Clancy?"

"Oh, and I also heard they're on the hunt for your girlfriend, Stacy, who decided to take a vacation right after she testified. She must've needed some mental R and R after Fitzgerald's vigorous cross." Clancy tapped his lips. "What color is her car again?"

"I have no idea about Stacy or her car." Malone's voice sounded like a low snarl. "I don't like your tone here."

"Okey dokey." Clancy grinned. "You know how I hate surprises."

"Just cut the bullshit and gimme a smoke."

Clancy lit a cigarette and handed it to him through the bars. Malone inhaled and stared at the ceiling. "You got me in a bad mood now."

"That means I'm doing my job."

Malone glared. "Word got back that Fitzgerald's been snooping around. You hear anything?"

"No?" Clancy wondered what that was all about. "Snooping around where?"

"If they had more evidence against me, she'd have to let us know, right?"

"Depends. If she's planning on using something for impeachment purposes on cross, she can do it without telling us in advance."

"Come again?" Malone flicked his ashes on the floor.

"She can surprise you on cross-examination. That's fair game, remember?"

"With what though? There's nothing on me unless Callahan made it up again. I didn't do nothing to Trevor Shea. He walked out of Jennianne's place alive."

"What if she brings up Drake Reed?" Clancy studied him.

Malone walked to the back of his cell and turned around. "So what if she does?"

"You've got to figure out what to say. You know as well as I that he turned up dead in Gloucester. What was he doing up there? Working some deal with Domenico? The jurors are going to be wondering about it because Fitzgerald will ask. I guarantee it."

51

ANNIE WATCHED THE jurors enter the courtroom after their lunch break. They all looked at her, seeming anxious for Malone's cross-examination. She could tell they had fallen under his spell. It was up to her to break it. She placed the two large paintings on the easel, one behind the other. The top one everyone had seen before; it featured Georgie Hurley, the red-haired boy on his back in the playground surrounded by the circle of kids. She paraded into center court and faced Malone.

"You're Charlestown's number one drug dealer?" Annie's voice carried across the courtroom. She would tear right through that fake skin of his and expose his rotten core.

"No." Malone met her gaze with equal distain.

"No? In the past ten years you've had a total of twenty-two convictions, twelve of which involved narcotics charges."

"That doesn't mean I'm a drug dealer."

"Really? Let's see about that." Annie moved toward the jury box and shuffled through Malone's prior convictions. She considered spewing them all over the floor as Clancy had done to Domenico, but decided to take the high road.

"In 2010, you were convicted of selling heroin in a school zone, am I correct?"

"I had heroin but I wasn't dealing. And, for your information, all of Charlestown is considered a school zone. My attorney told me to plead guilty."

"I see. By any chance, did that take place as you were playing basketball with the underprivileged kids at the Boys and Girls Club?" Annie grinned as she arced toward the jury.

"No."

"You've been convicted of possessing marijuana, cocaine, and heroin?"

"I was using drugs to fight my depression over my father's murder, but now—"

"In fact, Miles Domenico was one of the suppliers for your drug operations?"

"I had purchased a small amount of cocaine from him in the past for my own use, but that was it." Malone leaned back. "Look, Miss Fitzgerald, I did have a drug problem. I'm not proud of it, but I managed to beat it, unlike poor Trevor." Sympathy oozed from his mouth, making Annie sick. She gazed into the audience, making eye contact with Chris.

"You traveled up to Gloucester to purchase drugs from Miles Domenico?" she said.

"I did a few years back, but not recently."

"So." Annie cocked her head. "It was quite a coincidence that your fingerprints appeared along with Domenico's on the CVS bag?"

"I already said I touched the bag and his drug stuff when I was cleaning up."

"Oh, right." She raised her eyebrows. "You mentioned earlier that Domenico wanted to channel his drug operations through you. I'm curious, why did he choose *you*?"

Malone shrugged and appeared bored with the question. "I don't have a clue."

"He chose you because you operate a thriving drug trade. In other words, you make boatloads of money selling drugs in Charlestown."

"Objection," Clancy said.

Judge Killam took a moment. "This is cross-examination, she may have it. Answer the question, sir."

"You're wrong about that." Malone folded his hands on the witness stand.

"Then, inform this jury why Domenico chose you." Annie motioned toward the jury box.

"I don't know. Probably because I know a lot of people and I used to buy drugs from him. I'm not a mind reader, Miss Fitzgerald."

Annie stared him down. "You're familiar with a man named Drake Reed, formerly of Fourteen Old Ironsides Way?"

"I was."

"You grew up with him, didn't you?"

"Mmm hmm."

"He helped operate your drug trade?"

"No, like I said, there was no drug trade."

"You and Reed were arrested and convicted together eight years ago for distributing heroin?" Annie raised another conviction up.

"So? That doesn't mean we were working together." Malone grinned. "We just happened to be in the wrong place at the wrong time. Besides, I was using heroin at the time but never sold it."

"That's not what this conviction says." Annie walked up to the witness stand and slapped it down under Malone's nose.

"Objection!" Clancy stood.

"Overruled."

Malone ignored the paper, and kept his gaze fixed on Annie. "The DA was moving cases at the time and offered me a sweetheart deal, so I copped a plea."

"But it's fair to say you've associated with Drake Reed in recent years?"

"We were childhood friends."

"Reed was with you just prior to your arrest in this case?"

"At my ma's house."

"In fact he brought a gun to your mother's birthday dinner."

"Nope. I never saw a gun."

"Your mother told Detective Callahan that she saw him carrying a gun. Are you calling her a liar?"

"No." Malone pointed a finger at Annie. "You're the only one calling my ma a liar. *If* she thought she saw a gun, I guarantee it was part of his belt buckle."

"His belt buckle?" Annie cracked a smile. "You're telling me Drake Reed was wearing a belt buckle shaped like a gun?"

"Must've been because there was no gun." Malone sounded sarcastic.

"Reed took off just before dinner was served, am I correct?"

"He left."

"Can you tell us where he went?" Annie looked into the jury box; they were leaning forward, listening.

"No idea."

"Well, *someone* fired a shot through your mother's living room window."

"Objection." Clancy slapped the table.

"Overruled."

Malone snickered. "I heard the Boston Police fired that shot. They aimed at me but missed. Typical."

"Aimed at you?" Annie cocked her head.

"Yeah, that's right." He tapped his fingers against his chest. "Me."

"But you were facedown on the floor when the shot was fired."

"So? They could still shoot me." Malone glanced at the jury and then back at Annie. "They want me dead, Miss Fitzgerald. You should know that by now."

Annie paused to control her temper. "Tell us who got hit."

"Objection!" Clancy shot up.

"Overruled."

"A cop."

"It was Sergeant Thomas Amidon, wasn't it?" Annie savored the fact that she could now get this into evidence.

"I guess, but that doesn't mean they weren't aiming at me."

"Sergeant Amidon was standing ten feet away from you when he got shot down."

"I was lying facedown in a pool of my own blood after Callahan smashed my face over and over. How would I know where the cop was? I'm telling you, the Boston Police aimed at me and missed."

Annie made eye contact with the foreperson and walked toward her. "You sent Mr. Reed up to Gloucester to intimidate Miles Domenico from testifying the night before his scheduled appearance before this jury." She swung her arm back, encompassing the jury box.

"What?" Malone lowered his chin. "That's impossible. I was in jail."

Annie walked to her table, grabbed a piece of paper, and waved it in the air. "According to records from the jail, Reed visited you a total of sixteen times, including two days before Domenico testified."

"He may've, but I didn't send him up to Gloucester." Malone spoke quickly; he sounded agitated.

Annie closed in. "What happened to Drake Reed?"

"I don't know. I've been in jail."

"Oh, come on. You know as well as I do that Mr. Reed's body washed up on shore in Gloucester and he disappeared around the time of Domenico's testimony."

"Okay. I also read that in the papers, but I wouldn't know anything about it."

"Reed had no other ties to Gloucester, did he?"

"How would I know?" Malone raised his hands. "He was probably up there buying drugs. Drake's had an on and off drug problem for years."

Annie walked over to the easel where she had placed Trevor's painting of the kids in the playground. She glanced into the gallery and spotted Mrs. Hurley sitting in the front row. Annie was shocked. "Directing your attention to this painting. Do you recognize the boy lying flat on his back?" She pointed to George Hurley, the redheaded boy with the terrified eyes, and regarded Billy. When he looked at the painting his eyes widened and registered a hint of emotion. *Was it fear?* She wondered.

Malone didn't answer.

"Do you recognize that red-haired boy?" Annie touched the boy in the painting and raised her voice.

"No." Malone looked at Clancy and frowned.

"Come on. You grew up in Charlestown. Isn't that little Georgie Hurley?"

"Objection!" Clancy stood. "Relevancy?"

"Overruled," Judge Killam said. "Answer the question."

Malone regarded the painting again. "Could be, but if that's Georgie, it's gotta be a long time ago."

"Who's that boy sitting on his stomach?"

"After twenty years how do you expect me to know who that is?"

"Hmm." Annie gazed from Malone to the painting and back again several times. "It looks an awful lot like you, wouldn't you say?"

"Objection, Your Honor." Clancy placed both hands on the top of his head. "I'm not current with the statute of limitations for teasing a kid in the playground, but come on."

"Sustained. Move along."

Annie noticed perspiration on Malone's brow. She had discovered a chink in his armor. *Capitalize on it.* She saw the jurors studying the painting and Malone.

Annie touched the painting again and underlined the word *snich* with her index finger. She gazed at Malone as she dragged her finger back and forth. "What is a snitch, Mr. Malone?"

"You tell me."

"Answer the question."

Malone took a deep breath and exhaled. "We all know what it means, so don't get cute with me."

"What is a rat?" Annie raised her voice.

He gazed back at her with hatred.

"A snitch is a rat, isn't it?"

"I don't know."

"Inform this jury. What is a snitch?"

"Okay, Miss Fitzgerald, if you insist. I believe it means someone who tattles on somebody else."

"Would you consider Jennianne Smith a snitch?" Annie watched Malone's face darken—she was wearing him down.

Malone pursed his lips. Annie knew he was struggling to maintain his composure.

"Would you consider Jennianne Smith a rat?"

"I loved her."

Annie circled toward the jury. "Tell us how this witness against you died, Mr. Malone."

"I read in the paper that she was drunk driving and ran off the road into a tree."

"The truth is that someone ran Jennianne off the road!" Annie gazed into his eyes, challenging him.

"Objection!" Clancy yelled.

"Sustained."

Malone sprang from his seat. "Are you trying to frame me for that, too? Detective Callahan's setting me up again, isn't he?"

Judge Killam banged his gavel. "Sit down and be quiet! There's no question before you."

"I'm sorry, Your Honor." Malone glanced up at the judge and over at the jury, and resumed his seat. His chest heaved in and out.

"Jennianne Smith was the Commonwealth's primary witness in this case against you, am I correct?" Annie marched toward him, maintaining eye contact.

"I know she was a witness." He clenched his teeth. "I sat here and listened to her testimony like everyone else."

"And you had read the entire grand jury transcript from your jail cell before Jennianne's accident."

Malone paused. "I read it at some point."

"Therefore, you knew exactly what Jennianne was going to say on the witness stand."

"I knew it was all lies." His face turned red.

"That's why you had her killed!"

Clancy leaped up, knocking the table off balance. "Objection!"

"Sustained."

"You were afraid the truth would come out! The truth that *you* murdered Trevor Shea!"

"Objection!"

"Overruled."

"You're wrong." Malone pointed at Annie. "Dead wrong."

Annie stared into his eyes. Malone had emphasized *dead*. She wasn't afraid, she had power over him at this moment. They both knew it. Without removing her gaze from Malone, Annie sidestepped to her left and lifted the playground painting, revealing another giant canvas underneath. She placed the first painting on the floor, and leaned it against the legs of the easel. Annie grabbed the edges of the new painting with both hands and hovered over it. Malone blanched.

The judge and jurors leaned forward, studying Trevor's artwork. The painting revealed a scene outside the Celtic Tavern in Charlestown. A dead man lay across the sidewalk with arms and legs sprawled at crooked angles. Blood soaked his clothing and then pooled onto the sidewalk. It looked like it was still flowing; light reflected from the red tones. The flesh had been blown away in his chest cavity. A teenaged boy, obviously Billy Malone, kneeled over the body. He cradled the man, his hands and arms stained with blood. Inside the bar, dozens of faces peered out the large plate glass window.

Annie shivered when she regarded the dead man's open eyes. Trevor had painted them dead center. They nearly popped out of the canvas. So vibrant, so lifelike, so terrifying. Annie shivered again.

"Mr. Malone, have you seen this painting before?" Annie focused on him in an attempt to make eye contact.

Malone stared at the painting. He appeared comatose and unresponsive.

"It looks like you have seen it. Do you recognize this place?" Annie pointed to the Celtic Tavern.

"Hold on. Don't answer." Clancy stood with his palm extended. "Objection! This is absurd."

Judge Killam leaned way over the bench, studying the painting. "Grounds?"

"Relevance."

"But that's the Celtic Tavern. Right there." The judge pointed at the upper half of the painting. "You brought it up on direct, Clancy. Overruled."

"Interesting." Annie traced her fingers over the teenaged boy cradling the body, and regarded Malone. "That boy looks an awful lot like you."

"Why are you doing this?" Malone finally made eye contact with her.

"You're in both of these paintings, aren't you?" Annie lowered her voice.

"Clancy, what's this got to do with anything?" Malone gestured toward the defense table.

"Objection!"

"Overruled."

"Mr. Malone, how many other paintings are you in?" Annie asked.

"This is crazy. I don't have to listen to it." Malone covered his ears.

"Trevor painted unsolved murders, didn't he?" Annie faced the jury and shouted.

"Objection!" Clancy bolted up, sending papers flying. "This is pure speculation and prejudicial!"

"It's relevant to motive, Your Honor," Annie regarded the judge.

"Give me a minute here." Judge Killam raised a finger. "Overruled. She may have it. Answer the question, sir."

Clancy huffed. "Note my objection for the record."

Malone grasped the witness stand and gazed at both paintings. "I have no idea what Trevor Shea was painting, no damn clue." He shook his head from side to side as he spoke.

"Georgie Hurley." Annie raised the playground canvas with one hand and touched the red-haired boy with the other. "Tell me. Is Georgie Hurley still alive?"

"Don't know."

"Isn't that his mother right there in the front row?" Annie pointed to Georgie's mother, her face streaked with tears.

"Is Georgie Hurley still alive?" she repeated.

"No. But, what's that got to do with me?"

"He was beaten to death in this playground."

"Objection!"

"Sustained."

Annie set the painting down again, and touched the dead man with the gawking dead eyes in the other one. "Do you recognize this man?"

Malone stared at the painting.

"Who are all those people in the Celtic Tavern looking out the window?" Annie waited. "Who are they?"

Malone said nothing.

"Who is that boy kneeling over the dead body?" Annie pointed at the painting and moved toward Malone. "Answer the question. Who is it? Answer the question."

"Alright, that was me." Malone jumped up. "Fifteen years old and my father's lifeblood just spilling out between my fingers. Not one of those bastards came out that door, not one!" He extended his arm toward the painting. "See all those faces in the window? Not one of them saw a thing. They were all in the bathroom. A one-stall bathroom. Every last one of them."

52

CHARLESTOWN BECKONED ANNIE that afternoon. The vision of a fifteen-year-old Billy Malone cradling his bleeding father on the sidewalk outside the Celtic Tavern haunted her. She parked on Main Street in front of the spot where her parents' bookstore had been. She stared at the old brownstone, and remembered all the wonderful people who came in and browsed. Would Malone have grown up to be a different person if he hadn't held his dying father in his arms? It wasn't long after that when he killed Georgie Hurley in the playground. Is that why he had snapped? She pondered over how certain events set other events in motion. How would her life have been any different if that man hadn't come into the bookstore with the baseball bat on that hot summer day? *Charlestown, only one square mile. Don't hear anything, don't see anything, and never talk to cops.* Annie rested her head on the steering wheel and closed her eyes.

Someone rapped on her car window. *Buddy Clancy.* She turned her key and rolled down the window.

"Come join Rehnquist and me for a cup of coffee. I'll treat. We'll walk up to Sorelle."

Annie got out of her car and Rehnquist pranced, smiling at her with his tongue dangling off the side of his mouth. He sported a Red Sox bow tie.

"I've heard all about you, matching bow ties and all." She squatted and stroked the dog with both hands. He licked her nose.

As they walked along the sidewalk, people stopped and said hello to Clancy and Rehnquist as if they were celebrities. Annie was surprised anyone would speak to him. Didn't he represent the bad guys around here?

When they arrived at Sorrelle, Clancy placed a coffee and cranberry scone for Annie on a corner table next to the window. He draped his jacket over the back of his chair. Rehnquist sat next to Clancy and thumped his tail. Annie noticed Clancy's Red Sox tie; he had changed ties after court.

"Yes, I got something for you, too." Clancy broke off a piece of blueberry muffin and fed it to the dog. "You tried an excellent case, Annie."

"Thanks." She blew on her coffee. "So did you."

He fed Rehnquist another piece. "That was a powerful cross-examination of Malone today. One of the best I've seen in years." He took a large bite of his chocolate éclair; he had a cream puff, too.

"Can you believe I actually walked away sympathizing with him?" Annie said. "That painting of his father was so real. The blood, the eyes. I can't stop thinking about it."

Clancy regarded her for a moment. "Everyone has a story."

Rehnquist barked.

"Even Rehnquist." Clancy smiled. "Rescue dog. I've been known to bring him to court on occasion. Once I got away with hiding him under the table for a motion hearing. Judge Killam never knew."

"I can picture the look on his face if he ever found out. You would've been fined."

Clancy laughed. "Wouldn't be the first time."

Annie bit into her scone and fed Rehnquist a piece.

"He appreciates that, says thank you." Clancy sipped his coffee. "I'd like to see you enjoy yourself after this case. I've been thinking about you a lot lately. You're a terrific lawyer and a wonderful woman. You do have compassion, Annie. I was wrong in the beginning. No matter what happens with Malone, you need to get out there and enjoy life."

"I suppose."

"No, I mean it. I know what happened to your father at the bookstore.

It was awful, just awful for you to see that as a little girl. But, don't let it destroy you anymore. Your parents wouldn't want that." He smiled at her. "They were good people."

"I know." She knew Clancy was right. They sat in silence until Clancy changed the subject, telling her about some of his old courtroom war stories.

He finally checked his watch. "It's time for Rehnquist and me to go home. My wife will have dinner on the table soon. We're not supposed to be having treats before dinner, but you won't tell on us, will you?"

"I won't, but you'd better get rid of the evidence." Annie pointed to the crumbs on his trousers.

"Thank you." He brushed them off. "She saved us, Rehnquist." He and Rehnquist walked Annie back to her car. "Good luck on your closing argument tomorrow, and don't take anything I say personally. It's part of the job."

"I know."

"And remember what I said about enjoying yourself." Clancy winked. "It's a short life."

53

ANNIE REREAD THE notes she had prepared the night before for her closing argument. This was it. She wished she had more evidence against Malone, more paintings, more witnesses. She had a pit in her stomach, the guilty feeling that she could've done more, and that she'd crossed the line. Annie should never have pressured Jennianne like that in the ladies' room. The girl was throwing up. Her thoughts jumped to Chris and the basement. *Not now.* She didn't say anything to Chris when she passed by him earlier sitting in the front row. She was disgusted with him at this point. Annie had been dead wrong when she thought she could win him over in the beginning. He was bitter, pig-headed, and set in his ways. *She never should have kissed him.*

"Break a leg!" Callahan shouted out.

Annie looked over her shoulder to see him giving her a thumbs-up. Callahan sat next to the mothers in the front row. She walked over. "Did you find anything?"

"Nope." He wore a clean blue suit, but his eyes looked bloodshot and droopy like he hadn't slept in days. "Just knock the cover off the ball, will you?" He smiled.

Annie had hoped he'd find Stacy's car before closing arguments, and she'd be able to announce that Malone had ordered Jennianne's murder. *In a perfect world.*

"All rise!" Clerk Fallon rushed out of the judge's lobby a step ahead of Judge Killam. "The Superior Court of Suffolk County is now in session. The Honorable Conrad J. Killam presiding."

Annie studied the jurors as they trooped single file into the courtroom. They appeared rigid and serious. What were they thinking? Had they made up their minds?

"The court will entertain closing arguments at this time." Judge Killam addressed the jurors. "Remember, these statements are not evidence. Mr. Clancy?"

"Ah, that's me. Thank you, Your Honor." Clancy approached the jury box in slow motion. He straightened a navy blue bow tie with raised gold embroidered anchors on both sides. Annie wondered how he'd work the sailor theme in. Clancy reminded her of an endearing professor about to lecture his class on the ways of the world. She knew he would push the limits in his closing argument. He always did. She had to be careful not to object too much; jurors hated interruptions.

"Ladies and gentlemen, after this case, I'm retiring." Clancy enunciated each word, his voice boomed across the courtroom. "I've lost faith in the criminal justice system." He folded his hands and made eye contact with the jurors. "Thomas Jefferson once said, 'The jury is the only anchor by which a government can be held to its Constitution.'" He spread his fingers. "And this case is adrift." He lifted his arms over his head, swayed back, and wobbled. "It's up to you to anchor us and pull us back from the great abyss. Everyone deserves a fair trail. Everyone. A fair trail based on facts."

The jurors appeared spellbound with his speech. Annie had to think of a comeback for the anchor and Jefferson.

"This is nothing more than a frame-up job by the Boston Police. What eats at my conscience is the evidence that began building since November tenth of last year. Evidence of foul play. Evidence that Detective Callahan used Trevor's drug overdose to satisfy a vendetta against Mr. Malone." Clancy walked up to the defense table and pointed at Malone.

"'I'll get you, next murder in Charlestown is on your back, no matter who did it.'"

Annie wondered about those words. Had Callahan blurted them out in the heat of passion? Had he been misconstrued?

"Oh, Callahan kept his promise alright . . . that's why we're all here. But he shouldn't have invented a phony case." Clancy secured his thumbs beneath his suspenders and paced in front of the jury.

"His Honor will instruct you that the Commonwealth must prove its case beyond a reasonable doubt. Remember that, it's very important—*beyond a reasonable doubt.* This case is boiling over with reasonable doubt." Clancy stomped in front of the jury box. "Let's review the facts and I'll show you.

"Officer O'Neil reported Trevor's death an accidental drug overdose. The officers sloppily rolled the body, and may have stolen money from his wallet. The syringe probably fell out of Trevor's hand at that point, and one of them attempted to put it back. We have no reports of a body being dragged through the streets of Charlestown that evening. The notion of any path in the leaves is veritable make-believe. The wind would've scattered and dispersed them." Clancy fluttered his fingers. "Neither officer recalled finding anything in Trevor's front pockets."

Annie noticed the frowns and furrowed brows on the jurors' faces as Clancy spun the facts to fit his case. She also caught several nods, which wasn't a good sign for her.

"So, how did that empty packet of Nine-eleven heroin containing Mr. Malone's fingerprint *most conveniently* find its way into Trevor's pocket?" Clancy cocked his head. "Gee. Who found it?" He pointed into the gallery. "He did. Detective Callahan. What a surprise."

Annie watched the jurors look beyond Clancy's pointed finger and into the front row where Callahan was sitting. She hoped Callahan would maintain his composure. It was going to get ugly.

"Did the good detective hand this important piece of evidence over to Sergeant Sutton for fingerprinting at the crime scene? Of course not! Why? Because he never actually found an empty packet of Nine-eleven heroin in Trevor's pocket. I bet he found it in the trash can at Jennianne's apartment later on. Mr. Malone said he picked up Trevor's garbage after he left. That's how his fingerprint ended up on that heroin packaging. It makes perfect sense." Clancy smiled and closed his eyes for a moment. He turned around and faced Callahan. "Now, Detective, you must've fallen asleep during class, planting evidence 101. Next time, plant the evidence in the correct pocket! If Trevor had stuffed the heroin bag into his own pocket, shouldn't it be in his left pocket because he's left-handed?" Clancy held his left hand up and tried to insert it into his right pocket. "See?"

"Objection!"

"Address the jury, Clancy."

Annie noticed the entire jury panel smiling with Clancy. This was a disaster. She felt like hiding under her table. She pictured Callahan foaming at the mouth. She didn't dare turn around and look at him.

"So, why would a seasoned detective concoct evidence, and then take the stand and lie to you under oath?" Clancy scratched his head and made eye contact with each juror. "Because we know Callahan has been out to get Mr. Malone ever since he reported him to his superiors and the press for failing to properly investigate his father's murder. Was Callahan on the verge of losing his job over this? Perhaps." Clancy placed a hand on his hip and circled in front of the jury box.

"There's even more to the fix. Callahan employed a self-serving, perjuring drug dealer, Miles Domenico. He got a *Get Out of Jail Free* card and may have been bribed in exchange for his testimony."

"Objection!" Annie couldn't believe he said that. "There was no evidence of bribery. That's not fair, Your Honor."

"Sustained."

Clancy appeared unfazed. "We also know Callahan arrested Jennianne Smith for drug possession, threatened her with a murder charge, and kept her caged up like an animal for two whole days. Was Callahan credible when he told you he did *not* intimidate the poor girl? Did she panic when the detective towered over her and mentioned that Trevor ended up dead after he'd been to her apartment? And, what was going on between her and Stacy Black? We know they had a fight over Malone. Was Jennianne jealous or vindictive?" Clancy shrugged. "Detective Callahan gave Jennianne a way out. All she had to do was say exactly what he wanted her to say." Clancy spun around and faced Annie. "They both used her, played her like a pawn. Jennianne was a mess on that witness stand. You all saw that. Quite frankly, I felt sorry for her." Clancy's voice faded to a whisper.

"You know, it's quite sad. They applied all that pressure, but Jennianne's testimony didn't help their case at all. She did not witness Mr. Malone giving Trevor any heroin. She was in the kitchen when the heroin was produced. Jennianne witnessed Trevor cooking the heroin and injecting it into his own arm. That's exactly what Mr. Malone said. So, where's the crime?"

Annie counted more nods in the jury box. *Not good.*

"Please don't be fooled by the sympathy factor, either. That's what the prosecution is doing with the big paintings. Trevor was a talented artist, I'm not denying that. But this is not an art gallery, it's a courtroom. Cases must be decided on facts. We're not here to interpret the meaning of a painting. In fact, no one should be doing that because it calls for speculation. His Honor will instruct you on the law in a few minutes. He will tell you not to speculate. In fact, it's such an important part of the law that Judge Killam has warned time and again throughout this trial not to speculate." Clancy nodded toward the judge as if they were partners.

"All facts point to one conclusion: Trevor Shea injected himself with lethal heroin in the spot where the police found his body beneath the Tobin Bridge. This occurred over an hour after Trevor was with Mr. Malone at Jennianne's apartment." Clancy paused to allow his words to sink in. "The medical examiner testified that Trevor died at nine fifteen P.M. There was well over an hour gap between the time Trevor left the apartment at eight o'clock and his death at nine fifteen. In addition, neither Jennianne nor anyone else witnessed Trevor striking his head on a sharp object in her apartment. The medical examiner told you Trevor received the head wound when he collapsed during his heart attack. Sergeant Sutton testified that fingerprints last on human skin for an hour and a half at most. Two unknown prints were present on Trevor's skin at approximately eleven thirty P.M. That shows Trevor was in contact with two persons other than Malone between the time he walked out of Jennianne's apartment at eight o'clock and the time Officer O'Neil discovered his body."

Annie tensed. Jennianne hadn't been able to finish her testimony. If she hadn't broken down on the stand, Annie would've asked her what time it was when Trevor collapsed. She had testified before the grand jury that it was after nine. If only Annie had been able to get the grand jury transcript read into evidence. It wasn't fair. No doubt, Malone capitalized on the time element and made sure Stacy did as well. They corroborated that eight o'clock time as if they'd simultaneously checked their watches. *Come on*. Did the jurors really buy into that?

"Let's face it, both the police and prosecution had tunnel vision." Clancy gazed at Annie. "They zoned in on Malone and didn't explore any other possibilities. That is wrong. *They* should be sitting in those criminal chairs behind the defense table." He turned and pointed at a crimson-faced Detective Callahan in the gallery. The jurors followed suit.

"It's that very abuse of power that has veered our ship way off course. Our legal system is in peril. It's your job now as jurors to secure us from smashing up against the jagged rocks of a police state. Save us, please, the Constitution, *We the People*." Silence descended upon the courtroom.

"Thank you."

"We'll take a twenty-minute recess," Judge Killam said.

54

AS SOON AS the judge and the jurors left the courtroom, Callahan jumped out of his seat and pointed at Clancy. "Liar. You know he's guilty. You've ruined my reputation just to get Malone off again so he can go out and murder more people. How do you feel about that, huh?" Callahan's temples pounded; it felt like his head was about to explode.

Clancy waved him off. "Don't take it personally."

"What? How can I not? I'll sue you for defamation. You know I didn't bribe anyone."

"Calm down, man, he's not worth it." A court officer stepped between them. "We all know he'll say anything to win a case."

"Come on, Mike, let's go out for a minute." Annie motioned toward the hallway, and Callahan reluctantly followed her out of the courtroom.

"Son-of-a-bitch." He slapped the wall. "Clancy really twists everything around, doesn't he? Vilifies the police, warps the truth."

"He went too far this time," Annie said. "It'll backfire."

Callahan couldn't think straight. Now his hand throbbed and was swelling up, too. Maybe he broke it. "Why the hell couldn't we get Jennianne's grand jury testimony in? Trevor collapsed in that apartment after nine o'clock. The jurors should be able to hear both sides."

"I know." Annie sighed. "Clancy probably pointed it out to Malone. I thought it sounded rehearsed when Malone and Stacy testified that Trevor left the apartment at eight o'clock. I think someone on the jury will realize it. They know Jennianne never finished."

"We can't provide them with an explanation. We're stuck with eight o'clock because *he* killed her off. This jury'll never know the truth. That's why Malone's going to get off. It pays to kill off witnesses. All this was for nothing."

"No it's not," a woman's voice said.

They turned around to see Mrs. Reed standing with Mrs. Hurley. *Drake's and Georgie's mothers.* "Oh." Callahan was caught off guard. "Annie, you know Mrs. Hurley, but I don't think you've met Mrs. Reed."

"Nice to meet you." Annie shook her hand. "Thanks for coming."

"We appreciate what you two are doing here, more than you'll ever know." Mrs. Reed reached out and held both their hands. "This is the best shot we've ever had at Billy Malone. No one's taken him this far in the court system before. Remember, it's not all about winning one case. You're making big strides in Charlestown."

Mrs. Hurley nodded. "To see Malone break down on the stand like that yesterday . . ." She closed her eyes and swallowed. "It was . . . was worth it for me. After all these years, knowing how brutally Georgie was beaten. I always suspected Malone. Word on the street, you know? Georgie was just ten years old, Malone was sixteen. People say Malone snapped over something stupid. It was after his father was murdered, but that doesn't give him the right . . . Georgie was so . . . so sweet." She dabbed at the corners of her eyes with a balled-up Kleenex.

"So, Georgie would've been Chris's age?" Annie said.

"Yes, Chris and my Georgie used to play kickball together. I have a feeling Trevor saw what happened and painted it."

"You're probably right. Trevor would've been around six years old at the time. I'm sure it had a great impact on him." Annie checked her watch. "I have to get back in there and Google Jefferson quotes to one-up Clancy."

"You can do it." Callahan tried to muster up as much enthusiasm as he could, but his words sounded flat. He watched her head back in.

"By the way, what were you talking about this morning? I thought I heard something about a car?" Mrs. Reed said.

"We're looking for both Stacy Black and her car." At this point, Callahan figured, it couldn't hurt to tell them. "We suspect Stacy may've run Jennianne off the road, but we can't prove anything without the car. I had a tip that it was in a body shop somewhere, but I've been looking everywhere and can't find it."

The women regarded each other. "We'll ask around."

55

F OUR HOUSE be on fire, without inquiring whether it was fired from within or without, we must try to extinguish it.' That's also a quote from Thomas Jefferson." Annie stood before the jury.

"If our house be on fire." She paused and made eye contact with each juror. "Charlestown is only one square mile and it has the highest unsolved murder rate in the country. Why? Detective Callahan told you about Charlestown's code of silence. Don't see anything, don't hear anything, and never talk to cops. It's all about street justice. *And fear.*

"I suggest Trevor Shea witnessed this pervasive fear and he painted it. You can see the fear in the eyes of the people he painted. You also saw it on the witness stand. Think back to what happened when Jennianne made eye contact with Malone near the end of her testimony. She was too afraid to go on."

"Objection! Objection! Objection!" Clancy popped up. "This speech is inflammatory. It has nothing to do with the facts of this case."

"I gave you plenty of latitude, Clancy. Overruled." Judge Killam faced the jury. "Remember, closing arguments are not evidence." He turned back to Annie. "Please stick to the facts in evidence."

"Thank you, Your Honor," Annie said.

"The Commonwealth has proven its case of murder in the first degree beyond a reasonable doubt against the defendant, Billy Malone." Annie pointed at Malone. "His Honor will instruct you that first-degree murder is the unlawful killing of a human being with deliberate, premeditated malice aforethought." Annie paced a moment to collect her thoughts. She needed to explain a bit about the law.

"In this case, proof of murder comes in the form of direct evidence." Annie walked to the clerk's desk and lifted several evidence bags and photographs. "You also have direct evidence in the form of eyewitness testimony. You may also rely on indirect or circumstantial evidence, which means you may draw reasonable inferences based on other facts and your common sense and experiences in life." She hoped the jurors would think creatively. This was a tough case to piece together.

"Miles Domenico testified that Malone traveled up to Gloucester on the day of Trevor's death to purchase Nine-eleven heroin. The defense wants you to discount all of Mr. Domenico's testimony. I'm not going to stand before you and proclaim that he's an upstanding member of the community—*he's not*. Domenico's a drug dealer. However, I will tell you why his testimony is believable. He provided you with an accurate description of Malone's black pickup truck, and told you what Malone had been wearing on November tenth: jeans, work boots, and a navy sweatshirt with some kind of pub decal. This matched Jennianne's description. When Domenico sold the Nine-eleven heroin to Malone, he placed it in a plastic CVS bag, and Jennianne later witnessed an identical drugstore bag containing heroin. A CVS bag recovered from the scene contained fingerprints belonging to Domenico and Malone. Domenico's testimony jells with what other witnesses said and fits the physical evidence. He also warned Malone that Nine-eleven is so strong that he knew someone who OD'd on it and died." Annie noticed eyes glazing over; they didn't like the drug dealer. *Move on.*

"Let's talk about Jennianne Smith. She had the misfortune of getting mixed up with Malone. She told you that she overheard Malone say, 'Let's get this over with quick. I can only put up with this faggot for so long.'" Annie watched the foreperson nod—*a good sign.*

"Right after that, Malone appeared in the living room with that CVS bag, and ordered Jennianne to go into the kitchen and get more beer. She heard Billy say to Trevor, 'You done good lately—got something for yah.' When Jennianne reentered the living room approximately two minutes later, the CVS bag appeared empty, and Trevor held a bag of heroin, a syringe, and a cooker spoon."

Annie paused. "The medical evidence is clear that Trevor Shea was killed by that one lethal dose of Nine-eleven heroin taken in Jennianne's apartment. Dr. Joyce testified that the cause of death was heart failure, which occurred within minutes of a fatal heroin injection. We know Trevor received only one injection of heroin that evening since Dr. Joyce confirmed there was only one fresh track mark on his body. You can see that for yourselves in the autopsy photographs. Dr. Joyce further described what it looks like when one experiences heart failure due to a drug overdose: rapid convulsions, difficulty breathing, clutching of the heart, and then the body will collapse." Annie clutched her heart; one of the old ladies did the same.

"Jennianne's observations of Trevor's final moments are supported by the medical evidence and testimony of Dr. Joyce. Jennianne described what Trevor looked like within minutes after the heroin injection. He was unsteady, his face contorted, he convulsed, clutched his chest, and then collapsed."

Annie had to counter Clancy's time of death argument. She had to remember to speak slowly. "Now, the defense wants you to believe that Trevor was killed by a heroin injection that occurred somewhere outside Jennianne's apartment. They're basing their theory on Jennianne's estimation that Trevor collapsed around eight P.M., and according to Dr. Joyce, death occurred at approximately nine fifteen P.M. However, the medical evidence simply does not support that theory. Trevor received one heroin injection, and that's what killed him. Again, this is evidenced by only one fresh track mark on his body. According to nearly all eyewitness accounts, Trevor injected himself within Jennianne's apartment. What was Jennianne about to say next? You'll never know." Annie walked the length of the jury box.

"Malone had a problem that night—*a dead body*. He had to get rid of it.

Dr. Joyce testified that someone dragged Trevor's body due to the vertical scrapes and debris embedded into his back, postmortem. Detective Callahan described a narrow path in the leaves running from the street to the location of the body as if it had been dragged there. Also, if Trevor had simply walked out of Jennianne's apartment on November tenth as the defense wants you to believe, wouldn't he be wearing his jacket? It was cold outside." Annie caught several more nods.

"Next, we have the awkward placement of the syringe in Trevor's right hand. You heard testimony that Trevor was left-handed, which makes sense because the fresh track mark appeared on his right arm. Detective Callahan observed that Trevor was holding the syringe upside down in the wrong hand. Dr. Joyce said Trevor would've had a much stronger grasp around the syringe if he had died holding it due to rigor mortis. Thus, she believed that someone placed it in Trevor's hand after death had occurred. Think about that." Annie tapped her forehead.

"I agree with Mr. Clancy on one thing. The empty bag of Nine-eleven heroin was in the wrong pocket. If Trevor had stuffed the heroin bag into his own pocket, it should've been found in the left instead of the right because he's left-handed. Think about how you place items in your own pockets. The evidence suggests someone did plant that empty heroin bag in Trevor's pocket, but it wasn't Detective Callahan, it was Malone. He did it to throw off the investigation and make Trevor's death look like another accidental drug overdose. However, the forensic evidence foiled that plan. Malone left a fingerprint behind. *Whoops.* Of course, the defense relied on the old fallback: blame the police." Annie rolled her eyes. "Typical." She walked back to her table for a drink of water, and studied the jurors, searching for any clue as to which way they were leaning. Their faces resembled granite statues, hard and impassive.

"The defense made another big deal about the two additional fingerprints lifted from Trevor's body, which were unidentified. That does not negate all the evidence pointing directly at Malone. Perhaps Malone recruited another person to help drag the heavy corpse to its final resting spot beneath the Tobin Bridge. Perhaps someone came across the dead body, took a pulse, called nine-one-one, but was afraid to come forward." Annie spun around and stared a hole through Malone. He held her gaze.

Annie turned and exchanged eye contact with Callahan, seated in the front row next to the mothers. "There is one more issue I must address." She faced the jury again. "Mr. Clancy has bashed Detective Callahan's reputation in this courtroom. That's an age-old defense tactic. Don't fall for it. It should be clear to you that Detective Callahan has been working around the clock on this case. Malone resisted arrest and broke his own nose. But he wasn't the only one injured. Sergeant Thomas Amidon, another dedicated member of the Boston Police, was also shot."

Annie walked up to the clerk's desk. "The physical evidence is right here. Now it's your turn to administer justice. A trial by jury is the essence of our legal system and our Constitution. The defendant has taken great lengths to steal this case away from you and take justice into his own hands. Don't let him get away with it! Come back into this courtroom and declare that Malone is guilty of murdering Trevor Shea." Annie looked at each juror.

"Thank you."

56

RACHEL HAD FORCED herself to pay attention to Judge Killam's long-winded jury instructions. Most of her fellow jurors looked down as they filed out of the courtroom. She scrutinized Malone, who appeared to be sizing her up in return. His gaze neither implored her to accept his innocence nor revealed any hints of guilt.

She kept her chin up. He was guilty, no doubt, and invoked fear in all those around him as Miss Fitzgerald had suggested. As foreperson, she planned to move the deliberations right along. She pictured her desk piled high with paperwork and all those unopened e-mails in her in-box. This was worse than taking a vacation, because she hadn't been able to plan for it.

By the time Rachel entered the deliberation room, most of the jurors had taken seats around the long rectangular conference table. The two ladies with the matching white perms sat together in the middle on one side. Tim, the techie, took a seat in between a robust Coach Rob and Alberto; the two Asian women and the tall, pretty Russian girl sat opposite the old ladies. They were all involved with the arts somehow. Elaine grabbed a chair on the opposite end of the table next to Louie on her left and Julie, the grad student, on her right. Rachel felt sorry for the two who were chosen as alternates. She couldn't imagine listening to all that testimony and then not being allowed to deliberate. The alternates had been sent to a separate room, so now they had eight women and four men.

Rachel stood at the head of the table and cleared her throat. She felt formal, as if conducting an important business meeting. Clerk Fallon dispersed labeled evidence in piles within arm's length of each juror as if serving up a Thanksgiving meal.

"Okay, we have an hour and a half until the lunch break. Why don't we start by taking a vote?" Rachel looked around the table; most nodded or shrugged. She figured this would be the best road to take. If everyone voted guilty, they could go home.

"How many of you think Billy Malone is guilty?" She watched everyone look at each other. Alberto raised his hand first, followed by three others. "Okay, we have four. I'm voting guilty too, so that makes five. How many of you believe he's not guilty?"

Elaine's hand shot up. "Not guilty's my vote."

Rachel tensed; this was going to be a battle. She wondered if Elaine chose not guilty just to take sides against her.

"That leaves six of you undecided?" The remaining six nodded.

What to do next? At least she had four guilty votes on her side, but it had to be unanimous, and after practically three grueling weeks she would make damn sure it was. Rachel decided to put Elaine on the hot seat. She'd wear her down; that woman would never cut it in the business world.

"So, why on earth do you think the defendant is innocent, Elaine?" She placed her hands on her hips.

"I didn't say that." Elaine smirked.

"But you voted—"

"I voted *not guilty*. You must not have been listening to Judge Killam's instructions. There's quite a difference, honey."

Rachel gritted her teeth; she hated Elaine's condescending tone. "Don't call me honey."

Elaine rolled her eyes. "I voted not guilty because Miss Fitzgerald didn't prove her case."

"And, I listened to all the instructions." Rachel couldn't let that go.

"I think you missed some."

"What're you talking about?"

"First of all, we weren't supposed to be taking a vote. He wanted us to talk about the case first. Then, the judge said it was up to the Commonwealth to prove her case beyond a reasonable doubt. He stressed that a bunch of times, remember?" Elaine looked up and down the table. "Who doesn't have questions about this one?"

Elaine was trying to take over. Rachel wouldn't let that happen. "What are you questioning here?"

"Okay, to start with, why did Malone kill Trevor Shea? Can anybody tell me?" Elaine flipped her palms up and peered from side to side.

"He was after Malone's gal." Alberto grinned; his mustache stretched across his face. He had chipmunk cheeks.

"The artist?" Coach Rob shook his head. "No way. Didn't sound like he was into girls. I know the type. Besides, Malone wouldn't care; he was doing Stacy by then."

"He was what?" One of the old ladies put her hand up to her ear.

"Never mind." The coach smiled.

Alberto shrugged. "Malone's a ladies' man. He was probably planning on having them both. Maybe he thought Jennianne was into the artist. She seemed like it when she was testifying."

Several others agreed.

"I didn't think that," the Russian girl said. She spoke with an accent. "They were friends since childhood."

"Doesn't matter." Alberto raised his voice. "Malone could've been jealous anyway. He strikes me as the jealous type."

"Wouldn't want to make *him* jealous," the coach said.

Rachel pulled her chair out and sat down. Several jurors were having side conversations about Malone and his girlfriends. How long should she let them go before interrupting? She'd never done anything like this before. Was it all a part of a normal deliberation? She watched Elaine blabbing something to Louie.

One of the old ladies raised her hand. "I thought Jennianne mentioned something about trust?"

"Oh, you're right, Helen," her friend said. "Jennianne overheard Malone telling his brother that Trevor couldn't be trusted."

"I don't remember that," Elaine said.

"Me, either," several others said.

Rachel couldn't recall that, but maybe she'd missed it.

Tim the techie rubbed his beard. "To be precise, I believe Jennianne Smith said she overheard Billy and Frank talking when she first arrived and—"

"I thought that part was a little sketchy." Elaine raised her voice. How do we know that—"

"Let him finish." Rachel cut Elaine off and nodded at Tim. That woman had an opinion about everything.

"I thought Malone said that he couldn't deal with Trevor . . . something to that effect," Tim said.

"I thought there was an objection and it was sustained," one of the Asians said. "I wish Judge Killam had let us take notes. I would've written that down."

I thought. I thought. I thought. Everyone had a slightly different version of the testimony. Rachel listened to several people break into a discussion about the pros and cons of note taking. This group liked going off on tangents. "Let's get back to the testimony," she said.

"Malone mentioned something about not trusting Trevor when Jennianne first got there." Alberto pointed at Helen. "She was right."

"I don't think we should dwell on it." Elaine's voice bellowed above the others. "Malone could've been talking about anybody at that point. How did she know they were discussing Trevor?"

Rachel decided to butt in. "It was clear to me they were talking about Trevor."

"Yeah." Alberto raised a finger. "Because Billy said, 'Let's get it over with. I can't put up with that faggot for much longer.'"

"Can't really prove it," Elaine said.

"Wasn't that later on?" a woman said.

Rachel listened to the group break into another free-for-all. "I believe that was said later, after Trevor was sketching Jennianne."

"Who really invited him?" Coach Rob rose halfway from his seat.

"Yeah, who?" Elaine said.

"Malone did." Rachel thought that had been obvious as well.

"That wasn't clear," Helen said.

Several agreed with Helen and several disagreed. Rachel glanced across the table. Louie sat slouched in his chair with his eyes closed. *Was he taking a nap?*

"Forget about who invited Trevor for a minute." Elaine tapped the table several times. "Let's get back to what was said when Jennianne was in the kitchen. You know, 'Let's do it' could've meant they were about to leave Jennianne's."

Rachel felt a headache coming on. "I disagree. If you take those words in context—"

"There's another thing that bothers me about that." Elaine leaned way over the table. "Why would the Malones have said something so incriminating with Jennianne right there?"

"She wasn't standing in clear view," Tim said. "She overheard them talking from the kitchen."

Elaine laughed. "That's convenient. How do we know Callahan didn't tell her to say that? Huh?"

Rachel knew Elaine didn't like Callahan. "Now you're speculating. I recall the judge instructing us not to engage in such guesswork." She had to throw that jab in there.

"Well, that settles it. I'm sure your memory is superior to ours. After all, the judge made you foreman."

"Uh, that's foreperson, Elaine."

Elaine shrugged. "Call yourself whatever you want, honey."

Rachel wanted to claw Elaine to shreds.

"Why don't we review the evidence?" Helen lifted a photograph.

"Great idea." Rachel was relieved to change the subject. "We'll start with the first witness." She looked across the table. Louie still had his eyes closed. Was he listening? Should she say something?

"That drug dealer?" the Russian said.

"No." Tim raised a finger. "Officer O'Neil testified first."

"You're right, Tim." Helen smiled at him.

"Oh, we can skip O'Neil, can't we? He didn't tell us anything important, only that he found the body—big deal. If we rehash every single detail, we'll be stuck here another two weeks." Coach Rob checked his watch. "It's almost time for lunch now, and we haven't gotten anywhere."

"We can't just skip him." Elaine nudged Louie, startling him. "O'Neil was good for the defense. Not only did he steal money off a dead body, but he thought it was an accidental overdose. That's huge."

"True." Louie rubbed his eyes.

Rachel addressed Elaine. "You really think he stole money out of Trevor's wallet? I bet that was one of Buddy Clancy's smoke screens."

Elaine stood. "Oh, I'm absolutely positive he did. Them cops rolled the body lookin' for money, and they knew damn well it was against police procedure. They steal money from dead people all the time."

"I wouldn't be surprised," Alberto mumbled.

"And when they make a drug bust? If they find a box full a cash, they'll only report half of it. Lot a rich cops out there." Elaine rubbed her fingers together.

"There are plenty of honest ones, too. My uncle happens to be one of them," the grad student said.

"You're absolutely right." Helen tapped the table with her fingernails. "I've got a grandnephew on the force in Brockton, who just got promoted. He's as honest as they come. So, we have to decide whether the officers who took the stand in this case were truthful or not."

Several side conversations broke out about the police. Rachel liked them; she always got out of her speeding tickets. They probably doubled the fines for Elaine.

"Helen's right. There are plenty of good cops out there." Rachel raised her voice. She needed to get them back on track. "What do you think about Officer Twomey?"

"He seemed very tired. I think he'd been working all night," Helen said. "Don't you all think so?"

Most nodded. Rachel recalled the deep purple rings beneath Twomey's eyes. She heard someone expressing an opinion about all the extra police details in the city that taxpayers were stuck paying for.

"That guy Twomey was useless." Elaine raised her arms.

"Yeah," several others said.

"I also think he was coached to make up for all of O'Neil's screwups." Elaine waggled her finger. "Clancy did a great job on cross. There's no way in hell Twomey would've remembered all those details. They told him what to say during lunch that day."

"He was wrong about the weather." Louie sat up. "Everyone else said it was very cold and windy, but he claimed it was warm. I think he said mid-fifties. Now that's a big difference. Too bad we couldn't go back and check the weather charts ourselves."

"He also wasn't sure which hand Trevor held the needle in." Tim stood and raised the plastic bag containing the syringe. "At first he said the right and then he said the left."

Alberto scratched his head. "I thought it was the other way around."

"Twomey's biding his time 'til retirement."

"And getting paid good money to boot." Elaine shook her head.

More than half the jurors agreed. Rachel though so, too, but didn't want to agree with Elaine.

"I liked Buddy Clancy." Helen smiled.

"Oh, me, too," Helen's friend also had a wide smile. Rachel wondered if they both had crushes. She listened as the two old ladies had a side conversation about Clancy.

"Didn't it seem like the judge ruled against him a lot?"

"Yes, I felt sorry for him."

"Mmm. He has a dog with a matching bow tie."

"How do you know that?"

"My friend told me."

The whole room broke out into conversation about Clancy, his bow ties, and what type of dog they imagined he'd have. Rachel poured herself more water.

"I wonder if the judge knows Malone is guilty?" Alberto finally changed the subject.

"Probably. Judge Killam knows lots of stuff we don't. My neighbor's a lawyer, and he tells me they keep a lot of evidence from ever reaching the jury," the Russian said.

"Why?" Helen asked.

"Because it might unfairly prejudice the defendant's case." Tim sounded sarcastic.

"God forbid."

"Know what it boils down to?" Elaine grabbed the edge of the table. "They think we're stupid, like the law's too complicated for us. Lawyers and judges believe they're so far above everybody else."

Alberto nodded. "And then they pretend they're one of us when they try a case."

Rachel breathed on her glasses and rubbed them clean as the room broke out into a discourse on lawyers. Her head ached. They all needed to eat.

"I think Judge Killam knows he's guilty. Did you catch the way he looked at Malone all those times?"

Several jurors nodded.

"What does everyone think about the paintings?"

57

ANNIE GLANCED AT her desk clock for the hundredth time. It was five of three. The jury had deliberated right through lunch and into the afternoon. What were they discussing? Judge Killam would send them home in two hours, otherwise Johnny would throw a fit. She doubted they'd reach a verdict by the end of the day. She should've gone home. Her cell rang; it was Callahan.

"Hi, Mike." Annie sighed into the phone. "Nothing to report yet."

"Meet me at Drake Reed's house in Charlestown."

"Why?"

"Mrs. Reed says she has something to show us."

"What is it?"

"Not sure yet. Just drop what you're doing and head over now."

"Okay." Annie hung up and grabbed her pocketbook. She was supposed to stay in the vicinity of the courthouse in case the jurors had a question or reached a verdict. A quick trip over the bridge to Charlestown shouldn't be a problem.

Mrs. Reed greeted her at the door when she arrived. Callahan was already there.

"I wanted to wait for you," he said. "This'll be interesting."

"Follow me upstairs." Mrs. Reed led them up the staircase and into a bedroom.

Annie noticed the men's clothing scattered about the floor and bed. All the bureau drawers had been pulled open. The bedding had been torn from the bed and the mattress was still halfway off. She figured Agent Bertrand had searched it and left the mess for Mrs. Reed to clean up. Callahan would've done the same thing. She recalled his words during cross-examination: *standard procedure.*

Mrs. Reed grasped the bedpost. "I didn't like that FBI agent and the way he treated you." She regarded Callahan. "I didn't like the way he treated me, either. I'd just lost my son and he couldn't even say he was sorry." She peered out the window. "So, I decided not to help him."

Neither Annie nor Callahan said a word as they waited for her to continue. Annie noticed tears in the corners of her eyes. She knew it was painful for any mother to stand in her dead son's bedroom; it probably still smelled like him.

Mrs. Reed gazed at Callahan. "You showed me kindness when you came over here that day. It meant a lot." Tears rolled down her cheek.

Callahan nodded and patted her shoulder.

"I did my own search first, you know. Found a few things." She reached into her pocketbook, and withdrew a framed photograph of herself and a young blond boy. She appeared to be in her midtwenties, and the boy was a toddler. Both had been laughing. Annie figured it was her son, Drake.

"Those were better days," she whispered. "Anyway, I framed this for Drake and he kept it down in the living room. I picked it up when Drake first went missing and noticed the frame wasn't quite the same. It was similar. So, I took it apart and discovered this." Mrs. Reed reached into her pocket and pulled out what looked like a small earphone that had been smashed flat. She handed it to Callahan.

"A listening device." He held it up to the light and examined it between his two fingers. "What happened to it?"

"I squished it with my heel." She shrugged. "It was my instinct as a mother to protect my son. I knew Drake was heavily involved with Billy Malone. The feds had bugged the house."

"How'd you know it was the feds and not the Boston Police?" Annie asked.

"I didn't when I first found it, but when Agent Bertrand came to search the house, I could tell he was looking for it. He finally asked me if I'd taken a framed photograph." Her lips formed a tiny, devious smile. "I denied it."

"So," Annie said to Callahan. "Bertrand lied in response to my subpoena. I requested any information, including electronic surveillance. This means they have an active file on Malone."

"That's right." Callahan fingered the device. "I'm sure he'll wiggle his way out of it somehow."

"How about if I confront Bertrand since you're banned from the building?" Annie said.

"For eavesdropping on Drake Reed?" Callahan grimaced. "Not worth the hassle."

"No, for obstructing justice. My subpoena requested all investigative files pertaining to Malone, including information gathered via electronic surveillance. Reed was Malone's right-hand man, and anything obtained against him would go into the Malone file."

"They can still deny the existence of a Malone file."

"I'll bluff a little." Annie smiled. "I'm good at it—learned from Clancy." Callahan laughed. "Just don't start wearing bow ties."

"There's something else I have to say to you." Mrs. Reed stepped toward Callahan and placed her hands on his shoulders. "I'm very sorry but it was my son who shot your police sergeant the night you arrested Malone. I'm glad the man lived; I prayed for him."

Callahan's eyes widened. "We always suspected, but . . . how do you know?"

"I overheard Drake talking about it on his cell phone. I know I should've reported it. Perhaps if I had, my son would still be alive."

"Thank you for telling me now." Callahan hugged her.

Annie's cell rang; she recognized the clerk's number. "One minute, it's the court calling," she said. "Hello?"

"The jury has a question," Clerk Fallon said. "Judge wants you down here in five."

"Can you give me ten? I'm not at the DA's office right now—had an emergency."

"Better hurry." He hung up.

"Gotta go," Annie shoved her phone into her purse.

"Verdict?" Callahan followed her down the stairs.

"No, the jury has a question."

"What does that mean?" Mrs. Reed said.

"The judge'll announce the question in open court, and instruct them how to address it. Could be anything." Annie opened the front door. "Sometimes we can get a feel for what they're thinking or gauge how smart they are."

"And, if we're lucky, we can figure out whose side they're on," Callahan said. "Juries come up with the most bizarre questions sometimes. I've heard some wacky ones in my day."

"Hold on. Before you go." Mrs. Reed waved her hand. "I've got one more thing to show you."

Annie turned around as she jogged backward down the front walk. "I'll have to come back later. Judge Killam doesn't like to wait."

"It's a painting."

Annie stumbled, nearly falling over. Did she really say *painting*? "A what?"

"One of Trevor's paintings. It's still taped down to the underside of the kitchen rug." Mrs. Reed pointed to her car. "I put the rug in the trunk so Agent Bertrand wouldn't find it."

58

CLANCY WATCHED THE guard escort his client back into court. Malone looked like he hadn't slept in weeks.

"What's the question?" Malone plunked down into his seat.

"All rise for the jury," the clerk said.

"Stand up straight, don't slouch," Clancy said. "They're still judging you."

"I said, what's the question?" Malone's voice came across like a loud snarl just as the jurors entered. The first five looked right at him. They must've heard his angry outburst. Clancy smiled, nodded, and pretended everything was peachy.

"You'll find out soon enough," he whispered to Malone, without moving his lips. Clancy knew what the question was, but decided to keep his client guessing. He continued smiling as Judge Killam made small talk with the jury.

"Your question is can you give us more examples of what constitutes circumstantial evidence?" The judge said. "I've decided to repeat my instructions pertaining to direct and circumstantial evidence. Hopefully that will clear up any confusion you may be having."

The jurors nodded. It was an intelligent question. Clancy studied their expressions as Judge Killam explained about direct evidence and gave examples. They looked solemn, serious, and ready to convict.

Judge Killam cleared his throat. "Okay. You also have circumstantial evidence when a witness cannot testify directly about a fact that is to be proved, but you are presented with evidence of other facts and you are then asked to draw reasonable inferences from them about the fact which is to be proved. You are permitted to draw reasonable inferences or conclusions based on your common sense and experiences in life. In a chain of circumstantial evidence, it is not required that every one of your inferences and conclusions be inevitable, but it is required that each of them be reasonable, that they all be consistent with one another, and that together they establish the defendant's guilt beyond a reasonable doubt."

Clancy's mind raced. He glanced at Annie and wondered what she made of this. She had touched on direct and circumstantial evidence in her opening statement. Did that mean they were siding with her? Were they speculating? Looking for ways to find Malone guilty?

After providing several examples of circumstantial evidence, Judge Killam dismissed the jury, and the court lapsed back into recess. Malone glared at Clancy when the guard escorted him back out. He knew he had to make the dreaded trip to the cell and say something to his client.

Clancy grabbed a coffee from the cafeteria before heading to the cell. He let two ladies go in front of him in the line at the register, delaying the inevitable confrontation. Clancy would have to calm Malone down and give him false hope. It didn't look good. As expected, Malone was kicking the walls of his cell when Clancy arrived.

"What are they gonna do?" Malone panted. His face appeared red and blotchy.

"I can't predict what a jury'll do. You never know. We have to stick it out and hope for the best."

"They're gonna find me guilty—wouldn't even look at me." Malone's dress shirt stuck to his armpits; two wet semicircles had formed along his sides. "I paid you damn good money to get me out of here. I'd have been better off with a public defender. I'm innocent this time! Don't they get it? You picked a jury full of hard asses. I'm not going to jail for the rest of my life on this stupid drug overdose charge. Are you hearing me, Clancy?"

"Calm down." Clancy kept his voice even. Malone was lucky they abolished the death penalty in Massachusetts. If Bertrand had nailed him for murder in federal court a few years back, his client would've been six feet under with weeds growing up through his skull by now.

Malone circled the cell. "Who the hell are you to tell me to calm down?"

"They haven't found you guilty yet."

"It's obvious what they think."

"If they do, we'll appeal," Clancy said.

"Nobody wins on appeal. That's impossible."

"You'd be surprised. I've won several. We can take up the issue of all the publicity surrounding the case, and how you couldn't possibly have had a fair trial in Boston."

"And I'm stuck in the can while you're filing all your papers." He grabbed the bars and heaved his chest forward and backward. "Then we have to wait to get a court date. And, you'll screw me over with the legal bill. It's not fair. You should've kicked that big fat lady off the jury in the beginning. She hates my guts."

"The one who sits next to the foreperson?"

"Yeah, her."

"I had the impression she hated Callahan and could be on our side."

"She hates all men then because she's always sneering at me. You should've gotten rid of her. I got a bad feeling. Is it too late to kick her off now?"

"Yes. It takes more than one—"

"You should've kicked her the hell off!" The skin on Malone's face now appeared like it was ready to split open. His eyes had that crazed look.

Clancy turned away and linked his hands behind his back. His client couldn't be rationalized with at this point. He had tried a good case, he convinced himself. Win some, lose some—it was all part of the game. A hero when you win, a bastard when you lose. Malone would hire a team of lawyers, and they'd accuse Clancy of being incompetent, senile, insane, perhaps. They'd order a transcript, tear him to pieces, and drag his good name through the mud. Maybe they'd bring him up before the Board of Bar Overseers. He'd seen another appellate lawyer do that to a colleague just for the money and publicity. The poor guy had done nothing wrong, really, but he ended up losing his license to practice law. Clancy pictured himself spiraling downward just before his retirement. All for what? This guy? Billy Malone? *Not worth it.* Maybe he shouldn't take the big murder cases anymore. *Too stressful.* This would be his last one. He could spend more time with his wife, his children and grandchildren, and his dog. Of course, he'd said that before.

Clancy turned around and faced Malone again. "Do you want me to approach Fitzgerald about a plea bargain before the jury comes back? You never know, she may—"

"Get out!"

59

ELAINE DECIDED TO cut to the chase. "How can you call it murder when Trevor Shea injected *himself* with the heroin?" That was the crux of the case as far as she was concerned.

"Obviously, he didn't realize it was so potent." Rachel dipped her pointy chin when she wanted to make a point. Elaine hated it.

"I agree," Helen said.

"So what?" Elaine addressed Rachel, mimicking the chin dip. "Anyone who injects heroin takes that risk." *How naïve can she be?*

"Actually, I agree with Elaine on this point," Tim said. "Heroin is an inherently dangerous drug."

"Like playing Russian roulette." Elaine pointed her index finger and touched her temple, as if she had a gun.

"Good point." Tim leaned back and pinched his lower lip. "Let's say they were playing Russian roulette. Malone supplies the bullet and Trevor shoots himself. Does that mean Malone should be convicted of murder?"

"No," several jurors said.

Helen rested her chin on her fist. "Probably not."

Good. Now they were getting somewhere. It seemed like Helen always agreed with Rachel and Helen's new best old lady friend agreed with Helen. *A twofer.*

Rachel reached across the table and grabbed the syringe. She held it up between two fingers, and examined it for a moment. "That Russian roulette scenario is entirely different."

Elaine was so sick of Rachel and her highbrowed opinions. "It's exactly the same, *Rachel*."

"Oh no, it's not. What if Malone lines the bullet up in the chamber, so that when Trevor pulls the trigger it's a guaranteed hit? Now, that would make Malone a murderer in my book."

Annie couldn't wait to get back to Mrs. Reed's house to view the painting taped under the rug. It seemed like she hit every red light, and, to boot, the city was clogged with rush-hour traffic. The jury question had raised her mood. She hoped they were trying to piece together all the evidence, both direct and circumstantial, to convict Malone.

"Come on in," Mrs. Reed said as she held the front door open. "What was the question?"

Annie explained the jurors' confusion over circumstantial evidence, but didn't express too much enthusiasm for fear of getting Mrs. Reed's hopes up.

"The painting is in here." She motioned Annie into the kitchen. "We took it out of car and removed it from beneath the rug."

"Where's Callahan?"

"He got a phone call and rushed out of here. Didn't say why."

Annie wondered what had happened. Perhaps he'd been called out to another murder scene. She gasped when she saw the painting. It revealed a big man sitting on his front stoop, smoking a cigarette. His gray eyes stared out of the canvas, right at her. The colors within that gray paint appeared to be moving, dancing. His gaze chilled Annie to the bone. Trevor had painted the man's fear through his eyes, a fear of death.

"The eyes say it all," Annie said.

"It's what I call terrorism." Mrs. Reed touched the canvas. "That's John Eagan. His mother and I are second cousins. We used to play together as kids. She hasn't spoken to me since her son's murder."

"I remember this one. Eagan lived on Harvard Street—one of my unsolved murders from the nineties." Annie recalled the sparse file. The man had been shot and left to rot in his apartment for almost a week. A neighbor reported the stench.

"Everyone in Charlestown knows Malone did it," Mrs. Reed said.

"No witnesses, case closed."

"I pray to God you win, Annie."

"Me, too." She wanted this more than ever. Trevor's case was a culmination of all the unsolved cases. He was the voice of the victims. "I wish the jury could've seen this."

Annie's cell phone rang; it was Callahan. "Hello? I'm here with Mrs. Reed. What did you make of the painting?"

"I'm boarding a flight to Fort Lauderdale."

"What?" Annie assumed he was joking.

"We found Stacy Black."

60

WHAT ABOUT STACY Black? Did anyone believe her?" Rachel blew on her coffee. She still felt chilled from her walk to the courthouse. Sleet had melted in her hair, leaving it damp and flat. She eyed the box of donuts in the center of the table, and thought about rewarding herself with a lemon-filled. She could almost taste the tang on her tongue. *No, don't do it,* she told herself.

"Miss Black made some mistakes describing Jennianne's apartment." Tim raised several photographs. "She claimed the living room couch was maroon, but in these pictures it looks beige to me."

"Do you really think she was there that night? Jennianne never mentioned her." Rachel looked at everyone else eating donuts and longed for one. "I thought that was odd."

"Maybe she forgot," the Russian said, as she passed the photo of the couch along.

"How could she?" a woman mumbled. Several others agreed.

"Yeah, it was a slugfest between the girls. I would've paid to see that." Alberto bit into a chocolate donut. Crumbs clung to his mustache.

"She got real nervous toward the end when Fitzgerald went off about her car. I couldn't figure out why," Helen daintily dabbed the corners of her mouth with a napkin.

"I noticed that, too." Rachel counted several nods. "Stacy came across defensive. I don't believe any of her testimony, and I think somebody prepped her about what time Trevor left Jennianne's apartment."

"Why?" Elaine frowned.

"Because she answered way too fast. Her body language told me she was lying." Rachel sipped her coffee.

"I agree," two others said, in unison.

"You've got a point." Tim scratched his beard. "With all the commotion, I can't imagine her watching the clock."

"I agree. It sounds like she may've been coached," Helen said.

Rachel liked Helen; she was on her side. "Quite frankly, I don't think Clancy can hang his hat on the eight o'clock theory. I think Malone and Stacy said he left at eight o'clock to make it look like he died elsewhere."

"Defense lawyers are good at that." Alberto finished his donut and licked his fingers. Rachel noticed he still had crumbs on his mustache.

"You got that right," Coach Rob said.

Elaine reached across the table and grabbed another jelly-filled. "What about Clancy's other theory?"

"Which is?" Rachel noticed the sugar on Elaine's lips and wondered how many more donuts she'd down.

"The head wound." Elaine spoke with her mouth full. "Where'd it come from?"

"Maybe Trevor got it earlier in the night?" Louie said. "It was windy and cold. He could've fallen on black ice."

Tim shook his head. "No, because the medical examiner said Trevor injured his head right before death occurred."

"Right." Rachel could rely on Tim for getting the facts straight. "I think when Trevor was having his heart attack due to the heroin, he hit something as he fell to the floor."

Tim concentrated on the ceiling. "But Jennianne didn't mention that Trevor hit anything on the way down."

"Maybe she didn't see it," a woman said.

Tim shook his head. "There was no trace of blood anywhere in the apartment."

"Maybe Malone knocked him over the head with a hammer or something and got rid of it." Alberto demonstrated by swinging another chocolate donut like a hammer.

Elaine sighed. "There we go speculating again."

"It's not speculation, it's circumstantial evidence, right?" the Russian said.

"No, it's not," Elaine said.

"Why is the head wound so important?" Rachel wanted to get back on track with Stacy Black. "If it wasn't the cause of death, why should we care about it?"

Elaine pointed the remains of her donut at Rachel. "It *is* important. It bolsters Clancy's theory that Trevor's death occurred outside Jennianne's apartment. It makes his case."

"I'm Annie Fitzgerald, ADA, Suffolk County." She handed the receptionist her business card. "I'm here to see Agent Bertrand."

"Do you have an appointment?" The receptionist pushed her reading glasses down to the tip of her nose.

"No."

"I'm sorry, but you can't simply walk in here and expect to meet with him. He's a very busy man."

"I know, but this is urgent. Please tell him I have something that belongs to one of his files." Annie forced a smile.

The receptionist swiveled her desk chair away from Annie and picked up her phone. Following a brief, whispered conversation, she faced her again. "Which file are you referring to?"

"The Malone file." *Bertrand knew.*

The receptionist resumed whispering into the phone and addressed Annie again. "Agent Bertrand says we don't have a Malone file."

Annie fingered the transmitter in her coat pocket. "Tell him I found his favorite listening device at Drake Reed's apartment. I'm sure he wants it back."

The receptionist repeated Annie's words and hung up. "He'll see you." She gave Annie a knowing smile.

Annie followed the receptionist down the hall and wondered what Bertrand would do? At least she didn't have Callahan with her. She knew she had to corner the man and then give him a way out.

Bertrand waved her in. "Close the door," he said to the receptionist as he motioned her out of the room.

Annie walked up to the desk and opened her mouth to speak.

"Sit down." Bertrand pointed at a chair. His tone was commanding.

Annie hated it, and, therefore, remained standing.

He regarded her for a moment. "You have something of mine?"

Annie discerned the icy edge in his voice. "That's right."

Bertrand twirled a ballpoint pen between his fingers. "Callahan just won't give up, will he?"

Annie reached into her pocket and dropped the tiny transmitter onto his desk. Bertrand didn't flinch, but his eyes registered something. Annie couldn't tell what it was. *Shock perhaps?*

"This proves you lied in response to my subpoena." Annie maintained eye contact.

"Really?" He rubbed his chin. "How so?"

"You denied the existence of information obtained through electronic surveillance. This is evidence that you've been eavesdropping on Malone."

"But that came from Drake Reed's apartment, *so you say*." His tone sounded mocking now.

"That's right." Annie took a deep breath; she had to play her cards right. If she failed to control her temper, she'd end up in cuffs like Callahan. She sat in the chair facing the desk and stared at Bertrand's hard and impassible face. She pointed at the transmitter. "This is proof you had an active file on Malone. Drake Reed was his right-hand man." Annie decided to take it one step further to see how far she could get with her theory. "I also know Trevor Shea was one of your informants. He worked with you to build a federal racketeering case against Malone. Malone found out and killed Trevor with the Nine-eleven heroin to make it look like an accidental overdose. You knew all along and did your best to cover it up to save your precious case. You never came forward just like the witnesses in all my unsolved murders. They don't see anything, don't hear anything, and never talk to cops."

Bertrand rose. "You don't know what you're talking about."

"I know Trevor was disposable. His life, his art, meant nothing to you. You're more obsessed with catching Malone than Callahan." Annie paced for a moment, and then leaned over the desk. "Your best hope now is vigilante justice. Somebody will shoot Malone and he'll lie dead in the street, just like his father. All your secret files will be worthless. No pats on the back, medals, or pay raises. Only emptiness."

Bertrand blinked several times. His face turned red; he appeared to be holding his breath, containing his rage.

Annie had cracked him. Now she had to appeal to his emotions and provide him with a way out. As his lips parted, she decided to play her last card. "I'm going to tell you how Billy Malone got his start. Forget about subpoenas, transmitters, and cover-ups for a moment, okay?"

Bertrand stared at her.

"Years ago when Malone was sixteen, he got into an argument in a playground with a ten-year-old boy named Georgie Hurley. Malone started pushing the kid until he fell backward. He sat down on Georgie's chest, punched him in the face, and broke his nose. The kid was scared to death, he started crying, he begged Malone to stop . . . begged him. There were other kids there watching; a whole group of them. They had formed a circle around Malone and this boy. So, Malone, not wanting to get off the kid's chest, asked one of the little boys to bring him a large rock. The kid did what he was told." Annie pursed her lips as she visualized Trevor's painting. "So, Malone took that rock and smashed it into Georgie's head. He brought the rock down again and again until Georgie's screams stopped."

Bertrand swallowed and dropped his gaze.

"Georgie's parents buried him in St. Catherine's Cemetery three days later." Annie paused as she pictured Mrs. Hurley dressed in black, praying over the fresh grave of her only son. She recalled the Christmas candle in the window. "There were about a dozen kids who witnessed what Malone did to Georgie. He threatened them with their lives if they ever told a soul. As you can imagine, no one came forward. Justice was never served."

"Your painting," Bertrand whispered. It sounded like he was addressing himself.

"What about it?" Annie grabbed the edge of the desk.

"I came to court when you cross-examined Malone. Sat in the back." He met her gaze. "I saw Trevor's painting of the kids in the playground." Bertrand eased his chair out from behind the desk and stood. Without a word he walked to his window and peered out. He remained silent for several minutes. "Callahan and I have one thing in common. We share an obsession."

"I know."

"And, about Trevor Shea?" Bertrand turned around and faced Annie again.

"Yes?" Annie felt her muscles tense; he was about to tell her something significant.

"You and Callahan have this theory that the artist was one of my informants, and that's why Malone killed him."

"That's right, and I know it's true."

"Trevor Shea was an informant, but not one of ours."

Annie was speechless.

Bertrand looked out the window again. "I have another painting."

61

RACHEL REPRESSED A yawn. She couldn't wait to be released from jury duty, submerse herself in a hot bubble bath, and sip a glass of chilled Chardonnay.

"Let's organize the evidence." Tim stood and raised a crime scene photograph of Trevor's back.

"I wouldn't count that picture as evidence of anything," Elaine said. "I don't—"

"Let's put them in order and review all of them before we start talking about the individual pictures." Rachel was really losing patience with her now.

Elaine shrugged her shoulders and huffed. "Gettin' late."

"Remember the phone cord?" Alberto pointed across the table at an evidence bag. "He pulled that out of the wall, too."

"We don't have any proof that Malone actually did that," Elaine said.

No matter how hard she tried, Rachel couldn't get them to have an orderly discussion. Someone always had to skip from topic to topic.

"I think someone helped Malone drag the body out of the apartment." Coach Rob grabbed a magnified image of the scrapes on Trevor's back, and handed it to Alberto.

"Yeah, maybe that's why Malone asked his brother to be there," Alberto said.

"What about the fingerprint evidence?" Helen passed the fingerprint cards around the table.

"Malone looked like he'd seen a ghost when Fitzgerald cross-examined him on it."

"I agree with you, dear," Helen said to her friend.

Coach Rob rubbed his belly. "I wonder about the brother, Frank. He must've been arrested. I wonder why he didn't testify. Maybe he was tried already and found guilty."

"Yeah, I'd like to find out more about what goes on behind the scenes," Louie said. "I'd still like to see the weather charts."

"If we convict does Malone automatically get life?" someone asked.

Tim nodded. "Life without parole. But, remember, our job has nothing to do with sentencing." Tim cracked his knuckles. "That's up to Judge Killam."

"I wish we had some input." Coach Rob stretched his arms high over his head. "Malone already has a criminal record. I bet the judge'll nail him with the maximum if we find him guilty."

"I bet he'll be right back on the streets," Alberto said. "The jails are overcrowded; they're all getting out nowadays. I have a friend who—"

"Not for first-degree murder."

Rachel half-listened as they discussed parole and criminals getting off easy. Someone brought up another episode of *Law & Order*. She had to break in and get to the point. Otherwise, they'd be here for months. She'd rather be waterboarded.

"Let's get on with this." Rachel stood. "How many of you think Malone's guilty?"

The room fell silent for a moment. Seven hands went up. Louie raised his hand halfway and put it back down.

"How many of you are still undecided?" Rachel asked. The rest raised their hands with the exception of Elaine.

"We'll continue discussing the evidence." Rachel felt like they'd been going around in circles with the same arguments, pro and con. Would they ever agree on a verdict? She didn't want a hung jury.

No one said a word; they looked so tired.

"Back to the witnesses then." Rachel needed more coffee. "Let's see . . . we didn't say too much about Domenico."

"We should skip him altogether. He outright lied on the stand," Elaine said.

Rachel addressed Elaine. "I think the meeting between Domenico and Malone took place. That's where he got the Nine-eleven heroin, and it shows he had the intent to kill Trevor. Malone was carrying the CVS bag Domenico had given him because it contained both sets of fingerprints."

"She's right," Louie said.

Elaine shot him a dirty look.

Helen raised a finger. "That's why I believed some of Domenico's testimony."

Elaine squinted at Helen. "How can you believe only part of what a witness says? They're supposed to be under oath. Domenico got up there and lied about his perjury conviction. Same with them cops who exaggerated and embellished the truth. I say we have to believe either all or nothing."

"Then you'd have to say that about every witness for both sides." Rachel had to get tougher with her.

Elaine grinned. "If that's the case, we have to acquit because that means we have doubts."

"So, you're saying we shouldn't have any doubts at all?" Helen appeared confused.

"Not necessarily." Tim stroked his beard. "Judge Killam said that beyond a reasonable doubt doesn't mean beyond all possible doubt."

"I have doubts about certain things, but I'm convinced Malone is guilty." Rachel regarded Elaine.

"I also heard the judge say that Fitzgerald had to prove her case beyond a reasonable doubt." Elaine scowled.

"But how do you define reasonable?" Helen glanced at her friend, who looked confused.

. . .

Agent Bertrand opened a cabinet drawer with a key, removed several files, and pulled out a rolled canvas. Annie watched him unroll it across his desk. It was so large that it covered the whole thing. He weighted the ends down with several glass-framed pictures of his family, a book, and a pencil holder.

Annie walked around the desk and viewed the painting with him. It depicted a dead girl wrapped in a yellowed rubber carpet pad, stuffed into the trunk of a car. The trunk had been left open. It was nighttime and the dead girl's eyes reflected the orange streetlights. A man's shadow stretched across her body.

"Lydia Thompson." Bertrand outlined the girl's ashen face with his finger. "Looks exactly like her."

The man's shadow shot upward and mixed with smoke from a smoldering fire off to the right of the car. It looked like someone had been burning a circular pile of leaves. Annie could smell them smoldering. She leaned over the painting. *What was burning?* She made out some blackened items near the edge of the fire: the remains of a woman's high-heeled shoe, a piece of frayed rope, tied in a noose; scattered papers. *And . . . a hammer?* No, not a hammer. She moved even closer. It was a charred judge's gavel. Annie shivered.

"Someone dropped this painting off at my office about two weeks after we lost the case."

"That stuff. Right there, half-burned in the fire?" Annie pointed to the items. "Were they part of it?"

"Evidence that went missing. Yeah. She was strangled with a piece of rope, you know. That's why the judge dismissed the case against Malone. Nothing we could do about it."

"Trevor," Annie whispered. She recognized his signature in the corner.

"That's right." Bertrand rolled the painting back up. "Trevor wasn't one of our informants. He was working for himself, through his art, exposing Malone. A different kind of snitch." He handed the canvas to Annie. "Here. Take it."

62

I **THINK THEY** dragged Trevor out of the apartment like Fitzgerald said in her closing argument. They had to get rid of the body." Rachel poured the remainder of the coffee into her cup; it looked muddy, just like this case. It was four P.M., only an hour more to go before Judge Killam would release them for the day. The conference table was a mess with empty cups, pastry crumbs, and scattered evidence.

"Nobody ever mentioned a dead body getting dragged," Elaine said. "Are we supposed to jump to that conclusion based on a bunch of scratches on Trevor's back?"

"You sure, Elaine?" Louie asked.

"Yup, positive."

Louie rubbed his chin. "If Malone dragged Trevor out, could he have been alive?"

"I thought the medical examiner said that those marks occurred after death."

"Postmortem."

"Trevor died shortly after the heroin injection according to Dr. Joyce." Tim examined the death certificate.

"Maybe somebody else had it in for Trevor and knocked him over the head after he left the apartment," Elaine said.

Rachel sighed. "That brings us back to the head wound, which—".

"I know, I know. We can't seem to come up with an explanation for the head wound, which occurred before he died. Let's not rehash that again." Elaine stretched.

Most agreed. Rachel heard several mumbles and groans. They were getting too tired to think straight.

"I'm back to the same question: Why would Malone want to kill Trevor Shea?" Elaine asked.

"You're right, Elaine, the case is really weak on motive," Louie said.

Helen raised her hand. "I think it had something to do with the paintings. Remember Malone when he was on the stand and he—"

Elaine waved her off. "You're speculating about the art again, Helen. It was up to Fitzgerald to prove motive and she failed to do it. That creates reasonable doubt."

"The case does lack motive." Louie sighed and three quarters of the others sighed along with him. "And I wasn't crazy about those paintings."

"But, come on, don't you think he did it?" Rachel looked around the table. Would they give up now just because they were tired? Would they give in to Elaine?

"We'll never know for sure. Trevor could've killed himself for all we know to set Malone up for murder." Elaine shrugged. "Too much guess-work."

Louie stood and cracked his knuckles. "It's supposed to snow again to-night."

"I say we take it up in the morning when we're all fresh," Rachel said. "I can inform the judge."

Elaine stared hard at Rachael. "Let's take another vote right now."

63

"HELLO?"

"Hi Liz, it's Elaine."

"Can you believe this weather we're having? It's still snowing out there. I'm so sick of it—gonna move to Florida. By the way, how'd it go today?"

"Don't ever get on a jury if you can help it. I'm exhausted. Doubt I'll be able to stay up for *CSI*." She yawned. "At least we'll be outta there sometime tomorrow morning."

"Really? Have you decided on a verdict?"

"Just about. We have one holdout to convince. She doesn't want a mistrial, so I'm sure she'll end up siding with us."

"You ended up finding him guilty, I hope."

"No, just the opposite."

"You're letting Billy Malone off? But I thought . . . ?" She paused. "Didn't he kill the painter?"

"Probably." Elaine rummaged through the cupboard for a snack. "In fact, I'd even bet on it." She pulled out a box of last month's crackers. They were most likely stale, but might be alright loaded up with peanut butter. It was all she had. The trial had made her too tired to go grocery shopping.

"Then why are you letting him off?"

"Because the DA didn't prove her case."

"That's ridiculous, Elaine. It was obvious by just reading the papers. Look at the way they killed off the girl who went against him in court. *Jennianne.* And then there was that cop who got shot during the arrests. *Come on.*"

"It's too late to change my mind now." She scraped the bottom of the peanut butter jar with a butter knife. "Anyways, I've gotta hit the sack."

"Okay, talk to you tomorrow." Liz breathed into the phone. "Think about it good and hard before you make a big mistake."

Malone couldn't sleep; it was past three in the morning. Waiting for the jury was excruciating. Clancy had said the longer the wait, the better his chances for a not guilty verdict. It meant somebody was holding out, perhaps that one soul had reasonable doubt. Who could it be? He'd analyzed every glance, every raised eyebrow, every cough for the duration of the trial. He'd reached rock bottom after their question on circumstantial evidence, and thought they'd find him guilty right away. But, they hadn't. Someone urinated in the cell next to him; he could smell it. Malone hated the smells.

He couldn't bear another day of this. The waiting was beyond his control. He'd never come this close before. Was he ready for a lifetime in prison? He shuddered at the reality of lumpy cots with stained mattresses, cold cement floors, the permanent odor of antiseptic . . . for the rest of his life. He'd grow old there and die. He turned on his side and hyperventilated.

"Hey, come here," somebody whispered.

Malone rolled over. He made out the silhouette of a guard standing outside his cell. "Who's there?" he asked.

"Gimpy."

Malone pulled himself together and walked over. Gimpy was the nickname for one of the night guards, who teetered when he walked. He never said much, but when he did, Malone listened. He was a key link to the outside; Malone made sure he got paid well.

"Yeah?" Malone wondered what was up.

"Got news," he whispered.

"What is it?"

"This time tomorrow, you'll be out celebrating."

Malone's lips moved, but the words wouldn't come. He felt the rush of blood in his head, and for a split second he saw two Gimpys standing there. Could it really be true? He covered his face with his hands to hide the tears. Malone pictured himself leaping from the courthouse into a pile of fresh snow without shackles and guards. He could do whatever he wanted again.

After several minutes had passed, he regained sufficient control of his emotions to face Gimpy. "How'd you hear?"

"One of your friend's aunts has a cousin who's on the jury. They're coming back with a not guilty tomorrow morning."

"You're sure about this?"

"Positive."

Malone grinned. Now he could take his business to another level. Who could stop him now? He circled the cell with his hands on his head.

"But listen up." Gimpy paused. "You gotta keep an eye on Chris Shea. He's planning to take you out, and it might be right in court."

"How would he get a gun through security?"

Gimpy shrugged. "Just sayin'."

"He's a nutcase." Malone had noticed the way Chris had stared him down throughout the trial. "Just like his brother."

Gimpy checked over his shoulder, moved closer to Malone, and cupped his fingers over his mouth. "They wanna know what you want them to do. They can take care of him tonight."

Malone grabbed the bars and arched his back. What to do? No way he'd get a gun into court. Or, could he? The worst thing would be to get off and then get knocked off. But, if he had Shea killed tonight, it would be too obvious. He'd be back on trial for another murder. Malone would have to take the brother out, and soon, but he needed time to think it through.

"Tell 'em this." Malone placed his lips next to the bars near Gimpy's ear. "To get somebody who's not from Charlestown. We need to know where Chris Shea is and what he's doing at all times. Make sure they sit next to him for the verdict announcement. Gotta be ready for anything."

Gimpy nodded and left.

64

CALLAHAN RAN AS fast as he could; his lungs burned. He burst through the courthouse doors. He had to find Annie. People packed the lobby. He skirted the long line at security. The guard didn't bother him this time. Callahan pounded the elevator button. *Come on.* When it finally opened, he pushed his way though, and tried to close the doors, but people kept piling in. "Let's go," he yelled.

Callahan leaped from the elevator and ran down the nearly empty hallway toward the courtroom doors. He yanked both handles. *Locked.*

"You're about a minute too late, maybe less," a court officer said. "They're announcing the verdict."

"I gotta get in there!" Callahan pulled at the handle again. "Please unlock it! This is an emergency."

"Can't help you. Judge's orders. The court officer folded his arms. They'll all be out soon enough."

Callahan threw his car keys against the wall. *Always one step behind.* He backed to the opposite wall, ran as fast as he could, and slammed his body against the two locked doors.

"Hey!" The court officer grabbed him by the shoulder. "What the hell do you think you're doing?"

Callahan pulled away and pounded the doors with both fists. "Somebody let me in!"

Another court officer stepped out from the courtroom and relocked the door behind him. Callahan knew him, but couldn't remember his name. "What's going on out here?" Both men grabbed an arm, and dragged Callahan away from the doors.

"I have to speak with Annie Fitzgerald right now," Callahan said.

"You'll have to wait until after the verdict."

He twisted himself free. "Then it'll be too late."

The second court officer grasped his arm at the elbow. "There's nothing you can do about it now, Mike. The jury's already reached a verdict. They're about to enter the courtroom as we speak. You'll have to wait for the appeal."

"But Annie can't appeal a *not guilty* verdict." Callahan squirmed. "Come on, just let me in there."

"Look, there's nothing we can do. Judge Killam made it clear that no one is allowed in the courtroom once the jury has entered. I'm not going to risk my job for you."

Callahan had to reach her now. "Okay, I'll write a note. Just walk down the aisle and hand it to Annie. Please. You have no idea how important this."

"I don't know—"

"Come on," Callahan said. "Do it for all those mothers with the dead sons and daughters in the front row. Please don't let them down now."

"All rise!"

Clancy and his client stood. Judge Killam entered in his typical grandiose style, arms swinging, black robe fluttering behind him. He surveyed the packed gallery with the eight extra security guards lining the walls and center aisle.

"I will not tolerate outbursts or disruptions of any kind in my courtroom. I have instructed the court officers and guards to detain anyone who violates my rules. I don't care who you are. Do I make myself clear?"

Clancy turned around; people were squished into the benches. Mrs. Malone sat in her usual spot. Her lips moved in silent prayer; the rosary dangled from her clasped hands. Clancy recognized some of Malone's friends scattered about. Mothers Against Murder lined the front row with their yellow T-shirts. He exchanged eye contact with Chris Shea, who grinned at him, and came across a bit deranged. Clancy suddenly had a bad feeling about him. He hoped they had enough security.

"Court Officer, bring in the jury," Judge Killam said.

Johnny waddled to the side door. The jurors trooped in looking like straight-faced wooden soldiers. Silence descended upon the courtroom. Their gazes fixed on the floor, the wall, the swivel chairs, and their hands. No one looked at Malone. That was usually a bad sign for the defendant. Several made eye contact with Clancy, though, which could be construed as a good sign. The foreperson held the envelope containing the verdict slip, which she clutched in her hand, crinkling the paper. She looked angry. *So many emotions.* They collectively seemed more serious than past juries had for the formal announcement. Clancy wondered if they were at peace with their verdict.

After the jurors took their seats, Clerk Fallon stood and cleared his throat. "Madam foreperson, has the jury reached a verdict?"

The foreperson rose to her feet. "Yes, we have."

"Very well," Judge Killam said. "Please hand the envelope containing your verdict slip to the clerk."

"Sidebar!" Annie yelled.

Clancy nearly fell over. He twisted to his left. Annie waved a piece of paper in the air. *Was he dreaming?* In all his years no one had ever interrupted the verdict announcement.

Malone nudged him. "What's going on?"

"Miss Fitzgerald?" Judge Killam blinked several times. He also looked shocked.

"May I please have a sidebar?" Annie said again.

Clancy heard the desperation in her voice. He glanced at the jurors, who looked at her with their mouths hanging open. They appeared as dumbfounded as he and the judge.

"Approach. This better be good," Judge Killam said, when they reached the sidebar.

"Most respectfully, Your Honor." Annie coughed; her voice sounded scratchy as if she choked on her own words. "I'm requesting a brief continuance, sua sponte."

The judge stared at her for a moment. "On what basis?"

"Newly discovered evidence."

Clancy had to butt in; this was insane. "The jury is in! We can't call a halt to this now."

Judge Killam grunted. "He's right. The jury has already deliberated and reached a verdict."

"A verdict is not official until it's recorded." Annie stepped forward, toward the judge. "I'm requesting an opportunity to be heard."

Clancy gesticulated with both hands. "Official or not, it's still a verdict. I've been practicing law longer than anyone here, and I've never even heard of anything like this. It's a delay tactic."

"Why would I do that?" Annie addressed Clancy.

"Because you're afraid the jury's coming back with a not guilty! You're afraid of losing." He pointed at her.

"Don't you dare point at me!"

"The jurors were looking me in the eye; they wouldn't look at you. We both know what that means: you lost."

"Enough." Judge Killam banged his gavel. "I'm going to continue with the verdict."

"No, Your Honor," Annie lowered her voice to a whisper. "They just arrested Stacy Black—*for murder.*"

"What?" both Clancy and Judge Killam said.

"She confessed to running Jennianne Smith off the road. Malone ordered it. I'm requesting to be heard again on the admissibility of the grand jury transcript and to introduce newly discovered evidence."

The judge leaned way back in his chair and shook his head. "I'm calling a recess. I'll see you in chambers right now."

"This is ridiculous." Clancy couldn't believe the judge agreed to take a break.

"Thank you, Your Honor," Annie said. "I only need a minute to speak with Callahan before—"

"No."

Judge Killam turned toward the jurors. "I apologize for the delay, but an issue has arisen which must be resolved. The court is now in recess."

"Anybody know what's going on?" Alberto was the last juror to reenter the deliberation room. He slammed the door behind him.

Rachel stood at the head of the conference table and listened to the complaints flying from every direction.

"Never heard of anything like this." Elaine slumped into her chair. "What right does Fitzgerald have to stall our verdict?"

"She doesn't. It was our turn this time."

"Yeah, we did our job and now it's time to go," Elaine said. "I'm losing money by the hour."

"Me, too," several jurors said.

"I told my babysitter we'd be through this afternoon. Now I don't have coverage," the Russian said.

"How long do we have to wait?" Helen asked.

"I'm not sure." All eyes focused on Rachel. It was her job to take control of the situation and ease the tension. But what could she tell them? She'd never felt so helpless. "Clerk Fallon thinks it shouldn't be too long." Her words sounded feeble.

"He doesn't know squat," Elaine said. "You need to speak with the judge yourself. Tell him we won't put up with this nonsense. If you don't have the balls to do it, I will."

"Shut the hell up, Elaine! I'm sick of your bullshit." A droplet of white spit catapulted off Rachel's tongue and landed in the center of the table.

Helen raised her hands. "Calm down, everyone. Please! We have no choice but to wait it out. It's part of our duty as jurors."

"I agree." Tim addressed Elaine. "The issue must be important for His Honor to have called a recess like that."

"It's wrong." Elaine pounded the table, sending a paper plate flying.

"Did anybody overhear the conversation at sidebar?" Coach Rob asked.

"I thought I heard Fitzgerald say she had more evidence." Alberto rubbed his eyes. "I'm sick of this case. We made our decision; it's time to go home."

"He can't do anything about it now, can he?" Louie addressed Elaine.

"No way. Too late. Case closed. We've reached a verdict."

"The judge is probably covering himself by hearing Fitzgerald out." Rachel poured herself a glass of water. She hoped that's all it was. These people would explode, otherwise.

"I'm sure that's what this is all about." Alberto rolled his eyes. "Covering asses."

"They're the asses if you ask me." Elaine turned around and smacked her own behind.

65

ANNIE STOOD BEFORE Judge Killam to argue her motions in open court. The jury wasn't present. She couldn't believe this was happening. *No one could.* The judge had only given her ten minutes to prepare. If he ruled against her, the jury would proceed with their verdict announcement. If he ruled in her favor, he could allow the jurors to consider the new evidence and go back to deliberating or he might declare a mistrial.

"I'll hear you, Commonwealth."

"Thank you." Annie glanced at the scribbled notes in her legal pad. "I'm requesting permission to reopen my case to introduce newly discovered evidence. According to *Commonwealth v. Stewart,* when serious doubts are raised as to the integrity of the verdict, the judge may declare a mistrial, or alternatively, order further deliberations. Your Honor, as the trial judge, you have broad discretion to allow the Commonwealth to introduce evidence that rebuts the defendant's theory of defense even after the jury has purportedly reached a verdict. To qualify as newly discovered, the evidence must have been unknown and not reasonably discoverable throughout the course of the trial according to *Commonwealth v. Grace.*"

"What's the evidence?"

"Three of the victim's paintings."

"How did you find them?"

"I subpoenaed the Federal Bureau of Investigation requesting all records, files, documents, tape recordings, and other information pertaining to Billy Malone. The FBI replied in writing that they had no documents or recordings responsive to my request in their possession, custody, or control. In fact, they outright denied the existence of a Malone file."

Judge Killam grimaced. "So, you dropped the ball after that?"

"How did I drop—"

"You could've filed a motion to compel the Bureau to produce their file."

"My hands were tied because they denied the existence of *any* file."

"Did you employ any of your investigators to call their bluff?"

"I had no reason to believe they would lie about the existence of a file in the first place."

"Proceed."

Annie's mind went blank, and she forgot where she'd left off in her legal argument. She decided to resume somewhere in the middle. "The proposed evidence should be admitted for it is both material and credible and carries a measure of strength in support of the Commonwealth's case. Thus, there is a substantial risk that if this new evidence is not admitted, the jury could reach a different conclusion."

"How is it material?"

"The evidence is material and probative for it offers proof of motive, and will be used for rebuttal purposes. Further, the defendant will not be prejudiced by the introduction of this new evidence for he will have every opportunity for cross-examination and commentary through counsel."

"And credible?"

"An FBI agent will take the stand, and—"

"Whoa, whoa, whoa! Now you're talking out of both sides of your mouth. A few minutes ago you told me that the FBI lied in its response to your document request. Now, I'm supposed to believe they'll be truthful on the witness stand? Which is it, counselor?"

"It should be up to the jury to assess his credibility, as they've been doing with other witnesses such as Stacy Black."

Judge Killam grumbled and glanced at his watch, which was Annie's cue to wrap things up.

"I'm also renewing my motion to have parts of Jennianne Smith's grand jury transcript read to this jury."

"Why should I listen to *that* argument again? I already ruled that doing so would violate the defendant's right to cross-examination in violation of the confrontation clause of the Constitution. Clancy can't cross-examine a transcript."

"Circumstances have now changed. Stacy Black admitted to running Jennianne Smith off the road to stop her from testifying against the defendant." Annie pointed her entire arm at Malone. "He ordered her to do it."

Clancy jumped up. "And my client denies it!"

"Sit down, you'll have your opportunity."

"I have provided you with Miss Black's sworn affidavit." Annie watched the judge examine the statement.

"Tell me about the law."

"According to *Maryland v. Craig,* the Supreme Court held that cross-examination may be denied to further an important public policy."

"What is the important public policy here?"

"To prevent the killing of witnesses. To prevent the code of silence!" Annie focused on the judge and then took her seat.

"Attorney Clancy?

Clancy marched toward the bench. "The defense stands in fierce opposition to this motion. Allowing any of this allegedly new evidence, which consists of some *paintings,* will not comport with the principles of due process and will severely prejudice the defendant's case." Clancy extended his arm and index finger toward the ceiling. "*Commonwealth v. Carter!*"

Annie noticed the trace of a smile flicker across Judge Killam's lips.

"Let's do away with the theatrics for a moment, Clancy, and start at the beginning. Miss Fitzgerald relied upon the newly discovered evidence rule as outlined in *Commonwealth v. Grace.* Can we agree that the proposed evidence qualifies as newly discovered?"

"Absolutely not!"

"Why?"

"The evidence could've been discovered during the trial if Detective Callahan had done his job. Why should the defendant be punished for his laziness? I find it rather peculiar that someone of Detective Callahan's caliber couldn't find a couple of paintings scattered around Charlestown. The Commonwealth had ample time and resources to discover this evidence earlier. If they'd looked hard enough, they could've easily uncovered a federal investigation pertaining to Malone. It's common knowledge that Agent Bertrand and Detective Callahan don't get along. In fact, Bertrand just arrested Callahan. So, why should my client be punished for their little games of cat and mouse?"

"Objection!" Annie had to interrupt Clancy's tirade.

"This is a motion hearing. Please sit down. Now, it's attorney Clancy's turn." Judge Killam sounded like he was addressing two kindergartners. "Can you give me any reasons why this evidence should be barred? And, refer to some case law, Clancy."

"According to *Commonwealth v. Grace,* the judge must find that the jury would've reached a different conclusion had this new evidence been admitted at trial. In this case, we have no idea what the jury has concluded; therefore, how can we know if the jury could reach a different conclusion? Miss Fitzgerald is asking this court to second-guess the jury."

"I think Miss Fitzgerald is suggesting we use *Commonwealth v. Grace* as a guideline. If I find that the evidence was undiscoverable during the trial, tell me why it shouldn't be admitted?"

"Certainly. How can we find any FBI evidence or testimony credible at this point? The Bureau acted in bad faith when it denied the existence of its file. That bad faith on behalf of the FBI ends up prejudicing my client."

"How?" the judge asked.

"It's trial by ambush! I won't have the opportunity to investigate any witness or prepare for a thorough cross-examination."

"That's just what Miss Fitzgerald said about Stacy Black."

Clancy paced for a moment. He rubbed his forehead, appearing deep in thought. "Your Honor, every day I sat at my table listening to your strict instruction to the jury not to discuss this case amongst themselves."

"That's correct."

"At this stage, they've already discussed the case ad nauseam. To permit them to hear more evidence and deliberate further goes against those basic principles."

"If I allow any evidence in, I'll provide a limiting instruction."

"A limiting instruction will not override the prejudicial impact the evidence will have on the defendant's case. The jurors' mouths practically hit the floor when Miss Fitzgerald interrupted the verdict—*their verdict*. If you allow for this additional evidence, what will they think? This new evidence must be awfully important if the judge has directed us to tear up our original verdict slip. Why, it must carry more weight than all the other evidence introduced throughout the course of the trial."

Annie watched Judge Killam raise his chin, clearly contemplating Clancy's point.

"What if they all agreed, unanimously, on a not guilty verdict? If you make them redeliberate, they'll start wondering." Clancy placed his finger on his chin. "Hmm. The powers that be want us to go back in and second-guess ourselves? Perhaps the judge knows something about Malone that we don't. Maybe we should change our minds and find him guilty instead."

Clancy paused and looked at the judge. "It's wrong, Your Honor. Wrong. Allowing the Commonwealth to reopen her case after the jury has reached a verdict will desecrate the sanctity of deliberations, and therefore, taint the foundation of our judicial system."

"Thank you attorney Clancy." Judge Killam stood.

"The court will take a brief recess."

"All rise!"

"I can't believe this shit's happening to me." Malone circled the cell, around and around until he felt like vomiting. *Why?* "I should've been out of here by now. I'll sue the state and that bastard Killam for this."

"I've never seen anything like it," Clancy said again.

Malone sneered. "That bitch Stacy lied; either they forced her into it or paid her off. I didn't have anything to do with Jennianne getting drunk and plowing into a tree. Okay?"

"I know."

"Why can't you tell them that?"

"I did."

"What do you think the judge'll do? He always goes against me." Malone picked the skin at the corner of his thumb until it bled. "What's taking him so long now? I told you from the beginning that I didn't want Killam for a judge and look where we ended up? A normal judge wouldn't allow this."

"I've never seen anything—"

"Shut up!" Malone grabbed the bars. "I'm sick of hearing it!" He yelled so loud that the back of his throat hurt.

Clancy glared. "If Judge Killam rules against you, I'll request a mistrial."

Malone started circling again. "We'll have to do everything all over?"

"And so will the Commonwealth."

"We won't have Stacy Black this time around." Malone loathed her. This was all her fault.

"That's right." Clancy locked his thumbs behind his suspenders. "They'll also indict you for the murder of Jennianne Smith."

Malone would take care of that situation himself, he wouldn't fool around with the justice system again.

"You'd also be taking a big risk if you decide to testify a second time in this case. Fitzgerald can use the prior trial transcript to trip you up."

"Can they gather more evidence against me at this point?"

"Sure."

Malone rested his face in his hands. "If this jury found me innocent already, do you think they'll completely reverse their decision?"

"You never know. I'm not so sure about the paintings, but the remaining part of Jennianne's grand jury testimony is damaging, shows motive. On the other hand, the jurors didn't like their verdict being interrupted like that. It was finally their turn to speak, and Fitzgerald took that away from them. They may very well stick with their original verdict."

Malone had to make a decision; Clancy hadn't heard the rumor about the not guilty verdict. "I think we should stick with this jury no matter what. We can't do this all over again."

Annie checked e-mail on her phone as she waited in the courtroom for a decision from the judge. She saw the words, but their meanings didn't register. She was exhausted and her mind raced in all directions. Most people had cleared out to wait elsewhere, including Clancy.

"Did you know the verdict?"

Annie turned around; it was Chris. "How would I know that?" She was surprised to hear from him.

"I figured you did. Why else would you pull something like this?"

"No." She put her phone down. "It's kept secret from us, too."

"Ha." He smirked. "Nobody keeps secrets anymore. Even I knew it."

"Impossible."

"Everybody in Charlestown knows."

"That's crazy. I don't believe you."

"One of the jurors has a cousin who lives on Bunker Hill Street. She's blabbing like a canary. Do you want to know who it is?"

Annie studied him. Was he telling the truth? If so, she didn't want to know. It could further complicate things.

"Well?"

"No."

"I'm sure you must be curious—if you knew it could change everything for you."

Was he mocking her?

Chris opened the swinging gate to the lawyers' area and sat at her table. He picked up one of her notes and read it. *Very brazen.*

"What are you doing?" She grabbed the paper from his hand.

"Why weren't you at Jennianne's funeral?"

"Because I had to try this case."

"What about the wake?" He picked up her pen. "As I recall it was an evening affair."

"I was preparing for your brother's case."

He stared her down. "You couldn't show your face."

"You're looking at me like I'm worse than Malone."

"You are."

"Are you saying I shouldn't put a killer on trial because he'll kill somebody else? I had to put Jennianne under oath."

"The streets speak the truth, not this place. You blackmailed her. Everybody knows. I told 'em all at the wake."

"Why did you do that?" Annie noticed a crazed look about him; she felt uncomfortable.

Chris clasped his hands and smiled. " 'Oh, Mrs. Smith, do you want to know why your daughter's being lowered into the ground today?' "

"Why would you say a thing like that?"

"When you finish up in here and take a walk around Charlestown, they'll be watching you and they'll know."

"Why are you blaming it all on me? Stacy Black confessed to forcing her off the road. I told Jennianne not to leave the safe house, I told her to stay low. She'd still be alive if—"

"And where were you when all this went down?" Chris whispered. His words came across like a low hiss.

Annie met his gaze, knowing where she was. *The basement. With him.*

"You don't get it, do you?" Chris stood. "You played God and you lost. You lost her and you lost your case and you lost your soul." He bent over the table, facing her, until their foreheads nearly touched.

"Look at these." Annie stood and grabbed the two canvases she'd brought to court. She unrolled them across the table.

"Where did you get them?"

As she told Chris, she could see his facial features contort. His lips trembled.

"Chris, did you ever ask yourself, 'Why is my brother doing all this?' With every stroke, he's painting himself into the grave." She mimicked an artist painting with a tiny brush. "He knows it, but he still keeps on going. *If he had just painted anything else.* But, Trevor had to paint *this.*" Annie brought her palm down on the painting of Lydia Thompson wrapped in the carpet pad. *"And this."* She slapped the painting of the man smoking on his stoop.

"I told him to stop."

"But he couldn't. He didn't have a choice. This is the truth. This is what Trevor sees when he walks down the street." Annie touched the eyes in both. "What would you do, Chris? If you had the choice to undo all of Trevor's paintings just to bring him back from the dead, would you?"

The door to the judge's chambers opened. "Judge Killam wants to see you and Clancy now."

Annie gazed at Chris.

He had tears in his eyes. "I need to tell you something about my brother."

66

ANNIE ROSE FOR the judge and looked back into the gallery. Callahan gave her the thumbs-up. It was more packed than before. Extra security guards had been stationed throughout. She and Clancy had spent over an hour with Judge Killam going over exactly what would happen next. Annie had been ecstatic when he informed them that he'd allow her to reopen her case and read the remainder of Jennianne's grand jury testimony due to Stacy Black's arrest and confession. Clancy had exploded. Judge Killam ruled against her on the admission of the paintings as newly discovered evidence. She knew that would be next to impossible since it involved Trevor's art. *One step at a time,* she reminded herself.

"Be seated," Johnny said.

Annie noticed the frowns directed at her from the jurors. What could she do? If they held it against her, so be it. She would rather they hear the truth.

"Thank you for your patience." Judge Killam remained standing as he addressed the jury. "I have allowed the Commonwealth's motion to reopen her case and read the prior recorded testimony of an unavailable witness. You are not to draw any conclusions as to why this witness is not present here. Commonwealth, you may proceed."

Annie grabbed Trevor's pencil drawing of Jennianne and placed it on the easel facing the jury.

"Objection!" Clancy rose. "Prejudicial."

"This sketch has already been admitted into evidence," Annie said.

"But circumstances have changed." Clancy extended his arm toward the painting. "Come on."

"Overruled. Your objection is noted for the record."

Malone stood. "This is cruel, Your Honor, cruel."

"Sit."

Malone sat and scowled. Clancy whispered something to him.

Annie turned and faced the stone-faced jurors. "I'm reading from Jennianne Smith's testimony before the grand jury recorded on November twenty-first of last year."

She waited until she had their attention. "'What happened after you saw Trevor drop to the floor?'"

Annie changed her voice, and imagined she was Jennianne. "'I yelled out, "Oh my God! I'm calling nine-one-one." Then I ran over to pick up the phone, but Billy caught me by the arm and yanked it back so hard that it almost came right out of the socket. It hurt wicked bad. Then he yelled, "Nobody's calling nine-one-one." But I, I reached for the phone, you know, and said, "He's going to die, Billy. He's going to die."'"

Annie glanced up from the transcript. The jurors were leaning forward, listening. "'So then Billy . . . he grabbed a bunch of my hair from behind and said, "Control yourself, whore," and he pulled me by the hair into the kitchen. I still told him that we got to call an ambulance. I even picked up the kitchen phone, but he tore it right out of the wall. I said, I said . . . "We're killing him."'"

Annie recalled the terror in Jennianne's voice when she testified before the grand jurors. She could never do it justice. She inhaled and read the next section. "'Then Billy hit me with the phone. I fell on the stove, but I kept begging him: "He's going to die, Billy, you gotta call the ambulance." Until . . . Billy . . . he kicked me in the stomach, so I lost my breath, and couldn't say no more.'"

Annie heard her own voice wavering as she read. "'I remember Billy saying, "We'll take care of it. Just shut up and stay in here." So, I just stayed because I let myself pretend he wasn't going to make Trevor die. But I knew the truth . . . God help me.'"

Annie's fingers trembled. She touched Jennianne's portrait and said a silent prayer for her and justice. Several jurors were crying.

She faced the judge. "Sidebar?"

Judge Killam motioned the lawyers to the bench. "I'd like to call one more rebuttal witness. It will be very brief. It goes to motive, Your Honor."

"No way," Clancy said.

"Who is it?" Judge Killam asked.

"Chris Shea, the brother of the victim. He's on my original witness list." Annie explained what she expected him to testify about. He didn't have to be sequestered because he was a member of the victim's family. Clancy objected, but she had the judge thinking. He tapped his fingertips together.

"I'm not going to allow the other paintings in, I've already ruled."

"Yes, Your Honor," Annie said.

Judge Killam huffed and addressed Clancy. "Since I allowed the defense to add a witness, who wasn't listed, I'll allow the Commonwealth this one rebuttal witness." He turned to Annie. "Make it short. We've kept the jury waiting long enough."

Annie gazed into the gallery at Chris. She prayed he would do this. He hadn't exactly promised he would, but after listening to Jennianne's emotional testimony . . . *she hoped*.

"The Commonwealth calls Chris Shea." Annie held her breath; she couldn't look at him now. Would he get up? At first she heard nothing, but then came the sound of footsteps. Chris walked up to the witness stand and raised his right hand for Clerk Fallon. Annie exhaled with relief.

"Do you swear to tell the truth, the whole truth, and nothing but the truth, so help you God?"

"I do."

"Please introduce yourself to the jury," Annie said.

"Chris . . ."

"And your last name?" Annie could tell he felt uneasy.

"Shea."

"Did you have a brother?"

"Uh . . . yeah. Trevor Shea."

"Briefly, please tell us about your childhood." Annie was winging it. She hadn't had the time to prepare questions.

"We grew up in Charlestown and lived on School Street until our dad left us. He just vanished. I was nine and my brother was five. We moved over to the projects after that. Our mother became an alcoholic. Had it tough."

"Your brother had a gift?"

"Yeah, he liked to paint, he was always doodling as a kid."

"How many paintings do you think he did?"

Chris stared at the ceiling. "A lot. Thirty? Forty?"

"What happened to them all?"

"Some were stolen, destroyed." He shrugged. "I don't know."

Annie placed the painting of the kids in the playground back on the easel. "Do you recognize this?"

"Yes, that's one of Trevor's paintings. He got an award for it."

"Do you recognize the scene?"

"Objection!"

"Overruled."

"I do. I know it exactly."

"How?"

"I was there. I know all those kids, too. My brother painted it exactly as it was."

"Like a photograph?"

"Yes."

"What does this scene depict?"

"Objection." Clancy spread his arms. "Relevancy?"

"Motive," Annie said.

"Overruled. Answer the question, sir."

"That's the playground near the projects, on Bunker Hill Street."

"What is happening?" Annie noticed the jurors gazing at the painting.

"That's Billy Malone, right there." He tapped the figure in the painting.

"He's the older boy sitting on top of Georgie Hurley, the redheaded kid." Chris looked at Malone. "Georgie was only ten and Malone was sixteen. They got into an argument over something stupid. So, Malone started pushing him and jumped on top, hitting him."

"What were you doing?"

"Nothing. Just watching it go down, like everyone else." He touched a brown-haired boy in the painting. "That was me."

"What happened next?"

"Billy asked one of the little kids to grab a rock." He pointed to the rock in the painting. "See? Right there's the rock. Looks exactly the same."

Annie gazed at the rock. "What happened next?"

"So, the kid did what he was told. We were all afraid of Billy Malone, you know?" Chris's voice cracked. "Malone took that rock." Chris demonstrated by raising his hand high over his head. He looked at the jury and then at Malone. "He took that rock and brought it down . . . hard . . . on top of Georgie's head. He struck Georgie over and over and over until his skull was smashed in." Chris covered his face with his hands and cried.

Annie waited. She felt a lump in her throat as she imagined the scene. Some of the jurors were also crying.

Chris raised his head and looked at Annie. "That boy who handed Billy the rock was my brother."

67

ANNIE SAT BEHIND her table for the last time. The jury had reached a verdict. They had only deliberated for ten minutes. She had a pit in her stomach. Chris looked catatonic sitting in the front row next to the mothers. Mrs. Hurley was crying still. Callahan looked almost as bad with his hair sticking up all over the place. The trial had taken its toll on everyone. Guards loomed everywhere. Chris would have to be restrained if Malone ended up winning.

Clancy spun his hat around and around on his index finger. Annie couldn't imagine having to defend someone like Malone. How could he do it?

Guards escorted Malone into the courtroom. He nodded to his mother, who smiled, but quickly bowed her head in prayer over her rosary beads. Annie felt sorry for her.

"All rise!"

Judge Killam thundered up to the bench. "Again, there will be no outbursts in my courtroom. Mr. Clerk, are we ready for the jury?"

"Yes, Your Honor."

Annie knotted her fingers; she wanted this more than anything. The jurors shuffled into the room in single file. She searched for a clue, a showing of emotion . . . *anything*. Most looked at their seats or up at

Judge Killam. Not one made eye contact with Annie. Someone looked at Malone, then another, and another. What did that mean? They hadn't looked at Malone before. Did anyone even glance at Chris? *Not a good sign.*

"Madam foreperson, has the jury reached a verdict in this case?"

"Yes, we have." The foreperson stood and gazed at Malone.

Annie chewed on her knuckles. *Please find him guilty.*

"May I have the envelope containing your verdict slip?" Clerk Fallon walked toward the jury box.

The foreperson slowly relinquished her envelope. Clerk Fallon grasped it with both hands and carried it up to the bench. His movements appeared robotlike as he laid it down in the judge's outstretched palm. Annie leaned forward. Judge Killam opened the envelope with a shiny brass letter opener. He withdrew the paper and unfolded it. His head moved as he read it. Seconds felt like hours to Annie. When finished, Judge Killam reached for his pitcher, poured himself a glass of water, drained it, and smacked his lips. He refolded the paper and placed it back in the envelope.

Annie searched his face for a clue . . . *nothing.* Was the judge satisfied with their verdict?

"Will the defendant, William Joseph Malone, please rise and face the jury," Clerk Fallon said.

Malone rose and puffed his chest out as if to show he wasn't afraid of anything. Annie noticed the back of his hair clung to his neck, slick with sweat. Clancy stood next to him fingering his hat.

Clerk Fallon cleared his throat. "What say you Madam Foreperson as to count one of complaint number 12-8996K, which alleges that William Joseph Malone committed murder in the first degree upon the person of Trevor Shea? How do you find the defendant?"

The foreperson stared at Malone. "We the jury find the defendant, William Joseph Malone, guilty of murder in the first degree."

Malone's back arched and his arms went up like he'd been shot in the spine. "Noooooo!" He clutched his hair with both hands, teetered, and fell onto the defense table. Clancy had to help him back up.

The courtroom erupted into a pandemonium of muffled screams and clapping. "It's about time!" Several woman yelled.

Guilty. Annie was stunned. They did it. They really did it.

Judge Killam hammered his gavel. "Order! Order! Continue, Mr. Clerk." The courtroom roared louder.

"Are you all in agreement?" the clerk yelled.

"Yes," the jurors said.

Annie peered back in the gallery while Clancy polled the jury. The mothers sat arm in arm with Chris and Callahan. Mrs. Malone wailed across the aisle. Her rosary beads had fallen to the floor.

Malone flopped back into his seat with Clancy's help. His eyes appeared dim and hopeless.

Annie stood. "The Commonwealth moves for sentencing, Your Honor."

"Do you wish to be heard?"

"No."

Judge Killam peered down at Malone. "Will the defendant please rise."

Malone looked like a shell of his former self as Clancy yanked him up by the elbow to face the judge. Judge Killam stared him down as if relishing the moment. "William Joseph Malone, I hereby sentence you to life imprisonment, without parole."

Judge Killam's words echoed throughout the courtroom. Images from Trevor's paintings flashed across Annie's mind: Georgie Hurley, Lydia Thompson, John Eagan. She thought about Jennianne Smith, Drake Reed, and the folders of unsolved murders.

The guards shackled Malone and dragged him out of the courtroom to begin serving his life sentence.

When the judge and jury left the courtroom, all the mothers and Callahan huddled around Annie, hugging her. Most were crying.

"He did it. My brother brought Malone down when no one else could," Chris said. "I'm so proud of him."

"You're right." Callahan patted him on the shoulder. "He did something few would have the courage to do."

"We all did it." Annie motioned to the mothers. "Your testimony sealed Malone's fate, Chris."

"I want you to keep this." Chris handed Annie Trevor's framed self-portrait. She held it up and gazed at it. The colors were so vivid and beautiful, except for the part that hadn't been finished.

Annie smiled at Trevor. "It's time to fill in your eyes."

ACKNOWLEDGMENTS

I am grateful to all who have helped guide me through this long process of writing and rewriting. Thank you to my children, Sarah, Dave, and Kate Barcomb, for being the terrific kids that you are. A special thank-you to my friends from Charlestown who helped me with this book and asked to remain anonymous. I miss the Charlestown Community Garden!

Thank you to my friends at Mystery Writers of America for your community of writers and inspiring seminars. I appreciate the editorial help from my daughter Sarah, the Monday Murder Club, and Andrew Tucker. Thank you to Pen White for your special support and editorial critique.

The drama within this book derives from many days spent writing with my dear friend Avram Ludwig. We collaborated and turned *Under Oath* into a stage play. Thank you to the Actors Studio in New York for giving us the opportunity to develop our play and to our fabulous cast. You've made the characters come alive, and that is so special for me.

Thanks to Susan Gleason, my agent, for your wonderful insight into character development. I appreciate my editor, Bob Gleason, who comes up with all sorts of unique ideas. Most of all, Bob and Susan, I am grateful for your friendship. I applaud all the hard work and camaraderie from everyone at Tor/Forge, in particular, Tom Doherty, Linda Quinton, Katharine Critchlow, Alexis Saarela, and Patty Garcia.